The

"BE NOT CONFORMED"

Anthology

D. Gloria Elysée

2018

D. Gloria Elysée

The

"BE NOT CONFORMED"

Anthology

D. Gloria Elysée

D. Gloria Elysée

The **"BE NOT CONFORMED"** Anthology

D. Gloria Elysée

Acknowledgements

First, ALL glory, honor, and praise belong to God! Without His inspiration there would be no book.

To my parents: I would be nothing without your love and support. I am grateful and blessed to have you as my parents. Thank you for every sacrifice, every prayer, every hospital stay, and much more. I cannot put into words the measure of your worth.

To my extended family and friends: You have kept me going with your love and encouragement. Thank you so much for your continued support.

A special thanks to all those who helped contribute to my book in a tangible way: Nivdarla Anselme, Valerie Anselme, Gibson Bartelus, Tashi Bordenave, Henseley Elysée, Pierre Etienne, Chaniqua Nelson, Daniel Vieux, and Naomi Vilfort. You all believed in this book from the beginning, and put in effort to bring my book to life. I am truly grateful for each of you and the role you played in making this dream a reality.

Thank you all!

Foreword

Dear Reader,

First, I'd like to thank you for purchasing this Anthology of my first three books. I began writing this series in 2009, because I saw that many of the fiction novels dealing with Christianity were not very reflective of (my) reality. They seemed to deal with issues that did not resonate with people like me, and the stories often resolved with relatively little mess, while real life most often does not afford anyone the same opportunity. I felt the need to write for those whose background was similar to my own: young adult, Black, educated, professional, living in the city, attending church regularly. Often, we think that because people attend church regularly their relationship with God must be good. But the truth is that there are a rapidly growing number of young adults in church who attend church regularly out of habit, and not relationship. Church is a tradition, a social club, and not a highly anticipated "date with God." When people's spiritual relationship stays stagnant (or nonexistent), trials come along and usually end up pushing people out of the church altogether. The mass exodus of youth and young adults from the church cannot be addressed in the same way as in the past. It is time to meet people where they are, inside or outside of the church, and draw them into the life-changing love of God.

The "Be Not Conformed" book series is based on the verse in Romans 12:2, "And be not conformed to this world: but be ye transformed by the renewing of your mind, that ye may prove what is that good, and acceptable, and perfect, will of God." (KJV). In the New Living Translation, it states, "Don't copy the behavior and customs of this world, but let God transform you into a new person by changing the way you think. Then you will learn to know God's will for you, which is good and pleasing and perfect." In these last days, God is trying to gather together people who will stand up for Him in truth, honesty, integrity, and obedience. He needs people to call attention to His Word, His Will, and His imminent return. Time is short, and God desires His children to be ready for His Second Coming. You cannot get ready by trying to blend in with the crowd, refusing to be different. In this Anthology (and the three individual books), are the stories of Heaven Brown, Solomon Principle, and Gwendolyn Roberts. Each are different in their approach to their relationship with God. In "Words of Advice From a Jezebel," Heaven grapples with the dichotomy of backsliding while being a church regular. In "A King Among Men," Solomon shows the eternal search for security that we all have, and the unique battles that men face in their pursuit of Godliness and purpose. "No Better Than You" displays the other side of the church people you love to hate by revealing who the real Gwen is: to herself, and to you. In each story, God speaks, whether audibly, through others, or in His Word, showing that He is willing to go to the ends of the earth to meet us, heal us, and transform us into powerful tools that can reach broken souls in this fallen world.

Friend, I hope that this Anthology will cause you to think deeply about who God is, and how your life fits into His plan. I hope most of all, that it draws you into a deeper relationship with God, so that when He returns for His people, you will be saved. May God bless you and keep you.

-    D. Gloria Elysée

D. Gloria Elysée

Words of Advice From a Jezebel

D. Gloria Elysée

This book is for every woman who has struggled or is currently struggling with self-esteem, body image, or any kind of abuse. You are beautiful. You are loved. You are more precious than rubies.[1] Don't let anyone tell you otherwise.

---

[1] Proverbs 31:10, NLT*
*All Biblical references are in the New Living Translation unless denoted

D. Gloria Elysée

Prologue

I always wanted to have the perfect life. I know it doesn't exist, but I still wanted a good job, a great man, and a nice comfortable Christian life. So, you can imagine my surprise when I ended up here.

Wait! Where are my manners? Hi! My name is Heaven Leigh (pronounced "Lee") Brown. I know. Who names their child "Heaven"? And yes, I've heard the line "Your mama must've known you were an angel, 'cause she named you Heaven." Or the classic, "Mmmmm... I would DIE for a taste of Heaven. Wink wink!" Yes, someone actually *said* that! I hoped that he would be struck down by lightning for actually saying that foolishness out loud. Are men serious with these pickup lines?

Sorry, I got a little sidetracked. Anyway, I am 25 years old and I am in my first year of residency at Burrows Community Hospital. I'm a doctor intent on world domination- and of course, marriage, three kids, and a dog. Well maybe not the dog, but I do plan on saving the world. Well as much as I can, since Jesus did that already. My life is pretty simple. I have two siblings: Cameron Jr., 28, and Celeste, 30. Celeste is getting married next year, and my parents are making a huge deal about it. They were pressing me to finish school, not so I could become a super fabulous doctor, but so I could "meet a man and get married." (Get real!)

Anyway, my mom, Madelaine Channing Brown, and dad, Cameron Sr., have been married for so long that they think that we all should just rush out and get married, so we can bring them home some grandbabies. I guess they're bored at home, and are in need of entertainment. I suggested that they get a dog instead, but my mom gave me that, "I'll slap you into next week if you say one more word," look, so I took that as my cue to shut up. They are so touchy! I thought a dog would be a great way keep them entertained. That way, I won't have to distend my uterus for a few more years. But they're not buying it.

Anyway, on with the introduction! I am originally from Boston, MA. But when I was 16, we moved from our Hyde Park neighborhood to Northwest, Washington, DC. It was a tough transition, seeing how old I was when we moved. But it made sense since it meant a salary increase for my parents. That was necessary with my older siblings attending college. My mom is a nurse, and the nurse manager position was a step up with better pay options. So, the whole family picked up and moved. Well, my dad and I, since my sister was in New York trying to become the next Sandra Day O'Connor, and my brother was a business major at Morehouse. My dad found a job in a nearby auto shop (he's a great mechanic), and life went on.

After college, I decided to move back home to Boston. I live in the Jamaica Plain neighborhood now. I even go to my old church (Genesis Seventh-Day Adventist Church in Roslindale, MA). I call my mom all the time to update her on my life, and of course the church gossip, though she gets that from a few church people as well. My dad and I don't ever really talk, but we love each other, so that's all that matters. My mom and I are close though. She's the type that would have a meltdown if she didn't hear from me after two days. I tried to explain that I was a med student, and hardly had dispensable time. You would think we were married, the way she wants us to talk and carry on with each other all the time. Who needs a husband? I've got my mom! Ok, that sounded a little creepy. Moving on!

I love Boston and all, but it hasn't always treated me well. I've had a roller coaster of a year, with happy highs, and scary lows. Between meeting King, and the mess I went through with Hunt, and even my relationship with Mari, it has been one crazy year. There's no way I should've survived it. But then again, if I didn't, there would be no story to tell. It all began last May…

D. Gloria Elysée

Chapter 1
May 2009

I had just arrived home from a shift at Burrows Community Hospital, and I was tired! Working in the ER wasn't going to be easy! I walked into my apartment, and dropped my bag on the floor. On the way to my room, I bumped into my end table (next to the couch). It wasn't the first time, and I'm sure it won't be the last. It left a small tender area on my leg, so I knew that next time it would definitely bruise. I'm a little clumsy, but too lazy to push my furniture a few inches to the right so that it won't keep happening. Then again, it might be my schedule that makes me so tired.

Once inside my room, I changed out of my "outside" clothes, and put on some sweats. I went into my home office (a second bedroom that I can afford to pay for but don't really need) to check if I'd gotten any emails. I don't usually have time to check them because of my schedule, but I had finally gotten two days off, so I wanted to maximize my time. It was Friday afternoon, and the Sabbath would be starting soon.

I didn't really have a problem with doing things on the Sabbath that weren't church related. Although I'd grown up a Seventh-day Adventist, I still enjoyed a variety of activities on the Sabbath. I requested the time off from work citing my religious preferences, but I wasn't opposed to working on the Sabbath either. It was when I usually watched TV, went grocery shopping, or did laundry. I couldn't help it. They ALWAYS seem to give the best shows on Friday nights! And plus, since I am hardly ever home long enough to watch TV, this is the best way to catch up on the shows I missed earlier on that week. Not to mention, my hectic schedule meant that I didn't have much time to run errands, so the Sabbath was it.

Anyway, as I browsed through my email, I received one from Gwendolyn, this really annoying girl from church. I was going to delete it because she sends me so many forwards that I regret giving her my email address. But, seeing that there was no "Fw:" in the subject line, I opened it. To my surprise, it was a cleverly disguised forward, inviting some of the young adults at Genesis to go to a young professionals' mixer on Saturday night. It wasn't being hosted by any church, but was being hosted by the Young Urban Professionals Society, Boston Chapter. I considered it because it wasn't actually a church function. I wasn't really sure what the scene would be like though. To me, it sounded like a cocktail party, or happy hour, but since Gwen was interested it seemed like it could actually be VERY boring.

She's one of those super holy, uptight church people that never do anything even remotely fun. If it was a cocktail hour or club/lounge affair, I'm sure that she'd have a heart attack. Not that I have anything against lounges or happy hours. I enjoy them quite a bit, actually. But not with church folk. No way. I can't do all that with people I go to church with. If it were one of those types of events, I would opt to leave if Gwen decided stay. Well, maybe not because she'd be my ride, but I wouldn't be able to have my fun with her there. She's nice but can definitely be a killjoy sometimes. I know that it would get back to the church about my "heathen" behavior. Then it would get back to my mom, and then I would have to hear about it from her. I don't need that drama. It's happened before.

****

I mulled over the decision to go all through church the next day. Yes, even through the sermon. Pastor Morgan never seems to have anything to say that hasn't already been said. He's all, "Read your Bibles. Pray. Jesus said this. Jesus said that. He's coming soon." Blah blah blah. (Clearly paraphrasing, but it is like that a LOT.) But one thing I know: these hour-long sermons have got to STOP! I had enough of a hard time with the super long lectures in school. I don't need someone to bore me for an hour or two on my supposed day of rest. But then again, those sermons do facilitate some of the BEST naps I have ever had. I guess it balances itself out.

After church, Gwen approached me like, "Hey Heaven! Happy Sabbath!" *I wish you could see me internally rolling my eyes.* "Are we coming along to the mixer tonight?" *Who is "we"?* "I know you might be worried since it isn't being hosted through the church" *Are you kidding? That's the ONLY reason I'm even considering it!* "But I'm sure it will be a great way for you to network. I just hope that there won't be any alcohol served. It has happened before, unfortunately." *I need a shot to get me through this conversation.* "So will you come?" "Sure," I said. "It sounds great. Can I get a ride, though? My car is in the shop." *What am I getting myself into?* "Superb!" she cheerfully replied. *Superb? Who says superb? Really?* "Be ready by seven-thirty." As she walked away toward her holy roller friends, I wondered just how the night would actually go. Granted, I really wanted to go to this mixer, but I got the impression that she was the type of person to stay connected to my hip for the whole night. Plus, I couldn't stomach any more "superb" comments.

As I was walking out, Pastor Morgan called me over. *What does he want?* "Hey there Sister Brown! Just the person I was looking for! Happy Sabbath! How are you this week?" *He's making me late.* "Hi Pastor Morgan. I'm fine. I'm actually on my way out..." "Oh, ok Heaven. Well, all I need is a minute of your time. I know you've gone to this church for quite some time now, and I was wondering why you weren't more involved. If you're looking for a ministry, I know the youth department could definitely use some help. Gwen was just telling me that they needed volunteers for the upcoming church social." *Uh, NO!* "Um, *nervous chuckle* as much as I'd love to help out, I'm just swamped with work and I don't like making a commitment that I know I probably won't be able to honor to the best of my ability. You understand, right? I mean the Bible is always talking about fulfilling your vows and I don't like making vows I can't keep."

"Now don't go misusing God's Word for your pitiful excuses." *Sigh* "Sister Roberts. How nice of you to interject yourself into my private conversation." *She's such a-* "Pastor, you know that Heaven is not the type to help out in church matters. She's better suited in the back pews, observing her cell phone or sleeping like she does every week." *I need to go before someone gets punched in the face.* "Well it's been a pleasure but I have to go now. Bye!" I can't stand Sister Roberts. She's Gwen's mother. She's the one in church who says the loudest hallelujahs, wears the biggest church hats, and pretends to be the most sanctified, though she gossips like her life depended on it. And her daughter is turning into her. You see why I don't deal with church people? *sigh* Ok, I need to get ready for this mixer.

****

Gwen arrived promptly at 7:30. Thankfully, I am a punctual person as well. (Except when it comes to

21

church.) I dressed to impress. I wore a fitted coral dress with a lace overlay and rose-gold accessories. I noticed my low neckline was making Gwen uneasy. I had to restrain myself from laughing in her face when she asked if I brought a jacket. I did, but I wasn't planning on wearing it once we got to the venue. My large bangle bracelets were a great addition to the matching necklace I was wearing that dropped down into my cleavage. I think Gwen was about to have a heart attack. But I looked amazing, and if I got that reaction from her, I could only imagine what type of reaction I was going to receive when we arrived. Women usually envy me, and men find me irresistible. I couldn't wait to be the center of attention.

When we finally reached the place, the Knights of Columbus in West Roxbury, Gwen saw some of her friends, and walked over to them, squealing like a schoolgirl. *That's SO déclassé! Thanks for all the help. I'll find my own way around.* I thought to myself as she disappeared into the crowd. I didn't need her to babysit me, but I thought she would've introduced me to a few people before abandoning me for her own agenda. Honestly, I wanted to be the first to walk away. Thankfully, I heard someone mention an open bar, so I began scanning the room for it.

Just as I had located the bar, I felt a tap on my shoulder. A hand belonging to a man had found a way to rest on my shoulder. STRIKE ONE! As he introduced himself, he leaned in close to me. He towered over me. He was at least 6'2" compared to my 5'5" frame. "Hi. My name is Solomon Principle. You look a little lost. Can I help you with anything?" I shook off the scowl of annoyance that threatened to spread across my face. (I HATE when people I don't know touch me.) "Hi. I was just looking for the bar," I replied, eager to end the conversation. I could tell he was up to something, when, instead of pointing to the bar, he began leading me there, while complimenting me on my outfit. I'm sure he was actually complimenting my breasts, when he said, "nice necklace," and I'm sure if I had looked up, I would have caught him in the act. So shameless!

Now before you get all judgmental and whatnot, calling me conceited or a tease, recall that I hadn't been in the room for more than five minutes before he began his pursuit. Yes, he was attractive, and nice, but I simply was in no mood to converse with him. I was here to network, yes, but the compliments and the touching were quite unprofessional, and clearly, he was more interested in making a love connection, than a business contact.

Thankfully, just before he could ask for my phone number, or hand me his business card, I escaped into the crowd. I accidentally bumped someone and she turned around. Suddenly I was staring into a familiar face. "Marianne?" I asked. A look of recognition crept slowly across her face. When she realized that I wasn't a ghost, we began hugging and squealing like schoolgirls. I hadn't seen her since I was 16. Marianne Choux was my best friend before I moved to DC. We were really close, ever since the early days at the Baxter Elementary School. Poor Solomon was forgotten as I walked away with Mari.

We chatted about the years we had spent apart, and traded our contact info. Now that I had found her, I didn't want us to lose touch again. I wanted to know if we still had anything in common, since there was a large possibility that our paths had grown excessively different since we were 16. Being that we were 25, I wanted the opportunity to re-learn who my best friend was. I owed her at least that. But I did learn that she went to Mt. Bethel SDA church in nearby Dorchester. We were so close by, and weren't even aware of it. She was on her way out with her boyfriend Dwayne so we had no time to catch up. We made plans for dinner on Monday, since her law firm was only a few blocks from Burrows. She was working as a paralegal to put herself through law school.

We said our goodbyes and I decided to walk around the room and network. After mingling for a little while, a nearby conversation caught my attention. It was a discussion that was comparing the academic validity of historically Black colleges and universities to that of the predominantly White institutions (PWIs). This was a conversation I HAD to be a part of. As I moved closer, I heard a Black woman describe her Boston University education as a great experience, which is plausible, but when she went on to say that she couldn't understand why her younger brother wanted to go to an HBCU, I nearly fell over. Before I could step into the group and respond to her foolishness, I heard the voice that chilled my blood. It was his voice. Hunter Austin Black.

We used to go to Howard University together. Well, it goes a little deeper than that. There weren't many people who I hated, but he definitely made the short list. I met Hunt at Yardfest during the Homecoming of his sophomore year, while I was in my senior year of high school. We dated until the middle of his senior year, when he decided that having me for a girlfriend was no longer what he wanted. He would rather sleep with other women. So, he did. He left me to deal with my emotions alone. It was as if we were never in a relationship. I tried to win him back, tried to make him jealous, and tried to get my revenge on him, but to no avail. He graduated and went on continuing his life without me. I didn't try to keep tabs, because by the time he was finished with school, I was emotionally shipwrecked and plus, his friends wouldn't tell me anything. I called and emailed, but no response, and this was just before the invention of Facebook. Soon enough, I decided that I would be fine if I never heard from him again. Yet here he was, standing in this room that seemed to be getting smaller by the second, starting a monologue about the significance of HBCUs. I couldn't resist the urge to respond, though, and chimed in with my response (consequently making myself known to him).

I highlighted the rich legacy that HBCUs had, and how we turned out doctors, lawyers, philanthropists, artist, musicians, actors, and held the highest standards of success. I spoke about how necessary it was to celebrate the positive image of Blackness, in a world where we the media was more apt to show negative stereotypes. Even the excuse of having a Black President did not mean we were to stop addressing the needs of Black self-education, and now we needed to funnel our time in promoting the successes of institutions that served as a way to empower us, when we were restricted to lives of servitude.

Of course, this left her and the others speechless. Hunt couldn't contain his smug smile of satisfaction as the woman tried to stutter a response. As the crowd continued, I figured that my part in the argument was over, so I should move on to another conversation. As I began to walk away, someone grabbed my arm. *What is with all the touching?* "Hello Hunter," I said, still facing in the other direction. "How did you know it was me?" he replied. "Only you would manhandle a woman like that, with no regards to whether or not she wants to speak to you." I was irritated and was letting it show. "Oh, so it's like that?" he asked. "Precisely. Goodbye." I replied, wrenching my arm away. Still though, he grabbed for my arm again. As I violently pulled away from him, his expression changed, from a pleasant joking look, to one of surprise. "Calm down Leigh. I just wanted to say hi and to congratulate you. It's been a while." I was LIVID. First of all, he knows not to call me Leigh. Only my parents, and few others (a short list he *used* to be on) could do that. Second, I can't stay mad when he does that- and he knows it. His nonchalance was getting under my skin. I was trying not to cause a scene, but I did manage to catch a few glances from Gwen.

I brushed off the onlookers. I didn't appreciate his acting as if nothing had ever happened between us, as if I was some random old friend that he was catching up with. But what was really getting to me was his "been a while" comment. I was finished with this conversation. "Yes. It has 'been a while' since you broke my heart, moved on, and lived your life with no regards to me, or my feelings. It's been six years, three months, twelve days, and approximately 15 hours since you decided to sleep with other women, and remove yourself from my life." I said torpidly. As the shock registered on his face, it bought me the chance to turn around and walk directly to Gwen. "Are you ready to go?" I asked. Thankfully she was.

My emotions were supercharged and I did not want to cry in front of anyone. I was so anxious to get home. Trying to keep a brave face, I started for the exit. To my dismay, Gwen turned around and shouted, "Bye Hunter! I'll see you Monday!" I had a feeling that Hunt would be making more appearances in my life, but now that I knew he was here, I would make sure to be more prepared.

Gwen spent the ride home looking at me, as if she had a question that she wanted to ask, but didn't

27

know how. "How do you know Hunter?" Ahh, there it is. We were one block from my house, and I guess she couldn't resist anymore. "We both went to Howard together." I left it at that. She didn't need to know all my business. She wasn't buying it, though. "Looks like there was some history there. That conversation looked like it was way more than two classmates catching up." I was finished. Was she serious about this? It was none of her business. Thank God, I was almost home. I didn't want to be in her car any longer. "Don't worry about it." I left it at that. Maybe it was something in my tone that spoke to her, but the rest of the ride (all two minutes of it) was spent in silence.

I barely muttered goodbye to Gwen when we arrived at my house, and almost sprinted upstairs. Emotionally exhausted, I dropped my things on the floor, and headed for my bedroom, tripping over the end table and knocking over my lamp. I began to turn back for my purse, since my phone was in it, but I reconsidered after reaching the living room. I felt cloistered in my clothing, and felt compelled to undress, to help alleviate the trapped feeling I was having. Tripping again, I became angrier. As I flung myself onto my bed, I could not stop the tears that I'd been holding back. I could do nothing but cry myself to sleep...

Chapter 2
June 2009

I thought about him all day at work on Monday. He made me so angry, but he was looking so good. Seeing him again brought back everything. And though there were plenty of bad memories, I couldn't help but remember all the good ones too. Our moments hanging on the Yard, under the West Indian tree, going to Matchbox for great pizza, or even hanging in the Towers watching a movie, while snuggled up on his bed. Sure, I was young, but I was in love with him. We were together for two years, but I had wanted to save myself for marriage so I didn't want to have sex.

At first, I was what you called an "anything but" girl. But I didn't want to lose him, and I knew how many women wanted him, so eventually I gave in. It was dumb and I've never regretted it more. It hurt so much because he was my first love and (you know) my "first," but when I saw that he was tired of being with me, I emotionally shut off, and I decided that I was going to sleep with whomever I wanted, whenever I needed to. Now the reason for my emotional disconnect was back. I was as

29

torn apart now as when he'd first left. These memories were threatening to overshadow what was supposed to be a happy day- my reunion with Mari. I refocused my mind to our upcoming dinner date.

Mari and I had so much to catch up on. We decided to meet up at a small restaurant that was close to work, since I was going to be on-call. Over the course of our dinner, we talked about everything. I found out that she was still living at home with her mother while she went to Boston University Law School. She had been dating Dwayne for a year. Her dad still wasn't around, but she was okay, because she had Jesus. Well, that's what she told me. I realized that she was like Gwen: SUPER enthusiastic about Jesus. It's as if I attract people like that. Well, at least my female friends. Most guys I deal with probably never have stepped inside a church before. At least not outside of weddings and funerals. But Mari and I chatted about life, the past, and everything that had happened since we last saw one another at 16.

She still had her great sense of humor, and we spent a lot of time laughing. Though we were significantly different, we were still so much alike. I ended up telling her about what happened after she left the young professionals mixer on Saturday. She laughed at the story of the guy who unsuccessfully tried to pick me up, and rolled her eyes when I told her about the woman who thought HBCUs were pointless. "I wish I had the opportunity to go to an HBCU. I wanted to party hard with the Omegas too!" she exclaimed. I was trying to keep from rolling on the floor in laughter.

When I told her about the Hunter thing, she made one of those disgusted faces. She was familiar with who he was, since Boston is a small world, and though he looked great "on paper," she said that there was something about his charming demeanor that she didn't trust. She had "met his type before" and warned me that he was not only persistent, but dangerous as well, given the history we had. After I changed the subject, the remainder of our conversation was lighter and definitely less depressing. I was sad to see it end, but I had to get back to work. I had a long night ahead of me.

Wednesday morning, I re-checked my schedule, because I would be leaving work early. I had to pick up my car from the shop. Thank God, I wouldn't be subjected to public transportation anymore! Not that I'm not a fan of the T (how Bostonians refer to the public transportation system), but I enjoy a ride devoid of sticky floors, unidentifiable smells, and weird stares when I decide to sing along with my music. The day went along fairly smoothly, considering I work in an ER. I am destined to be a super fabulous doctor. My patients weren't insanely difficult, and other than a few annoying co-workers and superiors, work was pretty great. I left work an hour early. I know it seems crazy, especially since I just started, but I really needed to pick up the car before they overcharged me. I did my chart documentation during lunch and some of my resting hours to make up for it, so my charting was mostly done. The rest I could finish later.

31

When I arrived at the auto shop, they weren't done fixing my car yet, even though they had called me to pick it up. I headed over to the little waiting section, since it seemed that this was going to take a while. As I waited, I received a call from a Boston number I didn't recognize. Something told me not to pick up, but my curiosity got the best of me. "Hello? Who is this?" I asked. "Leigh! Don't hang up!" It was Hunt. He continued, "I just wanted to apologize. I was really young and stupid and didn't know what I had, and I treated you badly, and you definitely didn't deserve it. I just want to meet with you and formally apologize. That's all I'm asking for." Resisting the strong urge to curse at him and hang up on his face, I reminded him that he had a lot of nerve to call me. "How did you even get my number?" I asked, irritated and confused. He explained that he'd jumped through hoops to get my number. He got it from a coworker, after he'd confessed why he knew me. Apparently, she, far more forgiving than I, was won over by his charm and released my phone number to him. "Who is your coworker?" I asked, as a memory of Saturday night popped into my head. The one person in Boston that we had in common: Gwen.

I'm going to KILL her! How DARE she volunteer information to him? I knew she was stupid, but I didn't think she was crazy too! She was going to get seriously cursed out as soon as I got Hunt off the phone, which isn't an easy feat. Once he had dug his heels into something, there was no way to dissuade him. That is why he'd make an excellent lawyer, even though business was his chosen trade.

I was trying to keep my composure with this conversation because of the violent thoughts swimming in my head, along with my irritation at my car that was still not ready- an hour after I'd arrived. Hunt droned on about how he just wanted "one small lunch" so we could talk. "Talk about what?" I really didn't care to converse with him. Not now. Not ever. Unless his idea of talking included him on his knees begging my forgiveness, I wasn't interested. He sounded close to tears as he kept asking me to let him take me out to lunch to formally apologize and make amends. Exasperated with his persistence, I told him that I'd consider it. That satisfied him to the point where he told me that he'd call back with more details and finally hung up the phone.

Truth is, no matter how much I hated him, he was my first love and I still loved him. All those feelings I thought I'd gotten rid of years earlier were simply buried. Now they were resurfacing with a vengeance. It started when I saw him in his element, arguing passionately about the state of the Black race, and passionately vouching for his people. His passion, drive, ambition, charisma, and persistence were all such a turn-on that they almost cut through my anger, and were beginning to wear me down. Especially when he'd call me Leigh. It was the way he said it. It just made me melt a little.

But I came back to reality as the rude mechanic dangled my keys in front of my face. After having me sitting there for almost two hours, he had some nerve! I swear he's lucky I'm a Christian, or I would've had some choice four-letter words for him. I mean, I may not be a gung-ho Jesus freak, but I don't want people thinking I'm a complete heathen for cussing this man out. Jesus and I have an "understanding" so it's all good if I did. But this guy's tip was going to suffer for his rudeness, not his pride. In fact, since my dad was a mechanic, he taught me a few things, including reasonable prices for certain mechanical procedures, and with this rude man trying to rob me, I let him know that I wasn't having it. And he had no choice but to accept. So I paid him what I thought I owed him, and after a long discussion with the owner of the shop, I was able to have my way.

When I arrived at home, after a long day, I still had some unfinished business left. I still needed to have a little conversation with a certain person who thought it was okay to pass on another person's contact information without their consent. That was just tacky on her part. Still fuming, I dialed her number. "Hey Heaven!" she cheerfully answered. "Hey Gwen. Did you give Hunter Black my phone number?" I asked, cutting to the chase. "Yes, I did. He was just so pitiful. First, he tried to act as if it were for business reasons, but when he couldn't make up a good reason, he broke down and told me about his and your history. And you made it seem like he was just an old acquaintance! He just wants to apologize and make amends. You really should hear him out. It's the Christian thing to do."

NO SHE DIDN'T! "First of all, I don't appreciate you passing on my number to anyone. Even if it was my mama asking for my phone number, you still had no right. Secondly, you don't even know the story behind what went on, and you have NO idea what he did, other than whatever crap he told you. He lied to you at first, and yet you still thought him to be okay enough to give out my personal information? If I wanted him to have my phone number, I would've given it to him at the mixer. If you ever give out my number again to anyone, without my permission, I will yank out your hair strand by strand, and beat you with the Bible that you keep using to justify your stupidity. Do I make myself clear?" She was speechless. "I take that as a yes. Goodbye." As I hung up the phone, I couldn't help the smile of satisfaction that was creeping across my face.

After my day of waging war, I made myself a sandwich, had a cupcake, and checked my voicemail. Mari had called, inviting me to go to her church, Mt. Bethel, on Saturday. I wasn't too sure though. It's a Haitian church and I'm not Haitian. I'm African-American (well I'm an eighth French, on my mom's side, but can't speak or understand it), so it would be an issue if they started speaking in Kreyol or French. But as the message continued, Mari let me know that they held an afternoon service in English, so not only did I not have to worry about the language barrier, but I also could sleep late on Saturday, and not feel guilty, because I could still make it to church. Plus, as an added bonus,

35

she was hosting lunch at her house, after church. I guess she left me no room to decline.

When I called her back to confirm, I filled her in on the new chapter of the Hunt saga. She definitely didn't think it was a good idea for me to speak to him, much less go to lunch with him. She didn't think I could withstand his charm, and warned that the progress I'd made getting over him, could be undone with just one lunch. "I mean, look at what you went through when you saw him at the mixer. I could even see it in your face when you were telling me about him over dinner on Monday." She had a point, but I wasn't trying to hear it. "It's just lunch," I told her. "I'm a big girl. I can handle it." She sighed, and said, "Okay. If you say so." Her tone of voice made it clear that she didn't approve. I brushed it off though. I was grown, and didn't need her approval. She might know who Hunt is, but I knew how to deal with him. And I planned on it. After I hung up the phone with her, I called Hunt, accepted his offer to meet him for lunch on Friday.

****

Church on Saturday wasn't what I expected. It was a little more animated than most SDA churches. I was spoiled by the churches in the DC area, because most of them were so energetic, warm, and friendly. Genesis, my home church, was a little dry and impersonal. Mt. Bethel was somewhere in the middle. Since the service began at noon, I was well rested (for once) when I arrived for church. I was a little late (okay a LOT late), but I arrived in time for praise and worship before the sermon. The music there was on point! It looked like I found a new church home. The pastor had a thick accent, but I wasn't paying any attention to the sermon anyway. I was thinking of my lunch date with Hunt, the day before.

Hunt and I had gone to lunch in the "fancy" hospital cafeteria, since I had limited time, and needed to be close by if something happened with my patients. I had worked another long shift, so I brought a really cute outfit with me to wear. Well, as cute as it could be, since I had to wear sensible shoes. I had planned to change back from my scrubs before he arrived, but a complicated emergency patient took away any extra time I had. I was late to our lunch, but I was just thankful that I could make it in the first place. It was a rough day. As I checked the mirror, on the way to lunch, I realized I looked like I felt: exhausted, dirty, and overworked, but it was too late to do anything about it. He didn't seem to notice, and told me I looked great. I appreciated his flattery, since I felt ugly and nasty. He brought me a single white rose ("symbolic of peace," he said) and apologized. We barely spent ten minutes together, before I was being paged for something else.

As I rushed off, I told him I forgave him, but our friendship would have to be limited, since I didn't trust him. He would have to prove himself to me. He smiled, and said he was looking forward to the challenge, and was grateful that I'd even let him try. And so, I ran back to my job, and he left. I pushed him out of my mind for the rest of the demanding workday, but I couldn't seem to push him out of my mind during the sermon. I didn't hear one word, before the congregation stood for the benediction.

As the speaker walked up to the podium, I noticed it was a familiar face. I was in so much shock that I didn't even hear the final prayer. Apparently, I was at Solomon's church. I approached Mari after church, ready to ask some questions about why Solomon was here, but he was right behind me. He embraced Mari, and then turned to give me a "church" hug (a one-armed side hug, shoulder pat optional). We had a brief, but politely meaningless conversation. I must admit, though, that he was looking good. But he was one of those guys with no game, and made it way too easy. I like a challenge, and he was just a little too open and obvious with his attraction to me. I mean, he even pulled Mari aside, and call me crazy, but I did catch a few glances in my direction.

Mari, took it upon herself to be his personal hype man after he walked away from us. I stopped listening as she listed his "great qualities." "King is really great. He's so..." Blah blah blah... The more she spoke on his behalf, the less attractive he was becoming to me. I do my own hunting, and I don't need someone in my life that has to appeal to my girl to talk to me. My mind snapped back to attention as she mentioned that he and I "really should go out sometime." I think not.

Before I went to my car, I informed her that Solomon was the infamous guy from the mixer. I couldn't help but laugh at the expression on her face. That's when she dropped it. Thank God! I didn't need this pressure from her or anyone else, especially since Hunt was back in my life. Unnecessary complications were not my style, and this "King" guy was definitely that. Maybe I'd entertain him if he got some game, but no time soon. But the best thing to do would be to keep him around. He might come in handy.

****

I arrived at Mari's house for lunch. Her mom, Marie Joi, was warming up the food. Though she seemed happy to see me, I overheard her muttering something about Mari's "late" arrival. Mari was two steps behind me. As she tried to explain her apparent tardiness, (I was trying to figure out what "late" meant, since we'd left right after church), her mom snapped at her. She switched from English to Kreyol and back again. I'm assuming it had to do with the kitchen, because Mari rushed to the back of the house.

When Ms. Joi turned back around, she swept me into a big hug. "How are you my daughter?" she asked. I was taken aback by her display of affection toward me for two reasons. One, I didn't know that she recognized and remembered me. Two, because I had never remembered her hugging Mari like that- even when we were little kids. I only remember a kiss on the cheek, and that's because it's a greeting in the Haitian culture. "Fine. How are you?" I answered, as I snapped back to reality. She had me in the tightest bear hug. Talk about a grip! "I'm blessed. I'm just glad you're back in Mari's life. She needs a good influence like you around." *Good influence? Me?* "Maybe she'll finally get her act together." *I didn't know she wasn't "together" in the first place.* As she finished her sentence, Mari walked back into the room. Only then did Ms. Joi release her death grip and walked away with another barrage of Kreyol. "What was that about?" I whispered, as I shot Mari a look of confusion. But she only shrugged. "I dunno."

Lunch was ready, and we began to make our way toward the dining room. I wasn't the only guest there. There were a few other young adults there, and a few people who were her mom's age. We were set to eat together. There goes the conversation! As I sat down next to Mari, the doorbell rang. "I'm sorry!" she whispered as she ran toward the door. I guess not all the guests had arrived. As I wondered if I'd heard her correctly, I realized why she said an apology before she went to get the door. It was Solomon. *Great.* And because all the other spots were taken, she sat him next to me. *"Superb."* That man is harder to get rid of than a roach.

Turns out that lunch wasn't too bad. Haitian food is awesome, and even Solomon was so engaged in the food that I was able to get a few minutes of peace where he wasn't leaned in trying to talk to me. As soon as most of the meal was eaten, however, one of the other guests started a discussion. It was controversial, or that's what it sounded like. I never actually got to hear the conversation, because when the lady began to speak, my phone began to vibrate. I excused myself to the den to answer it.

It was my mom, calling to wish me a Happy Sabbath. She was being nosy and asking where I was, and what all the noise in the background was. After I filled her in, she said she'd keep it short. Thankfully, my mom isn't chatty at all, so after a brief conversation with her, I went to rejoin the others. As I returned to the commotion, I ran into Solomon, on his way to the "bathroom." "That was your man, wasn't it? He's a lucky man." Oh God. Is he stalking me? "I was talking to my mom. I don't have a man." I replied coolly. Why did I tell him that? That response made a smile of pure satisfaction creep across his face. You know: that smile that kids get when they get a cookie for good behavior or something? That was it.

I could see that he was choosing his words very carefully. "You seem like a great person, and I'd really like to get to know you better." I'm sure! "I would love to take you to dinner, just so we can get better acquainted with each other." *Yeah ok. I know what you want to get better acquainted with. You want to familiarize yourself with my body.* I was about to give him the polite blow off, until I realized that I had already admitted to not having a boyfriend. I could just kick myself. So, I did the next

41

best thing. I asked for his card, smiled sweetly, and said, "I'm really busy lately, but if I get an opening, I'll be sure to let you know." That seemed to pacify him, and we walked back to the conversation. *So much for needing to use the bathroom!* I knew he was lying.

Truthfully, I don't even remember what they were talking about once we got back to the table. I think I have a mental switch that turns off when I hear the word "Jesus" too many times. Go figure! Plus, they were all Haitian, and kept switching back and forth from Kreyol to English. I might've been offended if I was actually trying to pay attention. Anyway, I kept fiddling with my phone, tempted to text Hunt. Ugh! I watched helplessly as my fingers typed out words, and hit the "SEND" button. It kept happening until our correspondence had resulted in a dinner date for next Saturday evening. What had I done?

****

All the guests were gone, and I was helping Mari do the dishes. I told her about Solomon, whom she and every young person kept referring to as "King." (I hadn't mentioned Hunt because I knew she disapproved.) But she got way too excited about "King", and practically begged me to go out on a date with him. So much for not being his personal cheerleader! Her mom even chimed in. I didn't know she was part of the conversation! Ms. Joi's comment alluded to the fact that Solomon should date me because her daughter wasn't good enough for him. And how it was too bad Mari had "that ugly boyfriend" because she couldn't do much better than that. You could see the mounting fury in Mari's face. As I reached over and squeezed her hand, I decided to end the conversation by agreeing to go out with Solomon.

Satisfied, her mom walked out of the room leaving Mari and I alone. Noting the intense discomfort, and not knowing how to ease any of the tension, I decided it was time to make my exit. With a hug and a kiss, I headed home, but not before Mari had me call Solomon and set up the date in front of her. I was a little annoyed that she thought I wouldn't keep my word. *She knows me too well.* Dinner on Tuesday it is...

D. Gloria Elysée

Chapter 3
September 2009

Hunt and I have been dating since June. Don't judge me! There's a lot of history there, and I believe he's changed. He's faithful, attentive, caring, and romantic now. And he knows me so well. No, I'm not dealing with Solomon, or anyone else for that matter. One is all I need. I'm in my first year of residency, have no time, and need as few distractions as possible. I told Solomon that him and I were just friends, even though our dates (three to be exact) went pretty well. I learned a lot about him, and he might have won me over, but he was just no match for Hunt. I mean, Hunt had his MBA in Accounting, went to my alma mater, and was working for one of the most prominent accounting firms in Boston. Our history, his ambition, and his career were so stacked that Solomon couldn't compete even if he tried.

I was honest with Solomon from the beginning. I didn't give Solomon any specific details other than, "I'm giving my ex another shot," even though I thought Hunt was a much better candidate for my relationship. I mean

45

D. Gloria Elysée

Solomon did get a BA in Finance from Bentley University, but at 27 he wasn't doing what Hunt was doing. They were the same age, but light-years apart. Hunt was definitely more ambitious, and he was PAID! Trust me. I made the better choice, despite what Mari or the others thought. Last I heard, Solomon was dating one of Gwen's little friends. I guess he likes them "churchy." Further proof that he and I were incompatible.

The good thing is that Solomon and I hit it off as friends, so we're cool. I go to his church every week that I'm not on rotation, except for the third Sabbath in the month. I can't just leave Genesis hanging (even though I kinda want to). Once in a blue moon, we text each other. Usually, it's pretty generic. But those stopped once Gwen's friend entered the picture. She doesn't like me. But If I were someone else, I wouldn't want me hanging around their man either. I'm 5'5, a size 12 with a Coke bottle body, warm chestnut skin, deep brown eyes, and shoulder length hair that isn't store bought. I mean, let's face it- I'm the picture you see in the dictionary next to the words "gorgeous", "sexy", and "goddess of beauty and splendor!" Ok, maybe not that last one, but I am a head-turner. But I wasn't really trying to push up on her man. I guess pretty women intimidate her. Oh, well! She's not ugly, but King could definitely do better. Great. Now he's got me calling him King like the rest of them. He got the nickname from the kids at church when he was a kid. "King" as in King Solomon (in the Bible). Since I've gone to Bethel for a while now, and no one else calls him by his given name, it was inevitable.

But back to my man. Hunt and I are doing really well. I see him at least twice a week. There's even talk of him coming to church with me! I wouldn't hold my breath though. I laugh more at the thought of him in church, than me in church. I mean, I'm not a heathen (though I act like it sometimes) but I go to church more for the good music and for my mom's sake. And for the sake of not going to Hell. I love the music though. I'm an awful singer, but the sound system at church covers up my croaking, and the praise team is really good, and so they cover up all of my horrid tone-deafness.

Anyway, Hunt is up for a promotion, and I'm done with school and setting up my career. In fact, work would be virtually perfect except for Clarissa Rainier, the resident brown-noser at the hospital. She always has to be right. We never really liked each other, and I think she feels threatened by me. I don't know why. I don't have tons of money like her family does, and I don't get all the perks she does because her dad or granddad or uncle or whatever donated a wing or equipment or something to the hospital. Maybe it's because I'm Black. I know it seems cliché, but what else could it be? I guess the fact that a Black girl from the hood was doing as well as – or better than a trust-fund White girl drove her crazy. Oh well. Not. My. Problem.

My only issue with her is that she's my competition for head intern. It's not a fancy position, but it is almost like a guaranteed spot at Burrows after the internship process is over. I'm going to have to figure out a way to do better than she is, especially since we're dealing with actual patients. It's a matter of both pride and need. But I would never jeopardize the chance of getting that position. Oh, and the patient's lives too. But things are going quite well for me at the moment.

Mari, however, is a different story. She's fighting with everyone (except for me) lately. She and Dwayne aren't doing too well, and on top of that, her fights with her mother have driven her so far up the wall that she's had to crash with me a few times. That's fine because my apartment doesn't get much use since I stay at the hospital so often. Dwayne has been extra distant and moody lately, and is acting as though he'd rather not be in a relationship with Mari anymore. She's hanging in there though. With all the drama going on, she's been going on about Jesus a whole lot, always mumbling about him being a "fortress" and "strong tower" and all that other stuff. I say that too, but that's kinda automatic, because truthfully, I don't know what that means. I know that God takes care of us and forgives us and whatnot, but I have no clue what some of the stuff they have us repeating at church actually means. And don't let me get started on those hymns.

But Mari seems to know what all that stuff means. I just hope that she gets her issues worked out pretty soon. She really brings down the mood whenever we hang out. If she's not going on about a problem, it's about Jesus. Now I love our Lord and Savior and all that, but there are other things to talk about. We're gonna need new subject matter ASAP. I can't take too much more of her Scripture quoting. It's like she sees Jesus in everything. She saw a flower on the table on the restaurant, and started going on about how if God takes care of flowers, he cares about her, and will take care of her. Ugh! It was *just* a carnation! Hopefully she snaps out of it soon. I can only take so much of this...

****

Sound the alarm! Stop the presses! They've officially broken up. That's right. Mari and Dwayne are over. I feel really bad for her though. Especially since Hunt and I are doing so well. But I do know how she feels. I don't want to ever feel like that again. Hunt has made me forget (well- almost forget) the bad times. I've fallen head over heels with him again. It's been such a long time since I've allowed myself to be emotionally available to someone, and it feels so good. I even gave him a key to my apartment. He's always coming here anyway. But it saddens me that Mari doesn't have what I have. I'm so lucky to have Hunt.

Surprisingly, Mari doesn't seem to be too heartbroken. I guess since she's on the whole Jesus thing, she doesn't feel like it's as bad as it really is. She's moving on quite quickly. But that's a good thing though. Law school isn't something you can play with, and as she's in her last year, she really has to focus. Plus, she needs to find a man that can do for her what Hunt is doing for me. There's nothing like a good man to make a woman look more amazing. Especially when she's making big moves like Mari and I are.

We have a lot in common, but we're so different. We both grew up SDA; both are extroverts, passionate, and jokesters. But we channel our passions in different directions. She's all about church and God, and that's cool, but it's not where my passion lies. I love God and all, but she talks about him ALL the time. I mean ALL THE TIME! Sometimes, though, I wish I could see what she sees in God. My passion is medicine. If there was one thing I've always wanted to be, this was it. A doctor. And a wife. But it looks like that might not be too far off if things keep going the way they are with Hunt. No, I'm not jumping the gun. I know it's only been a few months but I'm counting the time we were together at Howard too. I think wedding bells are not a farfetched thought in the future. I'm keeping my fingers crossed...

****

Today was not a good day. Actually, it was a bad day. I've been so busy with Hunt lately that I skimped on my reading, and allowed myself to be distracted. I almost killed a patient today. What's worse is that Clarissa was the one who caught my mistake and fixed it. But of course, she HAD to publicly let the resident, Jack, know about it. I misread the chart, and was about to give the patient the wrong dosage of the medicine. It's a good thing I had prayed that morning, because had Clarissa walked in two minutes later, it would have been a bad scene. But the fact that Clarissa had caught the mistake was irritating. If it was the resident, I would've still been in trouble, but it would be different. Clarissa didn't even give me the chance to tell Jack. She decided to loudly proclaim my mistake, so now people think that I'm both illiterate and incompetent. I got into more trouble than I would have been in had I told him myself. Because she told him, it made it seem like I was trying to cover up my mistake. Now he thinks I'm sneaky, like I was planning to never say anything about it. But thankfully, nothing really happened, because Jack would be responsible for my mistakes. The bad thing is that he distrusts me, and listens her, and it doesn't help that she likes to wear her tight little scrubs and prance around. It's obvious he has a super nerd-crush on Clarissa, ad that she's taking advantage of it by flirting with him every chance she gets. She already has an advantage and preferential treatment. Now she's messing up my work relationships.

This is the hospital that I've always wanted to work at. I was born at Burrows Community Hospital, and as soon as I realized I wanted to be a doctor, I knew I wanted to work there. I guess I have to cut back my time with Hunt to make sure that this doesn't happen again. No more late nights when I have to work. But he doesn't like it when I scale back my quality time with him. It's a little unfair. It's like he forgot what it's like to be at the bottom of the work totem pole, having to be someone's flunky while you establish yourself. I never give him any grief when he cancels on me because of work. I wish he would have just a little more patience with me and all of my career woes. Oh well. No one is perfect. I don't let it get to me. He just wants more time with me. I can't blame him for that. What we have is more than what is missing. And you don't always get everything you want in relationships anyway. I'm just glad to have him. I could be alone like Mari. Thank God I'm not though. To me, even the empty meaningless sex of a regular booty call is better than being by yourself AND celibate. Sex in itself is great, but nothing beats sex with someone you love. I try not to do it, but who am I kidding? I like sex. I love Hunt. Why not? God will forgive me. Actually, I need to call Hunt. I could really use the stress relief right now...

****

Mari just can't catch a break! First Dwayne dumps her, and finds someone else (I think he found her first), and now this! So, Mari and her mom have never had the best relationship. They are always fighting and can barely stand each other. Well unfortunately, one of their arguments got so bad that Ms. Joi kicked Mari out. So now, Mari is living with me. She can barely afford to pay much for rent, and her job is how she affords to go to school, so she can't get her own place. But I guess I'm the blessing in her life, because I happen to have an extra (small) bedroom. It's actually the office, but I don't mind sacrificing the office space for her. This way, she won't have to keep sleeping on the couch. I think it's a good thing, her and I living together. We mesh well. Just as long as I don't have a lecture for breaking Sabbath and watching TV on Friday nights, I'm good. I don't do TBN or the Gospel Music Channel, or Bible DVDs. I do real, regular TV. Little Ms. Holy might have a problem with that.

I'm looking forward to getting real conversation. Not that her and I haven't had real conversations before, but it's kinda difficult to really talk about your business in a crowded restaurant, or in her house, when you never know who might overhear. Especially since it seems like Boston is SUPER small, and everyone has someone in common. Things get around way too quickly for my liking. So now, as immature as it sounds, I'm glad at the continuous sleepover that we get to have. Except when Hunt sleeps over. Then it gets a little awkward.

She doesn't think I should be fornicating. (I see why Dwayne dumped her!) I think she should get a man and try it. But that's just me. I don't know many man that I could introduce her to, when you disregard the ones outside of church, and the ones I've already ran through, or my fans. Most of my substantial guy friends have been eliminated because Hunt doesn't like it when I have a conversation with a male for too long, even if it's business or medically related. He's a tad bit on the possessive side, but I like it. He just doesn't want anyone else hitting on me. But although it's cute that he's like that, his temper is not. I can do without it. But he's my boo, and I love him. Even when I'm trying to focus at work, and even during church, he pops up in my mind. I'm happily addicted to him.

D. Gloria Elysée

Speaking of church and all that, Mari has gotten me all interested in some of the sermons. I heard a good one about having an "accountability partner." That's someone, particularly of your gender, who you can tell all your business to, and they're supposed to keep you in line (spiritually) and pray for the things you need extra help with. Basically, this person is your spiritual best friend. I told Mari she was mine, so that's another reason why I can't wait for our real conversations to start. I kinda feel burdened by many of the things I've done in my past, and have a huge issue with forgiveness, and I wanted to know if any of the "most holy folk" had issues with forgiveness like I did. I really want to stop being such a heathen. I mean it's fun and all, but I really don't feel like going to Hell, so I might as well have someone like Mari to help keep me in line, even when I don't want to be.

The hardest thing for me to give up will probably be the sex. Not that every other vice I have is any easier, but I REALLY love the sex, and I don't know what to do, because I really don't want to stop. I'd rather give up sarcasm. Plus, since Hunt and I have been having sex frequently, what am I supposed to tell him? That I changed my mind, it's wrong and we have to stop? He's not going to go for that. He doesn't like the fact that I'm not always ready to go, so how will he feel when I cut him off completely? Don't tell me that he's just going to have to accept it, because he's not the one changing the rules this late in the game. I got him used to the good stuff, and now I have to take it away.

I hope Mari has an answer, because no one else seems to be able to answer me, other than, "Just tell him, and he'll have to accept it." I wouldn't just accept that response, so how can I expect him to? But then again, I guess no one has been in this situation. They must all be in celibate relationships, or are dating someone who is either Christian or very understanding. I just don't see how this will work. He has to suffer because I decided to change my mind? That's how he's going to see it. But I hope someone gives me some real advice soon. I'm really trying to do better these days. I've even tried putting in Bible DVDs during the Sabbath, but I miss my shows. I guess I'll have to DVR them...

D. Gloria Elysée

Chapter 4
November 2009

Ok, so I have decided to really try to be serious about my relationship with God. It's high time that I did. Mari and I have stayed up for weeks talking about it. I told her some of my deepest darkest secrets, and the things that have been burdening me for a while now. She told me the things she was dealing with in her life, and we spoke about the concept of forgiveness: what it means to forgive others, and what it means to forgive yourself.

Surprisingly, she has just as many issues with the concept as I do. I guess we all have some issues when it comes to certain religious/spiritual concepts. She told me that I had the most issues with forgiving myself and accepting God's forgiveness of me, and that the guilt I was carrying around was a sign that I hadn't believed that God had actually forgiven me. This was weighing down on my perception of myself, and because I wouldn't forgive myself, and always dwelled on my mistakes, I made myself feel like I didn't deserve good things.

She said I had low self-esteem. I thought that was interesting because I actually love the way I looked, and made sure I highlighted my body and my pretty face as much as possible. She explained that many women highlight the physical because they feel that is all they have to offer. She said that by highlighting my curves, I was putting them on display to garner attention since I felt that was my only way of getting it. She said I felt my worth was wrapped up in my looks, and that I was looking for male attention to validate my self-worth. I think that's a stretch. I know I have a hard time with guilt, but saying I don't love or value myself is a lot. That still doesn't explain this nagging feeling I had when she said it though.

She told me that forgiving myself didn't mean that I wouldn't have remorse, but that I wouldn't have a burden anymore if I would just accept that I was forgiven, and move on. I guess she's right. Sometimes I can't help but feel that my sins define me, and that I won't make it into Heaven because of all the things I do.

I used to have one of those "why bother?" attitudes, because I felt like I'd gone too far, so God wouldn't want to forgive me. Especially since I grew up hearing that God doesn't forgive the sins that we knowingly do. In that case, I might as well not even ask. Every time I ask, there's nothing that makes me feel forgiven, anyway.

When I told Mari this, she looked surprised. She told me that if I ask God to forgive me, He would, because He is faithful to me, even when I'm unfaithful to

Him. She told me that if I'd just accept that He loves me like the Bible says He does, I would be able to wrap my head around the concept of forgiveness long enough to accept it. She added in that feelings were really not a good indicator of my spiritual state because they didn't always reflect reality.

She thinks that I don't love myself, because if I did, I wouldn't let mistakes define me, and also that I wouldn't be so tied down to sex because I'd realize how important it was to myself and my future husband. I think she might have a point about the forgiveness thing, but I don't see the correlation between that and my sexual activity. Oh well, that's just her opinion. It's not like she went to school for this.

She also told me to read the Bible for myself. I guess she has a point. All these things I should already know are just sitting there in the Good Book, but I can't seem to bring myself to open it. It's a little dry, and when I do read it, I can't understand the old English, or I can't keep myself from falling asleep. Plus, I do all this digging to find a verse, and when I find it, it's usually connected to a paragraph and it usually has nothing to do with what I thought it meant. It doesn't help that people walk around saying all sorts of things out of context. But I guess that's why I have to read it for myself- that way, I won't be one of those people. I can't pretend anymore. I'm literally sick of it. Being a hypocrite is a LOT of work, and I don't want to keep lying to people, or keep trying to be someone I'm not. It's not worth it.

Anyway, Mari is supposed to help me out, and we're going to read the Bible together. Nothing major, just a Psalm and a chapter from each Testament every day. We're just going to take our time, because I'm not trying to commit to something that I will break down the road. But Mari and I living together is actually great. She's been a lot nicer to Hunt since she's been living here. I guess they had a chance to talk it out, because he's usually here waiting for me when I get home, and since I gave his key to her, he had to learn to depend on her in a sense. (Don't worry it was only for like 2 weeks. I didn't really have time to make him a new key, but she did.) Either way, I'm glad that they are cool now, because it makes things a lot less awkward for me.

She's still pretty depressed though. Outside of school and church, she isn't really social. I keep trying to get her to go out and date, but the whole Dwayne thing has gotten her really down. It never ends! Apparently, he just got engaged to the girl he left her for. Mari is taking it especially hard, especially since her mother called her with an, "I told you so!" Yes. That really happened. Her mom called to rub it in her face. As nice as Ms. Joi is to me, that's how much she seems to hate Mari. And now Mari seems to hate her as well. She already hated her dad for being absent, and leaving when she was seven, but since then, her mom had gotten mean, and that phone call just pushed her over the edge.

Mari has no parental support whatsoever. She has no man. All she has is me. I don't think I'd be able to handle all that, but that goes back to the theory that God gives us lives that we can handle, and that He won't leave you hanging. Man, Mari has some serious forgiveness issues as well. I told her that if she didn't find a way to let it go, it would eat at her, just like my guilt was doing to me.

I just realized that this Bible reading thing is working. It must be. I don't usually have spiritual awakenings or revelations. It's starting to happen quite often now, and I don't know what to do with myself when it happens. I'm even praying longer too! I usually say the quick morning and bedtime prayers, but now my prayers have substance, aren't always repetitive. I actually kinda enjoy it now. It's not just a chore, but it's actually a part of my day.

Some of the church-ladies at Bethel and Genesis told me that life would get a lot easier if I became serious with God. Well, I think that's some great motivation, because life is a little difficult right now, and I could definitely use a break. Life just seems more burdensome these days, and a little unfair. At work, I have so many issues with just keeping up with the pace and material, and when I come home I have to deal with making sure that Mari isn't depressing herself even more. We never can talk about my problems, because she has so many. It's actually weird because she's so into God, but her life is sucking right now, and definitely not any easier than it was when we first reunited.

I think it's because Dwayne is a terrible person, her dad is a deadbeat, and that Ms. Joi is a bigger hypocrite than I ever was. At least I don't make my loved ones miserable. The worst things I ever got into were drinking, clubbing, and sex. Their choices have made Mari's life hard, not God. It's not fair to her. She deserves better. But her time will come, and so will mine.

I can't wait to be finished with this residency (yes I know it's years away), and specifically with Clarissa. She's got everybody watching me like a hawk, waiting for me to break. All this pressure on me, and I can't seem to get anything right. The most basic procedures that I used to be able to do, I'm struggling with now. And I'm afraid of the more difficult ones. I'm afraid to mess up, and my job performance is resting heavily on top of all this fear. Thoughts like *=your WHOLE future depends on this=* keep swimming around my head, and it's like I have performance anxiety. I try to encourage myself, by reminding myself that I've wanted to do this since I was three, have been working for this, and that the start is always a little rocky. That doesn't seem to help much.

Sometimes I wonder if God is really in all of what I'm doing, or if I'm just suffering the consequence of choosing my own path, and doing something I wasn't "Called" to do. What if God really wants me to be like, I dunno, a chef, and I'm so wrapped up in my idea, that

He's letting me fail before I get to do what I want to do? Or this could be what I'm actually supposed to do, and I'm letting my fears and lack of confidence keep me from being who I need to be, doing what I need to do, and accomplishing what I need to accomplish. My co-workers don't seem to have these issues. As much as I dislike Clarissa, I admire her confidence and her skill at all this. And here I am, wrecking this great opportunity, wrecking my career before it even really begins.

I pray about it every day, but it seems that as soon as I get to work and pick up a patient's chart, I freeze up. I can't evaluate, diagnose or treat without having the shakes. And I'm so insecure that if I make a mistake, get reprimanded or constructive criticism, a part of me breaks, and leaves me feeling down, long after the incident. I really feel as though I've fooled myself up until this point, and that I'm really not cut out for this job. It hurts when others doubt my ability, but not as much as when I doubt my own. I am ruining my career and my life, and I can't talk to anyone about it. I think I might have to go to the psychiatry department after work, and talk to someone there.

I can't talk to Hunt about this, because the last time I tried, he brushed it off and told me "everyone goes through it. You have to suck it up and move on!" And Mari has so many issues of her own, and I usually can't even fit in enough words to introduce my problem, because of her complaints dominating the conversation.

Truthfully, she complains so much lately, and it's starting to change her. She's distant when she's not complaining, and she doesn't even talk about Jesus like that anymore. We haven't had a late-night gossip session in a long time, and she doesn't open up anymore.

I think she's hiding something from me. She's always locked in her room. I think it's because Hunt is always here. Maybe she can't stand the sight of me being in a relationship when she isn't in one. I guess it hurts her that she's alone, and my boyfriend always being around is a constant reminder of her issues. But I thought they were getting along better. Now it seems that they don't want to be around each other at all. I guess her complaints are annoying Hunt.

But lately, he's no picnic either. I can't seem to win with him. He always has some "constructive criticism" that leaves me wondering what he's trying to construct. It feels like I disappoint him, and with all the stuff at work, and dealing with Mari's moodiness, I really don't have the emotional energy for this. He's upset because we've stopped having sex, he's upset that I'm trying to spend more time studying so less time to cook for him. My house is a mess, because I don't have time for upkeep, so he complains about that too. I can't do anything right. I think it might be time for him to get some "space" soon, but I don't want to be alone. Especially since Mari is so bitter.

But I really do have to clean the house though. I'm just so exhausted after work, and not just physically either. I told him that, but he said he managed to keep his place clean after working all day. True, but he's always here! When I told him that, he got upset. *Sigh* Another day, another argument. I'm sick of it. I can't seem to get any peace, anywhere I go...

****

I thought things were supposed to get better after you've given your life to God. They LIED! They said life improves. Well, it DOESN'T! I came home three days ago after a long day's work, to find Hunt in my bed: with Mari. I guess hers was too small, and they wanted an upgrade. The entire time he was distant and nitpicking everything I did. The whole time she was moody and locking herself in her room. All the criticism, complaining, isolation, sniping comments: EVERYTHING! It was all them! I was making myself crazy trying to keep everything together for their sakes, and they were betraying me by sleeping together.

She began to cry, apologizing, and saying that they "didn't mean for it to happen." He just stood there. No "sorry." No reaction resembling shame. Just stood there, between the dresser and the nightstand, pillow shams strewn all over the room, sheets disheveled and on the floor. He didn't even try to pick anything up to cover up his nakedness. Just arrogantly stood there, like it was my fault for interrupting them. As if I was an inconvenience, or I was in the wrong.

Meanwhile, my mind is shutting down while Mari is sobbing her apologies to me, and scrambling to put on her clothes. But my eyes were fixated on his arrogant stare. Still, he said nothing. That's when it all went dark. All I remember was my aluminum softball bat, a broken mirror, and a lamp flying across the room. And the police. But by the time they got there, I was by myself. I'm actually quite sad to say that I didn't hit anybody. Actually, I'm just pissed. Needless to say, Mari is officially homeless. I can't even front: I want to kill her and let her die a slow, torturous death. I gave her a place to stay when no one else would and *this* is how she repays my generosity. She's lucky she left when she did. If she'd stayed five minutes longer, I would've had a double homicide on my hands. (I had narrowly missed Hunt's head with the bat.) Meanwhile, he was cursing at me as if I were the one at fault. THE NERVE!

Since my neighbors had called the police, I was stuck with a fine for disturbing the peace, and now have that matter to deal with. I have so many cuss words swimming around in my brain right now I can't even begin to say them. I feel so betrayed. I can't go back into my room. I can't look at my dresser. My bed. I want to burn my sheets. I've been sleeping on the couch for the past three days. And yesterday, I killed someone. I was distracted at work, because of the homicidal thoughts about Mari and Hunter that I was having. Needless to say, wrong diagnosis, absent resident, wrong medication, and wrongful death. Now I have to go before the hospital review board on Monday.

There goes my career. My mom gave me that "He'll never give you more than you can bear" crap and I had to literally restrain myself from hanging up the phone on her. I'm so done with all of that. It doesn't work. Ms. Churchy McJesus Freak is in my bed having sex with my man, meanwhile she was the one telling me that I should stop the premarital sex. Yeah right! And now what am I supposed to do? Go back to church with her? Yeah okay. Not happening!

I'll go to church, but not hers. I'm going to try Genesis again, because there is nothing else in my life that is going well, but I tell you, Jesus better show up for this one, or I'm not going back. I'm so angry and hurt. So I'm not good enough for Hunt? He could just sit there and criticize me, and go on about all the things that were wrong with me, and meanwhile, sleep with my best friend in my bed? IN MY BED? I guess my room was clean enough for him *then*. I just can't wrap my head around his lack of remorse. What did I do to deserve a horrible man like that? And I feel so stupid, because it was my fault. I should have known better than to take him back. I should have known that people don't change. I should have known better than to trust a man. Well I won't make *that* mistake again.

These days I can't sleep. I've been up in the middle of the night watching all sorts of foolishness, from infomercials, to strange old movies, to ballroom dancing competitions. It's all I can think to do to keep me from having to think about what's going on in my life, and it's saving me from some violent outbursts that threaten to escape. It also is saving me from myself. I can't let myself be so fixated on this that I let my life go down the toilet. Oh wait, too late!

If my career ends on Monday, I'll have all the time in the world to be left with my thoughts. But I can't let that happen while I still have a chance. I can't believe that I let myself become so distracted that I let someone die. No- I killed her. She had a family, and a life, and my careless mistake killed her. And possibly my career. I can't believe I let Mari and Hunter's supreme betrayal distract me from my dream. And of course, Clarissa had to be the one who was so dramatic about it that I had to run to the bathroom to hide the tears.

The worst part in all this is that since my performance has been slipping lately, it seems like a trend, rather than an isolated mistake. I think this was the final straw. The way my job performance has been lately has been embarrassing, and now the review board? And I got my resident and attending in trouble too, so it really sucks. I feel really guilty about it. I feel like my career has ended, even before it has begun. All because to two very selfish, inconsiderate people couldn't keep it in their pants. Well this will all be settled next week, so I just have to pray about it and hope it works out for the best. But thank God, it's the Sabbath! No work-related ANYTHING until Sunday...

****

I woke up early the next morning to go to church. I had been so used to Bethel's late services that this felt a little foreign to me. But I did it, because I really needed some prayer. This wasn't the first time my patient died, but it was the first time that I had directly caused a patient's death. But church was normal. Pastor Morgan blabbed on and on as usual. I tried to follow, but it was one of those parables, something about a sower and some seeds, and I was in no mood to pay attention to it. I was sleepy, and plus, halfway through the service, Mari showed up. She didn't sit near me, but it did seem like she was looking for me during the service. I slid down in my seat. I didn't need any more mess in my life.

After church, I tried to rush out, but Mari caught me just as I walked outside. So, there we were standing in front of the church steps. Me, trying not to slap her, and her, with her, "Can we talk?" "Sure." I replied. "You have two minutes. Go." "Here?" she questioned. "Yes here. Actually, you know what? I don't have time for this." As I began to walk away, she conceded. "Ok ok. I just wanted to tell you how sorry I am. Please forgive me!" *Really? She wants to do this now?* "You won't answer my calls, and I can't stop by, but I just want to say I'm so, so, SO sorry! Please! You HAVE to forgive me!" *I don't "have" to do anything!* "I just want us to be friends again. I know you'll need some time, but will you think about it?" She was speaking in hushed tones. "This is why you've been stalking me?" I asked. "Well forget that. It's not gonna happen so **LEAVE ME ALONE!**"

I must have gotten loud, because people began to look at us. I guess she got embarrassed, because she started to get angry. "I'm trying to ask forgiveness here. This is really difficult for me to do. The least you could do is hear me out and not cause a scene!" *SHE DIDN'T JUST SAY THAT. NO. SHE. DIDN'T.* "The least I could do? **THE LEAST I COULD DO?** No sweetie. The least I could do is slap you into next week for sleeping with my man in my bed after I took your homeless behind into my house. The least I could do is publish a newsletter about your trifling behind, and put your mess on blast. The least I could do is ruin your life for wrecking mine, and taking away the peace I had in my own home. That's the **LEAST** I can do."

Now I was causing a scene. But I guess the truth hurts worse in public, because she began to get really angry. "Oh. So you're a saint now?" She replied. "That's funny. You weren't much of a saint when you were having sex with random strangers you met online. You've *just* started getting good with God. You've been righteous for all of two seconds, and you want to judge me? Your porn addiction doesn't seem so holy. You're nothing but a skillful whore who knows- correction- KNEW how to cover it up. Don't act like I didn't know what was going on. You told me yourself about how you slept with your professor so you could get a better grade. Don't go getting all brand new in front of these church folk. You ain't nothing but a 'ho in a church suit."

I felt like I was kicked in the stomach. Especially since the crowd we drew included the church board, the pastor, and of course, Sister Roberts. She knew my parents well, and whenever my mom knew about something going on at Genesis, it was usually because Sister Roberts had told her.

Mari stood with a smug expression on her face, and I couldn't breathe. I felt the tears welling, and all I remember was my mouth releasing a stream of expletives, my arms swinging out at her, and some people restraining me. I don't even know how I made it home safely, especially with my altered state of mind. I wasn't aware of anything but the ache in my chest. From the moment the lock clicked shut, the tears could not stop falling. I couldn't believe, after all that had happened, she could betray me even more. Sleeping with Hunt was bad enough. But I told her those things as my accountability partner, in confidence, so that I could stop judging myself and finally move on from the guilt I was carrying from them. I wouldn't even think to put her out there like that. Ever. Even after Hunter. But now she put all my business on the street. I can't ever show my face at Genesis again. All of them heard it. All of them were there. And the ones that weren't outside for that debacle would know by the end of the Sabbath. It wasn't just that they knew. It was that they were the ones who watched me grow up.

I'm still in a state of shock. How could she do that? She had no right to say that. I trusted her as my accountability partner. True, I was angry, and maybe said what I shouldn't have said, but I would've cooled down eventually. I just needed more time. Did she think I had forgotten so soon? It had been less than a week. I mean, had she not bull-guarded me at church, and had just let me breathe rather than stalking me, I might have had time to exhale, and maybe even have forgiven her. But there was no chance of any of that now. She can rot in Hell for all I care. She and Hunter deserve each other. But I can't afford to think about this anymore. I have other problems, like the possible death of my career to think about...

****

RING! *RING!* It was my parents calling. They did it every Sunday. I suppressed the urge to not answer. I needed a pick-me-up, and thought my mom could make me laugh. Especially since I had been in isolation since yesterday's fiasco. I just wanted to be alone, and cried nonstop all night. "Hey mom!" I tried to sound cheery. "Heaven Leigh." Two voices spoke. I tried to ignore the fact that I had been "full-named" (you know you're in trouble when your parents use your middle name too). "Oh, hey Daddy! I didn't know you were on the phone too. How are you guys? How was your Sabbath?" I was being chatty so they wouldn't notice my voice breaking, and maybe would be distracted.

"OK. Let's cut to the chase." My mom was all business. "I have been receiving calls from Genesis members since yesterday. What exactly have you been doing up there? Fighting in church? Whoring around with strangers? Is that what I raised you to be? A Jezebel with complete disregard to the Word of the Lord? We sent you to Boston to become a doctor. To grow in God. Not to go gallivanting around sleeping with everyone and then fighting about it at church. I know you think you're grown and all that, but have some sense. What were you thinking?"

I couldn't breathe. So, this is what a heart attack feels like. I could barely stammer out an, "I'm so sorry" amidst the tears and my mother's hysterical lecture. My dad just sighed and said, "I can't deal with this. I'm just so disappointed in you Heaven Leigh. I'm going to need some space. I can't- *Sigh*" (There goes that full name thing again). "See! Now you've gone and upset your father! How could you be so stupid! How could..."

As my mother continued with her angry rant, my mind was toward my father. I couldn't imagine what was going through his mind, but I felt SO bad about everything. "I'm very disappointed in you. You've embarrassed yourself and this family. And look what you've done to your father. He can't even look at the phone right now, let alone speak to you. I need some time to cool off myself. I'll call you when I've calmed down a bit. I'm just so disappointed in you. *Sigh* Goodbye." *CLICK*

Wait. Did that just happen? Did my mom just hang up on me? And did my parents just break up with me? This isn't possible. It can't be. And who told them? I'd bet a million dollars that Sister Roberts told them. I hate nosy people. I hate this. In fact, I blame Mari and Hunter for all of this. Neither of them has to deal with any of this. I'm sure Hunter's parents are still speaking to him. I'm sure Mari isn't having trouble at work because of this. It's not fair. It's just not fair. I can't stop crying. But I can't think about this. I have to go before the review board tomorrow, and I need to be able to focus on that. I think some vodka could be really useful at this point. I need to drink to forget everything that has been going on lately, but not too much. I have to wake up for work tomorrow. I hate this... I hate them...

Chapter 5
November 2009

Mondays are the worst! Notwithstanding the fact that it means your attempt at relaxation is over, it always seems to overlap into Sunday evening, leaving you with an even shorter weekend. And then you almost have to re-learn how to work. And it seems like everything goes slower on a Monday. As you can see, I abhor Mondays. Not just the fact that today starts another 32-hour shift, but that it also is the day where my fate is decided.

The hearing to decide whether or not I still get to be a doctor is today, and I am "sore afraid." I read that phrase in the Bible, and it made it seem like that fear was physically painful. But I definitely understand. That explains the headache that I'm having right now. (That or it's a hangover. Yeah, it's probably a hangover). But my physical pain can't be my focus right now. Nor can my emotional distress distract me. That's what got me into this mess in the first place. If I had better control of my emotions, I wouldn't need this hearing to decide my professional fate. Nevertheless, I'm learning that it depends on God's will for me, so I've been praying non-

75

stop since this morning. I even tried fasting on Saturday, but we all know how that turned out.

As the meeting started, my tension began to mount. Sitting next to my resident and my attending wasn't the best of ideas, but it also wasn't my choice. We had to sit together since we were the ones being reprimanded, and, plus, it gave the impression of a "united front". I'm praying that God will show up and put words in my mouth to tell them, because at this point I don't know what to say.

I don't want to lie (and plus God wouldn't help me lie in the first place), and I don't want to tell the truth, because I'll look really incompetent. How do I tell them that my "bad day" caused this to happen? It's not like there's much I can say to make it seem better. I was having emotional distress that caused me to misread the lady's chart, and in my attempt to be confident, and take more initiative, I gave her medicine she was allergic to, and killed her. Now the family wants to sue, and my job is looking a LOT less like a fixture and more like a memory. My mind isn't focusing on the hearing though. Oh wait, it's my turn. Okay God, I'm going to tell the truth. You'd better be with me on this one! Oh yeah... Your Will be done...

"I was in emotional distress due to certain issues in my personal life, and I was distracted when the client, Mrs. Jassen, came into the ER with Ms. Jassen, her daughter. She presented with a cough with green sputum, fever, shortness of breath, chills, chest pain that worsened during inspiration, tachycardia, and fatigue. I scanned over her chart and began treatment, since the ER was busy that day and the resident allows us interns a certain degree of freedom, granted that we check in, especially if we run into any problems.

"Mrs. Jassen's symptoms looked like pneumonia, so I took the initiative to diagnose and treat her alone. It looked pretty straightforward, and since I had only perused through her chart, and things looked fine, I didn't see any problems. I decided to prescribe antibiotics for her, and thought that amoxicillin would be best. It wasn't stated in her chart that she was allergic to penicillin, and the client or her sister never mentioned it. I don't explicitly remember asking for any allergies, but I'm sure I asked. I was distracted and busy with another patient when the daughter came up to me, and said that Mrs. Jessen was having labored breathing. I told her to go to the nurse, unaware that Mrs. Jessen was suffering from anaphylactic shock due to the amoxicillin.

"By the time I reached her, after the nurse came to get me, her airway was entirely collapsed, and I was unable to get a line down through her trachea. She died while we were trying to open her airways and reverse the reaction. The time of death was 4:49pm. I did what I could to save her, but it wasn't enough."

I'm guessing my openness about my compromised emotional state came as a shock to everyone. My resident and attending both vehemently denied knowledge of my compromised state. I understand though, because had they known, and thought I was a danger to my patients, and still had left me alone, they would be equally responsible. They were only looking out for their own careers, but it still hurt that, rather than back me up and say that I was a good intern, and that this wasn't a pattern, they kinda threw me under the bus, to save themselves.

Of course, Clarissa was all too eager to volunteer information about my past mistakes. The panel said someone had come to them in confidence to testify against me, and volunteered information about my ability as a doctor (or lack, thereof). They didn't say who it was, but there's only one person I know who would do something like that. Clarissa. My attending denied knowledge of my "history of mistakes", but my resident quickly cosigned with the "anonymous" tipper.

He painted the picture as though I was almost incompetent, and that my mistakes were "increasingly frequent and destructive." Of course, many questions were raised, including, "If you knew you were compromised, why did you continue to treat patients? Why didn't you go home or not come in at all, if you thought that you might be unable to do your job as you should?" They also had questions for my resident and attending. To the attending, "How were you unaware of this intern's mistakes? Shouldn't you be supervising your residents and making sure that they are actually teaching their interns?" To the resident: "If she was having so many problems, why would you leave her to treat these patients alone? Why haven't we heard about her problems? If she's so incompetent, why aren't you teaching her to do better, or at least supervising her so that things like this don't happen?" After we all struggled to find answers to these questions, it was time for the panel to deliberate.

****

Two days had passed, and it didn't look good. They had asked me, after the "trial" to take some time off, and to come back when they called me in. I'm guessing they wanted to speak with other people, like nurses and other staff, about my performance. Unfortunately, the stern look on their faces as we filed back into the room made me feel like I was being sentenced to death by a firing squad, or life with no chance of parole. I could then tell that the only miracle that would happen was if my career was able to resurrect from this disaster.

The chief of Emergency Medicine began to speak. "Due to professional incompetence, we will be terminating your residency contract at this hospital, due to the following reasons..." I couldn't hear anything as all the blood rushed to my head. I caught bits and pieces of words like "liability" and "lawsuit" and "malpractice" and "settling out of court," but I couldn't focus long enough to hear the rest, including what would happen to my resident and attending. Probably a slap on the wrist for my attending, and for my resident, I don't even know.

All I knew was that all I've ever wanted to do was be a doctor. And now, it was looking like it might not happen for me. I hated everyone that had to do with this decision. The panel. The ER staff. My attending. My resident. And especially Clarissa. I hated them all.

Funny thing, everyone was shocked at how severe my punishment was, as if it wasn't even realistic for me to be in so much trouble. In fact, many thought it was unfair, and that I should fight for my job back. Apparently, I was being made an example of, because the hospital was going through its accreditation process, and since the budget was tight, and I was a "liability," I had to go. After only being 5 months into my residency, though I "showed so much promise" because I was at the top of my class. I guess I had killed one too many people in too short of a time. I was deemed "professionally incompetent." I was a failure. I had no fight left in me though. I was glad that I wouldn't have to go to court for this.

When I walked by Clarissa, I said, "I guess you don't have any more competition for the spot of head intern." She couldn't help her smirk. She knew I was right, and it was then that I realized her hatred of me wasn't a color issue. It was a competitive issue. I was a threat. I outdid her as valedictorian at Harvard, and I was the likely candidate for the position of head intern (which isn't really a position, but it means a better chance of a great job, since many of them go on to have managerial positions). Word has it that she tried to mess up the career of one of her "closest" friends while at Harvard. I guess it really isn't a color issue. (My bad!)

She didn't like me because I was the best, and I was overshadowing her. Well, looks like she doesn't have that problem anymore.

As I cleared out my locker, every item I put in my little box built on the hatred and anger I was carrying in my heart. Hatred for Hunt and Mari. For my now former superiors and coworkers. For the pain I had to endure. For my dead career. For wanting to blame my dead career on budget cuts and accreditation, rather than my declining job performance. For the new job I would have to get since my dream died. For my trying to be honest and still having these consequences. For God, for not preventing or circumventing my punishment. For everything. For the fight that I couldn't fight, because in the end I was wrong, and that could be proven by my own testimony. I was consumed with anger.

It was all so morbid. I had to find a new way to pay rent, before I became homeless. I couldn't go crawling back to my parents in DC. They had their own problems. Plus, they weren't speaking to me, and I would rather wait tables than have to deal with that depressing silence. Anything but that.

And now I have nothing. Nothing except for bills: rent, cell phone, cable, internet, and LOANS that are now of no use to me. I took out loans to make it through Howard, and when I got a scholarship to Harvard, it was great. But I still had $60,000 worth of loans to pay back. I was jobless. No income. No career. No possibility of advancement. Do NOT pass GO. Do NOT collect $200. I was done. And I hated it. My life was now over. Finito. Kaput. I was nothing, a nobody, and it was all my fault. I went home and stayed in bed for three days.

****

Saturday morning, I decided to attempt to go to church. I didn't want to, but I thought a miracle could happen, and plus, I needed something in my life. I couldn't stay home and wallow in my funk any longer. And I'd always heard stories about how people would lose their jobs, but then when they went to church and prayed about it, somehow, there would be someone there that day that had an "opening" and then these people would get a job when they thought they had no possibilities. The thought of that happening was my driving factor. I figured that since I did what I was supposed to do, and got screwed anyway, that God owed me one, and He'd come through today.

I knew I couldn't go to Genesis ever again, but Bethel was my first thought. Bold with emotional courage, I decided to go brave Mari's territory. Maybe it was because I'd gotten up so late that I ended up going to Bethel, or maybe I was just trying to punish myself, but I decided to quell the thoughts that were trying to talk me out of going. I thought it was just the devil being a hater again.

As soon as I walked in, I felt a cold chill. But then again, it was the end of November, and Boston starts getting cold in September. I had gotten there early, for Sabbath School. I wasn't going to give God any reason to play me today. As I reached the door to the sanctuary, with my hand still on the doorknob, I ran smack dab into King. I tried to put up a cheerful front, as if I had not a care in the world. But it was to no avail. I was selling crap, and he wasn't buying it. He spoke only seven words to me. "I spoke to Mari. Is it true?"

My heart stopped. My legs almost buckled. His questioning stare burned straight through to my soul and I could look nowhere but down. His eyebrows expectantly raised, he stood, blocking the doorway to the sanctuary. What usually was a busy church now seemed deserted. It was only the two of us, and there was no one to distract him.

When I said not a word, he continued. "I knew it. When Mari told me, I didn't want to believe her. She told me everything you did. And she also told me why you didn't want to date me. You know what? I'm glad you were too shallow to go down that road with me. You probably saved me from an STD or something. You had the nerve to think you were better than me? I mean Mari is wrong for sleeping with your man and all, but you are all kinds of nasty."

I couldn't take anymore. I ran out the church, pushing past people, oblivious to their shock and anger at my rudeness. I had to get out of there. The way I sped toward my house, you would've thought that I would have been arrested for reckless endangerment or possibly, vehicular manslaughter. It's a wonder that I wasn't pulled over for violating every single traffic law known to man, or got into a car accident. But I arrived at home physically unscathed. However, I was emotionally broken beyond repair.

As I walked into my building, my phone started to vibrate. It was Gwen. I really didn't feel like dealing with her, so I ignored it, and went upstairs. The calls kept coming. And as I reached my apartment, the doorbell buzzed. Mentally exhausted, I decided to answer the door and the phone. I buzzed in the door, thinking someone was trying to get in to see someone other than me.

When I answered, Gwen said, "Coming up now!" I was trying to figure out what that meant, since my mind was in the midst of shutting down, when I heard a knock at the door. It was Gwen, along with a few others from Genesis. She dropped by my house unannounced with a church prayer group. "What do you want?" I asked brusquely. "We saw that you weren't at church today, and we know that you've been having a hard time, so we wanted to pray for you."

As grateful as I was for the consideration and the prayer, I was still irritated when she grabbed my hand and everybody began laying their hands on me. (I still hate when unfamiliar people touch me.) Gwen began praying. "Oh Lord God, Our Heavenly Father, we thank You this day for Your great and awesome mercy and love. We thank You for this Sabbath Rest that You have provided for us. We thank You for life, health, and strength to endure these trials that You've allowed us to go through. God, we bring before You our sister, Heaven.

"God she is lost and searching for You. She has fallen subject to the demons of addictions, alcohol, drugs, pornography, lust, fornication, hypersexuality, homosexuality, and all manner of perversion. Lord deliver--" *Whoa. Wait. WHAT?* "All manner of perversion? Homosexuality? What are you talking about? I don't know where you got that information from, but that is WRONG. That is NOT my issue. Never has been, never will be."

"Oh. I'm sorry," she said. "I guess I thought that I should throw it in there. I mean most sexual deviants deal with all of that. Oh, and can you not interrupt the prayer next time? Thank you." I was LIVID! You could even say, "my spirit was VEXED within me."

"Sexual deviant? I'M a sexual DEVIANT? So, you come into my house uninvited and throw this crap in my face? And add on sins I've never committed because it 'fits my profile'? You come in the name of God, calling me your sister, and then judge me and try to pray over me like you're doing me a favor? And then get upset because I interrupted your prayer full of lies? GET OUT OF MY HOUSE!" I didn't know what to do with myself. I never knew I could be so angry, and have so much hate in my heart. It was literally consuming me to the point of being scarily irrational. I was a hair away from committing a crime of passion.

Ms. Super Holy and those other Pharisees wanted to label me as a sexual deviant, perverse in all ways, and judge me, without ever getting my side of the story, and use prayer as a way to attack me. She, like everybody else, wasn't interested in my side. They had made up their minds about me. I was a Jezebel, and that was it. So yes. I kicked them out of my house. They're lucky that's all I did. I wasn't a deviant. I wasn't perverse. I wasn't a whore. I wasn't a horrible person. If anything, I was addicted to the attention. I could really care less about the sex. I just wanted to be successful, and wanted people to want to be like me. That was it. But they were taking things I did and were making it seem like I was this disgusting, indiscriminate whore. And they came up in my house, and had the nerve to throw God in my face. As if He hadn't done enough.

I was THROUGH. In a fit of rage, I threw my Bible out the window onto the street. I had had enough. Nothing good had come from my relationship with God. In fact, everything had gone from bearable to horrendous within a matter of weeks. I didn't need this in my life. Forget all of them, and anything that had to do with them. God included. I mean, he sent them, so he's responsible. I just can't take it anymore.

From now on, I'm all about me. No one else cares, so why should I? They've already made up their minds about me. I might as well let them think like that forever. It's all about what I want now. I can't be a doctor? Fine. Give me a few months. I'll be one somewhere else. I'll get a job in the meantime, and some way, somehow, I will get things done. I don't need God's help. Especially since he's making them like Gwen. If that's what it's like to be a follower of God, I'm GOOD. They can keep all that. I'm all about me now. Just me. I'm all I have. Just me. Just me...

D. Gloria Elysée

Chapter 6
December 2009

The holidays are almost here. And it's been rough. I've found a way to deal with all of this. I'm doing ok. I get out of bed every morning and go to work. I come home. I eat (sometimes). I watch TV. I'm doing ok. I'm coping. I got a job at the H&M downtown, and I'm making most of my payments. So what if I don't have enough money for groceries? I have Ramen noodles and cereal to tide me over. And it's not as if I have anyone coming over. Except those nights when I get lonely and go hook up with a guy. But usually I go to his place. So, see? I'm ok.

My only issue is that I still have trouble sleeping, so my doctor prescribed me some sleeping pills. Oh, and the fact that Mari still has my house keys. I mean, she's not trying to come by or anything crazy like that, but I really don't like her having them. I haven't had the time or energy to change the locks, let alone the money. But I told her that the bat would introduce itself to her head if she tried to come by unannounced, even though she still has a few things left here. She got a place of her own now. She finally stopped mooching off of people.

Funny thing. People I know from my past life (the church folk) keep updating me on things I don't care about, or care to know about. Like Mari. Why do people think it's cool to tell me how she's doing? I don't care! She doesn't matter. And people are telling me that I need to come back to church. *Not. Happening.* They say I'm in danger of death. Well to me, church is death so I'm good with all that. I don't care that they had Thanksgiving dinner together at church. Wanna know what I did this Thanksgiving? I worked, and then came home to a nice hot bowl of Ramen noodles, and a Cosby Show marathon on TV, rather than dinner with my family, who still isn't talking to me. My siblings know what happened and don't talk to me either. And since I have no friends, I just spent time giving myself thanks for myself.

But these church folk are out of their minds. I don't care that you still need help with your health ministry! I'm not a doctor anymore. I can't help you. Especially when you run into me when I'm at work at H&M. Clearly, I am not a doctor anymore. But, there are a few church ladies that I can't be rude to. They're the nice sweet ones, who only say, "I'm praying for you. God Bless you." and keep it moving. I can't be rude to them. But the people who say all that other crap, ask me for things, try to pressure me into coming back, and then try to update me on church gossip? I shut them DOWN. I don't do hypocrites.

I stopped living a double life, and only live for me now. I don't care about them or what they think. But out of respect, I leave the real church ladies alone. I just politely shut them down when they try to invite me to stuff. What I can't stand are the ones who clearly know I'm going through it, but tell me, "You've gained weight!" As if I don't own a mirror! I am well aware. And yeah, yeah I look "healthy," but that's just the old school way of calling me fat. I'm hip to the game, old people! I haven't gained this weight by eating my emotions, or gluttony. I actually hardly eat. Usually it's one meal, most likely dinner, and then I get ready for bed and go to sleep.

I'm putting in overtime at work because I need to get my bills paid, and it's a recession, and these creditors are knocking at my door, and there's no one but me to depend on. So, I'm on the grind, and I do what I gotta do. I work. I come home. And that's it. Oh, there are the late night escapades, but those are just because I need to relieve stress. I found a new group of people to hang with. These girls I met at the club one day. We have a lot in common. They're never fake about their lifestyle, and are just enjoying their adulthood, like me. Work, men, and sex dominate our conversations. We usually don't talk too much about work, though. But life is good. I do what I do. And that's all there is to it.

****

D. Gloria Elysée

Happy Birthday to me. Yesterday was December 16, my 26th birthday. No one called me and I have no missed calls, texts, or emails. I did get a voicemail from my mom, but it was rushed, and sounded like it was an obligation, not a genuine well wish. I deleted my Facebook account so nothing from there. So this is what it's like to be invisible. Does anyone actually care about me? They all either hurt me, judge me, or ignore me. I have nothing left. I can't do this anymore...

"Oh my God!!! Heaven!!!!"

What's all that yelling? It seems so far away….

"Hello??? Operator??? I need an ambulance!!! My friend swallowed all the pills in her bottle!!! I think they're sleeping pills!!! I don't know how long she's been like this. I just found her lying on the bathroom floor!!! I don't know what to do!!! Please help!!!! Send somebody!!! Quick!!!! My name is Marianne Choux. We're at…."

Why is she crying like that? It's not as if she cares…

"Oh God!!!! Oh God!!! PLEASE DON'T DIE ON ME!!!! PLEASE DON'T DIE!!!!!"

Don't cry! I'm finally going to a happy place…

"I can't take this!!! Heaven!! Don't you die on me!!! PLEASE just Stay awake!!! Help is on the way!!!! Oh God!!!! This can't be happening!!! Oh God!!! Heaven!!! HEAVEN!!!!!!!!!"

I'm so sleepy…

……………….."CLEAR!!!!"………………….

What is going on?

……………….."CLEAR!!!!"………………….

"Looks like an overdose on prescription sleeping pills."

……………….."CLEAR!!!!"………………….

"We're losing her! Push another amp of Epi!"

....................."CLEAR!!!!".....................

Am I dead yet? What is taking so long?

=Is she dead yet? What is taking so long??=

....................."CLEAR!!!!".....................

"OH GOD!! PLEASE DON'T LET HER DIE!!!!"

"Ma'am, you can't be in here. Somebody get her out of here NOW!"

95

....................."CLEAR!!!!"......................

=She wants to die. WHY AREN'T YOU LETTING HER????=

....................."CLEAR!!!!"......................

"Sinus rhythm! She's stable for now, but she's in bad shape. Send her up to Intensive Care. We've done all we can. Now, all we can do is wait to see if she wakes up from this coma. It's up to fate to decide what happens now..."

Beep

Why aren't I dead?

=Why isn't she dead?=

Beep

What kind of mess is this? I can't do anything right. I can't work. I can't be a Christian. I can't even kill myself. Who fails at suicide?

=Why isn't she dead? This isn't fair!=

Beep

Well God, since you're the one who's torturing me, why don't you tell me?

Beep

Well?

=She's mine. She should be dead. Let her die!!=

Beep

Aren't you going to answer me?

=She already rejected you Jesus! She doesn't belong to You anymore!
She's mine!!!!!=

Beep

**You must not exist. No REAL God would ever do this.
You are a HORRIBLE God.**

=Wait. Is she talking to You?=

Beep

**I know you are real. But You aren't good or whatever,
like the Bible says. It said "taste and see that the Lord is
good." All I've experienced is heartbreak and disaster
because of you.**

99

=She's mad that You didn't let her die, isn't she?=

Beep

Why aren't you answering me???

=Hahaha!! Oh now she's mad that You are silent? PERFECT!!=

Beep

=Can't you see He's ignoring you? He's taunting you. He doesn't care about you!=

WHY ARE YOU IGNORING ME?????

Beep

=Who does God think He is? He ruined your life. He took everything away from you. And now He doesn't want you to die. He wants to torture you slowly, and then kill you, and then send you to eternal death with me! That's who He is. That's why I left Him. You should tell Him that you want nothing to do with Him!=

HOW DARE YOU!!! Why would you do this to me? First, you ruin my life, and take away everything and everyone that means something to me. You destroy everything I touch, and then you won't even let me kill myself? What kind of love is that? You claim to be love but all you do is torture us until we want to die. Then you condemn us to eternal death. WHAT KIND OF A GOD ARE YOU?????

Beep

= Oh, this is going to be great. He HAS to give her to me now. YOU CAN'T SAVE HER JESUS!!!! SHE DOESN'T WANT TO BE SAVED!!! SHE'S MINE!!!=

D. Gloria Elysée

Beep

**WELL???? AREN'T YOU GOING TO ANSWER ME???
ANSWER ME!!!!!!!!!!!!!!!!!!!!!!!**

Chapter 7

"Who is this that questions My wisdom with such ignorant words? Brace yourself like a [woman], because I have some questions for you, and you must answer them.

"Where were you when I laid the foundations of the earth? Tell me, if you know so much. Do you know the laws of the universe? Can you use them to regulate the earth? Do you still want to argue with the Almighty? You are God's critic, but do you have the answers? Will you discredit My justice and condemn Me just to prove you are right?

"Are you as strong as God? Can you thunder with a voice like [Mine]? All right, put on your glory and splendor, your honor and majesty. Give vent to your anger. Let it overflow against the proud. Humiliate the proud with a glance; walk on the wicked where they stand. Bury them in the dust. Imprison them in the world of the dead.

Then even I would praise you, for your own strength would save you.[2]

"I Am the Lord Your God, who laid all the foundations of the Earth. I knew you before I formed you in your mother's womb. Before you were born I set you apart and appointed you.[3] I put my breath in you, so that you could be a testament to Me. And all you've done thus far is complain. You ignore what I say, but you still don't want any consequences. You pretend like My Words and laws are suggestions, and yet you still want Me to bless you as if you were righteous.

"You claim to be My child in name only, so you can reap My benefits, but you don't even love Me or want to be around Me. Being in My presence is a chore to you: a way to get blessings, and a way to skip out on Hell. But the very way you speak to Me shows your lack of respect, and even lack of belief in Me.

"The reason you are not dead is because it is not time yet. I gave you life, and only I have the power to take it away. I see your hurt and pain. I feel your anger and sadness. When you feel alone, I Am there. When you feel scared, I Am right beside you. Whatever you go through, whenever things happen, however things go down, whoever brings you sadness or anger, I AM always here.

---

[2] Job 38:2,3,4, 33; 40:2,8-14
[3] Jeremiah 1:5

"How could you think that I was cruel and that I was the type of God that would torture you? Don't you know anything about Me? All these years you spent talking about Me, and singing about Me, and praying to Me, and you still don't know Me? Not one thing about Me?

"I'm the God who sent his ONLY son to die for you, so that you could be adopted into My family. You're upset that I discipline you? Have you forgotten the encouraging words [I] spoke to you as [My child]? [I] said, 'My child, don't make light of [My] discipline, and don't give up when [I] correct you. For [I] discipline those [I] love, and punish each one [I] accept as [My] child'. As you endure this divine discipline, remember that [I Am] treating you as [My] own child. Who ever heard of a child who is never disciplined by its father? If [I] don't discipline you as [I] do all of [My] children, it means that you are illegitimate and are not really [My] child at all.[4] Think about it: Just as a parent disciplines a child, [I discipline] you for your own good.[5] You were comfortable claiming Me when I was blessing you, but as soon as things get a little rough, you accuse me of all sorts of horrible things. But I am true to My Word, and since you still represent me, I will not destroy you.

---

[4] Hebrews 12:5-8, Proverbs 3:11,12
[5] Deuteronomy 8:5, 6

"Therefore, I Am bringing you back. But not because you deserve it. I Am doing it to protect My holy name, on which you brought shame. I will show you how holy My great name is- the name on which you brought shame among [the people you know]. And when I reveal My holiness through you before their very eyes, then [they] will know that I Am the Lord. Then I will sprinkle clean water on you, and you will be clean. Your filth will be washed away, and you will no longer [put anyone or anything before Me].

"And I will give you a new heart, and I will put a new spirit in you. I will take out your stony, stubborn heart and give you a tender, responsive heart. And I will put My Spirit in you so that you will follow My decrees and be careful to obey My regulations. Then you will remember your past sins and despise [yourself] for all the detestable things you did. But remember, I Am not doing this because you deserve it.[6] You will be a testament to who I Am. Everyone you encounter will know that I Am God, and I alone have the power to change.

"All you need to do is repent, and obey, and you will enjoy all the benefits of what I have to give. Don't copy the behavior and customs of this world, but let [Me] transform you into a new person by changing the way you

---

[6] Ezekiel 36:22-27, 31, 32

think. Then you will learn to know [My] will for you, which is good and pleasing and perfect.[7] But don't just listen to [My] word. You must do what it says. Otherwise, you are only fooling [yourself]. What good is it, dear [child], if you say you have faith but don't show it by your actions? Can that kind of faith save anyone? So you see, faith by itself isn't enough. Unless it produces good deeds, it is dead and useless.[8]

"Look, today I Am giving you the choice between a blessing and a curse! You will be blessed if you obey the commands that I Am giving you today. But you will be cursed if you reject the commands and turn away from [Me].[9] Come now, let's settle this. Though your sins are like scarlet, I will make them as white as snow. Though they are red like crimson, I will make them as white as wool.[10] And [I], who began the good work within you, will continue [My] work until it is finally finished on the day when [My Son,] Christ Jesus returns.[11]

"Don't worry when trouble comes your way. Or when you have problems. The devil will always try to stop

---

[7] Romans 12:2
[8] James 1:22; 2: 14,17
[9] Deuteronomy 11:26-28
[10] Isaiah 1:18,19
[11] Philippians 1:6

you when you are serious about doing right. You will encounter all sorts of problems, but you are under My protection. Yes, and everyone who wants to live a godly life in Christ Jesus will suffer persecution. Evil people and impostors will flourish. They will deceive others and will themselves be deceived. But you must remain faithful to the things you have been taught. You know they are true, for you know you and trust those who taught you.

"You have been taught the holy Scriptures from childhood, and they have given you the wisdom to receive the salvation that comes by trusting in Christ Jesus. All Scripture is inspired by [Me] and is useful to teach [you] what is true and to make [you] realize what is wrong in [your] life. It corrects [you] when [you] are wrong and teaches [you] to do what is right. [I] use it to prepare and equip [My] people to do every good work.[12] And you can even look to nature to show how much I love my creations. If [I] care so wonderfully for wildflowers that are here today and thrown into the fire tomorrow, [I] will certainly care for you.[13]

"Now is the time for you to build up your faith. The world is soon to end, and my Son is soon to return. Your faith must be strong enough to endure all that will happen in these last days. There will be all sorts of deceit and sin running rampant, and as you see now, with all that is

---

[12] 2 Timothy 3:12-17
[13] Matthew 6:30

allowed in society, the images promoting sexual sin on TV, in movies, and the violent crimes that occur with no justice, even with nature rebelling, and global warming, THE END IS VERY NEAR.

"Patient endurance is what you need now, so that you will continue to do [My] will. Then you will receive all that [I] have promised.[14] Dear [child], be patient as you wait for [My] return. Consider the farmers who patiently wait for the rains in the fall and in the spring. They eagerly look for the valuable harvest to ripen. You, too, must be patient. Take courage, for [My coming] is near. Don't grumble about [others], or you will be judged. For look— [I], the Judge, [am] standing at the door! For examples of patience in suffering, dear brothers and sisters, look at the prophets who spoke in [My] name.[15]

"Don't worry about all the hypocrites. They will receive their judgments. Worry about making sure you are walking in my Will. Love the ones who persecute you, who hate on you for no reason, or hate you for trying to do right. When people do that, it means that you are living according to My Will, because people who are truly godly make those still stuck in the world uncomfortable. And

---

[14] Hebrews 10:36 NLT
[15] James 5:7-10 NLT

yes, someone can be in the church and stuck in the world. It isn't your place to judge.

"In fact, you should serve to inspire them. You were in the church your whole life, yet still in the world. But it is time for you to finally reject Babylon, repent, and accept Me. So think clearly and exercise self-control. Look forward to the gracious salvation that will come to you when [My Son] Jesus Christ is revealed to the world. So you must live as [My] obedient child. Don't slip back into your old ways of living to satisfy your own desires. You didn't know any better then. But now you must be holy in everything you do, just as [I] who chose you, [am] holy. For the Scriptures say, 'You must be holy because I Am holy.'[16]

"For [I] called you to do good, even if it means suffering, just as Christ suffered for you. He is your example, and you must follow in his steps.[17] You will be able to endure all that I bring upon you, because I know best, and I can see what you can handle. I would never harm you. I allow you to go through these trials to grow you into a person fit for my kingdom. I love you with everything that I Am, but you must understand and know Me in order to get somebody else to understand and know Me.

---

[16] 1 Peter 1: 13-15
[17] 1 Peter 2:21

"The end of the world is coming soon. Therefore, be earnest and disciplined in your prayers. Most important of all, continue to show deep love for [... others], for love covers a multitude of sins.[18] So humble [yourself] under [My] mighty power, and at the right time [I] will lift you up in honor. Give all your worries and cares to [Me], for [I] care about you.

"Stay alert! Watch out for your great enemy, the devil. He prowls around like a roaring lion, looking for someone to devour. Stand firm against him, and be strong in your faith. Remember that your Christian brothers and sisters all over the world are going through the same kind of suffering you are. In [My] kindness [I] called you to share in [My] eternal glory by means of Christ Jesus. So after you have suffered a little while, [I] will restore, support, and strengthen you, and [I] will place you on a firm foundation.[19] The world may hate you, but I will always love you. In me, you can go to bed without fear; you will lie down and sleep soundly. You need not be afraid of sudden disaster or the destruction that comes upon the wicked, for [I Am] your security. [I] will keep your foot from being caught in a trap.[20]

---

[18] 1 Peter 4:7,8
[19] 1 Peter 5:6-11
[20] Proverbs 3:24-26

"I Am sending you to be My witness among all the people that you know. You will represent Me, and be an example of the love that I have for all of humanity. So be strong and courageous! Do not be afraid and do not panic before them. For [I] personally go ahead of you. [I] will neither fail you nor abandon you.[21]   And know that [I] cause everything to work together for the good of those who love [Me] and are called according to [My] purpose for them. Nothing can ever separate [you] from [My] love. Neither death nor life, neither angels nor demons, nor rulers, neither [your] fears for today nor [your] worries about tomorrow—not even the powers of hell can separate [you] from [My] love. No power in the sky above or in the earth below—indeed, NOTHING in all creation will ever be able to separate[you] from [My] love that is revealed in Christ Jesus, [your] Lord.[22]

"Come back to Me, child, and I will restore you. I will forgive you and bless you. But you have to forgive those who have hurt you so your heart can be free for Me to do My work in you. You can't keep holding on to all of that hurt. If I could forgive you for everything you have done to Me, and the way you've treated Me, and for the sins that caused My Son to have to die, and your constant rejection of Me, you can forgive them for what they have done to you.

---

[21] Deuteronomy 31:6
[22] Romans 8: 28, 38, 39

"Remember, they are only human, like you, and are hurt, frustrated, confused, and sinful, JUST LIKE YOU. But, I can't make that choice for you. You can either side with what the devil has told you, or try Me, and experience true fulfillment. That void in you, was made by Me. It was made for you to recognize your need for Me. I promise, I will be everything you need, and much more. I will be a better addiction than sex, alcohol, attention, or anything else you can think of.

"Stop going back and forth between Me and the world. You have to make a choice. Remember Lot's wife. If you cling to your life, you will lose it, and if you let your life go, you will save it.[23] You can't keep doing what you want, but holding on to Me. You have to pick one. But the choice is yours. Make it soon, because time is running out, and you don't know if you even have an hour left, let alone tomorrow. Choose Me."

I don't know what to say. I didn't mean to come off like that God. I'm just so frustrated with where I am. I am weary, O God: I am weary and worn out O God. I am too stupid to be human, and I lack common sense. I have not mastered human wisdom, nor do I know the Holy One.[24] I know that you can do anything, and no one can

---

[23] Luke 17: 32,33
[24] Proverbs 30:1-3

stop you. You asked, "Who is this that questions my wisdom with such ignorance?" It is I—and I was talking about things I knew nothing about, things far too wonderful for me. You said, "Listen and I will speak! I have some questions for you, and you must answer them." I had only heard about you before, but now I have seen you with my own eyes. I take back everything I said, and I [humbly bow before you] to show my repentance.[25] But God, I'm afraid of getting broken. And I'm still so angry.

Choose Me.

But how can I face all those people? And how can I forgive Mari and Hunt and everybody else?

Choose Me.

But- -

---

[25] Job 42: 2-6

Choose Me.

Okay Lord. Okay. I will give it a try. Because somewhere in the Bible, you said to "prove you," so I will. I will. I will trust you. But when I don't, "help me overcome my unbelief!"[26]

---

[26] Mark 9:24

D. Gloria Elysée

Chapter 8

I woke up to my mom crying. Sobbing, actually. I felt so selfish for all I had done to her and everyone else. Especially to God. I didn't know if it was a dream I had woken up from, or a vision, or whatever it may have been, but one thing I was sure of was that God had spoken to me. And I knew that there was no time to play around. At first, she didn't notice that I was awake. She kept right on crying and praying. They had put a tube down my throat to help me breathe. I could only choke and gasp for air, so I tried to move my hands, and wave to get her attention. If you could only see the look of joy on my mother's face as she realized that I was awake.

She rushed to get the nurse, so they could take out the tube, all the while loudly praising God. Before, I would've rolled my eyes at her display, but after all that I'd been through, I finally understood her praise. She clung to me, like I was going to disappear if she let me go, but I didn't mind. God had given me back to her, and she didn't want to let me go. She only left to "get something I think you need."

I almost slipped back into that old mentality when she brought in Mari, but I remembered what God said to me about forgiveness. I had to let it go. Plus, she did save my life. The least I could do was talk to her. "Hey." It was all I could say. I was hoarse, and plus, I didn't know how to ask forgiveness, nor tell her how I was feeling. But thank God for whatever work He was doing in her, because, like my mom, no words were spoken, other than those in praise to God. She just rushed over and gave me a huge hug.

"Thank God! I was so scared you were going to die! I'm so sorry about everything! Just promise me that you won't ever do that again!" I could only nod and cry, and hold tighter to the both of them. I couldn't think of how to describe my encounter with God, but I realized that the point wasn't to tell them. It was to take everything that He'd told me, and finally begin applying it to my life.

They held me, and told me how Mari had found me, and how I was in a coma for 7 days. They told me about the people who came to pray for me, and how my mom had never left my side. When my mom left to go call the rest of my family, and inform the church that I was awake, Mari got really sad. "I know you probably could care less right now, especially since I'm partly to blame for getting you here, but I am SO sorry. I can't tell you how sorry I am. I'm trying to do better these days, and forgive people that have hurt me. I don't want my issues to ever spill over into your life again. But I do want to be in your life. "

"God has been working on me. I'm on my own now, and working and making it through my last year of school. I have started talking to my mom again, and I've decided to be by myself for a while and not turn to attention or sex to feel better about myself. I don't even speak to Hunt anymore, though I did relapse a few times. But he decided that he didn't want to be associated with me in any way, and that hurt, but it was what I needed to get back to God. And to you. I am so sorry! I know you need some time, but I hope you can find it in your heart to forgive me."

She sat there, with her head hanging down, staring at the floor. She looked so defeated. I reached out my hand to hold hers. "I forgive you. For everything. And if you ask God, He'll forgive you like He forgave me. Don't worry." The tears streaming down her face sent me into another round of sobbing. When my mom walked in, she didn't know what to make of the situation. But she came to my bedside and suggested we pray.

"Father God, we thank You for the grace and mercy You have shown us today, by returning Heaven to us. We thank You for your mercy and love that allowed us to see and experience You. We thank You for life and for forgiveness of our many, many sins. We just thank You oh Lord! We ask that You please forgive all our sins, and wash us in Your blood. Create in [us] a clean heart, and renew a right spirit within [us].[27] Cover us with Your righteousness, because we know that ours are worthless. Guide and protect us now, and through everything we do. Let Your will be done in our lives, and help us to forgive all those who have hurt us, so that we may be forgiven.

"Show us Your way out when we are tempted, and deliver us from all manner of evil things. Not that we deserve any of this, but we do pray in the holy name of Jesus. And now unto Him who is able to keep [us] from falling, and to present [us] faultless before the presence of His glory with exceeding joy, to the only wise God our Savior, be glory and majesty, dominion and power, both now and forever. Amen."[28] They left soon after, but I know that the presence of God was in that room while they were there.

I received many visitors over the next few days before I was discharged from the hospital. Gwen and her holy roller crew came, the pastors from Bethel and Genesis came, and my sister came up from New York to see me. Each time someone came, I felt the anger and hurt from before, but silently praying, I found a way to get through the visit. Some were easier than others. With the pastors, I didn't feel as much hurt and anger, so they didn't really annoy me or say things that would make me want to kill them. Not like when Gwen and her friends came.

---

[27] Psalm 51:10 KJV
[28] Jude 1:24, 25 KJV

It was sad. I was struggling to keep calm, and they were provoking me, even at my hospital bed. I realized that they might not ever change, but that wasn't good enough of a reason for me to stay the same. If you could only see how intently I was praying during that visit! I had to keep my mind in check, because the devil was preying on the fact that I didn't like them, and I'm sure he was using them to try to get me to relapse. Praise God for His strength, because I don't know how I made it through that visit without hurting them. Hunt never came to visit me, but it was for the best. I didn't need his negative energy in my life. Plus, I was going to forgive him anyway.

Meanwhile, the hospital had me on a suicide watch, and had Mari and my mom "suicide-proof" my house. They weren't taking any chances. I also had to meet with a therapist, and though she came by often while I was in my hospital room (carefully watching all my visitors), she told me that twice a week, for the next six months, I was required to meet with her.

The most nerve-wracking visit I got was when King came. I don't know why I was so on edge, but when he showed up, I had to pray harder than I had to pray before. His words had hurt me far more than Gwen, and I wasn't prepared to face him just yet. Nonetheless, he came, and so the confrontation was inevitable. For the first five minutes after he came in, he sat, and said nothing. He just sat down, and stared at me, and sighed, and then looked around the room, before resting his eyes on me again. He did this for five minutes, while I watched, silently praying, waiting for something to happen.

Finally he spoke. Well, he attempted to speak. He opened his mouth, but nothing came out. So he closed his mouth. He tried this again, but when I saw nothing was happening, I asked God to give me the words to say to him, and only the words God wanted me to say. "You're fine. We are ok. God used my selfish attempt to end my life as a way to reach me. I can't hold on to any more anger or hurt or frustration. I know I didn't always treat you the way you thought you should be treated, and I'm sorry, but that's all in the past now. Your words were out of anger, and I understand why you would want to lash out. True, you really hurt me, but I can't dwell on that, and neither can you. It's ok. We can work at being friends if that's what you want."

I'm guessing he didn't expect that from me. Not me mentioning God, or the fact that I was so willing to forgive him. My guess is that he expected me to throw him out. And the old Heaven would have. During the rest of the visit, he opened up more, and it turned out pretty well. I think he saw something different in me. I guess there is such a thing as immediate change in God, but it's also hard work. I still wanted to be mad, but at this point I had no energy left in me to hate others. That almost got me a one-way ticket to Hell by my own hand, and I wasn't going to ever let what others thought about me bring me to a place where I wanted to end my life.

Some people, like King and Mari, owned up to their part, and that was nice to hear- but not necessary. Others, like Hunt and Gwen, kept on doing what they did. They didn't not care whether or not their actions or words had led me to where I was. But ultimately, I was the one holding the power. It was my choice to feed into what they thought about me, and my choice to try to end my life because of how I was feeling. It was my choice to push away God so much that I felt desperately hopeless, and then learned to hate myself after I'd pushed everyone else away. I chose not to rebuke the anger welling up inside me because I wanted to place blame on others. I didn't want to be the sinner. I wanted to be the misunderstood but good human.

Truthfully, God put it in perspective for me. I was a sinner, so I deserved to die. Point blank. I didn't feel like one, I didn't think I was that bad of a person, but by rejecting the One who made me, I was rebelling against God. I allowed the devil to feed me the lie that I was "self-sufficient, in need of no one, and not a bad person." Therefore, I had no need for God, and had I not gone through all that mess, I would've never recognized how much I needed Him in my life, and how much He loved me.

I was finally in a place in my life, where I could finally be of use to God. Granted, I never wanted a testimony. I never wanted to go through any trial, or ever feel like this, but God did turn it around. The subsequent week, I started going to therapy (mandated by my doctor), and I also started going to the Bible study at church. I realized just how crazy I was without God in my life, and refused to be anywhere but with Him. So, you can say I overdosed on God. I was at church on Sabbath, at Wednesday night prayer meetings, and even at Friday night Bible study. I even got up early for Sabbath School. To some people, it seemed extreme, even to my therapist. She tried to tell me that it wasn't okay to go from one extreme to the other, but all I knew was that God had saved me when he could've let me die. I owed it to Him to be desperate, almost like a stalker.

Actually, yes- I stalked God. He thought He was omnipresent? Well, wherever He was, so was I. I was pressed to go to church. I did my best to shake off the stares, the whispers and the looks of disgust as I openly praised Him. In church, I tried to sit in the front, so that when I was saying "Amen", I wouldn't have to deal with the people in front of me turning around to look at me. Do you know that some people thought that I was making fun of the church, or that I was trying to be a distraction? People thought I was demon possessed, and some even would pull me aside after church to ask me to tone it down. But none of them understood. I finally got what all those hymns were talking about: I once was LOST, but now I'm FOUND, was BLIND but now I SEE!

I was miserable and He came and rescued me from the grip of death itself. Even people who came to visit me in the hospital still asked me to tone it down. Maybe my praise was making them uncomfortable, but I knew where I had been, and I wasn't about to let anyone tell me that my God didn't deserve my loudest praise. People get super loud when their favorite song comes on the radio, or their favorite team is winning the game, but are extra quiet in church and act like they can't open their mouths. This time, when I answered the altar call, I was serious. I wanted to be baptized, and started Bible study. I even started reading the books by Ellen G. White. She was a prominent leader in the beginning of the Adventist movement, and had a gift of prophetic knowledge. She wrote plenty of books that provided insight on the Bible.

Before, when people would bring her up, I didn't want to hear anything they'd have to say. That was because people would take her words (usually out of context) and beat me over the head with it. But as I grew in God, I realized that she was inspired and that her books were helpful. I also realized how misquoted she was, and how many people misunderstood the context, the content, and the origin of her work. Her words were NOT the Bible, but she was inspired by God and had brought clarification to a lot of Biblical concepts. I realized that the misuse of her words by others had caused me to almost write her off entirely, but her words still were poignant and did a lot of good to my Bible study.

I also learned to love the Bible. Every time I opened it, after praying and asking God to send in the

125

Holy Spirit to speak, I would always find something of use. I realized that the reason why I had never really received any new insight was because I wasn't really looking for anything. I was just doing what I thought I had to do. Basically, I was performing an automated task. Read the Bible? Check! The difference was so crucial! I had to be intentional about what I was doing, or else there was no point. If I didn't fully commit my heart when I was serving God, He didn't want any of it.

I was new. Brand-new. And everyone noticed it. People at the church might have been hating (except for the few older ladies who were just happy that I was back) but they noticed. People at my job, including my newer, flaky "friends" noticed. They got upset when I didn't want to party with them anymore, or didn't want to close out on Friday nights and work Saturdays, because I wanted to keep the Sabbath. Oh well! But I had finally realized the freedom in practicing what I preached, and the benefits of not lying to people. Honestly. I was still a little sarcastic, but before, I usually kept my feelings to myself. I began to be a little more honest with people after my attempted suicide. I wasn't going to be afraid of them anymore. I wasn't going to seek attention from them anymore. Other people were no longer my priority. I'm telling you, I changed. And I was so happy to have gotten the chance to.

It wasn't all rainbows and butterflies though. Don't let all this happiness fool you. My life was far from being a fairy tale. I was under constant supervision because of my attempted suicide. My mom had to move in with me for a month, so that they could be sure that I wasn't trying to kill myself. They removed knives from my home, along with any sleeping pills, cleaning supplies, and belts. They even spoke about getting me to move back to DC to live with my parents, just so that they could keep an eye on me. I had a curfew, and my mom obsessed over every detail of my life. I had gone from feeling alone, to constantly being watched. All privacy I had was virtually erased when she was with me, and of course, they got Mari to "drop by" just to make sure that I was okay.

Things with my brother improved, and he came to see me when he got some time off. You could see that there was tension, but it wasn't anything that I couldn't handle. By the end of the visit, we were almost back to normal, teasing and poking fun at each other and getting into stupid arguments about nothing. The only thing that was pressing on my mind was my relationship with my father. While all this was going on, he was basically absent.

Sure, my mom called him and updated him every day, but he always "had to go" before he could talk to me. One time I had to snatch the phone just to speak to him, and he barely responded. I had cut him deeply, but he was mortally wounding me. I missed my daddy, and with his quiet demeanor becoming frigidly cold, I didn't know what to do. I would cry, and my mom would tell me, "He loves you. Just give him some time." I would wonder if he would ever forgive me, and if he still loved me. True, he wasn't a man of many words, but he became the man of no words. He spoke to everyone else, but I was the prodigal daughter that he didn't want back.

Late at night, I'd hear mom arguing with him about it. She told him that it was killing me, and that I could relapse at any moment. I felt so bad. I didn't want him to be forced to talk to me. I wanted him to forgive me on his own. I was struggling to forgive everyone for the hurt that I had felt, but he wouldn't even try. It was making me sad and angry. I would stay up and talk to God about it, but kept getting the answer to forgive him anyway.

It didn't make sense, and it wasn't fair. I was doing my part, and he wasn't even trying. He was my dad. How could he just give up on me like that? How could he just rule me out and make me irrelevant? I know he couldn't come up with my mom because he had to work and take care of the house, but not once did he try after she returned. No phone calls. All I could do was tell my mom to tell him I loved him at the end of every phone conversation, and hope that it would get through to him. It wasn't likely, but hope was all I had at this point. I just had to start working toward mending the broken bridges I had left behind me.

Chapter 9
March 2010

With the new year came new problems. Work was pretty standard, but I had begun looking to re-apply to residencies. I prayed about it, and I was sure that this was what I was supposed to do with my life, but it still wasn't working out the way I thought it should. I wasn't a prime candidate like I was the year before. I wasn't at the top of my class, and I had a record that wasn't pretty. I had been fired from one job, and usually people don't want to hire someone who couldn't make it through their first year on the job. I was afraid. I couldn't lie, and I had no real reason for people to let me into their program other than, "I'll try really hard." Truthfully speaking, if I was to get into another program, it would be only God that got me in.

Socially, I was doing a little better. King and I were on good terms again, and I think there might be something there, but I'm so afraid to trust again, that I don't want to go down that road until I'm SURE that he's the one that God chose for me. I can't risk opening up to another man and getting my heart splattered all over the floor. Mari and I are working on our relationship. Honestly, I do have to keep rebuking that anger that starts to well up inside me when I see her, and I have to literally restrain myself from throwing what she did in her face whenever we argue. I'm tired of the struggle sometimes, and just want to say what I want, and I do slip up, but God (and Mari) forgive me, and help me through all my mess.

King has been patient, even though he still doesn't trust my motives (he thinks I can't tell.) Though he wants to start something, I know I'm just not ready to. He wants to be physical, and though I want to as well, I know that if I'm not ready to be in a relationship with him, I'm not ready to have sex. And of course, God says no, above all else, so there you go. Plus, Gwen's friend hates me even more now. I'm the woman in the Bible that lacks discretion, like a pig with a gold ring in its snout.[29] I'm the Jezebel that stole her man.

I can't shake that title. I looked her up, but Jezebel doesn't exactly mean whore. She was actually a queen of Israel. True she was a pagan, and had the worst influence on her husband, Ahab, and most of his horrendous and sinful behavior can be traced back to her: but she wasn't a whore. That was Gomer.[30] Jezebel was ambitious, and crafty, a go-getter by any means necessary, and believed in her gods, even though they let her down. She liked painting her face, and doing her hair, and she even tried to die pretty, but she was not a

---

[29] Proverbs 11:22 NLT
[30] see the book of Hosea, chapters 1-14

whore. [31] That's all I'm saying. She was NOT a whore. But I digress.

Things with my dad aren't much better, but at least he's been speaking to me. He doesn't call, but I will take what I can get at this point. God must be working in him, because I don't know why he would want to talk to me now. But Hallelujah, Praise be to God anyhow! I'm just glad that he spoke to me. I know people who have been estranged from their family for a lifetime with no possibility for reconciliation, and have only God to call Father. For some people, God is all the family or friend they have in this world. I feel blessed and privileged to know Him, and to also be blessed with my family.

It could be a million times worse. I could be an orphan. Or worse, be rejected by my existing family, orphaned by their choices. No one deserves that, and I thank God that He is still there, even when we don't have anyone else. I just pray that I don't take what I have for granted ever again. I'll try to tell others about God. It's a little embarrassing, but I'd rather be a lame and get to Heaven rather than hold on to what others think of me and stay here and burn. I'm telling you: I refuse to take things for granted...

****

---

[31] 2 Kings 9:30; 1 Kings 21:7, 25

I am devastated. Heartbroken, and words cannot express how much grief I am in right now. I just got a phone call from my mother. My daddy is dead. He got into a car accident this morning, on the way to work. It wasn't raining, or snowing. There was no ice on the road. Someone simply wasn't paying enough attention, and ran a light, right into him. He was taken to the hospital, but there wasn't much they could do. My mom could not stop crying. My brother and sister are already on their way, and now I have to go bury my daddy.

We just started to get close again. I had *just* started to reclaim my life and was starting to be happy. I was just getting used to my new life. And now this. I don't know what to do with myself. I want to call someone, 'cause I don't want to pray.

Talk to me, or call Mari.

=*Call King.*=

I know it seems hypocritical that I'm upset at God for not letting my dad live, but I just don't understand why he couldn't live a little longer. Maybe I'm selfish, and my view is limited. Maybe I just don't want to accept that he's gone, and anger is the best way to not let grief overtake me, but I am angry. I am angry with God.

I wish my daddy could still be alive. I wish I could still work on my relationship with him. I don't even know if he forgave me all the way, and that's what's making me crazy. I don't know if my father and I were on good terms. He was still angry with me, and though he never really gave me much attention in the first place, it was clear that his frozen demeanor had never thawed completely. He still had an air of coldness to his tone when we spoke. I felt like our conversations were a little forced. I don't know if he ever forgave me. And I don't know if I can ever forgive myself if he didn't. I know it seems crazy, but I somehow feel like this is my fault. Last night I was angry with him because he wasn't as receptive as I wanted him to be, and I yelled at him. We didn't end on a good note. I was angry, and now I feel responsible. I have all this anger and frustration, and no one to direct it to. I guess that's why I'm so angry at God.

I have so many unanswered questions. Why I was allowed to live and he wasn't? Did my dad actually forgive me before he died? Why did family have to suffer even more this year? I had put them through so much, and now this. God wasn't playing fair. THIS WAS NOT FAIR! I had put in time to spend with God. I was living right, as best I could. I changed my attitude about a lot of things, and I even changed my behavior to glorify God. I expected other people not to like me because that's what the Bible said. It hurt when people thought I was weird, crazy, lame, or whack, because of my new lifestyle, but I was still trying. I stopped having sex, even with myself, and I cut out the porn, and most of the dirty jokes. I had cut down on sarcasm, and was trying to keep my life holy, and here God was, taking away my dad. It just wasn't fair. I was holding up my end of the bargain. I didn't think he'd live forever, but I thought the deal was that if you serve God, you will live a long life in the land of the living. I think I read that in Psalms somewhere. I just didn't think it was fair.

Now I have to go to DC, and spend time making the arrangements with my mom. I can't imagine what she's going through right now. I need someone to be with me tonight.

Talk to me or call all Mari.

=Call King.=

I think I will call someone.

Talk to me or call Mari.

=Call King.=

I just can't be alone right now. I just can't do it...

****

I did something I shouldn't have. I want to blame it on grief, but I'm the one who's responsible. And King, I guess, but mostly me. I slipped up and had sex last night. King and I had promised we weren't going to, but I was so sad and I needed some comfort. I just wanted to be close to someone. It was inevitable once I made that phone call. I couldn't stop it. But then again, I wanted it. I REALLY wanted it. For as many emotional reasons as physical ones. Now, I have to deal with the guilt, on top of the guilt with my father. And since I had been celibate for so long (four months seems like an eternity), this slip-up can very well send me right back to where I was.

=WHORE. You have NO self-control, do you?=

Honestly, I'm kinda ashamed to ask God for forgiveness. Especially since I was so angry yesterday and I said/thought some things that I shouldn't have. I should've have listened to the voice telling me to call Mari yesterday, but no, I decided to call King. Knowing Mari, she would've come over and held my hand, cried with me, and then prayed with me. I think I subconsciously knew that calling her would have me ending up praying, so I called King, knowing what I wanted to do. Anticipating- no, PLANNING what we were going to do.

And now it's awkward because now that we've done the deed, but aren't dating, and I don't know where we are, and it's too much to handle because I'm still trying to wrap my head around my dad's death. I feel like I'm going crazy, and now I want to drink, to forget everything that has been going on lately.

=One drink won't hurt.=

Honestly, I'm struggling so hard not to make myself a martini, or drink the rum straight from the bottle. I need a strong drink, not one of those girly sweet ones. Well, I don't need it, I just want it really bad.

You don't need it.

=You need it. You need to unwind and relax. Especially after all this. Trust me.=

I have to keep telling myself that I don't need it, but since I haven't asked God forgiveness yet, it's hard to convince myself.

Just ask.

=He's not going to forgive you anyway. It was premeditated. Plus, you deliberately ignored Him. That's blasphemy. It's unforgivable. Doesn't the Bible say that if you grieve the Holy Spirit, God won't forgive you? Well, what do you think you just did?=

Just ask.

I'm just going to have to suck it up, and admit I'm wrong, before I really go crazy and do something stupid. Well, something *else* that's stupid...

****

After the funeral all the people left and it was just my mom and siblings and I. We assembled in the living room of my parents' house, still trying to wrap our minds around what happened. Angry, with no real outlet or recipient (and overwhelmingly sad) my family tried to cope with the loss of the quiet but strong presence that was my dad.

I don't want to say that his death hit me the hardest, because he was closest to my brother, married to my mom, and my sister knew him longer. I guess it had a lot to do with the guilt I was feeling. I felt overwhelmingly guilty about our argument that we had the night before he died. It was about me messing up. I asked if he was ready to start calling me again, and got angry when he said he didn't know. It was March! He hadn't called me since before all the drama, and I was asking him if he could call me the next day. When he said he didn't know, I got angry and asked him if he'd punished me enough.

The argument snowballed after he said that I had embarrassed the family, and he still needed time. I told him that God had forgiven me, and asked why he couldn't forgive me as well. It hurt my feelings, especially since I was emotionally fragmented and trying not to use male attention as a substitute for his affection. His indifference or lack of forgiveness pushed me over the edge. I told him that if he'd paid more attention to me growing up, that I wouldn't have needed to sleep around to feel wanted by a man.

That really hurt him, and I could tell. I regretted it as soon as I said it, but I was still so angry. After that, he sat in silence so I told him that I had to go. He died on the way to work the next morning. My heart has been wrenched in two. I really hurt him, and I never got to ask forgiveness, and didn't get to make peace with him. So now I have residual anger along with my overwhelming sadness and guilt. Thinking spiritually, I don't know what his last conversation with God was about, and if he had the chance to forgive me before he died. I know that people won't go to Heaven until Jesus comes back, and the dead in Christ will rise[32], and all that, but if he didn't forgive me, he won't be counted in the righteous. That scares me. What if I've messed with my daddy's salvation?

I feel such extreme guilt. I can't look my mom in the eye. I can't stop thinking that I would be responsible for his eternal damnation.

=You Are!=

I feel so bad. I'm tired of feeling like it's my fault.

=But it is!=

---

[32] 1 Thess. 4:13-18

I feel like I'm going crazy, and I don't know what to do. I have no motivation to pray, or sing, or try to read the Bible-

=Who needs that stuff anyway?=

-and it feels like there's a war in my head. I'm tired. I'm so tired. I can't take much more of this. It's overwhelming in a way that I've never felt before.

=You need to drown your sorrows in a drink!=

I'm so sick of this grief, and the hurt and pain that I've caused everyone.

There's still tension within the family, and it's all my fault. It's like I'm reliving all the drama again, except that I added my dad's death to the mess I've caused. I'm sick of being the family screw-up. My sister is seemingly perfect in my parents' eyes. One night, a few weeks ago, when my mom was hanging up the phone after our conversation, I heard my father ask her where they went wrong with me, since Celeste and Cam Jr. turned out so well. I can't tell you how much it hurts to know that I will always be the disappointment, the loser, the black sheep.

=You'll NEVER be seen for anything but your mistakes.=

139

My mistakes will haunt me FOREVER. And I'll never get to move on and live my life with the forgiveness that God gave me, because to everyone else I'll just be Jezebel.

I might as well change my name. I don't deserve to be named Heaven.

=Heaven? You'll never get there. You? Ha! Don't kid yourself!=

According to everyone else, I'll never get there.

=Give up...=

I don't know if it's worth all of this. I don't think I can be saved if I caused someone else to not be saved.

=Give Up.=

I don't know if he forgave me, but if he didn't, I know it's my fault. I egged him on, and I hurt him. I should have known better. God. I'm tired. I have no motivation to talk to You. This is as much as I can give right now.

=Give Up!=

God, I don't know what to say. I'm tired, and I just want to go to sleep, wake up again, and have this be just another bad dream.

God. I don't even know anymore. I'm going to bed. If I wake up, that'll be great. If I don't, maybe it won't be so bad. Or it will, because I'll just be causing my family more problems. God. Just do what You want. You always do, anyway…

****

My mom is such a woman of God. I don't even know where to begin. Speaking with her was what I needed to do. It's a little strange that the woman I was supposed to be comforting was the one who had the most strength out of all of us. After the funeral, it was time for us to go back to our respective homes. My mom sat us down to have a talk. My sister went first, and it was full of a lot of hugging and crying and the sort, so I thought that it was going to be the same for me.

My brother was teary-eyed afterwards, but tried to hide it and be a "man". Sometimes men just need to learn to let their emotions show. It doesn't make you less of a man because you cry. It shows you are comfortable with being yourself and expressing your feelings. Anyway, when my mom called me in to talk to her, I thought we were going to sit down and have a heart to heart. But it didn't quite go down like that.

"Do you know why I named you Heaven?" She asked. I heard this story so many times, that I could almost repeat it with her. "I named you Heaven because I wanted you to always remember your goal. You were a constant reminder to look to God. I added the "Leigh" in to make sure you acted in a way befitting a citizen of Heaven." Though I knew where this was going, I restrained myself from reverting to the old me, tuning her out and daydreaming until it was over.

"I should have named you Beautiful, so that you would know your self-worth." As the shock of what she had said, registered to me, she continued. "You are so beautiful, so precious, but you act as though you are not. Why don't you know your value? Have I not told you how valuable you are? Or is it that you don't believe me or the Bible when we say your worth is immeasurable? Honestly, you act like you don't know this, but you're so valuable that Jesus died on a cross for you. How can you still not get it? Do you know Jesus? Like, really know Him? We sit in church and sing about how we love Him, but honestly, sometimes I know that's a lie. I can't love someone that I don't know. I might love the idea of Him, but not Him for who He is. I believe you are my daughter in that respect. But looking for a god to fit your standards always leaves you coming up empty. If God was who you wanted Him to be all the time, not only would you never need Him, but in fact, you'd HATE Him. We blame God for much of what we ask Him for. Like a little kid, we beg for candy, and ice cream, and cookies and cake, and junk, and then overdose on it until we are sick to our stomachs. Then we are angry that we're sick.

"Sweetie, it's not up to me to save you. Truthfully, you made your father and I so angry that we didn't want anything to do with you. We got over it, but our humanness couldn't do much for us- let alone for you. I see you're trying to get on the right path, and I'm here to encourage that, but I want you to be sure that you want this. It won't get any easier. In fact, if what they said you did is true, those sexual urges, the need for attention, and all your temptations will hit you harder and faster than ever before. The only way to get through it is if you learn to depend on God completely.

"Now, I don't have any tricks or secrets or anything, because I'm trying to sort my way through all the stuff the devil has set up for me. We may be dealing with similar issues, but your temptations are always specific to you, catered to trip you up and turn you away from God. You need to be aware of what you want, what is out there, and the difference between them.

"We are living in the last days, and it's no longer okay to live underneath the radar. You can't be so afraid to be disliked that you choose to blend in with the crowd. There is nothing about God that can blend in with the world. NOTHING. You can choose to dress, speak and act like everyone else or you can be the type of 'peculiar person' that God requires us to be. In the Bible, it says, "But you are not like that, for you are a chosen people. You are royal priests, a holy nation, God's very own possession. As a result, you can show others the goodness of God, for he called you out of the darkness into his wonderful light. Once you had no identity as a people; now you are God's people. Once you received no mercy; now you have received God's mercy.

"Dear friends, I warn you as "temporary residents and foreigners" to keep away from worldly desires that wage war against your very souls. Be careful to live properly among your unbelieving neighbors. Then even if they accuse you of doing wrong, they will see your honorable behavior, and they will give honor to God when he judges the world."[33]

"You have to realize that everything that the world celebrates (and I do mean everything) has a spiritual component to it that is contrary to the Spirit of God. From Satanism, New-Age "non-religion", polytheism, astrology, spiritualism, witchcraft, sensationalism, atheism, scientology, and a whole rack of other anti-Christ philosophies, you are receiving their anti-Christ messages everywhere you go.

"I am proud to be Black, and don't you ever forget it, however, that has no weight over my relationship with Christ. It's hard to say this in a world that denigrates our culture, our skin, our existence. As proud as I am, and as vocal as I am, I need to be sure that the love I have for Christ is more than the love I have for my culture. Not everything associated with my culture is good, though we often try to celebrate every aspect of it

---

[33] 1 Peter 2:9-12; Hosea 1:6,9; 2:23

because of how the rest of the world vilify us. But though I choose to embrace and celebrate the rich culture God has blessed me with, my choice to live a life honoring God is my most important priority. That's why if there is anything about my culture that threatens to usurp God's position, or is opposed to what God says, I reject it. I'd rather not embrace something contrary to the only sure thing I have in this life.

"Honestly, I am not so current with the music, but I do know that anything that promotes the glorification of self, the idea that money is the most important, or that we are all gods, is a tool of Satan, and must be rejected. There is NO grey area. There is room for human error in the eyes of God, but you will be held accountable for what you know. If an actor or musician talks about "channeling" the character, or something/someone "taking over", know it is not for you. Yes, I'm restating the obvious because we live in a desensitized world where even the obvious is rationalized away. Blatant Satanic worship, and jokes about Jesus are explained away, or ignored. You will be told by many that you're looking too deep into it, and that things are just as what they seem to be- entertainment, a joke, a nice beat, FICTION. It's a Satanic tool to keep you in a deluded state.

"Now's not the time to be distracted by all that. We're not supposed to be like everyone else, and sometimes that sucks, but we have to be different. You must not let the world dictate your dress and your speech. The world in which we live in isn't pretty. It's full of deception, sin, and full of people who don't like you and never will. But remember that who you are in God is enough. You may not always be liked, but when it all comes down to it, if you follow God you will be saved. That's the goal.

"You can't please everybody. Making one person happy will make another person unhappy and leave you more miserable than before. Rather, you should make God happy, because in the end He's the only one that matters. I'm not saying it's a sin to be current, relevant, or fashionable. In fact, you should be those things- so long as they don't conflict with the Word of God. And with the sexual desires: if you begin treating sex like it's sacred, it will be. If you think of non-married sex as a sin punishable by death you will be less willing to venture down that road. Even more so, if you esteem God so high that you really do want to love Him, you'll want to listen to Him because He wants what's best for you- even more than I do.

"Your father forgave you after that argument and expressed that he wanted to apologize to you. I need you to know that. Now, Daddy may be sleeping peacefully until God comes back, but we have more to do, so don't get caught up in other people's foolishness. The time you waste will have to be explained to God. Remember- that's who you will be representing to the world. Your rebaptism is your declaration that you belong to God, and are His representative for others. You can't take Christ's name and defile it anymore. He says not to take it in vain. I love you but I can't save you. Only God can do that. Okay, I think that's enough for now, but you must remember that this is not easy, and it's not a joke. But it's getting late. Don't forget about what I've said."

As I turned to go, I couldn't help but process all that she talked about. It was like a sermon. It was a sermon. And parts of it hurt, some of it definitely made me uncomfortable, but I did have both truth and hope in the end. I guess that's the characteristic of a truly Spirit-led sermon. If a sermon only uplifts or only condemns, it is probably not of God. Even in the Bible, when God was reprimanding His people, there was always a message of hope afterward, that would always say that if you changed your ways and turned back, He'd restore you.

But my mom's words cut like a razor in some places. I was so used to living under the radar, and blending in with the world around me. I didn't want to be disliked because I was "too amped for Christ." I knew people like that. They never went anywhere, did anything fun. They didn't joke, and dressed like pilgrims. They didn't watch TV, listen to secular music, or go to the movies, and if they did, it wasn't something worth watching anyway. They were boring, mundane, irrelevant, and a chore to be around. They usually had an unrealistic view of the way people should live, and left no room for error. Everything was in black and white, and no grey areas ever could exist. They were

147

cutthroat, and usually I could feel them judging me, with cold eyes, and a holier-than-thou sneer on their face.

I didn't want to be one of those people. But God showed me something different. My mom was one of those people. She had a great sense of humor, and joked all the time. She loved people, and was always opening up her home to people. She was one of those warm, friendly types that struck up conversations with people on the Metro, just because they were sitting close to her. She was fashionable and modest at the same time, and looked good for her age. She ate well, and exercised, and she was involved with a lot of church ministries that served people outside the church. She liked prison ministries, and children's ministries. She would offer up advice when asked, and though it was rigid in her opinion, it would communicate love rather than judgment. She was the type that didn't joke about everything, didn't watch just anything, didn't drink or smoke, and wore nice-looking clothes that weren't distracting, and yet she was great to be around.

She didn't wear jewelry, but sparkled like a diamond. She had a love for God and for people, and yeah she made mistakes, and sometimes let her habit of gossip, or her temper get out of hand, but I really did see that she was a true follower of Jesus. She was proof that it could be done.

I used to cringe whenever anyone would mention Ellen White, but honestly, reading her stuff, she is right about so much. She said, "Many young men and women who profess godliness do not know what it is to follow

Christ. They do not imitate His example in doing good. Love and gratitude toward God are not springing up in the heart nor expressed in their words and deportment. They do not possess the spirit of self-denial, neither do they encourage each other in the way of holiness. We do not want young people to engage in the solemn work of God who profess Christ but have not the moral strength to take their position with those who are sober and watch unto prayer and who have their conversation in heaven, whence they look for the Saviour."[34]

Yet and still, as true as her words, and my mom's words are, I'm still feeling some kind of way right now: a little afraid of the radical change that I know I have to go through, especially since I know I will lose friends over it. Yet I'm also excited that I can finally be free from the judgment of others. It's scary to know that I have to change, and that I will lose a lot in the process, including friends, job opportunities, and my reputation (what's left of it) would take a hit. But I look at who I was just a few months ago- so miserable that I wanted to kill myself, and I know that life without God is far much worse.

I may not be perfect now, but I'm willing to start looking for better. I'm willing to give God what He asks, because there is no better option. He said that love equals obedience, so I have to be willing to give it a try.

[34] Testimonies, Vol, 5. Chapter 13, pg. 111, White, Ellen G. (Sept. 5, 1879)

Man, I have a lot to think about. I only have a few more weeks of Bible study before the big day, and I have to prepare. And "watch and pray" and make sure I stay in the Word. Thank God for praying mothers, right? Even if my own mother wasn't praying, I knew that some of the older ladies at Bethel and Genesis were praying for me. And that was enough. I just hope God gives me some new friends if I have to replace mine, because I don't think I can go this race alone...

Chapter 10
April 30, 2010

My nerves are jumping. Tomorrow is the big day!! No I'm not getting married. I'll be getting re-baptized tomorrow, on May 1, 2010. I'm excited, because I'm finally ready to take that plunge. I know that a few weeks ago I was freaking out because people wouldn't like me, but Mari and King and a few others have proven to be headed in the same direction as me. God brought me new friendships to replace the ones I had lost, and renewed the ones I had broken.

I am so excited. Since today's a Friday, and since tomorrow is so important, I'm doing all the cooking for Sabbath lunch now. I'm hosting it myself. Don't worry, since I'm not a gourmet cook, Mari is volunteering her help. She's bringing her Haitian dishes, and I'm making the soul food. The next few weeks will be celebrations. Mari will be graduating law school on May 8th, and with my re-baptism, my sister's impending wedding, and (hopefully) re-instatement into a residency program (I'm waiting to hear back from a few places), I will be spending every weekend of May celebrating something.

I'm a little sad that my sister couldn't make it to my baptism, and that my brother would rather stay in a hotel than with me, but I'm not mad. This just means I have time to cook and clean before my mom flies in tomorrow morning (early). She was trying to not travel on the Sabbath, but had to push back her flight when some sort of crisis thing happened at the hospital. God worked it out, though, so she'll make it just in time for church.

Anyway, I'm excited about everything that's going on. King and I decided to fall back a little, because I needed to work on my relationship with God. He was a pleasant distraction, but a distraction nonetheless. Plus, there was so much pent-up negativity and hurt feelings between the both of us, that if we continued down in that direction, it could've been devastating for both of us. It's crazy when you realize that you shouldn't be with someone, even though you really want it to happen or work out. I'm glad that I prayed so much about him, because even though I want to be with him, I am learning that God has my best interest in mind, and plus since He can see down the line, He might be saving me for something better, or even an upgraded version of King.

It's <u>really</u> hard though, I'm not gonna lie. Honestly, I'm trying not to be sad, because I really did like him, but I trust that God will reunite us down the line if it's really going to happen. It's a little tough sometimes, especially when he talks about the girls that approach him, but I keep a brave face, because I appreciate his friendship, and positive spiritual influence on my life. There are so few people who are really trying to be about God, so I'm not about to let him go because we aren't dating.

I did need a little break from him, though, but now we're on tentatively good terms. Mari and I are getting closer and being way more open again. I still don't really trust her after all that has happened (God's gonna work that out!), but we did talk about King, and I told her some of what I was going through with him. She's being so supportive. On the other hand, I've been encouraging her to talk to her mom again. Yes, her mom is a little on the crazy side, and yes, she may not be receptive, but Mari has to try. That's her Godly duty. Haha. Listen to me! "Godly duty." I'm spiritually progressive now. I'm dishing out spiritual counsel! Me! I'm even going to join a ministry or two at Genesis. Though I love Bethel, it's not where I am meant to be. I might not like those people at Genesis (Lord, forgive me), but I do have a responsibility to that church. Which is why I've been going back there. I had the pastor at Bethel talk to Pastor Morgan so my transition would be smooth.

I'm thinking of becoming a deaconess. Yes, me. A deaconess. I am as qualified as anyone to do it. When I asked Pastor Morgan about it, I waited to see if his expression would change, you know, a raised eyebrow, or a stiffened spine, but he smiled and told me it was a great idea. You know, he might not be so bad after all. I am ready to take this plunge and start doing what I must, to get to where God wants me. Even in the presence of Sister Roberts, Gwen, and the other holy rollers. I have to find a new name for them because I feel little bad for judging them- even though they treat me like I'm a whore. Yeah, I still get the whispers, the eye rolls, the sneers, and all that. But I think that since I have so many haters, I must be doing something right.

I feel like I'm beginning to walk up a mountain path, maybe the path up Mt. Everest. I want to be in a relationship again, but I get the feeling that God wants me to spend some alone time with Him. You know, talking to Him, doing His ministry, and focusing on the things that I should be focused on. It's tough because attention is one of my biggest addictions. I guess it makes sense that I need to focus on God so I don't value the gift more than I value the giver. I should be desperate for His attention more than anyone else's. If I was in a relationship with anyone now, my life would more than likely become all about them. God wants me all to Himself, I guess. I mean He did send His Son to die for me, so I guess that gives Him the right to be jealous. Oh, and, of course, He made me, so uh, that gives Him every right to be demanding. But all He demands is love, and obedience. That's not much compared to how He treats me.

Wait! Was that the doorbell that just rang? It's only 7pm, but to me, it's late. I didn't invite anyone over. I'm so tired though. I'm halfway through the collards (vegetarian of course), but I still have the cornbread baking, the yams roasting, and of course, the chicken to fry. It's probably just someone who needs to get into the building. I'll just let them in. I hope they're not a serial killer.

Now back to this food...

****

Imagine my surprise. I am standing in my living room, face to face with the man who got me here in the first place. No, I'm not talking about Jesus. I meant the one who caused all the trouble. Again. Hunter Austin Black. I thought I'd forgiven him, but as he stands in my living room, I realize that I still despise him. And I'm staring into his eyes, silent, waiting for him to state his reasons why he's here.

"Hi Heaven." *I really don't have time for this.* "I know I did you wrong again, and I know it's too much to ask for your forgiveness again-" *Are you for real right now?* "-but I figured that since you've been going to church and doing that Christian thing, you might possibly find it in your heart to forgive me." I was shell-shocked. *This is ridiculous.* "I know I don't deserve it-" *YOU SURE DON'T!* "-but I need you to forgive me." I didn't know what to do with myself. Part of me wanted to kill him, part of me wanted to seriously injure him, and the other part of me wanted to emotionally wreck him.

Almost every part of me wanted to exact revenge on him, so much so that I had already begun planning a vicious, vindictive, shockingly cruel plan. Too bad that now that I'd started listening to God, I couldn't turn Him off. Yes, the little nagging "forgive him" in my mind was beginning to overpower the renewed hatred that was brewing. He went on and on, but I stopped paying attention, focused on the battle in my mind.

=It's just a trick. See how he always does this? He's got you right where he wants you. He thinks he can just ask for forgiveness and get it? Don't you remember everything that he did to you? Kick him out, shut the door, and NEVER look back!!=

And I almost did exactly that. I was so caught up in what he'd done to me that I forgot what the actual point of forgiveness was. Still, I wasn't trying to hear God, or forgive him. He didn't deserve it after all he'd put me through.

Now you know better than to not forgive. Did I ever withhold forgiveness even though you spent an entire lifetime rejecting me? Did I ever hesitate when you did me wrong? Didn't I say that revenge is mine to handle? Don't you think that the miracle working God who sees all can have better revenge than you, who can't even see past your own self? Why would you throw away your own salvation for this? You know I said that if you don't forgive others, I won't forgive you. In fact, you said it yourself: "Forgive me AS I forgive others."[35] Do you REALLY want to throw everything away because of him? If he's not

---

[35] Matt. 6:12

worth your time, why are you making him worth your salvation? Forgive him.

Wow. I'd been ignoring the truth. I mean yeah it sounds nice if I said I immediately forgave him, took him into my arms, hugged him, and then became his best friend, BUT LET'S BE REAL. I didn't think I had it in me to forgive him. I was having a hard enough time trying to stay Mari's friend. I wasn't trying to go against God, but honestly, I'm not God and my capacity for love/forgiveness is nowhere near His. The best I could do was attempt to forgive, but even so, I REALLY didn't want to even try. The thought, "why should I?" kept running through my mind. Of course, to that I heard "because I said so" and "because I did it for you," but I wasn't convinced.

In the midst of my internal battle, Hunt just kept right on talking. I wasn't even pretending that I was paying attention. He kept droning on about how I was the one that got away, and how sorry he was to have hurt me, and a whole other rack of foolishness that I no longer cared for. A few months ago, I might've bought into it. But I was finally learning to love myself, and I finally knew that I could do better. Soon, though, I tired of his droning, and had to stop him. "Why are you even here? You've had all this time to ask for forgiveness, but you never did. Why now?" I expected to hear a dramatic answer, like, "I got HIV" or "I had a life-changing

157

revelation" or even "I got in a car accident and realized that life is short."

In all actuality, this negro said, "I heard about what happened to you, and I thought that if I got you to forgive me, it might help you move on, and give you closure. I mean I didn't think what I did could affect you so much. I knew you cared for me, but not enough that I shattered your existence. That's why I stayed away. I didn't want you to think that my visit meant that I wanted to get back with you. But now that you're all in church again, I thought it would be safe to hash these things out and give you're the closure you need."

He wasn't sorry. He in his conceit, thought he was doing *me* a favor by asking for forgiveness. In his mind, I was the desperate crazy girl who needed to get over him. As livid as I was, I realized that he was trying to be honest with me, and was right in his own mind. I had to get *over* him? I couldn't believe how arrogant he was, to think that he was the sum of my discontent with myself. He thought that what he'd done had devastated me so much that I attempted suicide.

As he went on, all thoughts concerning forgiveness quickly exited my mind. I didn't want to. Now, not only was he taking up my time, but now my food was starting to dry out and burn. I rushed to the kitchen, and he followed me. I was through. All the joy I had about my rebaptism was long gone. I was tired, a headache was mounting, I was irritated that my food was slightly burnt, and he was getting on my last nerve. Mid-sentence I interrupted him and asked why he mistreated me and cheated on me. His answer was, "Because I could. You let me. And plus, you bored me."

As I tried to keep my composure, he kept trying to make me lose it. But despite all my anger, I wasn't about to let him keep me out of Heaven. He was NOT worth losing my salvation. Nonetheless, though I was going to try to forgive him, there was nothing in the Bible that stated I had to *like* him. I wouldn't hate him, I would tolerate him. But as for now, it was time for him to leave. I had things to do and he was taking up too much time and mental problems. "Look, as it is the Christian thing to do, and required by God, I will forgive you. But don't think that you're ever going to be a part of my life ever again. No drop-bys, no phone calls, no contact unless initiated by me. By the way, you were never the source of my problems, and whatever you broke, Jesus found a way to fix. Your time in my life has been a lesson, and now that I've learned it, I have moved on.

"I honestly suggest that you confront all of your demons and go find Jesus, or else your life will have no meaning. Trust me, I've lived enough without God, and in the short time I've really gotten to know Him, He hasn't let me down yet. I've finally learned to love myself, and I deserve much better than anything you have to give me. No offense, but just like the living don't hang around the dead, the spiritually living has no business hanging around the spiritually dead. God bless you anyway. Now, it's time for you to go. Goodbye!"

And with that I walked toward the door and let him out. I guess this closure was necessary. I know it seems crazy that I could try and forgive him despite his asinine and arrogant statements, but I guess I really have grown in God. Otherwise, I would've thrown the lamp at him again. I could've sworn I saw him flinch every time I passed a lamp. He must remember last time.

Anyway, I do believe that I have started to grow. It takes all my strength to maintain my friendship with Mari, and yeah, I've forgiven her (mostly), but there is still a huge part of me that doesn't trust her. If I was still living without God, I would have no qualms about moving on without her in my life. However, God has given me the strength and endurance (and crazy peace) that allows me to keep going when I want to snatch her breath from her throat. (I'm really not as violent as I seem- I promise!)

I was watching one of those talk shows, where a girl had been in a similar situation as Mari and I, and I found it funny that though I related to her, there was something about my relationship with God that made it much easier to let go of all that pain and anger. But I guess that's the difference those of us who carry God in our hearts, and the rest of us who are just "living," I don't think it's farfetched to believe that those in Christ may have an easier time forgiving others, since we have so much reason/motivation to do it. It goes along the lines of "peace that passes understanding" and "joy unspeakable." I praise God that I have the opportunity to even get to know Him.

Whoa! Where is my mind? I have to finish getting ready for tomorrow. The Sabbath is almost here, and I must respect God's wishes. I just have to put Hunt out of mind for the time being. I won't let the devil take away the joy of my spiritual rebirth. I guess I have to just turn up the music, head back into the kitchen, and worship my way back into a happy mood...

D. Gloria Elysée

Epilogue
September 2010

Life has gotten back to normal (somewhat). I don't chill with King anymore, as he has a new girlfriend. Though it still stings a little bit, I respect him (and his relationship) enough to back off. Mari and I are basically back to where we used to be. She had a conversation with her mom about her father, and finally asked why her mom hated her. No, they didn't cry and make up and are the best of friends. They are trying to work through their issues. Ms. Joi is still crazy, but at least Mari has some truth to why her mom is the way she is. At least they're on the right track.

Mari and I decided to try the "accountability partner" thing again. It's hard to keep my heart open to trusting people when I've been hurt so many times, and hard to keep my heart open to love, but I guess that's the beauty of God. He keeps His heart open for us, so that we can keep our hearts open for Him and other people.

My sister is married, and I'm sure there's a baby on the way. My brother (finally) met a woman that he actually thinks will be around for Thanksgiving (since they never last that long). My mom is doing well, and comes to visit periodically. And we all lived happily ever after...

Yeah right! I'm still having problems at work, but I have a resident that is willing to teach me. I work at a smaller hospital, in nearby Milton, MA. I've learned more with her than I did with my other resident. I work so hard during the week, but one good thing about the strenuous work week is that I FINALLY understand the joy of the Sabbath. Every Friday afternoon that I'm not working, I clock out, go home, cook, clean, and when the sun goes down, I REST. I pray, I sing, I sleep, and I spend quality time with God since every day I'm usually rushing some portion of my morning worship.

I go to church on Sabbath morning, and I worship. I don't think about work, my problems, drama, or other people. I think about God, and I rest my mind and my soul in the Lord. It's things like the Sabbath that remind me why I serve the Lord: He mandates time to rest, for my well-being, and for meditation on Him as my Creator. Because of Him, I've learned to truly love and appreciate my life. My life is still tumultuous, and I still struggle with my sins, but now I have hope. Hope for the future, on Earth and for Heaven. (No pun intended.)

I am not the same Heaven I was last year. I'm not the same Heaven I was 6 months ago. God has blessed me beyond belief. No, my life isn't perfect. Far from it.

But I think that's the misconception that everyone seems to have about being a servant of God. People think that life gets better, easier, and everything you want works out. That's probably why many people don't stay in church, or don't go to church at all. We're all so hurt by life, and all sinners, so when we get together in church, though we recognize who we worship, we are still the same flawed people, struggling with the same mess we came in with. We grow only if we surrender to God. But the rate of our growth isn't the same, just as our struggles aren't the same.

We are all seeking for the same things: love, acceptance, attention, validation. In some form or another, we all crave it, center our lives on it, and hurt when we don't find it. We all want magic solutions to the problems we face every day, especially in this world of instant gratification, and/or we all want to escape the negative situations in our lives.

Realizing that the church isn't a quick fix, nor will it guarantee a life without speed bumps, we become disheartened and go back to what we were unsuccessfully using to fill our voids. God created the void in us so we would turn to Him, the only One who can fill it and leave us satisfied. I was so busy looking for it in men, that I never gave God the chance to fill His own shoes. Not until He turned my life upside down and emptied it of all the things I was using to substitute for Him. He changed my life for the better.

165

Don't get it twisted: there's no instant "magic" solution to life- not even Christianity. I thought that giving my life to Christ would mean that I'd be happy from then on. I thought everything would suddenly "click" together, and that I'd have everything I ever wanted. It was this shallow thinking that made me so angry at God. I didn't understand that his plans for me didn't have anything to do with what I wanted. I wanted a man who I realized didn't love or respect me. I wanted to be rich, married, beautiful and successful (according to the world's standards). I wanted everyone's approval, attention, and admiration. I wanted to serve God on my terms.

If God hadn't ripped my life from my hands, I wouldn't have the blessings I have now. No, I'm not rich, famous, married, or skinny. I don't have a man, I have a job again, but not at the same hospital, and I'm about 20 pounds heavier than I was before. My job is ONLY by the grace of God, and life hasn't gotten any less dramatic as before. However, I have peace, joy, and love in my heart. And most importantly, I have an actual relationship with God.

Most of my trials were direct consequences of my insubordination and my insolence toward God. I gladly ignored His Will for my own (temporary) pleasure. I finally get it now. I couldn't ask Him to let me act a fool, reject Him, despise Him, and then get mad that I had to deal with my actions. At my job, I wasn't doing what I was supposed to do, so I had to deal with the consequence. In my relationship, I was allowing behavior I didn't like go unchecked, undisputed, and unchallenged, so I had to face the reality of the situation. My God didn't love me less by letting me deal with everything I had been doing to myself. In fact, His love was letting me learn my lesson, so that there would be no "next time" and I could learn to focus on, and trust Him above all things. I had to realize that my actions were leading me in a destructive way, and that even though God didn't allow me to pay the full penalty (death), I still had to pay for my actions, to grow, to learn, to correct my ways. It hurt like crazy, and felt like Hell (literally), but if the Bible is quoting that we are gold that is tried through the fire, I don't expect that "fire" would be a pleasant experience.

I was created to stand in a stark contrast from the "real world," but failed at representing God accurately. I was trying so hard to belong to it, and tried my hardest to fit in with the people I was supposed to be helping. Rather than showing them a way out of their mess, I was telling them that their mess was enjoyable, as good as it gets, and that there was nothing else to look forward to. And when things went wrong, I blamed God. Never mind that I never blamed the devil for his part, or took responsibility for the decisions that I made, and chose to blame God for letting sin run rampant, but I ignored every warning God would give me. Honestly, especially being someone who was raised in the church, it's really sad that I never respected God until after my suicide attempt. I didn't even hear Him, until I was forced to be aware. I'm sure that I had almost gotten to the point of no return, and that if it wasn't for some praying family and church ladies, I might have never made it. It's a wonder that He is still giving me chances.

Don't think I'm perfect, or milestones away from where I was last year. I relapse all the time, and fall back into the mess He pulled me out of, but now I know to ask forgiveness and believe that I'm forgiven.

I finally learned how to tell a man I'd been intimate with "no more sex." You see, if sex is such a determining factor in the relationship, and he can't respect me or LIKE me enough to stay in a relationship without it, we had no business being together in the first place. God would never create a man for me that didn't have a heart for Him, or one who thought sex was more important than the one they were having it with. I know I'm worth waiting for, and though I have slipped up quite a few times, I know that I am trying to save myself. Whoever God has for me is worth the wait. God would not ordain His daughter to be united with someone who had no respect for Him, or me, who isn't part of His own, and who isn't progressing in a forward direction toward Heaven. My God made me great, so I'm holding out for the greatness I deserve.

God truly changed me, my mindset, and consequently, my actions. I could've gone on living in the way I was before: oblivious to what true joy, peace, and happiness were. I could've died, in church, without ever knowing God. God has blessed me. I don't have everything I want, but I have everything I need, and never knew to ask for. I can't thank Him enough.

As I look at the way this world is deteriorating, it worries me that so many people just don't care about God enough to change. Like me, they were comfortable doing what they knew they shouldn't, confident that God would bend the rules for them. Time didn't matter. The fact that planes flying into buildings were a prophetic indication of Jesus' imminent return didn't mean much.

I did it too. Walking around claiming that it was "the end of the world," but would revert back to my own ways, clubbing, sexing, and all that "fun" stuff. I was having so much fun but hated myself for the fun I was having. I was seeing all the signs of Jesus' coming, and Pastor Morgan spent all his time talking about it, but even with the crazy weather patterns, the devastating natural disasters, the corruption in politics, the war on terror, the systematic genocidal racism against people of color, and the economy failing, I went on doing what I was doing. Somehow, I got it into my mind that my life on earth was more relevant, urgent, IMPORTANT.

I was spiritually sleepwalking, and unaware of all the danger I was in. But God woke me up. I didn't like His chosen method, but then again, no one likes to be woken up out of a good dream. Many people would rather stay in that dream state, because at least they'd be able to enjoy this earth on their terms. So, they trade their birthright for a bowl of soup like Esau did[36], and

---

[36] Gen 25: 27-34

sell their souls for fame, earthly success, love, and fun. Or they get so distracted in the bills, the day-to-day errands, the jobs, the church ministries, the "form" of holiness, and/or the fast-paced nature of society and forget that God is supposed to be the focus.

I have been praying that God allows me to speak to others about Him. Now I might have a past, but this is the real world, and almost everybody I know has some sort of baggage that they're carrying around. It's time to bring the Gospel to real people in a real way. I don't like to talk about my business like that, and most people don't like putting themselves in a vulnerable situation, but I'm realizing that if Moses wasn't a murderer, and David wasn't a philanderer, we wouldn't know that God restores any and everybody. Not that God wants us to go out there and start sinning so we can relate to others, but God loves us and uses us despite our pasts.

Maybe my life story can change your life story. Maybe it can show a young woman that she is valuable, whether or not anyone has ever told her so. Maybe it can tell a young man that he should keep going despite all the roadblocks in his life. Some people think they can't do anything right, and are so ready to give up or abandon the plan because it's not working, but maybe if you looked to God for His plan, you would see that your failure is His tool to make you a winner.

Everyone has a testimony that holds weight, and every Christian's duty is to tell their story. We never know who we impact with just our own story. The one that we take for granted, devalue, and try to cover up in embarrassment. God wants to use your spiritual poverty to bring someone out of theirs. God wants people who want to be spiritually awakened, purified, ready for His use. He wants people who love Him, who want to talk to Him. People who don't think it's an obligation to spend time with Him.

You are busy, going about your business, fun-loving, and there is nothing particularly wrong with that. But you are also a sinner, who can't help but make mistakes, who needs to recognize that there is a way out of your despair and pain. Don't let the devil shame you into putting God aside. No one of your friends or family members can save you. No one of them can send you to Heaven. They can't even rescue themselves or keep from making their own mistakes. Don't worry about what other people have to say. They'll attack you, not because you are such a bad person, but because you want to be like God.

There isn't much time left for this world. Prophecy is being fulfilled every minute, and just turning on the news you can see that the events spoken about in the Bible are almost complete. You don't have time to lose. It's time to really make a decision. Don't follow my bad example, especially seeing how miserable I really was. You don't need that in your life.

You now know all my business. You know who I am better than my family and my friends. Take it from me, once you are where I am now (in Christ) you will **NEVER** want to go back to who you were before. You will **NEVER** find more peace, joy, and love. I don't care how happy you think you are now. You will **NEVER** truly know what happy is unless you are in the Will of God. So, take it from me: don't get so caught up in your life, that you lose out on your *LIFE*. Just a few words of advice...

"And know that [I] cause everything to work together for the good of those who love [Me] and are called according to [my] purpose for them. Nothing can ever separate [you] from [My] love. Neither death nor life, neither angels nor demons, nor rulers, neither [your] fears for today nor [your] worries about tomorrow—not even the powers of hell can separate [you] from [My] love. No power in the sky above or in the earth below—indeed, NOTHING in all creation will ever be able to separate [you] from –[My] love that is revealed in Christ Jesus, [your] Lord."

-Romans 8:38, 39 NLT

D. Gloria Elysée

A King Among Men

D. Gloria Elysée

This book is for all Christian men in the world (especially Black men) who struggle to maintain a Godly standard of manhood in a world full of sub-standard principles, little integrity, and lacking in both discretion and direction. I applaud you for your persistence in a world that does nothing but try to denigrate you. I also dedicate it to all the men who grew up without a father or a strong male influence in their lives. Remember that God is your Father, and is always with you, "even unto the end of the world."[37]

---

[37] Matthew 28:20

D. Gloria Elysée

Prologue

We don't talk about him. Ever. We pretend as if he doesn't exist. But, somewhere in the recesses of my mind he does. They both do. I guess it's safe to say like father, like son in this case. Father gone. Son gone. Father living a fast life. Son repeats all the same mistakes, and adds a few of his own. Father dead. Son- well, I don't know where he is or if he's even alive at this point. But that just means that it's all left to me. I guess I'm the legacy. I'm left to be the King among women. There just aren't enough men left.

My name is Solomon Principle, but my friends call me King. That nickname was given to me a *really* long time ago. It started at church one Sabbath when a lady was telling the story of King Solomon. I guess some kids thought it was funny, and started calling me King as a joke- until it stuck. It was only my 3rd week of church. EVER. My mom had just found Jesus. She was hypervigilant because my father had just been killed in a prison fight as he awaited deportation to Haiti. Plus, my 15-year-old brother was deep into his rebellious teen

179

phase, staying out all night, and scaring her into religion with his antics. So now, at the age of 10, I was an involuntary Christian. I didn't mind going as much as I hated the fact that my mother was now obsessed. She woke us up every morning by singing at the top of her lungs. Whenever we misbehaved, she began a LONG prayer session that included 10 songs, 3 psalms, and an extremely drawn out prayer. Did I mention this was all in FRENCH? The whole thing took about an hour and a half. Now, this doesn't mean that I didn't pray. I did! Every night- especially for my brother, after he stumbled home one afternoon, badly beaten- even though he refused to tell me what happened. I still helped him clean off all the blood before my mother came home- we couldn't afford to have another torturous prayer session. I didn't know if all the blood was his or not, but I was too afraid to ask. When I asked what happened, he shrugged his shoulders, and shot me that infamous smirk, "You know- things happen!" I never found out what happened that day. I can only speculate that it was illegal. After all, he was my father's son.

Anyway, enough with the stroll down memory lane- dwelling in the past will do nothing for my future. I didn't become a successful marketing specialist by dwelling on my less-than-stellar upbringing. Staying in the past has caused many people to fail. That cannot be me. I refuse to ever go back to my former lifestyle. And will never allow my children to grow up the way I did. I am, after all, a King...

Chapter 1
September 2013

The cool Monday in September started pretty uneventfully. I had some paperwork to complete before I had to meet with a new client. I'm a Senior Associate and brand marketing specialist at Court, Locke & Stone Financials. I spend most of my time consulting the advertising executives of startup companies about branding. Basically, I make my living teaching people how to stand out. That's funny, because when I was younger, I was pretty invisible. I was easily forgettable in high school- nice to people, but not so nice people thought I was a pushover. I had just enough of a smart mouth to get me in and out of trouble with ease. I looked so unassuming that when I said something, people usually looked through me to figure out who said it. I had a few girlfriends, who usually moved on when they realized I wasn't going to upgrade their social status, or that I was broke. I was on the basketball team, but I wasn't a starter, or even in the game for a long time. This makes the fact that I make a living by teaching others how to stand out in the market, quite ironic.

Being 30, however, made me hungry for success, and even if I couldn't stand out, I'd make sure my work with my clients would do that for me.

My new client was running late. I had done some research on him, though there wasn't much information to find. Known as C.B. Stone, he was a young entrepreneur that had begun a small social media networking website. I was unsure of the details of his product, even with the research I'd done. All I knew was that some guy named C.B. was now pulling in a LOT of money and was trying to create a more diverse market for his product. Oh, and the most important factor: C.B. was the prodigal son of Mr. Phillip Stone, the Chief Financial Officer and Partner at my firm. So now I was stuck babysitting my boss' son, and would be responsible for his financial future. If I succeeded, it would solidify my future at Court, Lock & Stone Financials. I could either make partner, or build enough venture capital (and clientele) to start my own marketing firm. If I failed, my career could end. I could be fired, blacklisted from all the other firms, and end up making a living off of cheesy advertisements from local mom-and-pop shops. Talk about pressure!

I might've been flattered for the vote of confidence from Mr. Stone if I wasn't sure that my getting assigned to C.B. was because none of the other associates wanted this job. Since I was consistently singled out for the projects no one wanted, and always "under supervision" (despite the fact that I was great at my job) I assumed this was the same. I guess a young educated black man really is a threat. I wouldn't have considered race if it wasn't for the fact that 1. I live in

Boston, and 2. I usually get partnered with a Junior Associate (Read: assistant, who then gets the majority of the credit) because some clients feel uncomfortable working with me alone. I usually get assigned a partner, always of another race, usually Caucasian, to "lessen the blow" or to make meetings with me less menacing. Apparently, the smart Black man isn't qualified to handle to caseload himself. But since this is somewhat of a babysitting job, they left me to wait for C.B myself, who was now 25 minutes late to our first meeting.

We were set to meet at 1pm. Apparently, using the company table at Meritage wasn't sufficient for C.B.'s taste. Instead, I was seated at Mr. Stone's personal table in The Café at the Taj Hotel. Sure, it had an incredible view, but that view wasn't keeping me from getting restless at the tardiness of my new client. Not to mention, this business lunch was threatening to offset my other work. Although this client was to be given the utmost priority, my other workload was not to be diminished. So, the fact that this rich pretty boy was late was starting to get under my skin.

My back was to the door, and I had begun to tire of craning my neck to turn and look. I was about to signal the waiter to pay for my cranberry juice when I noticed an attractive blonde woman standing next to me. She was all body, in a curve-hugging blue dress. It wasn't exactly modest (though her hourglass figure might've had more to do with that), but exuded a high-class, almost unattainable sex appeal. Her jewelry suggested exquisite taste and old money.

As I ran my eyes back to her face, she smirked and sat down. "I'm sorry-" I began to let her know that the seat was taken. She held her hand up to silence me. "No need to apologize. I'm the one that's late. You are Solomon Principle, correct?" I was confused. "I thought I was meeting with C.B. Stone. Are you here on his behalf?" She raised an eyebrow. "Perhaps I was unclear. My name is Charlotte Blaire Stone. My father is Phillip Stone, of Court, Locke & Stone Financials. I had a 1 o'clock appointment with Solomon Principle. I assume that is you. I don't know where you received the misinformation that I was his son. Although, knowing Daddy, this could just be wishful thinking on his part." I was stunned. I had to fix this or I could lose my job.

"I'm so sorry for the misunderstanding, Ms. Stone. I assumed, based on the use of your initials, and surprising lack of background information available, that you were Mr. Stone's son. In fact, no one at the office corrected me when I first referred to you as- well. I'm so sorry Ms. Stone. I hope this does not reflect negatively on the firm. I hope we can start over. My name is Solomon Principle, and I assure you, I am the best man for the job." "I both doubt and yet am sure of that fact," she replied. "So, who did you piss off to get stuck with me?" I was stunned. Was I really supposed to answer that? "I know my father. I know he considers me a nuisance. Let me guess. You are to keep me busy enough to make me think I'm doing something, but should not let me get so involved that I want to stay around for long. Nor should you do anything to make me request any more money. I am neither to be seen nor heard. You are to make me successful enough to satiate my curiosity in this subject until I, "as usual," find another hobby." (She imitated him perfectly.) "And under absolutely no circumstances are you to allow me to drop-in on Daddy's office without an appointment scheduled at least 2 days in advance, so he can have time to reschedule me or make up a business trip. He *hates* it when I show up and he has to cancel on his flavor of the moment tramp! Am I right?" She was right on target, but of course, I couldn't let her know. "Actually, Ms. Stone, I thought that your company could have the same impact that Facebook™ and Twitter™ have on social media. I asked for this job because I welcome a challenge. What exactly sets your company apart from all the other social networking sites?" "Oh! You're good!" She spoke with a slight French accent.

I heard that most of the high-powered and wealthy couples rarely raised their own children. I assumed she was educated at one of the finest European boarding schools. I didn't have time to daydream, however, since time was no longer on my side. "Ms. Stone-," I began. "Please. Call me C.B. We will be spending lots of time together, I assure you, and formality will only waste more time." She was really straightforward. I was impressed. I was expecting a spoiled brat with a superiority complex, not a bombshell with a brain. This was going to be interesting.

185

"Okay, C.B. What makes your company a good fit for Court, Locke, & Stone? As she began describing her brainchild "Kandid!" the hint of French deepened, becoming more and more pronounced as she passionately spoke about her idea. "Kandid! is the type of website that rivals Instagram™ for pictures, but specifically targets the seasoned traveler. It is the way to document your travels and interact with other travelers. I want it to be like Groupon™, Pinterest™, and Instagram™ all rolled into one, but for travelers. So, you can take pictures of places you travel to, bookmark the places you want to visit, and even buy tickets for entry to tourist spots, shows, and eventually, restaurants! I must admit, I did not write the program for the website, however, my associates who did, will meet with us at a later time. For now, you just have the brains- and beauty I might add, behind Kandid! and Kandid.com."

I expected to hear about some fru fru site, something girly, concerning clothes, maybe accessories or jewelry. Something only marketable to heiresses and rich socialites. But this was amazingly impressive. A website that was geared for travelers was exactly what was needed in today's market. Here you had a growing trend of traveling on a budget, of tourism extending beyond the traditional monuments and museums. A person could use this website to chart their trip, buy tickets to events, food options, accommodations, and tours before they left for their vacation. Or they could reach the destination and find local deals in real time, where they were. This could mean advertising revenue from restaurants, hotels, and tourist attractions, since the traveler could "check in" to their location, and give an impromptu (rave) review. I did not expect such a thoughtful and inspired idea from my boss' progeny. And of course, the company was aptly named, as C.B. was certainly very candid, though she remained professional.

"First of all, C.B. I must start off by saying that your idea is fantastic, as I'm sure you already know. Kandid! is a really good concept, however there's a lot of work to be done in order to develop it into a brand that will rival the other social media networking sites. I think the first order of business is to narrow down the vision into a specific primary goal. Let's say, we focus on eliminating the ways it mimics the other sites. This way, we highlight the differences, which will draw the clientele of the other sites to it. If we continue to describe it using our competition as the benchmark, we teach our clients to do the same. That'll make it seem like an imitator or that we're re-inventing the wheel. Investors will not want to heavily invest in a knockoff of a successful technological venture. We want them to see that it has the potential to break through social media networking to possibly become part of the infrastructure of tourism itself. If the European Council on Tourism and Trade and the English Tourist Board were on board with Kandid!, perhaps that could revolutionize the tourism industry altogether. This is not easy, simple, or small. This is major. Your brainchild is exactly what this firm needs and, naturally, vice versa. I will do everything in my power to convince the senior partners of this- after we've worked out the kinks, of course."

She straightened up in her chair, although she, by no means, was slumped over in any way. She held a steady gaze, her piercing green eyes staring directly into my eyes. "I wasn't aware that Kandid! was flawed," she responded defensively. "I have done extensive research on this project-" Now was my time to interrupt. "I am not implying that your hard work has been for nothing. I'm just trying to elevate Kandid! from a social networking site to an integral part of the tourism industry. It needs to be so ready that even your father can't help but sign off on it." What could she say to that? She smiled, and held out her hand. "In that case, Mr. Principle, I believe we will be unstoppable." As I stood, I took her hand, contemplated kissing it, but simply held it long enough to help her out of her seat. "It was a pleasure, C.B. I will contact you shortly about our next meeting. I look forward to it." "Don't wait too long, Solomon. I don't think I could stand that."

As I watched her walk away, I couldn't help but admire her firm behind. She has a distinct sway, not quite like a *sista*, but definitely had its own quality. I couldn't help but notice how well she pronounced my last name, and how familiar she became as the meeting ended. I know when a woman is flirting, and she was *definitely* flirting. But I need to stay focused. Flirting with the boss' daughter is a dangerous game. I can't afford to trip up now. Not with so much riding on this...

Chapter 2
September 2013

Back at the office, I was busy in my cubicle finishing my other marketing projects. But I couldn't stop thinking of the meeting with C.B. I was contemplating resuming work on the Kandid! account so I could see Charlotte again, but I knew I needed to focus on my work. She was cute, but not enough to make me lose my job and end my career. She was a trap that I wasn't interested in getting caught up in. As I looked over one campaign (Helchem Laboratories, an up-and-coming pharmaceutical company, trying to make a name for itself), my coworker Mark Stratford stopped by. "So, how was she?" he said. "You knew C.B. was a girl?" I exclaimed! "I've been walking around for a week calling her a guy!" "Wait," he said, "You seriously didn't know? I just thought you were calling her a guy because you saw her pictures as a kid. Yuck!" "No," I replied. "I didn't know. That almost blew up in my face. Next time, I'd appreciate the heads up." He smirked, as though he wasn't even listening. "So, is she as ugly as she was when she was a kid?" I didn't have time for this. I should've known he'd never correct me.

As the only other Black man in the office, he acted as though there could only be one of us in a high-ranking position. Sometimes I felt as though the partners at the firm felt the same way. Not to mention, his lighter skin and prep school background seemed to be more appealing to the partners, the clients, and even my coworkers- despite his shady ways. No matter how polite enough he was to me, I knew that he was not to be trusted. "Mark, I have a lot of work to do." Meaning: "I really don't have time for this." "Is there anything specific that you needed?" "No," he replied. "Just that Mr. Stone would like to see you in his office. Now." Great. And of course, he'd wait until to tell me this. "Okay. Thanks. Bye." I needed to hurry. Who knew how long Mr. Stone had been waiting.

As I walked into Mr. Stone's office, he yelled, "It took you long enough to get here. Close the door behind you." This wasn't starting off well at all. "How did things go with C.B.? Tell me everything I need to know. Now." I cleared my throat. "Mr. Stone, C.B. has developed an idea for a website that could rival all the social networking sites that are out there today. If it succeeded, it would be a hit with the tourism industry. It's actually quite an amazing-" "Let me stop you right there. How much? That's what I want to know. How much will it cost me? How long is C.B. planning on staying here? When does C.B. plan on stopping by? I don't care how good you think the idea is. I want to know the important things." I cleared my throat again. "Honestly, sir, I haven't gotten that far yet. I was trying to finish my other assignments, like the Helchem Labs and the Fuller Media campaigns. I was planning on starting on C.B.'s Kandid! campaign as soon as I finished all the other work." "Well that's not going to work for me. I need all your attention on doing whatever it takes to get C.B. out of my hair, so Helchem and Fuller are now Mark's. Your only responsibility is to make whatever foolish idea C.B. has thought of cost the least amount of money. And make sure C.B. does NOT stop by my office unannounced. Keep C.B. occupied, and try to minimize any office visits. I'd like to keep my office C.B.-free. Do NOT let me down. Understand? Good. Send Mark back in." And that was that. He turned and answered his phone, and dismissed me. Now all my hard work was going to Mark, and I was left with only the Kandid! account. If I screwed this one up, I would definitely be fired. God, sometimes I <u>hate</u> working in this place.

****

For my Thursday afternoon meeting with C.B., I was prepared. After lunch, we met in the courtyard of the Boston Public Library, to discuss our upcoming meeting with her web developer, and to talk about the numbers. My focus was on doing my job: promoting the brand while saving my client (and my boss) money. She had a ton of new ideas she wanted to incorporate, however my goal was to start small, because it would be best to developed it over time. The longer we waited to launch, the more likely the idea would be ripped off by someone else. Although she wasn't too fond of that idea, she knew it was what was best. "I trust you, Solomon. Don't let me down."

It was the story of my life. I seemed to be the depository of others' hopes, dreams, and successes. My job was to protect others' investments and make their dreams come true, but I wondered sometimes if I was doing what I was supposed to do. You know, what *God* wanted me to do. Sure, I was good at it. It was almost as if God had given me the ability to mold a vision until it reflected the client's ideals. And I was doing so, successfully working my way up the corporate ladder. But when people told me they trusted me and not to let them down, something about the *way* they'd say it just didn't sit right with me.

The meeting continued quite uneventfully. We discussed her business model, the estimates for the development of the web page, the networking she'd done and her potential advertisers. We also discussed her company budgets, staff, the location of Kandid! headquarters, and the web designer's role in the future of the company. By the time we were finished it was dinnertime. I had planned to go grocery shopping and then head home to cook (yes, I cook- and well!), but C.B. decided that she wanted to continue working over dinner. There wasn't much left to work on, since we weren't going to hear any estimates from the web developer or anyone else until at least next week. But she insisted, and so we headed to Sorrelina restaurant, since it was across the street. I knew that I could use the company card for business meetings, since Mr. Stone had insisted I not bring her to the office for meetings. He gave me an expense account so that everything could be done out of the office. Still, I hated spending money- even if it wasn't my own.

The food at the restaurant was great despite its teeny tiny portions. I still preferred home cooking, though. Something about home cooked food: straight from the pot, in steaming heaps on your plate, and made with love! There was nothing like home cooking-especially Haitian food. I much preferred home cooking to fine dining, no matter how good it was. Since I missed a good plate, so I decided that after church this Sabbath, I was going to visit my mother. She always had a potluck after church anyway, so I knew there'd be plenty of food. Plus, it'd been a long while since my last visit. Come Saturday, I'd be eating like a king.

****

I arrived at church early on Saturday morning. I attend Mt. Bethel Haitian Seventh-Day Adventist church. We have multiple services, but I chose to attend the early one, since by the time it ended, my mother's potluck would be starting. She goes to another Haitian church outside of Boston- Calvaire SDA Church, in Easton, MA, which is a bit of a drive, but it was worth it today.

The service itself was good. My ability to understand and speak Kreyol is pretty good, but not as good as I'd like it to be. I can follow along in the service, but I am much more comfortable with the afternoon service (my regular service) because it is in English. I understood most of the sermon, which focused on being a good steward, or manager.

193

It was the story of the man who went on a trip after giving his servants some money, and when he came back, he asked what they did with it[38]. Long story short, two of them invested the money, multiplied it, and returned a hefty profit. The other just left his money tucked away somewhere, and then returned it to the boss with an excuse of "'...I knew you were a harsh man...I was afraid I would lose your money, so I hid it...Look, here is your money back.[39]'" So then he's reprimanded, and then the clincher verse: "To those who use well what they are given, even more will be given, and they will have an abundance. But from those who do nothing, even what little they have will be taken away.[40]" I didn't understand why someone who had little would get that taken away, but I got the point: use it or lose it.

During the remainder of the service, I struggled through remembering the French hymns (most of which are a series of noises I make while singing, rather than words with meaning). My mind was a little distracted from my thoughts about C.B./Kandid!, but mostly from last visit with my mother.

A month ago, my mother told me that my brother was up for parole soon, and asked if I could attend his hearing. I was really busy with a project so I said no. The thing with my brother was he kept getting into trouble, and then asking us to vouch for his character at these meetings. I was tired of having to use my money to bail

---

[38] Matt. 25:14-30
[39] Matt. 25:24
[40] Matt. 25:29

him out, or wasting time with court dates and parole hearings. This was only his second strike, but his 8-year stint in prison had given me the time to finish school and regain control of my life. To keep giving him my time and enable his behavior was to do myself a disservice. When I told my mother all of this, she called me selfish and tried to guilt me by saying he's my older brother, and that God did not approve of my behavior. That was the last time I visited. I called her a week or so later, and I call her every Friday afternoon, but I always hung up the phone when she started talking about my brother. That was not what I needed in my life. I had finally broken free of the need to say yes to him- yes to borrowing money, yes to borrowing my car, yes to his crazy schemes and "business ventures." I was coming to see my mother, and eat some good food, and not worry about my brother.

After church let out, I ran into my friend Marianne Choux (Mari). She was talking to Grace Jean-Joseph, a newer member of Mt. Bethel. Mari was having a potluck at her house in a few weeks and invited me. Home cooking? I was there! I said hi to her mom, and a few others and then headed to my mom's house. She had been living there since I started college. She moved out of our Washington St. (Dorchester, MA) apartment to come to suburbia (Randolph, MA). I think she hosted potlucks because she needed the feeling of a full house. She had no one around, except for the older lady she took care of (state-funded, of course).

There were at least twenty people in the house. I walked into the kitchen, kissed my mom on the cheek and hugged her from behind. "Who's that?" she asked in her heavy accent. When she turned around, she has such a look of surprise and joy that I felt like a little kid again. She hit me with a towel and swatted me on my behind as she chastised me for staying away so long and making her worry. And then she told me I looked like I was getting skinny and made me a plate. You gotta love Haitian moms- they know how to feed you. I ate two plates of rice and beans, fried plantains, baked macaroni and cheese, and fried turkey in cashew sauce. Of course, my mom put some in a large aluminum pan so I could take home and eat during the week. That food would be gone by tomorrow night. My mom can throw down. Since there were other people there, we didn't talk about my brother much. Of course, there's always that one person that asks how he's doing, but my mom usually responds with a, "He's good, praise God. Just keep praying for him." I knew, however, that if I stayed and helped my mom clean up, I'd have no choice but to talk about it again. But I'm a good son, so I stayed, because there'd be no one to help her clean, and though she's only 55, I can't help but want to make sure she's taken care of.

"Junior is coming home. They're letting him out." She had just closed the door after waving goodbye at the last guest. She didn't waste any time. "He's coming home and staying with me until he gets on his feet. In two weeks, he will be here. I want you to be there when I go get him. I'm having a potluck that Sabbath too. We should all go to church as a family, together. I don't care how you feel about him. He is your brother and I am your mother. You don't want to do that for him? That's fine. Do it for me." I knew anything but a yes would only cause a fight at this point. So I nodded, and we started clearing the table in silence. I hoped that she wouldn't keep talking about him, because I still had to process that David (Junior) was coming home. Unfortunately, I wasn't so lucky. "I'm not going to keep Anna in the house either. I don't think they'll let me take care of her with Junior in the house. Oh! I want to change the papers on the house and put his name on it too. He should have something in case I die. I'm getting older and I think I should put his name on the house and the car too." I had enough. "No mom. Absolutely not. You know he first chance he gets, he's going to sell the house and use that money or that car for his foolishness. Don't you remember when he tried to get you to take a second mortgage on the house so he could post bail? Are you seriously telling me that you think leaving the house in his name is a good idea? You can't be serious!" Now she was upset. "He's my son too! If I leave everything to you, he is going to get nothing because you don't love him. You already refuse to support him and I'm not even dead yet! If I don't leave something for him, he will have nothing. That is not good. He is my firstborn. So, he makes mistakes! You think I'll just abandon my child because he makes mistakes? You are why I have to leave the house to him. You have your own job and apartment and car. You don't need it. He has nothing." "HE has nothing because he throws it all away!!" I was furious now. "I make

197

something of my life and I'm punished because he keeps conning you into enabling his behavior? Of course, he has nothing for himself! You give him everything. You won't let him deal with the consequences of his own choices, and then yell at me because I do. You enable him and make him worse than he is. I have my own because I had to struggle to build it- just like you. He throws away his life and I'm supposed to feel sorry for him? He's a grown man, mom. He's 35, and he can deal with his own choices."

That got her so riled up that she went off on a tirade about forgiveness, prodigal sons, and how he's changed and given his life to Christ. She said I needed to forgive and forget, and move on. "Yeah, like you moved on from dad, right?" Her shoulders slumped, like I knocked all the wind out of her. As she turned away, the look on her face read with so much pain that I ran and embraced her. "I'm sorry mom. That was unfair. I'm so sorry mom. I do love Junior. It's just hard for me to show it sometimes. I'll be there, though. I'll support him. Please don't be sad. I love you mom." The conversation was over. She hugged me back and then finished washing the dishes. "Don't forget your food!" she called out. As I kissed her goodbye, I wondered how things were going to be once my brother got out. I was a rising success, and despite what my mother said, I knew his presence in my life could only lead to trouble. After all, it was what he knew best.

Chapter 3
October 2013

He stood before me. At 6'5, he only had a few inches on me, but he was much bigger than I remembered. I guess that's what prison does to you. All he did was work out, so his muscles were much bigger than mine. "What up Son?" He smiled at me. I nodded my head. "Hey bro. Good to see you man." He hugged me and smiled again. "It feels good to be out. You don't even know. Don't ever go to jail man. It ain't even worth it, nah mean?" Like I didn't already know not to sell drugs and go to jail for possession. Seriously? I knew his smile, though. That was his, "I'm friendly but you should give me all your money and sign your life away smile." It was the same smile that got people to trust him, got us to bail him out, and got his baby's mother to drop the charges for nonpayment of child support. Of course, my mother and I had to pay *for* him, but that smile? *That* was how he made his living.

When we got home, he helped himself to everything in the fridge as my mom stood beaming, in the doorway, as this was her finest moment. She hadn't given me that look before, not even when I received my

199

MBA. She was sad that day, and said "I wish your brother was here to see this." I got a sad smile, while he got a radiant smile for his greatest achievement yet-coming home from prison. AGAIN. I was so disgusted, but I had promised to stay a little while longer. I was counting the minutes until I could leave.

"So, how many girls you got on rotation, Son? I know you got a few of them on deck. They must be cute even though you like them uptight chicks. How's that Carine chick you were dealing with?" "First of all, I'm your brother, not your Son, so stop calling me that. Anyway, Carine and I haven't been together for a while. That was five years ago. And no, I don't have a 'rotation.' I'm grinding it out at work for a promotion. Then I can focus on finding a wife." "Wait. You ain't got none in five years? You *must* be gay. or got a serious case of blue balls, man. *'I'ma work, and then find a wife.'* I ain't about to waste my time with only one chick. I'm in my prime. You see me settle with Trina? Even when she had Kristal I still wouldn't marry her. That's just stupid. I don't even know who you are anymore. *'Focus on finding a wife.'* Forget that!"

I tried to keep my cool. "No. You don't know me. I'm about my money- you know, that thing you ask for whenever you need us to post bail? Who do you think pays for that? And who do you think has been paying your child support to Trina? I don't have time to find a wife, or have a 'rotation' cause I'm too busy cleaning up your messes. Maybe if *you* could get your life together, I could find someone."

"Solomon, stop-" my mother interjected on his behalf. "Don't talk to him that way. He just got home. You shouldn't-" "Ma, chill. I'm good." He chimed in. She muttered to herself and swatted me on my arm as he continued talking to me. "You don't need to get so sensitive, Son. I was just saying, you're too young for all that wife talk. Take it easy. Live a little. Have some fun and *then* shackle yourself. There's a time for everything. I read that in the Bible once. You know I'm Christian now? Gave my life to Jesus and everything. But, yeah, I'm just kidding, Son. You ain't got to get all mad." "STOP calling me son! You know what? I don't have time for this. I need to get back to work. Sorry but I gotta go." I couldn't stay there any longer. I wanted to reach over and massage his throat until no air could get through, but I couldn't afford to since I'd be no better than him if I did. I needed some air. I kissed my mom, nodded in Junior's direction and left. I didn't even take any food. That's how irritated I was. But the drive home did me some good. By the time I got to the grocery store and then home, my anger had subsided.

My brother and I didn't always have a strained relationship. We were fine until he started coming home late, telling me to lie for him. I did it, though, because he was my big brother. When all the kids at church started calling me King, he started calling me "Son." He said if I was "King," I was his "Son" since David was Solomon's father in the Bible. I always hated that name, but he knew how much it bothered me and kept doing it until I was really mad. And then, he'd switch it up and flash his

201

signature smile. "I'm sorry bro. You know I'm just playing. But bro I need you to... [Inserts shady request] ...for me. You know you're the only one I can trust. Don't let me down." And like a sucker, I'd lie for him, be his alibi, sneak him money (when I was working my way through school), and later on in life, let him use my car.

Letting him use my car almost cost me my future. In my last semester of college, he borrowed it one day, and the next thing I knew the police were at my door. He'd been arrested with weed and a gun in the car. Since it was registered in my name, they came looking for me. I went voluntarily, so they didn't arrest me and I wasn't charged for anything. I was so angry during the trial, though. According to the police report, he'd tried to assume my identity so he wouldn't "technically" be in trouble. By using my license (since we looked so much alike) the record would fall under my name. He got caught when he was fingerprinted and his priors from juvie came up. I was a college senior then, and could've gotten a record. And he said that he did me a favor by leaving my name out of it, and that he could've told them I was involved. He said my taillight had gone out which got him stopped in the first place, so I was to blame for this. He claimed that if he hadn't made sure I was cleared by the police that day, he wouldn't have been the only one with a record. I'd have been the one with the ruined life. He tried to tell me that he saved me, and that I owed him for it. That he took the fall for both of us. That he told truth even though the police said he didn't.

That was when I saw him for what he was, and saw that if he had the chance he'd sell me out too. Even after I spent my savings to bail him out of jail. Even after I stood by him through all his trouble. Despite all the times I was his alibi. He was only out for his own gain, and would use anyone and anything to his advantage to get what he wanted. Even his brother, who had always supported him. Even though I was younger and he was supposed to be looking out for me. I'd always thought him to be selfish, but this was far beyond. He was a narcissist.

But even though he had failed in trying to implicate me, I still suffered consequences. The police presence in my apartment made me the object of suspicion among my neighbors. All of a sudden there were complaints being lodged against me every time there was excessive noise or a stranger in the building. I never really had guests, so it was frustrating when a noise complaint brought the police to my door, though the music was down the hall. After a few months, however, it stopped. Coincidentally, that was when my nosy elderly neighbor, Mrs. Kinsale, passed away. Good thing, because I was considering moving elsewhere. Also, I almost ended up losing my work study position at my school. They said that it wasn't a good look for the school for one of their students to have the police sniffing around. But since the semester was close to ending, I could stay on until the end of the semester. The only reason why I stayed on after that was because my professor went to bat for me. That was when I was done with my brother- for good.

D. Gloria Elysée

It's not that I don't have love for him, I mean he *is* my brother. My dad is dead. I don't know any of his family, and my mom's family is in Haiti. They're the only family I have. I have church family, and my friends from school, but they're the only blood relatives I know of. My brother just has a way of pushing away anyone who wants good things for him. He wasn't willing to let mom help him out or show him affection unless it was in the monetary form. Take his work history, for example. He got his girlfriend Trina pregnant at 19 and attempted to get a regular job. His juvenile record didn't leave much to be desired, but he found work at a construction site. Unfortunately, working a "regular" job wasn't providing enough money for his taste, so he went back to selling drugs.

His affinity for the criminal began at a young age. At 15, he started coming home with blood on his clothes, and lots of money in his pockets. I didn't ask many questions, but I knew it was probably illegal. And at 16, when he went to rehab and then juvie for possession of illegal substances (weed), I knew that he wasn't going to stop. When I visited, he told me that he had claimed a drug addiction due to my father's death so they would put him in rehab instead of sending him to jail. He was pretty convincing at the hearing. He even shed tears when he was talking about our father's death. He could've gotten an Oscar for his performance. He would've made a great actor, the way he'd play the sympathies and emotions of everyone around him. Even back then he was ever the charmer.

He came home different. At first It was slight, almost unnoticeable, but it became very pronounced as time went on. After having spent almost 2 years in rehab and the juvenile delinquency center, he had become distant, aggressive, and violent. He'd lash out at us, throw things, and pace around the house in the early hours of the morning. On one occasion, I had the misfortune of waking up to pee at 3am. I ran into him in the hallway on the way back to our room and he attacked me and started kicking me. I was screaming at the top of my lungs for him to stop, but it was to no avail. My mom was the reason why he stopped. She calmed him down and sent him back to bed. She suggested I stay home for a few days after it happened, but I opted to go to school after one day. With him being home, I didn't want to spend any more time alone with him than I was required to.

I swear he had PTSD, but you know Haitians: they're not about to go share their all their business with a therapist. "Why do these people keep saying he needs therapy? We have God. I didn't get therapy and look at me. I'm okay! Do I look crazy to you?" My mom's philosophy was her truth. But I knew something was seriously wrong. His erratic behavior got so bad my mom actually kicked him out. It only lasted 3 months, because soon he was back, giving her the sad puppy dog eyes. And of course, she let him come back home. Things calmed down for a while, though there were occasional incidents. I learned to keep a bucket in my room in case I woke up to use the bathroom. I also kept a couple of snacks/drinks in case I got hungry. I wasn't going to risk another beating like that again.

For the next five years, I felt like a prisoner in my house. But I loved my brother, so as he started to get back to normal we began talking more. We would talk about everything: life, Dad, sex- everything except for what happened in juvie. We never broached the subject of the night he snapped on me. In my house, there were things that we just did NOT talk about. In many Haitian households, there is a culture of silence. So, I wasn't surprised when we didn't talk about things. I never knew much about my family history, and I think that had a lot to do with why I was so introverted growing up. I never really felt like I knew who I was because I had no clue where I came from. My mother's refusal to talk about her past, my father's past, and their respective families made me think something was wrong.

I wasn't given the opportunity to discover what made the past so unspeakable. To celebrate graduating high school, (and to discover my roots) I bought two tickets to Haiti to visit my mom's family. I surprised my mom with it for her birthday. She completely flipped out and ripped up both tickets. I barely got a refund for the money I'd spent, and no explanation as to why she was so adamant about neither of us going to Haiti. She never mentioned it again, and never let me talk about it either. I knew that she didn't talk to her family, but I figured it was because they didn't have access to a phone. I didn't know that she would react so strongly to the trip. I kinda was expecting happy tears, maybe a hug and a few kisses. I felt bad that she got so upset. She didn't talk to me for 2 weeks after that. Of all her reactions, that one made me the angriest. I didn't want her to be mad, but it felt like she blamed me for trying to do a good thing. I couldn't understand why she reacted so strongly, and why she wouldn't talk to me. Nonetheless, I learned my lesson. Since then, I don't surprise people with anything. My ex-girlfriends always complain that I'm not spontaneous, but after slaving away to surprise my mom with plane tickets and getting that kind of reaction, there was no way I was opening myself up to that again.

At 18, I was going off to New England Union University and going to live in the dorm on an academic scholarship. My brother was having some legal trouble with his ex-girlfriend Trina. Even though he wasn't in jail, he never saw his daughter Kristal or brought her any money. The year before, my mom had kicked him out. For a few months, he had spent his time living at Trina's, playing the part of the family man. But, as usual, he started making reckless decisions and she kicked him out. Now he was back at home and Trina was suing him for nonpayment of child support.

That was an interesting turn of events, considering the fact that my mom and I combined our resources and gave him money to give her every month. But she said he gave nothing. Despite her perpetually sour disposition, I believed her story more than my brother's. I know that seems wrong, but his track record was proof that he was capable of stealing his daughter's child support money. My money was on the line here, and I was not playing any games.

I tried to convince my mom to write Trina a check every month, but up until the lawsuit she always declined. "Junior is going to think we don't trust him. I just got him back. I don't want him to leave again." Clearly her favoritism was clouding her judgment. It wasn't until we were served with the court papers for nonpayment of child support (for _two_ years) that she changed her mind. Even then it was a fight. She wanted to give Junior a blank check (she didn't know how to spell Trina's full name), and I flipped out. Giving a con-artist a blank check was signing over your life! I took over the payments from then on. First, I met with Trina and explained the situation. I worked out a payment plan with her to repay the money (using some of my scholarship money), on the condition that she drop the charges. Then, I told my mother and brother alike that I would handle all future transactions with her, and money for child support would go through me. Junior didn't like that.

Now that I was eighteen, I realized that I could not afford to let my life fall apart. I'd begun working at fifteen years old and was anal about my money management. With this whole Trina fiasco, I wasn't playing any games. My mother would give me her portion of the payment, I would deposit it into my account, and then I'd write the check for Trina, keeping record of my payment. In retrospect, I probably should have written a contract mandating Junior to repay my mother and myself when he got a job, but knowing him, it would never work. He'd either just ignore my contract (and I wouldn't be able to enforce it), or he'd just use his drug money (which I wouldn't accept). I knew that I'd never get that money back. Either way, since my mother decided to place all hopes and dreams about him not returning to jail on me (not him!), I had to do my best to negotiate with Trina and hope that she'd put her anger (and her lawsuit) aside.

It's sad that as a teenager, I was more responsible than my brother. I realized that I had to do what I could to climb the corporate ladder, and distance myself from all the drama of growing up. I secretly wished my brother would just hurry up and do something stupid (again) to get arrested (again) so I wouldn't have to deal with him. I know. It's a *horrible* thought, but it's the truth. My mother clearly enabled his behavior, and then spent hours on her knees praying loudly whenever he got in trouble. She never would do anything proactive about it, and "left it to God" to fix him. I guess she was afraid that if she kicked him out for good and something happened to him, it would be her fault. She had put my father out of the house, and then he got arrested which led to the fight that killed him. I think she blamed herself and refused to do the same to my brother. Either way, her blatant favoritism and enabling of his antics made it certain that I could not continue to be a part of the cycle.

****

The potluck was a welcome escape from the drama with Junior. Of course, I didn't tell him about it. He would certainly use it as an opportunity to charm an unsuspecting church girl out of her clothes (and money) and I didn't need any more Junior-related problems in my life. In fact, since he's been back, my mother has been overdoing it with the mandatory "family time" and insisting that I begin attending her church and her potlucks on a weekly basis because "Junior is new and doesn't have friends and you should be there for your brother." It's not my fault that he's been locked up for 8 years and hasn't been socializing. I didn't care that he needed to "find the right girl and settle down." So, I ~~lied~~ told my mother that I was unable to accommodate her requests due to my position at church. I said that I would try to come see her when I didn't have any church obligations during the Sabbath.

Of course, I was just sparing her feelings (and my sanity). The only obligation I had was to stand at the door as an usher every third Sabbath, and occasionally be on the pulpit to do a welcome or Scripture reading or something. I just refused to be tied down to Junior for every weekend until he ended up back in jail. Cynical? Probably. But was it the truth? Absolutely.

This potluck was to erase all of the negativity I'd been dealing with since his return. Mari could throw down, and plus she was known for inviting interesting (and attractive) friends of hers to church, so I knew it would be a great day. Especially with the crazy potluck conversations we usually have. Today, I was seated next to Grace. She, like most Haitian women, was a nurse. No disrespect to her- I just notice that most Haitian (or foreign for that matter) women gravitate to nursing as a means of stable income.

She was pretty funny, and actually quite beautiful. She wore her hair naturally in a curly afro, and had a loud laugh that reminded me of my mother's (in her happier days of course). I don't remember many specifics about the conversation. I just know it was fun. She was funny. I was funny. And everyone else had a great time as well. Even Heaven Brown and her man were laughing, and they aren't even Haitian. I guess she's been HBA (Haitian By Association) for so long that she's picked up some of the language. It's nice to see her happy. She had a rough time a few years back, but her and I have actually become pretty good friends. Mari and I of course go way back. But Grace is a few years younger than we are, so I guess that's why I hadn't really noticed her before.

Grace had actually grown up in my mother's current church, Calvaire. We never moved in the same circles, even though I knew her older brother Peter. He was Junior's age, and they had a pretty serious rivalry in the church basketball league many years back. I didn't know she existed until she'd graduated from college (one of the UMASS's I think), and moved to Boston from Easton, MA. She was three years younger than I was, but was mature. I could tell she was a really great person to know. Not quite my type, though, but definitely someone I'd hang out with. She just had this thing about her- like the church-girl-traditional-valued-intellectual-who-knew-how-to-be-submissive-but-still-was-a-great-partner-type-of-woman. *But like I said*, she wasn't my type.

The conversation turned into career-talk: how we got into our specific career paths, and how we knew God chose us for the jobs or career we had. Everyone

211

had their stories. Of course, Heaven spoke about what she went through with her life after medical school, and how God brought her through and changed her career path. Mari spoke about how she was blessed with her job as an immigration lawyer, mostly because she knew she couldn't take the emotional strain that came with practicing family law (divorces, custody battles). She spoke of her struggle in law school, and how God revealed to her that her duty was to help those who had no voice for themselves, and then sent her an old lady at church who was about to be deported, and that's how she knew.

Grace spoke up and said she had always known her job was to be a caretaker, and that's why she'd decided to become a nurse. She also mentioned that she was in graduate school for social work and how she couldn't wait to help underprivileged children. She was working as a visiting nurse to pay her way through school to do what she really wanted to do. She was in her field because she truly wanted to be there, and not just because it was "stable."

A few others spoke, and then the attention was on me. I felt a little embarrassed. I had no revelations, no assurance that this was where I needed to be, so I made a joke to try to deflect. "Now you know this is the Sabbath, and we're supposed to be RESTING from work, including conversations about it! Um, I just know that God is leading the way. Besides, I doubt I'd have gotten this far if I wasn't where God wanted me to be, right?" Everyone smiled at the joke, but Grace said, "Well, I know that God sometimes allows people to stay in situations that they've chosen until they're ready to be receptive to His

Will, and then He tells them where they need to be." **My eyes narrowed and I tensed up, but I tried to play it off. Seriously? Who asked her? Heaven piped in, "Actually I can agree with that. I was sure of my success for a long time. I was top of my class at Harvard Med, and yet because I wouldn't listen to God I tanked at Burrows Hospital. I'm grateful because I know that it was the will of God to move me, and I'm in a *much* better situation. But back then you couldn't have paid me to believe that I wasn't supposed to be an award-winning ER doc at Burrows. It was my dream, so of course I pursued it and assumed God put His stamp of approval on it because I wanted it. I'd definitely pray more on that if I was you, King."**

I was irritated. I'm a successful, young, Black man, who is working his way up the corporate ladder- in *Boston*, no less, and I'm getting a lecture about God's will for my life? "You do realize that God did want us to be successful, so we can help out the less fortunate, right? I mean, who's to say I'm not in the right place, just because I hadn't had a vision or a revelation about it?" "I meant no disrespect bro," Heaven replied. "I'm just saying it's something to think about. You know it's all love though, King. I'm sure you're right where you need to be." It was a little tense in the room. I relaxed back into my seat a little, and made a casual joke about having God, "...Write the vision, and make it plain...[41]" which seemed to dissipate the tension, until it was time

---

[41] Habak. 2:2 NKJV

213

---

to go. I said my goodbyes, thanked Mari and her fiancé, and left with the conversation still on my mind.

Grace didn't even know me and then had the nerve to question my life? She didn't know how long I was in the church. Didn't she know I was an integral part of the church? I read my Bible. I know my Scriptures. I just didn't like her insinuations that I was unsure because God had been trying to reach me and I'd been ignoring Him. In fact, it was the opposite. I'd been praying to God for guidance, and every time I would, I'd be promoted, or given a huge case to work on, or get some accolade or bonus for my work. Who was she to question that? At least Heaven and Mari knew me, and had major life experiences to back up their advice, however unwarranted it was. But not Grace. I really wasn't feeling her anymore. Pretty face or not, she didn't know me well enough to judge me. Anyway, I wasn't worried about her. I still needed to work on the Kandid! project with C.B. That's probably what got me so riled up in the first place. Oh, well! After the sunset, I need to kick it into high gear.

Chapter 4
January 2014

C.B. and I met again. We had been meeting twice a week for over four months now. I'd already met her business partners, and technically should've been meeting with everyone involved in the Kandid! project. But it was usually just C.B. and I (and convenient excuses as to why no one else came). Thank God for the company card! I could barely afford a drink at most of the restaurants she chose, let alone the gourmet food. I preferred larger portions of food to the small, expensive portions that were provided in fancy restaurants. Especially considering the exorbitant amount of money being spent on these meals.

Anyway, over time, she'd asked me to call her Charlotte, and of course, I obliged her. She was openly flirtatious with me. Well- as open as a reserved socialite can be. We both knew that mild flirtation was as far as it could go. But now she was getting a little bolder. She'd let her hands linger on my arm as she leaned in closer to read the documents. She began wearing clothing that revealed more cleavage than was appropriate for an afternoon business lunch. She began suggesting dinner

215

meetings instead of lunches. I had worked with enough blue-bloods to know when something was out of place.

Okay, so I was making assumptions about the change in her behavior. But, I knew that whatever it was couldn't be good for me in the long run. She's my client (and my boss's daughter), and that was a line I wouldn't cross. It didn't matter if she wasn't, because Charlotte Stone was not what I had in mind to date. Too bad my body didn't get the memo. She was fiiiiine. Her curve-hugging dresses, jewel-tone green eyes, and the intoxicating way she said "Solomon" were constantly fighting my resolve. I had to mentally prepare myself (and pray!) before our meetings in order to stay focused on the work. She definitely wasn't making it easy on me tonight. She wore a green dress that clung to her like it was attached to her skin, and her perfume was definitely turning me on.

"Charlotte," I began. "We've been working on this Kandid! account for four months now. In about two months, we can present Kandid! to your father and his partners, and can launch the newly revised website soon after that. What is your vision for the launch party?" She paused, leaned back in her chair, and smiled. "You like to plan ahead, don't you? Well, I'd like to make it nice. Perhaps the Museum of Fine Arts, since the MFA is a prominent tourist site, and would be a great feature for Kandid! I also see a great food. I'm thinking world-class chefs and restaurateurs, and perhaps a 5- or 7-piece orchestra. Are you getting this down? Good. Of course, it would be a black-tie function. All our investors would be invited, and the developers, and of course the press."

I'd thought she'd be thinking along those lines, and shared the proposal I'd worked on for the launch party. "I took the liberty of drafting up a proposal for the launch party. Let me know what changes I need to make before the pitch. I'd like to make sure that the party stays within the budget we've set."

She was impressed. "Solomon, you really understand me! This is so amazing. I could kiss you!" She became flustered. "I mean, I appreciate all your hard work. Thank you for everything." She rushed out, nearly knocking over her glass of water. As she hurried to the door, she glanced back at me before she exited. The scent of her perfume still lingered in the air. I sat for a few minutes, enjoying it, before calling the waiter over for the check. I guess she really is feeling me. I can't blame her, I certainly don't mind, but that's probably the last thing I need right now...

****

I came home and took my phone off Do-Not-Disturb, only to find 5 missed calls from my mother. It was only 9pm, so I know she was still awake. As I hurried and dialed her phone number, I wondered what this could be about. She did tend to be a little dramatic most of the time. It could very well be nothing. "Hello mom?" She picked up. "Solo, where is Junior? Where is your brother?" How the heck should I know? "Calm down mom. I don't know where Junior is. I haven't seen him since the last time I came over. And plus, I don't think he knows where I live."

I could hear her hyperventilating over the phone. "Solo, I need you to find him. I haven't seen him since yesterday. Some people came to see him today. They do not look like they are good people. Big. Ugly. Like Lougawous" [Werewolves]. "I don't want them to come back. They say they are his friends, but I don't think so. I need you to find your brother." "Mom, I don't know what you want me to do." She sighed. "Well, I thought he might be with you. My keys to your house are missing so I thought he was with you. I cannot take it if he is dead or in jail." I tried to comfort my mother. "Mom I'm sure he's okay. He's probably at Trina's or something. And don't worry about those guys. You said it yourself. Junior's changed." I hoped my words didn't sound as meaningless as they felt.

Truth is, I knew Junior was just being himself. I knew he hadn't changed. His whole "I love Jesus" scam was probably to get him paroled early. But random guys showing up to my mother's house? That was not okay. I could kill him myself, if I knew where he was. I tried to convince my mom to come stay with me for the night, since I didn't want her to be alone. She kept declining. I insisted, and told her I was coming to get her right now. I would drop her off at work the next morning since her car was out of service. I was not having my mother out there by herself.

As I hung up the phone with my mom, I noticed something different in my apartment. My two TVs, my Xbox, my DVD/Blu-ray player and my brand-new sound system were all missing. My house wasn't ransacked, my lock wasn't tampered with, yet my things seemed to have walked out of my apartment by themselves. And then I remembered my mom mentioning that the spare keys to my apartment were missing. The spare set of keys that I kept at her house in case of emergencies. That could only mean one thing: Junior was back to his old ways. Again. And I was paying for it. Again.

Somehow Junior always found a way to try to ruin my life. Thank God I had my laptop with me for my meeting or it would've been stolen too. First thing in the morning, I'd call my landlord and a locksmith to change my locks. Since I live in a three-family home, I'd have to pay a ton to change the locks since the other 2 apartments in the building share the main entrance. But I'd rather pay the money and have the peace of mind of the extra deadbolts I'd be installing.

On the ride to my mother's house, I became more and more angry. Junior was endangering my mom's life. Her hypertension was getting worse, and the goons who showed up at her house were definitely not helping! But he didn't care, and never assumed any responsibility for his actions. He stole from me, and probably would've stolen my mom's car too, had it not been out of service. Now I was driving to pick my mother up to bring her to my home in Roslindale. She calmed down a little on the

219

ride to my apartment, but I could tell she was still on edge. She was hypervigilant and beginning to nitpick when she noticed my TV wasn't in the living room. I'm sure she knew I was lying when I said I got rid of it because it was distracting. She certainly knew what happened when she overheard my conversation about the locksmith with the landlord the next day. She's a smart woman, and put together the missing keys and the missing TVs.

I ended up working from home the next day. I called my boss and said I had a family emergency, and then dropped my mother off to the hospital. She works at Klinton Hospital in nearby Milton, MA. It's a small partnering hospital in the Burrows Medical Network. IT was mid-afternoon when the locksmith came to re-do the locks. (Expensive, last-minute, and extensive work. Great!) I called my mother, letting her know that I'd pick her up from work if I could (trying not to mention the locksmith), but if she could, to find a ride home. I had a lot of work to do on the Kandid! account, and all these costs and unexpected distractions were not helping! I just hoped that I'd be able to pull it off. No sign of Junior all day though. I was hoping that was a good sign...

****

She called me, frantic. It was Ms. Marie Joi, Mari's mother, and the lady who usually gave my mother a ride home from work. "She had a heart attack! She's at the hospital. You need to come now! She's at Klinton Hospital in the emergency! Come now!" I could barely understand her shrieking. But this was BAD. I rushed to the ER at Klinton. I tried to not hit the other cars on the road as I sped to the hospital, and barely missed getting pulled over by Milton police. My mind was rushing. Was she okay? Was she dead? What caused this? My mind was racing with a million questions.

When I was finally in the room with my mother, I fought to hold back my tears. She looked so weak and tired, and had all sorts of machines hooked up to her, beeping, and hissing. She tried to sit up and speak. "Mom. Don't talk. It's okay. I'm here." Choking back tears, I hugged her as I sat beside her on the bed. I tried not to squeeze too tightly, but it was difficult not to hold her tightly now that I knew she was alive. She had on an oxygen mask, and kept trying to remove it to speak. "Mom, you can't-" I began. "Tande'm." (Listen to me). Somehow her sickly whisper seemed like a shout. She continued in Kreyol. "Junior-" "Junior did this mom? Did he do this to you?" "Tande'm, pitit." (Listen, child) "Where is Junior? Is he okay? Was he inside?" *Wait, she's lying in a hospital bed, and asking for him? I guess I'm not enough of a son for her.* "They broke into the house. They broke things. I came home and everything was broken. My heart started to beat so fast and hurt. Solo, I need you to go find Junior and make sure he's okay. I'm worried about him. Find him before they do something bad to him. Please. Promise me."

Seriously? At a time like this, with Junior almost certainly being the cause of this whole mess, she wants me to find him? After he broke into my house and stole my stuff? After his associates broke into my mother's

221

house, causing her heart attack? She still wanted me to risk my life to look for him? I tried to hide my anger as I helped her replace the oxygen mask. "I'm not going anywhere right now, mom." She attempted to sit up. "Don't worry mom, I'll look for him, but right now my only priority is making sure you're okay. I'm staying the night, and tomorrow I will go find Junior. No mom, there's no use in arguing with me so you just sit back and get comfortable. I need to go find your doctor."

As I spoke to her doctor in the hall, my mind raced with fear and anger. Fear that she could die. Anger at Junior. I was overwhelmed by the information about how to care for her after this. There was a significant risk of a second heart attack or stroke occurring. The doctor was going on and on about the expected length of her hospital stay, insurance information I needed to complete. I told him that some things might be in her records in Human Resources and the Electronic Medical Records because she was a current employee of Klinton. He didn't know who she was, but said I still had to get it done within the first 24 hours of her hospital stay. I was in no position to handle this. It was too much for me. I needed to pray. I decided to go back into the room with my mom, and knelt at her bedside.

I took her hand in mine and began reciting from memory. <<L'ange de l'Éternel campe autour de ceux qui le craignent, Et il les arrache au danger[42]>> <<...Si Dieu est pour nous, qui sera contre nous?[43]>> It means

---

[42] Psalm 34:7, LSG
[43] Rom. 8:31, LSG

"For the angel of the LORD is a guard; [He] surrounds and defends all who fear [Him].[44]" "...If God is for us, who can ever be against us?[45]" My mom had taught us to recite it since she first started coming to church. In fact, every prayer ended with those verses. I figured that we both could use an army of angels to surround us right now. My mom was in pain, but had fallen asleep so I didn't want to wake her. I decided it'd be better to pray silently.

"Dear Heavenly Father. Thank You for saving my mother's life. For giving me life, and allowing us both to see a new day. Lord, I don't know if I can handle all of this. My mom shouldn't be in the ER. She should be at home, cooking, and gossiping on the phone with Ms. Joi. She should be healthy, not hooked up to all these wires and machines. Father, I need You to heal her. PLEASE heal her. Fix her. Make her better. I don't want her to die. I need my mom. I know I get mad at her because of Junior, but she's all I really have. God please don't take her away. Please forgive our sins and make us new in You. Cleanse us from all our unrighteousness, and help us to love and obey You always. In the name of Jesus, I pray. Amen."

As I said "Amen," I took a deep breath before I opened my eyes. I kissed her hand as I got up. I probably should've prayed for Junior, at least to find

---

[44] Psalms 34:7
[45] Romans 8:31

him, but I really couldn't deal with him with all of this. I could've tried calling his cell phone, but I honestly didn't need the drama or the reminder that this was his fault. I needed to focus on my mother, not on his being a failure of a son. I needed to call my job. There was no way I'd be able to come into work tomorrow. I needed to make sure my mother had what she needed. My first priority was to make sure that her health care proxy and health care directive were completed. We'd never discussed what she wanted in terms of care, so when the doctor asked, I didn't know what to tell him. I didn't want to disturb her now that she was resting. But when she woke up in the morning I would get the information I needed so that I could better help her.

As I sat and watched her sleep, I began to doze off. I didn't notice I'd fallen asleep until a hand was shaking me. Confused, I saw my father's face next to Junior's face, merging until they were one. As I blinked, startled, I realized it was just a dream. The night nurse was asking me to move so that she could do another ECG. I checked the time. I'd forgotten to call my boss and let him know I'd be out for a while. It was 11pm, so I decided to call the office.I left a message on Mr. Stone's answering machine that I would be out for the next few days. I went to the bathroom, and went to the nurses' station to ask where I could find water and maybe some crackers to eat. I also called down and left a message for food services to deliver some breakfast in the morning and made a mental note to ask my mom's nurse about any food restrictions. I heard the mention of my mother being NPO, but I wasn't sure what that meant. I knew I needed to get some rest. It was going to be a long night.

****

In the morning, I woke early. I didn't want to, but the people kept coming to check my mom's vital signs, administer medications, and draw blood. I was woken up every time someone came in, so my sleep was terrible. It was almost 7am, so I decided to call down to food services again. I wanted to have breakfast waiting for my mother when she woke up. As I was looking for the menu, the nurse came in and said, "Remember-she's an NPO patient." I told her I had no clue what that meant. She explained that due to the procedures that needed to be done on my mother she wasn't allowed any food, or broth, or juice. She told me that I was free to order a guest meal, but I couldn't share with my mother until the doctor changed the NPO status.

It made me feel uncomfortable at the thought of eating in front of my mother and not sharing. She'd raised me to feel that it was rude to eat in front of people who did not have food without first offering them. I couldn't offer her food if she wasn't allowed to eat, and I doubted that my Haitian mom understood food restrictions. I once dated a vegan girl, and my mom kept offering her chicken and turkey when she came over for dinner. I explained that she was vegan, and my mom said, "I know. But it isn't meat! It's chicken!" To my mother, dietary restrictions that aren't allergen-based were basically ignored. But I digress. I decided to order breakfast anyway.

The day progressed slowly. I tried to let my mother rest as much as possible, and took a few naps myself. In the moments when we were both awake, we got through the insurance questions and the health care proxy/advance directive. The advance directive details what procedures/ lifesaving measures a person would want or not want if they are unable to speak for themselves (i.e. if they're unconscious or unresponsive). A healthcare proxy is someone you designate to advocate on your behalf and make health decisions for you if you become unable to make them yourself. I understood the need for this to happen, since a lot of families get caught up in disagreements about treatment strategies. Sometimes it ends up in court, and the patient deteriorates because they are unable to receive help until the court decision (which can take months). It is necessary to have someone you trust as a proxy, in case there is a "next-of-kin" that you do not want making decisions for you. Some people live the nightmare of having a family member go against previously expressed wishes. That's why it was important to me to get my mother's wishes down, and be her health proxy. I knew it would be a complete disaster if Junior had to do it.

We had a witness come in so my mother could sign the papers. I'd written them out for her, and read it back to her to be sure. I had to be sure that she got what she wanted. After the nurse left with the papers (and the good news that she could have "thin liquids"), my mother grabbed my hand. "You need to find Junior. Last night he was in the house. I saw him leaving through the back. I don't know if he saw me. He was taking the TV, Solo. It looks bad. I think he needs money. You need to find him and help him. If they could do this to my house, they will do much worse to Junior. I don't want them to kill my baby." It's commendable that in the midst of her heart attack, her mind was on her son. But I wish she'd never told me that he was at the house. That she caught him stealing her TV. That his life was worth more to her than anyone else's- including her own. And now she wanted me to risk my life to help the ingrate that almost ended hers.

I tried to smile, weakly, and squeezed her hand. "Okay mom. But I can't make any promises." I had absolutely no intention of looking for him. I'd much prefer that he'd be caught breaking into somewhere else and go back to jail. He was my brother, so I didn't wish him death. But I wouldn't mind if he was beaten (badly) by the people he owed money to- as long as they didn't kill him. Maybe *then* he'd learn his lesson and stop sabotaging his life and everyone else's. I was tired of having to deal with his mess. He almost got my mother killed. What if she was home when they ransacked the place? What if they had attacked her? What if she had died from the heart attack, or had a stroke? Do you know that they are monitoring her for risk of a stroke because of her history of high blood pressure? Junior is lucky he's not here. He's smart enough to stay away, so I have to give him credit for that. But if my mother dies because of this, I'll be the one going to jail- for putting him in the ground myself.

I needed to cool off after this conversation, so I told my mom I needed to call work again, and left the room. I walked down the hall to the "family room," where patients usually receive visitors. Thankfully, it was empty. I was so angry that I sat there for an hour. I had my laptop with me, open to the Kandid! launch party pitch. But I couldn't do any work. My mind had simply shut down. I sat there for hours. I got up from time to time to check on my mom. Her co-workers kept stopping in to see her (thanks to Ms. Joi). Then came the Pastor (also thanks to Ms. Joi). In between, I told her to rest, and I'd take care of everything. That way we wouldn't have to talk about Junior.

As it neared 7pm, I relocated to her room. I'd managed to get some work done after all. I closed my laptop and decided to head back to my mother's room. Unfortunately, my phone rang as soon as I reached the door. "Hey, Sol, what's good?" "Junior? *'What's good?'* Are you serious? My place was robbed, you go missing, some goony-goons messed up mom's house and now she's in the hospital! You went MIA, and now you want to know what's good? Tell me something, do you even care that your mother almost died last night because of you? First your 'business associates' stop by the house and scare mom. Then, she comes home to a torn-up house and sees you leaving with her TV? My stuff wasn't enough for you? You had to steal from your own mother? Did you know she had a heart attack because of you? You're lucky I'm a Christian or I'd kill you on sight. Seriously, don't even bother coming to the hospital. You're not wanted here." I had to walk back into the family room so that I wouldn't be screaming in the halls.

"So, it's like that? You won't even let me see my mom? Who do you think you are? You think raising your voice scares me? Don't forget, *Son*, I was locked up for a while. Don't let the church *act* fool you. You try to play me, and you'll have a real problem on your hands. Now, I'ma come see my mom in about a half hour, so if you got a problem, you can be somewhere else when I get there. Or you can man up and *'kill me on sight.'*" He was always this arrogant, but this pushed me over the edge. "Listen, my mother is not going to have another heart attack because of you. I've been here all night. I'm the one that has sat here with her. I didn't disappear for 3 days- you did. Don't think that I can't notify the front desk to not let you in to see her. You want to try me? Fine. But don't get it twisted: I may be a "church boy" but if you call me "son" one more time, I have no problem beating you bloody."

I was livid. But I decided to play it smart. Sure, he could come by. But I'd limit his time. True, visiting hours could be extended for immediate family. But I made sure to let the nurses know that he couldn't stay more than 20 minutes. I didn't need my mom getting worse because he was asking her for money. I notified the nurses at the station, especially my mom's nurse. Since she was on a monitor, I told them if my mother's heart rate increased during his visit, he should be asked to leave. If necessary, he should be escorted out. I warned them that he was very persuasive, charming even, but no exceptions were to be made. Since I was officially my mother's health care proxy, I didn't want anything to compromise her well-being- especially him.

I returned to my mother's room, creeping in quietly to not disturb her. I glanced at her bed, but she was still asleep. As I returned to my chair at her bedside, my phone vibrated again. "What now, Junior?" I replied exasperated. "Junior? Solomon, where are you? What's going on?" It was C.B. calling. "What do you mean, Charlotte?" "I've been waiting at the restaurant for you for twenty minutes. Are you almost here?" I'd completely forgotten that we were supposed to meet again today. "I'm so sorry Charlotte. I'm actually not coming. I'm at the hospital with my mother. She had a heart attack two days ago, and I've been here with her ever since." "Oh no! I'm so sorry Solomon. And here I was thinking that you were off doing who knows what! How is your mother doing? Is there anything I can do to help?"

I appreciated the concern. "No. I'm just here at the hospital. I'm just getting some work done while she's sleeping. I'll be back to work next week. I've been working on your account, so no worries." "Oh no, Solomon! You should be focused on your mother's well-being right now. But it's nice to know that you're trying to be productive. What hospital are you in?" "Work is helping me stay calm, actually. We're at the Klinton Hospital in Milton. I just hope my mom gets better. I just want to know that she's okay." "I hope so too. I pray your mom feels better. I won't keep you any longer, Solomon. Let me know if there's anything I can do to help. And give me a call when you can. Goodbye."

I smiled when I hung up the phone. It was nice to know that she was concerned about my mother. My bosses were very nice, but they still insinuated that I should hurry to come back to work because we had deadlines. Plus, the Kandid! meeting with Mr. Stone had been moved up to next week. The launch party was two months away, so I know his mind was on that. I glanced at my mother to see if she was still asleep. She seemed peaceful.

About forty-five minutes after Charlotte called, I was feeling a little restless, so I decided to take a walk to the vending machine. I was a little hungry, and since dinner was around 5pm, I figured a trip to the vending machine was in order. True, there were some snacks in the little patient fridge area, but the good vending machines were in the area next to the cafeteria, so I headed there.

As I reached the elevators, they dinged and opened. Charlotte hurried out with bags in her arms, and plowed into me. I was about to speak when she grabbed my arm and exclaimed, "Hi love. I'm so glad to see you!" and pressed her body up against mine. I was confused, but before I could even think, Junior stepped out of the elevator. He smirked and nodded at Charlotte. "Oh, that's you? Never mind, gorgeous." Immediately I understood. Before Charlotte could respond, I said, "Mom's in room 1103," and stepped onto the elevator. Charlotte hadn't detached herself from me yet, so she followed.

231

When the elevator door closed, she let go and fixed her dress and hair before she spoke. "I'm so sorry about that. I usually don't behave that way. That guy saw me in the lobby and followed me. He was so persistent and wouldn't take no for an answer. When I saw you, I figured you'd be a great way to get him to go away. But apparently, I was wrong! You know him?" "Yeah. He's my older brother. We don't get along. It's complicated. Anyway, what are you doing here?" I was still carrying the bags that she brought. I'd taken them from her as part of the ruse. "I came to see you. I brought some flowers for your mother. And since you couldn't come to the restaurant, I brought the restaurant to you." "Ah, so *that's* what that smell is! I was actually headed to the cafeteria vending machines for a snack. We can stay there and avoid Junior for the time being."

We spent the next two hours talking, laughing and eating. It wasn't until a hospital worker yelled, "Hey. You can't be in here!" that we realized it was almost 10pm. As we gathered our things to leave, I breathed a sigh of relief. "Thank you so much for this Charlotte. I would've had to make it through the night on junk food if you hadn't brought this amazing food with you." "It was my pleasure Sol. Thank you for rescuing me from your awful brother. I can't believe you two are related. You're nothing like him!" She had grabbed and squeezed my hand as she thanked me. I smiled. "I know. But still, thank you so much. I really appreciate it!"

As we reached the lobby, she released my hand to give her ticket to the valet. "Are you okay to go home Charlotte?" She smiled. "Yes, I drove here. I know my way around. Plus, I have GPS." "Still, please give me a

call when you get home, so I know you arrived safely."
She smiled wider and said okay. When the valet pulled
up with the car, we said our goodbyes. As she began to
turn toward the door, she hesitated and craned her neck
upwards and kissed me on the cheek. Then, she turned
and ran to her car.

That night, as I watched my mother slept, I didn't
bother trying to stop the thoughts swirling around my
mind. I was impressed that Charlotte came to the
hospital with flowers and dinner. She was really
considerate, and I appreciated that. She was also really
down-to-earth. We'd spoken about everything that night.
About her upbringing, and mine. About my relationship
with God, and her belonging to the Presbyterian Church,
but more in name than in faith. We even spoke about my
decision to practice abstinence until marriage. She
thought it was funny, and laughed aloud, until she
realized that I was serious about it. Then she regained
her composure and called it "sweet" and said that not
many men would be able to have that type of self-
control. I explained that I was trying something new, and
trying to depend on God to make it. Since I wasn't
interested in dating just to date, but for marriage, it
would make all the difference. She seemed impressed
that I was actually looking to settle down. She said I
wasn't like other guys.

Our conversation flowed so smoothly that we got
lost in time. We probably would've continued for
another hour if that guy hadn't interrupted us. But I

wasn't sure if this was a good idea. She was my boss' daughter, my client on a major campaign, and from an entirely different world than I was. I only wanted to entertain serious potential partners. Though she was great, beautiful, smart, funny, and super sexy, she didn't have the most important factor I was looking for: a solid relationship with God. Plus, I couldn't imagine her and Junior being in the same room together, let alone family. But I was getting way ahead of myself. She was *just* a client, and soon she'd be gone, back to her upper crust world of fine cuisine, haute couture, and limitless funds.

I tried to push thoughts of her out of my mind to go to sleep, but the more I fought, the more I was losing the battle. But I couldn't accept my feelings for her. She was *completely* wrong for me. Well, she was mostly right, and only a tiny bit wrong for me. Really, she was amazing and her *only* strike was that she didn't share my faith and didn't have a relationship with God. She was unsure that He existed at all. But, that wasn't such a big deal right? There were many people who ended up learning about God from their romantic partners. That couldn't automatically rule her out, could it?

Do not be joined together with those who do not belong to Christ... How can one who has put his trust in Christ get along with one who has not put his trust in Christ?[46]

I'm not going to make any decisions tonight. Who knows what the will of God is. I mean maybe that verse is right,

---

[46] 2 Cor. 6:14, 15 NLV

=Don't you wives realize that your husbands might be saved because of you? And don't you husbands realize that your wives might be saved because of you? Each of you should continue to live in whatever situation the Lord has placed you...=[47]

But I'm jumping way too far ahead. I just need to chill and not worry about her. I mean, I need to focus on my mom and my work anyway. I'm just gonna do that. I can't let her be a distraction. I have WAY too much going on already...

---

[47] 1 Cor. 7:16,17

D. Gloria Elysée

Chapter 5
March 2014

It had been two months since my mother's heart attack, and my life had finally adjusted to all the changes. My mother was back home, and a visiting nurse came three times a week to help her. The Kandid! Presentation had gone well, and our launch party was in three days. Charlotte and I had been (officially and exclusively) dating since she came to the hospital. As a bonus (or not) there'd been no sign of Junior since the hospital. My mother never mentioned him, so I just let it be and enjoyed my life.

It was a little tough being in a relationship with Charlotte. There were so many aspects of my life that she couldn't relate to or didn't understand. For example, I don't think she realizes that once the Kandid! business dealings are over, we can't regularly dine at her preferred expensive places. I wonder how she will react once the expense account closes and I can't afford The Taj and Sorrelina, and all the other high-end restaurants she's used to. Sure, I could dip into my savings and take her to places like that, but I had a budget and I wanted to stick to it. That doesn't mean that I was trying to go to fast food restaurants or anything crazy like that. But my idea of a moderately priced restaurant was (in her perspective) "slumming it."

I'm not typecasting her as shallow or anything, but it is a real observation. She thought I was joking when I suggested a reasonably priced restaurant that I loved, because it didn't require a specific dress code and didn't have a valet. I convinced her to go anyway, and she enjoyed it. That is, until she realized that this was the new status quo, with the exception of special events. I guess she didn't realize that the expense account was paying for our meetings, and not my own pockets. Her father had given me the expense account only for the duration of the Kandid! account as a means of making sure his daughter had no reason to complain. The expense account would be gone as soon as the launch party began.

As someone who rarely had to worry about money and budgeting, it was a struggle for her to understand my financial issues. I was doing okay for myself, and had a good job, but I was still on a tight budget. My mother's medical expenses, and the cost of living in Boston were draining my pockets. I could afford nice things, yes- but it was impractical to spend all my money frivolously. She did have financial and business sense, but her budget completely eclipsed mine. She received a monthly allowance from her maternal grandparents. Her Kandid! project was fully funded by that allowance. From her parents, she also received a fully furnished brownstone in the Back Bay area, a brand new Mercedes Benz SUV, and a generous spending allowance. Her parents were from money, and she was expected to inherit even more when they were gone. She'd always had money, and it was very likely that she'd always have it. She just didn't understand the struggle.

Another issue we had was that she didn't really understand how serious I was about my relationship with God. She didn't understand why I wouldn't skip church to go shopping with her, or why I didn't want to go out on Friday nights. I explained to her that I was a Seventh-Day Adventist, and that my faith was extremely important to me. A major part of that was to "Remember to observe the Sabbath day by keeping it holy... The seventh day is a Sabbath day of rest dedicated to the LORD your God. On that day no one in your household may do any work... For in six days the LORD made the heavens, the earth, the sea, and everything in them; but on the seventh day he rested. That is why the LORD blessed the Sabbath day and set it apart as holy."[48]

I tried to explain that the Sabbath was a special day that was set apart for God so that we could rest from all the everyday work we do. She argued that going out with her wasn't the same as working. I told her that it was my special time with God, like a date. I invited her to join me at church, and told her we could host a potluck afterwards. Her response was less than satisfactory. "So, you can hang out with other church people after church, but you can't go shopping with me? How is that

---

[48] Exod. 20:8-11

even fair? It's not like I'm asking you to work. All I'm asking is for you to spend time with me on your day off!" I understood her point, but she refused to see things from my perspective. I told her that God was important to me, and that fellowshipping with other believers and talking about the Bible wasn't the same as shopping or going to a movie. The point was to stay focused on God during that time. She was dismissive, but I let her know that I wasn't planning on changing my entire belief system because she didn't like having to adjust to fit my schedule.

She also wasn't that impressed by my unwillingness to have sex with her. When I reminded her of why I was abstinent, she told me I was lying, and accused me of sleeping with someone else. I told her she was insecure. (That didn't help.) I had to keep reminding her of who I was, and what I believed in. I guess she thought that her looks would be enough to make me lax on my principles and that time with her was worth skipping church and disrespecting the Sabbath, because she complained that I didn't care about her whenever I stood firm. I guess that whole "unequally yoked" thing is real. If this is going to last, we're going to go through a lot of changes last.

But I couldn't dwell on our relationship issues. They'd have to be sorted out once I was finished with the Kandid! launch. The party was imminent and there was a ton to do to prepare for it. I didn't need anything to distract from it. The good thing is that I got the launch party to be on Saturday night, after Sabbath ended. The museum is closed by 5pm, and the party begins at 7:30pm (until midnight), though most people should be gone by 11pm. The publicist and event planning company we used have assured me that everything will be ready in time for the event, and they came highly recommended, so I trust them. I even have time to run any last-minute errands before the party if necessary.

I was supposed to meet Charlotte in an hour. A short time after that, we would be having our final meeting about the launch party the publicist and event planner. I wanted to have some time alone with Charlotte beforehand, because our last conversation didn't go so well. She has asked about the party, and said she couldn't wait for us to make our entrance. I told her that it wasn't the best idea to announce our relationship at the event. She got angry, accused me of trying to hide our relationship, and (once again) accused me of cheating on her. I know she's had some bad experiences in the past, but I was getting a little annoyed with her constant accusations.

Today, I was going to have to explain what I meant. The truth was that Kandid! was like her child and she'd worked very hard on making it a success on her own merit. I didn't want our relationship to be the primary topic of conversation when the focus was supposed to be on her and the Kandid! brand. If everyone was gossiping about us, the focus would be shifted from the brand, making the launch a disaster. Plus, it might put Kandid! and my firm (and me) in a negative light. When the time was right, we'd bring our relationship to light. But now wasn't the right time. We

241

should each arrive and leave alone. We could interact during the evening as long as physical contact was kept at a minimum. It was her night, and I wasn't trying to take that away. I just hoped that she'd be more understanding this time.

****

The museum looked awesome. There was a red carpet, the press was everywhere, and the food was great. The Kandid! party was definitely a success! I worked my way around the room, stopping frequently to speak to familiar faces, coworkers, former clients, and of course, my boss. As I scanned the room, I saw Mark speaking to a woman. I was about to head in the opposite direction when the woman turned and then waved me over. It was Gwen Roberts, a girl I knew from a neighboring church. Great. Now I *had* to go over there. I wondered how she knew Mark, but I know Boston is small and that she works in finance, so it wasn't impossible for them to know one another.

As we chatted, and of course made the requisite, "How do you know...?" banter, I realized that I would rather be talking to anyone else here- even my bosses. See, Gwen's good friend Carine is my ex-girlfriend. Gwen is not someone I'd consider a friend, and I didn't really care for her. She was a super pretentious, extra "holy" and generally not a pleasant person. The combination of her and Mark (and unwillingly divulging personal details of my life to him by manner of the "how do you knows") was sinking my festive mood. I turned the conversation to the company and my work, but of course Mark was more interested in the personal. Gwen didn't seem to take a hint that I was trying to change the subject, so she volunteered the information about Carine, instead of leaving it as "We know each other from church," as I had previously stated.

Bored with the conversation, Mark excused himself to get a drink. Leaving Gwen to question me about my current love life, and update me on what Carine was doing. Before I could change the subject again, I felt someone standing behind me. *Of course* Charlotte would arrive now. I didn't hear of her arrival, but here she was, standing directly behind me. I introduced Gwen to her quickly, hoping that it would read as "she's not a threat, so don't get crazy in public and ruin your party." The introduction made a welcome break in the previous conversation, but not for long. Thankfully, Mr. Stone was on the stage, calling for everyone's attention as he introduced the guest of honor, his daughter Charlotte.

As she walked away, and I said a quick, silent prayer of thanks. Mark returned to where Gwen and I were standing. He was engrossed in what was happening on the stage. I knew Mr. Stone wasn't *that* fascinating, so his focus was probably on Charlotte. All he'd seen were pictures of her when she was still an awkward teen (since Mr. Stone didn't have any recent photos), so I bet he was surprised at the beauty she became. Part of me wanted to brag about how she was all mine, but I remembered where I was, and snapped out of it.

After the toasts, the food was brought out. Somehow, I ended up next to Gwen again. As soon as Charlotte saw this, she made a beeline for us. Mark soon followed. I was hoping Charlotte wouldn't make a scene. She seemed very intent on questioning Gwen and my history, and didn't seem satisfied with the fact that there was nothing to tell. Mark was really focused on Charlotte. I hope he wasn't picking up on her jealousy. I really didn't need this getting out. But, he ended up inadvertently rescuing me by informing her of some important person across the room who wanted to speak to her. Still, I felt uneasy as he began whispering to her as they walked away. And since Gwen didn't know many people at the function, guess who she hung around the whole night? That's right. Me. I knew I'd pay for it later, so I decided to circle around the room, even if it meant Gwen would follow. I'd be in less trouble if I was in a group with her versus standing by ourselves, right?

I had to make my rounds to speak to my bosses, colleagues, the publicist, the caterer, the press, and more. I tried my hardest to lose Gwen in the crowd, hoping one of the introductions I'd made would lead to a conversation she couldn't resist. Thankfully, she was enthralled by a museum curator (I can't remember from which museum), and left me alone long enough for me to find Charlotte. She did not look too pleased to see me, but tried to hide it well. By miracle, her father interrupted us before we could begin speaking. She needed to take a photograph for her feature in The Bostonian magazine, and get quotes for the article. I was flattered to be in the picture as well. At least work was a success. Mr. Stone congratulated me and whisked

Charlotte off again. That was the last time we spoke that evening.

I was one of the last people to leave. Though I was not an event vendor, I wanted to be sure things were okay before I headed home. In the morning, I'd have to go see my mother and deal with Charlotte. I know she'd have a lot to say, but I was hoping the success of her event would erase all (or at least most) of the things she made up in her mind about Gwen and me. I hated being accused, especially when I didn't even do anything- and *especially* when I didn't even like the person I was being accused of cheating with. I needed Charlotte to understand that I was telling her the truth, and not responsible for the guys from her past. I refused to pay for anyone else's mistakes. Junior taught me that lesson the hard way. I wonder where he is, anyway…

****

Charlotte and I are not on the best terms right now. It's been three weeks since the launch party and she's been upset about it ever since. It didn't matter how many times I explained that there was nothing going on with me and Gwen, and that I had not invited her as a date. I couldn't understand why she wouldn't leave it alone until she told me that she was afraid I'd leave her for someone else. I assured her that there was no one else, and that I wanted to make things work with her. This turned into the, "Why haven't I met your mother? I didn't even get to see her at the hospital when she was there. And why can't I tell my dad about us?" argument, which led to the "You're hiding me!" argument. So, I've decided to ask my mother if Charlotte can come over for dinner, so she can shut up. I'm tired of this argument. If that goes well, then we can have dinner with her father and tell him. I wanted to save money for that dinner. I knew that I would be paying the tab when went out, and they both had a taste for the expensive. I wanted to be able to afford whatever bill was handed to me at the end of the night. I assumed Mr. Stone would be that type of guy- "If you can't afford dinner for my daughter, you shouldn't date her."

Honestly, I didn't think we were at the "meet-the-parents" stage yet. That's why I was in no rush to introduce her to my mom. And in even less of a hurry to tell her dad. But Charlotte was clearly on a different page. She would constantly bring up "the future," and incessantly told me she loved me. I tried to tell her I needed more time, and that I was trying to be careful to not commit too soon, but all she heard was, "I don't know if I want to be with you." This would set her off again, and I was growing tired of the cycle.

Don't get me wrong, she's an awesome woman. She's super sweet, intelligent, and one of the most beautiful women I've ever dated. I just get annoyed by her baggage. But I guess if she could be understanding about the whole Junior thing, she's not a lost cause. Anyway, dinner is supposed to be tonight, so I'm getting ready to meet her at my house, and drive over there with her. She's extra excited because she said she'd been studying up on Haiti, and she's sure she'll impress my mother. I doubt it, since my mother isn't the type to be interested in facts, but I didn't want to burst her bubble, so I said nothing.

I'll be driving Charlotte's car, even though she turned down her nose at the idea of taking mine. She tried to hide her negative reaction when I suggested driving, but I saw right through it when she insisted that we take her car instead of mine. I guess the thought of my Toyota made her cringe. I drive a new Venza. But I know she's used to her Benz, so I didn't push. I just hope the night goes well.

****

We arrived and parked in front of my mother's house. The driveway had her (broken) car in it, so we parked on the street instead. As I walked around to open the door, Charlotte clutched her purse, and clung to me like her life depended on it. "Are you sure that the car will be okay out here?" I sighed. This was exactly the reason why we should've taken *my* car. "The car will be fine, Charlotte. This neighborhood is nice. Don't worry. On the other hand... You have insurance, right?" The panicked look on her face told me my joke wasn't funny. "I'm sorry, honey. I was just kidding. Don't worry, hon. I promise you, everything will be okay. I was just kidding. I promise." We hadn't been here for two minutes, and I was already apologizing.

We rang the bell, and walked up the steps. I could smell the food as the door opened. It was Grace.

Charlotte's eyes narrowed. "Hi Grace. How are you doing?" "Fine. How are you? Come in! I'm just getting ready to go home." I turned to Charlotte. "Charlotte, this is Grace. She goes to my church, and is the nurse that takes care of my mother. Grace, this is-" "I'm Charlotte Stone. So, you're the nurse? You won't be staying for dinner?" It was a question, but it sounded like a statement. Grace shot me a glance and then looked at Charlotte. "Yes, I'm a nurse, and no- I won't be staying for dinner." "At least take a bowl home, Grace," my mother called from the other room. "You helped make it, so you should at least get to eat some of it. And take some for Peter." Grace disappeared into the kitchen. She returned with my mother, kissed her goodbye, and with a filled bowl wrapped in a plastic bag, she left.

Charlotte stepped forward and forcefully hugged my mother. My mother gave me a questioning look as she let go. "Hello, you must be Charlotte." It came out sounding like "Shah-low," which made Charlotte stiffen up. "It's pronounced *Charrrrlotte*," she said, drawing out her "r." My mother shot her a questioning look. Charlotte began to speak rapidly in French, while grabbing my mother's hand, as though they were old buddies. Confused, my mother pulled her hand away. "I'm sorry, Shah-low, I don't speak French. I speak Kreyol." "I apologize, Madame Principle. I thought French was the national language of Haiti." "It is, but mostly the rich people speak it. Kreyol is the language of the common people." Neither Charlotte nor myself knew what to say to that, so I said, "Why don't we eat?"

After I kissed my mother, she beckoned us into the dining room. I hung back and grabbed Charlotte's coat to put on the rack with mine. "Solo, why you don't pull out Shah-Low's chair?" Charlotte flinched again. "That's *Char*-lotte, Mrs. Principle. Charlotte." She drew out each syllable very slowly. My mom looked at her like she had two heads. "I know. That's what I said. Shah-Low." "Well, actually-," Charlotte began to correct my mother. I cleared my throat. "Uh, why don't we say grace so we can eat?" I interrupted the awkward exchange. "Grace already left," my mother joked. "No, Mrs. Principle, he meant a prayer over the foodf," Charlotte interjected. My mother narrowed her eyes, and glanced at Charlotte, and then at me. "Ok. I'll pray," she said. "I hope you don't mind if I speak Kreyol.

[In Kreyol] "Before I begin my prayer, I just have one thing to say. I don't know if this girl is stupid or she thinks I'm an imbecile. Solo, you better tell your little girlfriend something before I kick her out of my house. Please. My heart's already not good, and you bring home a girl who talks to me any which way? Father God, give me strength to finish this meal with this girl. Bless the food. And hold on to me so I don't say anything to this girl that you don't want me to say. Okay Lord. Amen."

I hoped that Charlotte wasn't trying to use her French to translate that prayer. My mom was not happy. As my mother served the food, Charlotte kept declining most of the dishes offered, and picking at her food. Clearly, she wasn't informed about the fact that if a Haitian woman offers you food, you take it, whether you want it or not. I tried to warn her, but it was to no avail. She kept asking, "What is this?" and "What's in this?" That would've been fine, if her facial expressions weren't a wrinkled-up nose and a frown, like she was smelling something bad. I was surprised that someone so "refined" and classy could behave like she was. When my mother mentioned a dish that Grace made (potato salad with beets), Charlotte quickly spoke about how it didn't measure up to the other food. The problem was that it was still my mother's recipe, and a favorite at that.

The night continued as Charlotte tried to impress my mother with the facts she learned about Haiti, It bored my mother, but she humored Charlotte anyway. The night took a turn for the worse when Charlotte brought up the Duvalier era, the TonTon Macoutes and asked what life was like growing up under a dictator. My mother's face went ashen, and she quickly excused herself from the table. I wasn't sure what it was about, but I knew it was bad. I told Charlotte that she needed to back off, and to leave it alone. She didn't understand why, and ignored my request. When my mother returned, she clarified that she was, "so fascinated by the article about François and Jean-Claude Duvalier," she wanted to know about it from someone who lived it firsthand. My mother told her that she would rather not speak about it, and then the table went silent.

We sat until my mother asked (in Kreyol), "Have you heard from him?" It had been almost three months since she'd asked for Junior. I reached over and squeezed her hand. "No mom. I haven't. I should be asking you the same." I answered in English. She responded in Kreyol: "Don't answer me in English when I spoke to you in our language. I said it like that for a reason." I apologized to her, but the damage was done. Her foul mood had gone from bad to worse. Thankfully, the phone rang and my mother went to answer it. Charlotte said she felt uncomfortable, and that we needed to leave. "Your mother hates me." The dinner wasn't halfway done yet, but she was adamant- she was leaving. Now I was angry. Not only was she cutting short the dinner she badgered me into happening, and acting jealous of Grace, she was now threatening to strand me here if I didn't leave immediately. I knew I shouldn't have come in her car, with no other options for a ride back. She wanted to go wait for me in the car, but I told her if she was leaving, she'd better tell my mother to her face. I was not doing her dirty work for her.

As my mother returned, Charlotte stood, and told her that she was leaving with a flimsy excuse of having to work early in the morning. She didn't know that my mother saw through it. My mother asked if she'd like to take some food to go, but she quickly declined. I told her to go ahead into the car, after I pressed the remote starter, but she didn't budge. I went into the kitchen with my mother to get my takeout plate. I wasn't going to leave without all that food, especially when there was a ton of food and no one but my mother to eat it. My mom gave me a long hard look, but stayed silent. It wasn't an angry look, just a mix of quizzical disappointment and sadness. It was everything she could say in a lecture, but ten times more potent. "I know, mom. I know," I sighed. "I love you. I'll call you when I get home, okay? We'll talk."

I was silent for the majority of drive back to my house while Charlotte tried to offer explanations for our sudden departure. "I really do have to work tomorrow, you know. And so do you. We couldn't stay there all night. Plus, it was *really* awkward and your mom obviously doesn't like me. I bet she wishes you were with someone like that" (she curled her lip and said disgustingly) "nurse. She didn't seem to have any issues being warm and cozy with her. I bet that's why she was so cold to me. In fact, the nurse couldn't stop looking at you. They're probably plotting to get rid of me so the nurse can have you."

"Her name is Grace," I finally spoke. "And you're being absurd. There's nothing going on there, nor is my mother acting out against you, despite the way you insulted her." "Insulted her? She was calling me shallow the entire night!" "She did not. She called you by your name. She speaks with a heavy accent. As many places you've lived in, no one has ever said your name with an accent? And she kept trying, but you were rude to her and spoke to her like she was an infant." The fight continued with her defending her behavior. I kept refuting her statements with the cultural violations that she claimed she'd studied. She blamed me for not adequately preparing her to meet my mother. I reminded her that this dinner was her idea. When I tried to help, she brushed me off because she'd "studied the Haitian culture and history enough to impress anyone from the island."

Of course, she only became angrier as time went on, and her voice kept getting louder and shriller. By the time we arrived at my house, I had a headache. I was already stressed because of my mother's health, and her sudden mention of Junior. But I was also going back to my regular work schedule, and wasn't really excited about the increased workload and office politics. I was thinking about quitting, and becoming an independent branding specialist. I considered possibly using my savings to start my company and pay my bills until it was self-sustaining. Part of me even considered giving up my apartment and living at my mother's house to help care for her and save money, but I quickly dismissed that idea. I had a few former clients that would be willing to leave the firm with me if I decided to make that move, but I wasn't sure if it was the right time, or the right decision.

This relationship with Charlotte wasn't supposed to be this difficult. I know that. I had to explain to her that her irrational fear of me cheating was pushing me away. Surely a woman as beautiful and intelligent as she was couldn't be so insecure that she'd ruin a good thing because of fear! (I hoped.) She calmed down after that, and began to cry. I hate crying. Through her tears, she reminded me about how hurt she was. Every single man she'd ever dated had cheated on her. Growing up watching her philandering father made her feel like all men are the same. I told her that there was a difference between a guy and a man, and I was a man of my word, and a man of God, so she could trust me. True it was a heavy claim, but I needed her to stop punishing me for what other men had done to her. A hands-off conversation in passing with a woman was not cheating. If she couldn't control her insecurities long enough to stop blowing things out of proportion, I'd have no choice but to leave her...

Chapter 6
June 2014

I've been working really hard since I've gone back to my regular schedule. Mr. Stone and the other partners have been giving me bigger projects, and consistently letting me take point on key presentations. I'm finally beginning to feel like I'm where I belong. I just finished an awesome rebranding project for a non-profit for young boys. The client, Clinton McFadden, is a really nice guy. He used to be an investment banker, but when his nephew was murdered, he gave up his job and created a non-profit and a shelter for young guys. They're admitted into the program from age 8 to 21 years old. The government doesn't fund any of the boys over eighteen, but Mr. McFadden believes that eighteen years old is too young to kick these guys out of the system. He currently has about fifteen charges, and five full-time employees, and everyone else just volunteers. And get this- it's called the "League of Lost Kings." (Or, the LLK.) I was so impressed that I began volunteering a few times a month. It seemed like a cool place to work, and Mr. McFadden is a really great guy, so I really liked getting involved in this.

My one concern about joining the LLK was that I barely had enough time for myself. Of course, Charlotte was extra upset that I was so busy. Between her, my job and my mother's health, I didn't think I'd have any time to volunteer. But I managed to squeeze out a few hours twice a month (for the past two months) to play ball with the boys. She's been increasingly difficult to deal with since she met my mother. I don't know if she's more difficult, or if I have less and less patience, but I know that things are more difficult than they were before. They're *definitely* more difficult than they had to be.

Charlotte and I haven't revealed our relationship to her father yet. I'm not going to lie, I am grateful and happy that he (or anyone at my job) doesn't know. What I don't understand is that she isn't even close to him, and yet she was pushing to make our relationship public. Don't get me wrong- our relationship isn't completely private. I try to invite her to church with me, and she doesn't want to go. She hates my choice of restaurants, but goes anyway, and I treat her to her favorites on occasion. But I don't know many of her friends, and my friends are mostly from church, so unless she comes with me, she probably won't know them. I told her meeting my friends could help put her fears at ease, but she isn't too keen on stepping out of her comfort zone.

The good part is that after the fiasco with meeting my mother, I think she realized how overzealous she was and decided to enjoy the stage we were in. I plan on being very strategic when it comes to her father. I don't want my job to be in jeopardy. I know that I'm not with her to "get ahead" in my company, but I need to make sure that that's not the perception. I'm actually pretty old fashioned. I'd rather not introduce or be introduced to the family until the relationship is serious and has a solidified commitment. Plus, there's a certain preparation that is warranted when meeting the parents. That's why things didn't go so well when she met my mother. If Charlotte and I survive this stage of our relationship, I'll be sure to wait a very long time before I reintroduce her to my mother. Her blood pressure can't take another visit from Charlotte.

My mother's health isn't getting much better, and it just makes everything more stressful. I've spent much more time there with her, which I think helps. By default, I also end up spending a great deal of time with Grace. Don't worry, we both understand that I'm in a relationship, and it's nothing like that. We just hang out and talk from time to time. I think I misjudged her. She's really cool, and funny. And she's all about God. Like a walking Bible encyclopedia. But it's nice to have someone I can talk to about the craziness, who can bring it back to God and not just throw around religious clichés. But I don't want to jeopardize what I have with Charlotte, so I don't really let my mind dwell there. Even though that's the most fun I've been having lately. It's just so much easier.

I don't just want to take the easy way out with Charlotte. I'm not meshing with Grace because I need a break from Charlotte. At least, I'm not looking to find common ground with Grace. But it's hard not to see the major problems I have with Charlotte. She doesn't respect my relationship with God. She doesn't understand why I want to wait to have sex. I'm happy that I haven't given in because she's crazy- though I've almost slipped up on *many* occasions. I'm starting to see that the confidence she had when we met was a sham, and she's really insecure. She's stopped accusing me of cheating, which is good. But now she's turning into one of those nightmare movie girlfriends who try to "drop-by" unannounced, or who try to check phone messages. She actually wanted to come back to my mother's house, but I put my foot down. I told her that my mother's health was not a game, and her house was off limits. No one needs that much stress in his or her life.

But I'm a man of my word, and until God makes it painfully clear that she's wrong for me, I will stay with her. I will not entertain the idea of another woman, even if she's as awesome as Grace. But that's something I need to pray about. Well, another thing I need to pray about. I'm starting to understand the proverb that says, "It's better to live alone in the desert than with a quarrelsome, complaining wife."[49] We aren't even married, but I can't imagine life like this. It's "as annoying as constant dripping on a rainy day."[50] This shouldn't be this hard. I read that, "the man who finds a wife finds a treasure, and he receives favor from the LORD," [51] but I think Charlotte is more in the category of the first wife. Always picking fights, argumentative, and annoying. I know that every

---

[49] Proverbs 21:19
[50] Proverbs 27: 15
[51] Proverbs 18:22

woman can be annoying and nag sometimes, but she does it constantly. And we're not even married yet. Nowhere close! On top of that, we don't have much in common. We usually end up in an argument for no reason.

She's the type of person that always goes from 0 to 100 in 3.5 seconds. I was starting to realize that she vacillated between extremes. One minute, we'd be relaxing, having some fun and joking around, and the next minute she'd spiral into angry, irrational, accusatory behavior. The catalyst was always another woman, or the status of our relationship. She always brought up the interaction I had with Gwen at the party, or with Grace at my mother's house and it would set her off. Or she'd "jokingly" say, "Aren't we awesome together? We should just elope," or something similar, and then get angry when I'd dismiss the joke/suggestion. I wasn't mentally/emotionally there (or *anywhere* near there) yet. She'd then accuse me of being unfaithful. It was becoming a consistent cycle of nonsense, and I needed this to end.

If I was honest with myself, I'd come to terms with the fact that my relationship with Charlotte was probably a bad idea from the start. I should have never crossed the boundaries beyond mild flirtation. I'd have to find a way to end this relationship, and hopefully not lose my job in the process. I sometimes get the feeling that Charlotte might try to get me fired if we were to end our relationship- let alone if it was my idea. I guess I needed to go on faith, and break it to her as gently as possible. Hopefully her class and poise would help her stay calm, and would keep her from doing anything reckless.

****

He's reappeared. After almost six months of radio silence. Junior dropped by my mother's' house last night. She called me when he left, crying. I had to calm her down, and decided that I would stop by her house after work. He came back to ask her for money. Somehow, I knew he'd be back to ask me. I wasn't surprised that he wasn't answering questions about his whereabouts for the past six months. That was never his forte. He was the one who usually did the asking, and it always had to do with money or valuables. Or women. I had a date with Charlotte, but I'd have to cancel. Unfortunately, that meant I'd have to feel her wrath, and that I'd never hear the end of it.

I called during my lunch break, and took my tongue lashing like a man. I reminded myself that my focus needed to be on my mom and the Junior situation, and not on my relationship problems. After a few deep breaths, I went back to work until the end of the day. As I packed up my things, my phone rang. "Hey little brother." Junior was calling. "I need a favor. I know you've been doing your thing, working and all, but I need you to help a brotha out. I need a couple grand. I'm in a bind- but I can get it back to you in less than a month. I just need about 5 Gs. Don't act like you ain't got it- I know you be saving your money."

I could've had a stroke right then. "Let me get this straight, Junior. You disappear for 6 months after my house is robbed; mom's house is ransacked and she has a heart attack after two guys come looking for you, and the only thing you have to say is give me $5,000?" "I told you, I'm in a little bit of trouble, and I know you got it- don't even front like you don't-" "Whether or not I have the money is beside the point. I'm not giving you *anything*. Where's my TV, Junior? Where's my Xbox? My home entertainment system? You steal from me, and then you ask me for money and think that because I *might* have it, you should get it?" "You do have it. I see you with that rich white girl. You can't keep a girl like that without money. It'd be a shame if something were to happen to her though. Don't she work with you, or something?"

Now he was threatening to harm Charlotte? I was beyond furious, but I had to play it safe. "You think I have money, but the truth is I don't. In fact, all my money goes to mom's medical care and bills. You'd know that if you hadn't disappeared. I might even have to move back in with mom. I can barely afford life right now. And for the record if you EVER threaten my girlfriend's well-being, you won't have to worry about the people who you owe money to. *Trust.*" "Oh, you mean you pay for that cute girl with the booty to take care of mom?" "Don't even think about it. Don't even think about thinking about it. Anything happens to her and I'll kill you myself." He chuckled. "Oh, so you got something on the side with the nurse, huh? Maybe I was working the wrong angle with this. Look. I need this money in 3 days, so I'll call you with the details- and no checks. Cash only. I'll come get it myself." *Click*

I had no words for what just happened. Was Junior out of his mind?? To think that he could cause this mess and then demand money, while making threats? I couldn't believe this. He was insane. There was NO way on this earth that I was giving him any money. No way. As I drove to my mother's house, I decided that I wasn't going to mention it to my mother. No need to cause her any more stress. I'd let her vent to me about his drop-by, but it just wasn't smart to bring up his demands for money. My mom was a sucker when it came to him, and I wasn't going to let her sell her car or do something crazy like put up the house again.

When I arrived, Grace was in the living room, curled up on the couch, reading a book. "Hey Grace. Where's my mother?" She furrowed her brows. "Um, she's taking a nap upstairs. She's not doing so well today, so I decided to stay here until you came." I nodded. "Yeah last night she had a little bit of a shock. But is she okay?" "She's managing. I'm checking her vitals every hour just to be sure." She paused. "Can I ask you a question?" I sat next to her on the couch. "Sure. What's on your mind?" "Well," she began, "I really don't mean to pry, but your mom was telling me about your brother, and I just didn't understand. Why is she so upset that he visited her last night? I thought his return was a good thing. He seemed pretty nice to me."

Now I understood why Junior called me. Junior hadn't been able to ask my mom for the money because Grace was there when he stopped by. "You really don't know my brother, do you? I don't expect you to. His return would have probably been better received if the circumstances of his disappearance weren't so bad. He got into some bad things, and some guys came looking for him here. They scared my mom and kept asking questions. The next day, she came home and the house was ransacked. That's what caused her heart attack. And to make things worse, Junior has been missing since then. He came to the hospital once during her stay, about 3 days after she'd been admitted. We haven't seen him for almost 6 months since that visit."

Grace tilted her head and looked deep into thought. "Well, you can't say that was his fault." "Yes, I can!" I snapped. She looked startled. "I'm sorry Grace. I didn't mean to get so upset. I tried to leave out some of the details because I wasn't trying to air out *all* our dirty laundry. The truth is, two days before my mother's heart attack, I was robbed. No one broke in, no sign of forced entry or anything, and my spare keys had mysteriously disappeared from my mother's house around that time. In fact, all of my electronic devices were stolen. TV, DVD player, Xbox, Sound system. He took it all. I had to change my locks just to be sure."

"That sounds more like speculation to me, still. Your brother is still your brother. You can't tell me he's really that bad." "You have no idea. He is a professional con man. Yesterday, he didn't ask my mom for money, probably because you were there. But he called me today and told me that he needed $5,000 cash in two days. So yes, he is *that* bad. You weren't there when he tried to pin his drug arrest in my name, or when he borrowed my car for a drug run. You weren't there when my mother had to take a loan out to pay his bail. You weren't the one who's been paying his child support for him. So, brother he may be, but I'm not having any part of that. No thanks."

She sat in silence for a minute. "I'm sorry," she said softly. "I didn't mean to overstep my bounds or make you upset. I'm just an optimist. I like to think that forgiveness and unity are more important that being "right". You know, "Love... keeps no record of being wronged."[52] But in light of all the information you gave, you are right- he does not appear to be a good person- no matter how charming he was. But I still think you should do your best to forgive him. I mean, "...if you refuse to forgive others, your Father will not forgive your sins."[53] That says a lot, doesn't it?"

All the Junior talk was starting to make me feel claustrophobic. And I really didn't want to think about forgiving him. Definitely not feeling that. "I need to get some air. This is all just a bit much. I need to go for a walk or something. What time will you have to take my mom's vitals again? Would you like join me?" She smiled. "I have another half-hour until I have to re-check her vitals, so I'll join you on that walk."

As we strolled along the Randolph neighborhood, we switched topics and spoke about everything under the sun. I told her about Mr. McFadden and the League of Lost Kings, and my first days there. She thought it was awesome, and said I should try to get more involved than my twice monthly commitment. "You never

---

[52] 1 Corinthians 13:5
[53] Matthew 6:15

know the amount of influence a Godly man can have on young boys. **God can be using you to rescue His children."** I laughed and said Charlotte wasn't too happy about her new competition, so twice monthly was what I could afford. Grace gave me a questioning look, and then quickly changed the subject to her school days, when she had no time to volunteer.

About 15 minutes later, we were back at the house, and sitting on the open porch. I told her about how I really felt at Mari's potluck, but she knew. "I'm sorry I spoke so matter-of-factly about your life and your calling. I have to do a better job of remembering that my experience may not be everyone else's. So, I apologize. Still friends?" She held out her hand and smiled sheepishly. I grabbed her hand and shook it, and we laughed.

"So, this is you taking care of your sick mother?? Cavorting with *that* nurse? No wonder you didn't want me to come here! *She's* the reason why you cancelled on me?" It was Charlotte. She was standing at the bottom of the stairs in front of my mother's porch. Great. *Of course* she'd show up and find me shaking Grace's hand! I sighed, already tired of this conversation. "Please keep it down. My mother is sleeping inside. And we weren't doing anything. I was shaking her hand. So, don't jump to conclusions."

That made her furious to the point of losing all composure. Her WASP-y veneer broke, and her voice became loud and shrill. "Jump to conclusions? You call me and break our date and say you'll be with your mother, and yet I find you here with her nurse, holding hands. If either of you cared about your mother, who probably isn't even home anyway, wouldn't at least *one* of you be with her? How can you do this to me? I bet this was your mother's idea. She hates me and I bet she loves this nurse because she's black and can give you black babies!" Whoa, what?

"You are such a lying pig! All of your, "no sex till marriage" crap sure goes out the window with her I bet. I mean black girls do get around a lot. She probably does all the things I was raised to never do. That's why they all get pregnant and carry STDs. I can't believe you'd trade all this-" She jumped back, startled, as Grace began to stand and move toward her. I had to physically restrain Grace from jumping off the porch. As I pushed Grace into the house, I told her I'd take care of it. But before I could, a voice came from the window. "You come to my house and disrespect my family. You say all these nasty things about people you don't know. You wake me up out of my sleep with your craziness. If you don't leave now, I will call the police and let them take you." My mother had woken up. She was leaning out of her bedroom, window, visibly upset. I needed to get rid of Charlotte ASAP.

I ran down the stairs and she backed into the street, towards her car. "Listen. I don't know what your problem is, but if you EVER disrespect me, my mother, or Grace like that again, you and I will have serious problems. My mother was asleep so I went for a walk. I did nothing wrong, and yet you still come here, disregarding my specific instructions. If my mother has another heart attack because of this, you will regret this decision more than you regret anything else in this life. I've been nothing but faithful to you and you treat me like a criminal. Well clearly, you're a racist, so I guess that makes sense. I'm done with you, you psycho. Leave. Don't come back. Don't call. Don't text. I'm done." I walked away as she tried to stutter an apology and as she attempted to grab my arm, I pulled away and walked into the house.

She stayed outside, banging my mother's' front door for almost five minutes. First, crying and begging me to come talk to her, and then, like a spell had been broken, her WASP veneer returned and she left. Inside, Grace had gotten my mother to calm down long enough to take her vitals, but as soon as she came downstairs and saw me, she got riled up again. I had a super long lecture, until Grace convinced my mother that she was raising her own blood pressure and needed to go relax. I knew my mother wasn't done, but I was just glad for the break.

When Grace returned, she began packing her things to leave in silence. "Grace-" I began. She turned to the side slowly, long enough for me to see the tears. "I'm fine. I don't want to talk about it. But if I catch her on my own, she's got another thing coming." Her voice broke as she spoke. I knew she wasn't fine. But her tears weren't from sadness.

Those were tears of anger and bitterness. I was very familiar with those tears. I'd swallowed enough of them in my profession. Every black person living in America has had moments when all you could do after a racially charged confrontation was vent your anger through tears. When the success we've built for ourselves is overshadowed by our skin color. When stereotypes were assumed to be truth, and people acted as though it was our reality. Moments when we were victimized, but the law was not on our side, and so a government full of systemic injustice toward us prevailed. When police brutality caught on film was explained away, and the victims were blamed, criminalized even, for the injustices committed against them. When fear of our skin color merited our murders, mass incarcerations, and constant systematic and institutionalized barriers. When words like justice, equality, and post-racial society, were shoved in our faces accompanying the image of a black president, without the actual liberties granted for our use. Sometimes, tears were the only language we had left to deal with the weight of having a Black existence in a world where Whiteness was seen as the normative standard.

I got up to hug Grace. I couldn't stand to see her hurt and angry as an innocent bystander in my drama. She pushed me away though. She wiped her face, grabbed her things, and ran out the house like she was in a marathon. I apologized, but my, "I'm sorry" felt like I had a lead tongue- heavy and useless. I didn't have her

269

number to call and apologize. I needed to make this up to her. This was my fault. I should've never gone down that road with Charlotte. As I headed upstairs to say goodbye to my mother, I resolved that I would make this up to Grace. She didn't deserve to be caught in the crossfire like that. No matter what, I just needed to make things right.

****

I walked into the office late the next morning, and the first person shoving a ton of fakeness in my face (as per usual) was Mark. He seemed particularly cheery today, which was annoying. He kept chuckling to himself, and saying cryptic messages, like "This is gonna be good," and "This is hilarious." It wasn't the first time he acted this way. He had a tendency of doing that when he was planning to sabotage someone. A true coward, he would leave cryptic hints to his "victims" until it came out how he'd stabbed them in the back. But today, I had no time for games. After yesterday's fiasco, a terrible night's sleep, and running late this morning, I wasn't interested in office politics. Not today.

I planned to spend the first half of the morning organizing my upcoming projects. I said a quick prayer to refocus myself, asking God to help me make it through the day. I really didn't want to be here, but since Mark was *clearly* up to something, I was hoping to get the bad news soon so I could deal with it and move on. There was too much stuff on my plate as it was. But I couldn't afford for the sabotage to catch me unfocused and unprepared at work.

About an hour after I'd gotten settled, (about 11:30 am) Mark came back. "Mr. Stone wants to see you. NOW." Great. Here goes. "I'll come as soon as I can. Let me just finish-" "No Solomon," he interrupted. "NOW. Immediately. Hurry up. He's not happy." I'd wanted to pray again before I went in, because a sinking feeling in the pit of my stomach had been growing since I walked in this morning. I said a silent prayer anyway, as I walked to Mr. Stone's office. Mark was behind me as I entered the office, and then went and sat down at the desk. Mr. Stone called me over. "Solomon, sit down. I need to clear up something with you. I heard something this morning that I hope isn't true. Mark told me that he received a phone call last night from my daughter..." My stomach sank into my feet.

As Mr. Stone continued, Mark's fake-concerned face kept slipping into a knowing smirk. "I took a chance on you when I hired you. You weren't the best candidate, you know. I usually hire graduates of Ivy League schools, but you seemed like a good risk. Please tell me that you haven't betrayed my trust, and soiled our company's good name by dating a client. And my daughter, no less. Using her for a promotion? Well? What do you have to say for yourself?" As I opened my mouth to speak, the door burst open and Charlotte ran in. She was closely followed by Mr. Stone's personal secretary, in a failed attempt to keep her from barging in. I let out a heavy sigh. "Yes, it is true. We were in a relationship for six months though, it wasn't a fling, or one-sided. And I assure you, I didn't do it for any form of reward. It was a real relationship. You can ask her yourself."

She stood at the door, eyes narrowed, looking in confusion between myself, Mark, and her father. "What's going on?" she demanded. "Mark has informed me of your relationship, and how Solomon had taken advantage of your position as client and my daughter to angle for a promotion. He says you called him last night, heartbroken, and in tears after you realized that Solomon was using you. Solomon has just stated that you two were in a real relationship. So, which is it?"

She looked shocked and taken aback. "It was real, at least I thought it was until I caught him with another woman last night-" "You caught me with nothing. I was shaking her hand." I interrupted her quickly, (and angrily). "You met my mother. We were together for six months. I didn't even initiate the relationship. I don't know what lies you and Mark have conspired to get me fired, but you should at least have the decency to set the record straight in person." "Decency? Decency-" before she had the opportunity to begin her rant, Mr. Stone stood and yelled, "That's enough!!" "I've heard enough from all of you. I don't care if it was six months or six minutes. You began a romantic relationship with your client while you were supposed to be working, putting the reputation of the company at risk. I assume your multiple dinner meetings are actually dates that you went on, and used an expense account that was strictly for business purposes for your own personal gain. That, in itself, merits termination. Include the fact that in the past few months your performance has declined, you've been late to work multiple times, and overall your client satisfaction rate hasn't met the same level as your peers, I think it's time that you were let go from the company. You're fired."

I sat there, shocked, but this wasn't a dream. My professional life just ended on the false testimony of a co-worker, and the mistake of a relationship. As I returned to my desk to collect my things, I could hear Charlotte arguing with Mark. "I came to you in confidence. You said you'd help us get back together. You weren't supposed to go to my father!" Soon she was standing behind me. "I thought Mark was your friend. He promised to help us get back together. He betrayed me too." I paused. "I told you Mark and I were not friends. Why would you think we were friends? Have I ever mentioned Mark in a positive way?" "Well, you two have so much in common..." She trailed off as I turned around. "The only thing we had in common was that we are both black and both worked here. Perhaps you need to understand that not all black people are "besties." How many more stereotypes do you have left in your bag?" I grabbed my things, and she began crying.

As I left the building, box of belongings in hand, my thoughts rushed at me like an ocean wave crashing into the shore. What would I do now? How would I pay my bills? How could I help my mother with her medical bills now? I knew I had savings that could last me a few months of rent and utilities, but there was no guarantee that I'd find a job in this economy. And I was almost positive that Mr. Stone would blacklist me from the other firms. I didn't know what I would do. I needed a job. I needed it. I drove to my apartment and sat in the car for twenty minutes before going inside. I had no idea what to do. All I could do is pray. And hope that I hadn't thrown out that last bottle of Barbancourt rum that my mom's best friend brought back from Haiti...

Chapter 7
July 2014

It's been two weeks since I was fired. I must admit, I took it pretty hard. I drank a quarter bottle of rum after I got home, and avoided people's calls until I passed out. And then woke up in a pool of my own vomit, with a monster headache. That's when I decided to make a plan. I went to visit my mother, so I could let her know. Grace wasn't there when I stopped in, but I had to tell my mother anyway. So, I strapped on her automated blood pressure cuff and told her I was fired. Of course, her first instinct was, "so you're moving in!" I thought she was crazy, but after thinking about it, I realized that could be for the best. I wouldn't have to worry about rent or utilities, just my cell phone, grad school loans, and gas. I could focus on finding a job, and maybe even start my own marketing firm. Plus, I could keep an eye on my mother and it would cost less for care, since Grace wouldn't have to come in so much. So, I decided to pack up my things, and within two weeks I was living in Randolph.

Life with my mother was awesome for the first three hours. She cooked my favorite meal. She was great, until it was time to clear the table and do dishes. Then I was thirteen instead of thirty. I know that this is just her way of fussing over me, and feeling important, but it is annoying. And it's going to make finding a woman to settle down with all the more difficult, even though I have no plans to be in a relationship for a *very* long time.

I've been sending Junior's calls to voicemail as well. He came by the house yesterday, trying to extort now $7,500 from me. Almost doubled since the last time we spoke. He tried charm and pity. He told me he was in deep trouble and he really needed it- his life depended on it. I told him that it was time for him to take on his own responsibilities, and that I wasn't going to carry any of his consequences anymore. I was done with his poor decision-making, and I couldn't afford to fund his future and mine, so I was choosing mine. When the sob story didn't work, he tried convincing me that it was a temporary loan and he'd have the money back to me in no time. When I wouldn't budge, he mentioned my "little white girlfriend." He wanted me to ask her for the money.

When I refused again, he switched gears. The boy who beat me in the hallway on my way to the bathroom had returned. He got in my face, and told me that if he didn't get the money he'd go after Charlotte. And Grace. And he'd make it look like I did it. I was done with the whole conversation. I punched him in the face. I swear, if my mother hadn't returned from the grocery store with

Grace, and screamed bloody murder, we would've killed each other.

He left shortly after. At least he had the good sense to not ask my mother for the money. He swore that I'd better watch out, because he'd get me back. It was almost comical, like a movie villain upon capture: "I'll get you for this, if it's the last thing I do!" That's not what he said, but still. It was pretty funny, and I started laughing, which pissed him off even more. I still had to calm my mother down. Grace got her into bed, and then I pulled her aside to talk.

"I'm so sorry for everything that's happened, Grace. You got caught in the crossfires of an insane jealous woman, and I'm sorry she said those things. Clearly her warpath wasn't complete with the surprise visit though. She got me fired too. But I'm really sorry. I'd like to make it up to you somehow. I'd surprise you, but I've had my fill of surprises for the week. How can I make it up to you?" She smiled. "I thought you were on vacation, and thought it was sweet that you decided to spend it here. Um, no need to make it up to me, though. You didn't do anything wrong. She saw our handshake and jumped to a million conclusions. That has nothing to do with us. Plus, her racist rant was from her own ignorance. We're good. No worries. I'd offer to shake on it, but we say how that turned out last time." I laughed. "I think it's safe, but let's not chance it." She laughed and grabbed my hand anyway. As she shook it, I winced in pain. I think during the fight, I might've hit the

277

refrigerator or counter, or maybe it was Junior's cement block head that was so hard.

She went to get some gauze and peroxide to bandage my hand. And my face. Thank God I didn't have to worry about work, because my face would probably be swollen for days. She sucked her teeth as she cleaned the wounds on my face and hands. "You know you shouldn't be fighting. I mean, look at you." "I know," I replied. "But you should see the other guy." The look on her face made me realize that she didn't think my joke was funny. "Okay, I shouldn't have hit him, but he thought he could come in and extort me, and then threaten to harm y-." I paused before I revealed too much, and sighed. "I had to draw the line somewhere."

She nodded her head. "Don't let it happen again. You're supposed to control your anger and your impulses, not feed into them. It lowers you to the same level he's on. It reminds me of that verse, "Don't answer the foolish argument of fools, or you will become as foolish as they are."[54] He's not worth it. You need to remember that "a person without self-control is like a city with broken-down walls."[55] You can't continue to let him get to you like that. Your mom almost had another heart attack, catching you two like that. I know that's not what you want to happen. Just try not to let him get under your skin. I know, easier said than done, but still, it'd make your life a whole lot easier."

---

[54] Proverbs 26:4
[55] Proverbs 25:28

"You know what Grace? For someone with such a big head, you sure are wise. Must be brains in all that forehead." She feigned anger and swatted me on my forehead. "Ow. Ok! Ok! I get it! No more jokes." She laughed. "Sorry. But you're one to talk. I know everything will work out between you two. If anything, you remember what the Bible said about being good to your enemies, heaping coals on their head.[56] If you leave things in God's hands, you'll get the last laugh." She was right. God would handle Junior. I just needed to focus on my own life, getting a job, and moving forward with my life.

****

It never ends. This afternoon, my brother, David Principle Jr., was killed in an attempted armed robbery of a bank. I'm supposed to be sad about this, but I feel overwhelmingly angry. Once again, he's found a way to disrupt my mother's life. Again. His selfish decision now has my mom in the hospital with atrial fibrillation. She had a crize (a huge emotional display expressing grief), and then she passed out. Grace and I had to call an ambulance. If I lost my mother, I don't know what I would do. But once again, Junior's decision had complicated everything.

I didn't think he was *that* stupid. Or that desperate for money. But he chose to rob a bank, and was killed

---

[56] Proverbs 25:21,22

by the police as he attempted to leave. How could he be so stupid? So selfish? Sure, he'd come to me for the money, but I had none to give him. He'd taken enough from me as it is, and now he was gone. The worst part about it was that now that he was gone, the money was going to him *anyway*. My mom couldn't afford to fund a funeral herself. I'm sure I couldn't get donations to bury my armed thief of a brother, so my savings were going to him anyway. And since my mother would be in the hospital for another week or so, I had to organize and plan the funeral myself.

Don't get me wrong, I was sad, but the blinding rage I felt was much stronger than any feelings of grief I had. When I went to go identify the body, I could almost feel him telling me that it was my fault- if only I'd given him the money when he'd asked. That made me even more angry. I was now stuck with the task of making him sound like a decent human being. I had to create a falsified obituary, and basically lie through my teeth about who he really was. If there was one thing I hated was when people lied and created angelic new personas after death for people who were horrible in real life.

I wanted to write. "He was a charming con man, able to separate any sucker from their hard-earned money. He was a career criminal from childhood, educated in the fine arts of thievery and lying at the best correctional institutes that the Boston area could provide. He was a fan of creating debts he could not repay, and skilled in the area of disappearing inconveniently. His career triumphs included robbing his own brother, and ransacking his mother's house, causing her to have a heart attack. His life was tragically cut short during his final attempt at ill-gotten gain. He will truly be missed."

I didn't send that to print. I'm not crazy. It was how I felt, but I wrote an annotated version. I needed my mother, because I didn't know who to call, what family names to include in the "The *blank* families thank you" section. My mom had no family, and all we had was church family. So, his obituary looked more like this:

"David Principle Jr. was a charming and charismatic man. He was very personable, engaging most of the people he met, and leaving a lasting impact wherever he went. He was extremely motivated and skilled in the art of fundraising. He was eccentric, often withdrawing into solitude in deep thought and reflection. He made many mistakes, though he struggled to overcome his personal troubles. Unfortunately, he eventually succumbed to them on July 17, 2014 at the age of 35. He leaves behind a daughter, Kristal Larson, his brother Solomon, and his mother, Marie Josée Principle. He will be sorely missed."

It was the only way I could maintain my integrity and not add to the swarm of lies that surrounded me. It's not like everyone wouldn't already know. It was on the local news, so everyone heard about it within a few hours. And of course, the footage was terrible. Him barreling out of the bank, bags in hand, gun in the other. The officer yelling at him to drop his weapon. His pause, where he made that final choice. And in an instant, it was over. It was like a scene from a movie. My mother hadn't seen it. She had the "crize" and then we had to rush her to the hospital. On the other hand, I couldn't stop replaying it in my mind. And if, for a moment, it wasn't at the forefront of my mind, there was always a reminder- someone calling with sympathies, or even the news replaying the video. And there were the people I unfriended on Facebook because they kept sharing the link.

In death, as in his life, Junior had found a way to dominate the conversation, and every aspect of my and my mother's lives. He'd brought unnecessary attention to the aspects of life I'd have rather stayed private. And much like when he went to jail, everyone couldn't stop calling or stopping by with what was meant to be comfort. It only made me more uncomfortable, and that made my anger grow. My mother liked the comfort and support, but to me it felt like these faces were the ones who would spread the news of my dearly departed criminal. I guess he really did take after our father.

I felt like I was under a microscope, the subject of gossip and even worse- pity. I never liked when people knew my business and so I kept to myself, and stayed private. When my father died, I was 10 years old. Of course, I didn't understand everything that was going on, but I had learned early on that we didn't speak about his prison years. After his funeral, my mother joined a new church, made new friends, and very few people stayed in our lives from before then. I didn't even talk about my father's death at school, until my mother came in for a meeting with my teacher about my sudden poor performance. When we got home, my mother told me that no matter what happened in life, I must always hold it together in the public eye, because "société" (society) was unforgiving and took advantage of weakness. I was not to let people know about the negative aspects of my life. I carried that credo with me into my adulthood.

I struggled with allowing God to use my life story as a way to reach people. I guess that's why I was so fascinated with the League of Lost Kings. Mr. McFadden was really up front with his life story in our branding meetings that it intrigued me. How could he share so many personal details of his life without batting an eye? All I knew was that though Junior had died, a small part of me was extremely relieved that he was gone, unable to cause more problems. It sounds horrible, but I just meant that now I didn't have to "explain" him to anyone, and didn't need any more disclaimers to my friends, coworkers, or significant others about his comings and goings. It's extremely tiring to maintain a clean image when someone else is intent on messing it up.

So, I focused on being strong. Holding it together for my mother. Accepting the flowers and food that people dropped off. Handling the conversations that I zoned out of for self-preservation, the pitiful stares and the crocodile tears from people who'd never met him. I didn't cry, even though every old lady that came to visit kept hugging me and telling me to let it out, before they started wailing like banshees. I kept it all together, as my mother came home two days before the funeral. Grace, who I'd barely seen since the day we found out, had offered to pick us up from the hospital, since my mother now had an oxygen tank to carry around.

We drove in silence, broken by the occasional wail that came from my mother. Grace had on her Melody Laure CD, playing the title song, *"God Is In Control,"* but I wasn't so sure at that point that He was. I was terrified that my mother wouldn't make it through the funeral. I was carrying so much anger, that my tolerance for the forms and functions of funerals, the ceremony of it all was leading me to my breaking point. I could take only so much more of the, "sorry for your loss" and "it happened for a reason" mantras. Yes. My brother's death happened for a reason. It happened because he was a selfish, stupid criminal who made horrible decisions. I just needed to make it past these next few days, and get my life back...

****

The day of the funeral was here. I was really on edge, but I tried to be a support to my mother. Grace came about an hour before we had to leave, to help my mother finish getting ready. I was really grateful, because she really didn't have to do any of it, but she came. She brought a little boy with her, and apologized for the inconvenience, saying that her mom was supposed to watch him but couldn't this morning. I didn't mind. He was half asleep anyway, and fell asleep on the couch as soon as he got there. I just hung out in the living room until Grace came down with my mother. She said she'd meet us at the church, she just had to go get ready, so I got my mother into my car and left.

On the way to the church, my mother stayed pretty quiet. About five minutes before we reached Calvaire, she spoke. "Did I do everything I was supposed to do for him? Did I make a mistake in not giving him the money?" She wasn't speaking to me, per se, but I had to respond anyway. "Mom, you know it's not your fault, right? Junior made his choices. When he got out, he said he changed, and started on the right path. He got a job and everything. But he chose to leave that job. He chose this. It's a tragedy, but you cannot blame yourself. He was a grown man. It's not your fault. I don't even want you to think that way."

She nodded, tears streaming down her face. "I prayed. I prayed so hard for him. I just wanted God to save him. I just wanted him to want better for himself. He was so smart. He was so good. I don't know. If David had not gone to jail, he would've been different. He was just like his father. They just made the wrong friends. I should've prayed harder. He was such a good boy."

It hurt to see my mother in so much pain. She kept saying, "God has His reasons, why He took Him. God knows." It's not that I don't believe that God had His hand in this- I just believe that everything that happens isn't God's true Will for us. People make choices, and there are consequences to those actions. My brother chose to break the law *repeatedly*. He chose to steal, to rob a bank. And his death was a consequence. One allowed by God, but a consequence nonetheless. Not every bad thing that happened wasn't a "furnace of affliction."[57] Sometimes the "afflictions of the righteous"[58] that we claimed to have, were actually the consequences of our foolishness that God was allowing us a taste of. We loved to pretend we were righteous, but never wanted to claim our responsibility for our actions. We enable bad behavior in ourselves and others, and then become surprised when we reap the harvest we've been growing. King David (in the Bible) understood. He committed adultery and murder, and then tried to cover it up. Soon after, his sons were killing each other and trying to kill him.

Consequences were nasty things that impacted whole families, not just the one who made the bad decisions. King David's whole family fell apart because of his decision to commit adultery and murder. In fact, the entire kingdom suffered. My brother knew what he'd been choosing. He chose repeatedly until it killed him. It might've been a mistake at first, but at some point, it started being his character. That's why I was so uncomfortable with the pretense that my brother was "gone too soon" or "the good die young" or "he made a mistake" foolishness that people were spewing. But I had more to endure for today. I knew that it would wean itself within the next few weeks. Soon, we wouldn't be the subjects of attention. I couldn't wait until then.

The service was very short. The service was in French, and being that it was a Friday morning, the attendance was low. Of course, the members of Calvaire attended, and so did a few from Mt. Bethel. I saw a few

---

[57] Isaiah 48:10
[58] Psalm 34:19

friends. Mari, Grace, Heaven, and even Gwen came. Grace didn't come back with the little boy, but she did sit behind my mother, and bring her water and tissues a few times. I saw Trina and Kristal sitting a few rows behind us. I guess Trina didn't want to come sit with us. It felt awkward sitting on that front pew, just my mother and me. We had no other family, no spouses, and our only other family member was in a small urn in front of us.

Thank God, it would be over quickly. I didn't need the wailing and crying dragged out. Did you know that in Haiti, and some other countries, people were hired to cry at funerals? I was glad we didn't waste any money on that. But that was to no avail. There is this one woman at my church. We call her, "The Wailer." She wails, hollers, and screams herself into a "crize" at every funeral, whether or not she was personally acquainted with the decedent. Guess who showed up and had to be escorted out (yet again!) from another funeral? But I think she realized this wasn't that kind of funeral, and when she returned to her seat, she sniffled and shed tears, but much quieter.

I was much more concerned with the eulogy I was supposed to give, but thankfully The Wailer had struck midway through the eulogy, so I rushed the end. After the pastor spoke, and a prayer, it finally ended. Trina brought Kristal up to see my mother, and told me they couldn't stay. That was the first time we'd seen her in ages, since she didn't stop by the house in the week since Junior's death. But she was already leaving and taking Kristal with her. My mom burst into tears when she saw Kristal- the spitting image of her father. So, she started crying, probably startled and overwhelmed by everything. I hoped it wasn't the last we'd see of Kristal, but a sinking feeling told me that it was. And just like that, they were gone.

Since we'd decided on a private cremation, there was no burial, so everyone went down to the basement of the church for the reception. It was a wonder how people switched gears from being mournful to jovial so quickly. As soon as they saw the food, they were hugging, laughing, and it was almost as though the funeral never happened.

I stood by, watching people argue across the table about sports and politics. My mother and I were at a full table, where other than the occasional woman bringing food and a kind word, no one but Grace spoke to us. "You were really strong up there," she leaned in and whispered. "I think your mom will really need that strength after all this is done." She was seated next to me, across from my mom. My mom was flashing her weak smile, clenching her Bible so hard I could see the whites of her knuckles. "You okay mom?" She looked at me with such dearth in her eyes that I decided we'd give it another half hour, and then I'd take her home. It wasn't even 1pm yet, but it was clear we'd had enough.

After the requisite goodbyes, we went home, with Grace in tow. "I can't stay long. I need to pick Peter up at 3, but if I can get my parents to do it, I can stay. I really think I should stay." I appreciated everything. She really didn't have to do so much. When I told her that, she looked at me like I had three heads. "Your mom is a second mom to me. You guys have been through so much. I don't mind this at all! You should know better than that." "I know," I said. "I just don't want to inconvenience you or your brother." "My brother?" She gave me a quizzical look. "Yeah. Peter. Your brother. Isn't that his name?"

She paused. "Yes, I have a brother named Peter, but that's not the Peter I was talking about. I'm talking about my son. You know, the little boy who was here earlier? Who did you think he was?" I shrugged. "I didn't ask. I don't know. I just assumed when my mother talked about Peter, that she meant your brother. I didn't even know you had a son. This morning I just figured he was a cousin or nephew. He was asleep the whole time, so it's not like we talked or anything." She smiled. "That's my son. He's turning 7. And before you ask, I had him at 20 and no, his father is not in the picture. But my parents helped out with raising him so I could finish school and become a nurse." I was a little stunned but more impressed. "You got one degree and are about to pursue another degree while raising a child? Wow." She smiled again. "Is that all you got out of everything I said?" I laughed. "Well, I'm a little surprised, but life happens. Whatever." "I usually get, 'But you're such a good girl!' and 'But I thought you were raised in the church!' or worse. You and your mom are one of the few people who didn't automatically assume something negative about me." I smirked. "My brother was just

289

killed in a bank robbery. We judge NO ONE!" My chuckle suddenly trailed off, and the conversation took a more serious note.

"How are you doing? And I know, 'You're fine.' I want the real answer." She grabbed my hand and stared in my eyes until it was uncomfortable and I looked down. "I don't know how I feel or how I'm doing. I'm just numb. And angry. Actually, I'm really pissed at him for doing it again. He always knew how to wreck my life, and was always so selfish. And once again, I'm left to take care of my mother, alone. I can't even vent about it to her because she'll just defend him again and then I'll be the bad guy. Again." It all just spilled out. For the first time since his death, I spoke those words out loud. For the first time since Junior died, someone asked how I was doing and cared enough to not let me get away with an automated, generic response. She squeezed my hand. "I can imagine how angry you are. He was your older brother, and you always had to clean up his messes and be the responsible one, instead of the other way around. And your mom coped with his behavior by praying and trying to show more love and attention to him instead of disciplining him. That must've been difficult. And now you're caught somewhere between grief from missing your brother, and anger at him for his selfishness."

I was surprised she understood. She was really intelligent, and had a lot of wisdom. I wonder how much having a kid had to do with it. Truthfully, I was just glad to talk to someone about it. Someone who didn't automatically judge me for it, like Carine did. I appreciated Grace more than she knew. I guess I'd been staring at her for too long, because she suddenly pulled her hands away and stood up. She cleared her throat, smoothed her dress, and said, "I think I need to go pick up Peter right now. I forgot that traffic is going to make me late. I have to go. Tell your mom I said bye." She rushed out of the house in a whirlwind.

I sat there for a few minutes, trying to figure out what happened. I think I might've been staring at her pretty hard. And I wasn't talking. I must've looked like a creep to her, holding her hands, staring at her in silence after all that, "Wow, you really understand me," stuff. I hope she doesn't think I'm a stalker. I hope it won't be awkward when she comes by the house. What if she quits? I know I didn't do anything wrong, but her reaction made me nervous. I couldn't think about that right now. Then again, I'd rather think about Grace than about Junior...

D. Gloria Elysée

Chapter 8
December 2014

I finally found a job. It's nothing fancy. In fact, I hate it. I work for a company that fundraises for various organizations by calling people. Yes. Soliciting people in a call center. I'm not one of the callers. I manage a group of them. I'm glad I have the opportunity to work here, even though I hate my job. I know they needed someone in a pinch, so they asked me to run the call center on a temporary basis. It sucks. But it pays the bills, and plus I needed something to do all day. If I stayed home all day, we'd have no need to keep Grace as a caretaker for my mother. None of us want that.

I'm not gonna lie. I *really* like Grace. We got through the awkwardness of what happened the day of the funeral. Turns out, as I was giving her the *look*, she was trying not to give me the *look* right back. She liked me, but wasn't ready to have feelings for anyone, so she ran. Factor in that I'd just lost my brother, and her having a son, she figured nothing good could come from taking our friendship into any other realm. I would've agreed if I thought my feelings for her had occurred as a result of her "being there" after my

293

brother died. Truth is, I'd wanted her much longer than that. So, though she backed off, I haven't given up.

I think this could be something real. I mean <u>real</u>. I understand and appreciate her precaution, but I wasn't about to let her go. So, I took it upon myself to convince her that this wasn't about my grief, nor was it about loneliness. It was about me, and it was about her. It was about how great she was, and that I could see a real future with her.

She'd been bringing Peter with her in the afternoons since her regular babysitter moved away, and her mom had to work, so I'd gotten the chance to get to know him. He was such a good kid. He was quiet at first. He sat with his toy truck, rolling it back and forth. I figured he needed another toy, so I grabbed the old G.I. Joe action figure from my room, and gave it to him. Junior had drawn over it with permanent marker, so it wasn't a collector's item. Peter's eyes brightened when I handed him the toy. Soon, he was playing with truck and driver, and began asking me about myself.

He was really smart for a six-year-old, and so I'd sit with him, helping him with his homework (yes, kindergarteners get homework). Then he'd play trucks, pausing every so often to ask me questions like, "Why does it rain?" or "Why do we have noses?" I figured the amount of questions I got was a tiny fraction of what he asked Grace on a regular basis. But he was a good kid, so I asked Grace if I could get him some Magic School Bus books and DVDs, since I loved the show as a kid. She said okay, and looked at me strangely, but I knew that she was impressed.

A few months later, she's *feeling* the King, and I'm definitely not about to let her slip out my fingers. She's so much more than just her looks. Don't get me wrong, she's gorgeous. But she's also intelligent, God-fearing, funny, loves my mother, my mother loves her, a great cook, and did I mention absolutely beautiful? And she doesn't know it yet, but she *might* just be my wife.

I know it's a really ambitious thing to say, especially since we just started dating, and she has a son, but I don't see Peter as a setback. We're taking it slow, so there hasn't been much commentary from outsiders. My mom knows, though. And of course, she's thrilled, but she told me to be careful, because I wasn't just dating Grace. It was a package, and I had to make sure to always be aware of that. We'd just taken a huge step by having Thanksgiving dinner together. Her parents had invited my mom, since they were friends, and knew her situation probably wouldn't allow for her to make a full meal. I, of course, attended. In a way, we might've made her parents aware of our relationship, but I was just glad to be there. Plus, it was one of the first times it felt like family. Her older brother came with his fiancée, and between my mom and little Peter, we were one big happy family. I think that solidified what we had, but of course Grace was still wary.

She'd had many reservations. I guess in her past, many guys started off enthusiastic, and then bailed as soon as they realized what dating a woman with a child meant. I know it'll be tough with all the cancelled dinners we've had already: she couldn't find a sitter, or he was coming down with a cold, or *insert valid parental issue here*. But I saw something in her that I could not let go of. And Peter was an awesome kid, so if there ever was a packaged deal that looked good, this was it. And better yet, I prayed about her. In fact, I prayed about her every night. She made me want to be a better man. I wanted to be the type of man she deserved, so I began reading my Bible every day. I had fallen off my daily reading plan in the past few months, but now I was determined to stay on course.

I wanted to improve myself, and she was a great motivator, but my relationship with God wasn't based on my relationship with her. I knew some guys who were like that. Extra holy, doing Bible studies and reading Scriptures so long as they were with a woman who demanded that type of devotion to God. But the moment they got her, their devotion to God mysteriously disappeared. Or maybe they kept up the charade until they broke up, and they'd regress. I'd seen that happen with women too. They had no spiritual legs to stand on, and pretended to have a relationship with God, rather than actually having one. Their walk almost never matched their talk, and it usually became a sore point in their relationship if their partner was truly committed to living a Godly lifestyle and being obedient.

Now, my relationship with God was far from perfect. I never fasted (unless someone made me), and I could be a little lazy with my Bible reading, but I tried to at least pray and listen for God. I know I needed a lot of work, and that God was the only way I could make it. I am still so messed up over Junior, and I struggle with feelings of hatred toward him. Grace picks up on it, and tells me that I need to give it over to God. Picking up the Bible regularly can definitely help that. I hope I can make it through. I'm good most days, and then I hear my mom crying at night, or he crosses my mind, and then I lose it and spend my time cursing through my tears. I'm mad he chose to live his life that way. I'm mad that he died in such a publicly embarrassing way. And then I miss him, and my heart hurts. And then I'm mad that I miss him so much. I'm mad that I hate him, and I'm mad that I love him. I have so much anger, that sometimes it's hard for me to function.

So though Grace does encourage me to be better, I do it for me. I do it so that this anger doesn't consume me and turn me into something God wouldn't approve of. The Word says, "...Watch out that no poisonous root of bitterness grows up to trouble you, corrupting many."[59] I'm sure being this angry will mess up my relationship with Grace, but my biggest struggle is that I feel like I have a right to be angry. Junior messed things up for me and for my mother. He had a history of choosing to be a criminal, to cause hurt and embarrassment to his family. Robbing his brother, causing his mother's house to be broken into, causing her heart attack. All these things were proof of his selfishness, and I had every right to be mad. I had every right to not want his name brought up. To try and forget the shame he brought by removing the reminders of him around the house. My mom could

---

[59] Hebrews 12:15

keep up the pictures of him when he was younger, but the recent pictures in the past few months, she'd have to keep to herself. I didn't want to see them. They were just another reminder of the lies he told, and the pain he'd caused. To see the makeshift family picture that we took on the day of his release was an insult.

Rather than argue with my mother about my brother, I found a reason to change the subject or leave the room when she'd bring him up. I moved all the recent pictures of him into his old room, except for the one from his prison release. That one, my mom wanted in her room. Grace tried to talk to me about it, but I was firm. There was no room in my heart for Junior. He'd made his choices, and now I needed to focus on my life, so I wasn't going to dwell in the past. She thought I was running, but I knew that I was just fine.

But the insistence from her and my mother to talk about Junior made being at the house more and more difficult. I started picking up more shifts at work. I did that for my peace of mind. Plus, I hadn't been working for a while, and during that time, Grace paid for a few dates. I *hated* that. Most of my savings had been used for the funeral, so I couldn't always take her out. She'd grab the check and slide her card in with such fluidity that before my hand was fully extended, the waiter had already taken the check to be processed. We argued about it the second time she'd done it. Now that I was working, I was determined to not let that happen again. I didn't care that she was making money as a nurse. I told her that her job was to use her money to take care of her son, and not to pay for our dates. She didn't like that very much. Now it's almost a battle every time we go out. I've had to pull aside the waiter or waitress to tell them to hand me (and only me) the check when we go out. And pre-order our movie tickets when we go out for a movie. I tell her she can pay for the popcorn. That's my one concession. But I can't have my woman paying for our dates.

That's why I took this job and have been working as many hours as physically possible. Most days I work until the call center closes (at 8pm). I am there from about 9am, so that's a good amount of time and money. Since my job is to set up accounts with the organizations we are fundraising for, I usually have nothing major to do by 4pm. I then do "quality assurance" on the phone calls, and pull aside the slackers to give them "encouragement" and throw them back into the waters. I truly despise this job. I hate having to be condescending to the people who are trying to raise money in a recession. The people on the other end aren't very receptive, and sometimes are really belligerent. And to tell them to do better, when I myself probably couldn't do their job, sucks.

But it's a job, so I am not complaining. Now, I see Grace on the weekends, and since our time is so precious, there isn't much talk about Junior. I get home around 10pm every night, so after the prayers with my mom, and the phone call to pray with Grace, I get to sleep. Only on Fridays do I have to spend time avoiding the Junior topic. I get off at 4pm on Fridays. When I get home, Grace is getting ready to leave, and my mother is primed and ready to spend quality time with me. That means that his name will probably come up.

Sometimes I just let her talk about him, and I zone out, but I draw the line at that. She needs to vent, so I'm here for her in that aspect, but I'm not going to pretend to be super sad when I feel more anger than any other emotion. I'm really trying not to be bitter. Is it working? Probably not, according to the new best friends (my mom and Grace). Grace thinks I need grief counseling, but thankfully, my mother doesn't cosign that idea. She recommended that both of us try and see a counselor, but my mother shot her down immediately. Still, she keeps trying to convince me to go.

Now the word on the street is that I'm a workaholic. Grace says it because I don't spend enough time with her, or Peter (though I spend Sabbath with her, and Sunday afternoons playing with Peter). And my mom says it because she's lonely, and heard Grace call me one. It almost makes me want to work Sundays at my job, for more overtime pay. But it would only be for about five hours, so I doubt it'd be worth it (or the headache my ladies would give me if I did). I just know that bills need to get paid- and so do the dinners, movie dates, and other activities. I appreciate when we go to Sabbath potlucks, because I can save the food for another day. But then people want to go out after Sabbath ends, so I try not to stay long. I never, ever volunteer to host, though. That would just be a bad idea.

My mom hasn't had one of her potlucks since before Junior disappeared. I'm glad about that because our groceries and money need to be kept at home so she can get better. She thinks I haven't noticed that she's more tired lately. Her last doctor's visit ended up with an increased dosage of her heart medicine. But her boredom is what she's most concerned about these days. She suggested hosting a potluck, but I told her that it was out of the question. She wants to cook the food, and spend money we don't have on random people. People who stopped calling a week after her son's funeral. People who, at the funeral, sat at the table next to her laughing loudly, discussing sports, politics, and foolishness while she suffered in silence. I refuse to host *those* people in my house. She thinks I'm overreacting, and that because it is her house, she will do what she wants. I guess she's right about that.

It's funny, because I moved in when I lost my job, to save money and to help out, because she was sick. Now I feel like a teenager. She's begun her "it's my house" rants, and I'm considering moving out again, now that I have a job. Truth be told, I'd probably have to take the Sunday shifts in order to afford my old apartment, but I'm trying to decide if my sanity is more important than poverty. A man was not made to live with his mother after a certain point. She will treat him like a child, forgetting that her job of raising him is done. I mean, who tries to give a 30-year-old a curfew? Only a Haitian mom.

I spoke to Grace about the fact that I was considering moving out and she, in true woman fashion, flipped out. She was upset on behalf of my mother. She

301

said I was being unreasonable and unfair to my mother. She said that my mother was sick, and this could worsen her already weak heart. She said I was being selfish, and that I wasn't letting my mother regain her life. Apparently, we'd shifted the focus of the argument to the potluck now. I was told that I had to respect my mother's wishes, especially since it was her house, and if I didn't want the potluck, "too bad."

I wasn't given a chance to explain myself. She made me feel like I was a barbarian, or an ogre. I was told that not only was this potluck happening, but it would occur within a week. Grace would be helping my mother with the grocery shopping and the preparation of the food. And then I was uninvited from the potluck and told that if I couldn't be supportive, I wasn't allowed to come. In my own home? I couldn't believe what I was hearing. I was trying to keep my mother's health intact, and trying to save money in the process, and I was being treated like I was an enemy. So, I decided that I'd use that Sabbath afternoon to go somewhere else. Maybe I'd go hiking in the Blue Hills, and clear my head.

God knows I need direction. And peace. This is getting too much for me. All I do is get attacked, told I'm angry, bitter, selfish. Everyone just expects that the hard decisions are made, but no one wants to make them, and when I do, I'm the bad guy. I'm the one who said no potluck, but no one cares why. They just want what they want and don't realize that I've spent the last few weeks trying to convince the insurance company to not cut some of my mother's benefits. They want to remove Grace from her service at my house. My mom would be left with no help. Or I could pay out of pocket for a visiting nurse. And trying to convince an insurance company that my mother (who despite her fatigue was still going to church and trying to host potlucks) was still sick enough to need a visiting nurse, was getting impossible.

But every story needs a villain, and I guess I was it. I was going to need to come up with the money by the end of the month- or forfeit the service. Grace would be fine, reassigned to another person in need in no time. My mother, however, would be alone for the majority of the day. And if she was tired now (with all this help,) I didn't want to know what could happen if she had to do everything herself. I was trying to negotiate to see if I could keep the visiting nurse service if only once or twice a week. But they said that Grace would be transferred to someone who needed full-time care, and they'd send a part-time person instead. And that they'd send them on Saturdays or Sundays- the *only* days we didn't need the help.

My catch-22 situation was tough. I was trying to tell Grace of the situation, but she was too involved in defending my mother. She said that my actions were keeping my mother from healing quickly. Apparently my "negativity" was making my mother stressed, which was bad for her heart. Of course! *I* was the reason my mom was sick. Not my dead brother who ransacked the house and caused the heart attack, or who robbed a bank and got killed on TV. It was me. The one who'd been working my butt off trying to make sure that she'd have proper care for as long as she needed. Who spent all his spare time on the phone, going back and forth with the insurance company and with the Visiting Nurses Association, trying to work out a deal.

It was a shame. I'd thought she understood where I was coming from. I guess my feelings were only valid for the first month after the funeral, but now I guess I'd become a nuisance, and my grace period had just ended. I resented her for telling me that it was okay to open up about how I felt, and then using my words to attack me. Telling me that I needed to change because my feelings. Calling me bitter, and negative. And spending all her energy telling me what was wrong with my actions, without even taking the time to ask me why I did what I was doing.

No one asked why I did what I did. No one asked me about anything other than Junior, and then spent forever telling me that I needed to forgive him. No one told me *how* to forgive, but they could tell me that I needed to "let it go." I prayed about it. I'd <u>been</u> praying about it. But nothing was working. Nothing. Not my prayers. Not my Bible reading. Not me dropping an anonymous prayer request into the prayer box at church. Nothing. No "positive thoughts." No sunshine and rainbows. Certainly not my girlfriend or my mother. Peter was just about the only person I could stand to be around lately. And he was six.

I was tired of holding on to all of this stuff. First available opportunity, I was going to sit my mother down and tell her about the situation we were in, and have her make the decision. She could have her potluck, but I wouldn't be continuing Grace's services. Or, she could stop trying to make herself sick and enjoy her help while we could still afford it. If she was upset, oh well. I was tired of carrying this by myself. She wanted to be queen of her castle, fine. She could make this decision *herself*.

I had to make sure that Grace wasn't around when I spoke to my mother. It had to be on a day that she didn't come in, or after she left. My mother liked to treat her like she was an equal party in the household, as though she were her daughter. This was family business, and I needed it to stay in-house. If Grace had an issue with it, she'd have to get over it- she wasn't a Principle *yet*. The best time to have that discussion would be a Friday afternoon. But that would be too late, seeing how my mother wanted the potluck for this Sabbath. She'd surely be enlisting Grace's help. I decided that I'd work a half-day and be home by 5pm, so I could talk to her today.

****

The mountain air was crisp. Well, the Blue Hills weren't actually mountains, but the air *was* crisp. I didn't actually hike. In December, that'd be pretty difficult. I just drove up and parked where I could look over the city, and still see trees. I sat, trying to clear my head. I needed to spend this Sabbath in solitude. No mother, no girlfriend, no church building. Just me, my God, and His creation.

I tried to focus on my surroundings, but I kept reverting to the argument I had with my mother. I had informed her of the financial situation we were in, and the decisions that needed to be made. She took it really badly. First, she told me I was exaggerating. Then, she told me that I was trying to raise her blood pressure. I tried to tell her that we needed to make some tough decisions. She decided to brush me off and have the potluck anyway. She said that God would provide, so there was no need for her to get worked up about it. And how dare I try to get Grace fired, knowing that she had a young son. She said Grace deserved to be here for this conversation, and that I should know better.

I tried keeping it objective, but she wasn't interested in being rational or logical. Her emotions had taken over, and now there was no reasoning with her. I was trying to keep Grace on, but she was accusing me of trying to fire her. I was looking out for her best interest, but she told me I was being selfish. It was the same old conversation that kept rearing its ugly head. And then she called Grace. As though my night couldn't have gotten worse.

They spoke for a few hours, and my mother calmed down for a little while. She still wasn't speaking to me, but she did let me come in and measure her blood pressure and give her the last of her medication before bed. I'd received a text message from Grace, and planned on returning it, but fell asleep before I could. That was Tuesday. It was now Sabbath morning.

I had worked doubles on Wednesday and Thursday, and my usual Friday shift. But Friday afternoon, I decided to go hang at the League of Lost Kings. It'd been awhile since I saw the guys there. Honestly, it was difficult to see them now that Junior was gone. They reminded me so much of him. And, of course, they would have questions about him. Everyone saw the tape. Most people had let go of it, but I hadn't seen them since before the incident. I was sure they'd have questions. I was sure Mr. McFadden would have questions as well. I'd let him down, and my commitment had waned. I knew he'd be disappointed. Part of me wanted to stay away longer, but I knew that the last place I wanted to be was home, where my mother and Grace were preparing for the potluck.

When I got to the LLK House, the guys barely looked up as I walked in. Mr. McFadden wasn't in, but a few of the older guys said hi, and then went to the back to play a game of pick-up basketball. I watched them play for a half hour, and then decided to head home. I wasn't comfortable at the LLK, and I figured if I was going to be uncomfortable, I'd rather do it in my own home.

The drive home took forever, which usually put me on edge, but I welcomed it today. I knew that Grace would be angry that I had barely texted, let alone called her in the past few days. And of course, my mother was still angry. Plus, I figured Peter would be there, and they'd want me to watch him while they cooked. Don't get me wrong, I really enjoy spending time with Peter, but today I just wanted to avoid everyone, and the last thing I needed was to babysit. It was probably selfish, but it was no less true. I needed REST this Sabbath.

When I finally arrived at home, my mother and Grace were in full force, and the house smelled amazing. I almost wanted to reconsider going to this potluck, but I knew I'd have to stick to my guns. My mother didn't look at me when I kissed her hello. In fact, she stiffened. But I brushed it off. She'd cave soon enough, and then all would be well again. Grace shot me a look that meant I was in trouble, but I kissed her anyway. "Where's Peter?" I asked. "He's with my parents for the weekend. Good thing, seeing how you like to pull disappearing acts and don't know how to let everyone else know that you changed the plan." I sighed, partly of irritation, but mostly of relief. "So, no babysitting duty? Word. I'm upstairs. Call me when you're done helping my mom. Oh, and save me plate! Thanks!" Her look said it all. I needed to get out of there, and fast.

I went to my room, and passed out. Next thing I knew, it was morning. I helped my mom get ready, and dropped her off at church, with another reminder to save me a plate. Then I headed to the Blue Hills. I brought my Bible, my Hymnal, and my Gospel music, and some snacks.

I've been sitting here for about a half hour, thinking, and people-watching. I saw some people inner tubing, some skiing, and some brave and adventurous people attempting to hike the snowy hill. I stretched my legs for a while, and then I went and sat in the car. I was considering going to Dunkin Donuts for some coffee or espresso, since it was freezing, and I didn't want to waste my entire gas tank on trying to stay warm.

After thinking it over, I realized that I could still make it home before all the potluck-ers, and make myself some coffee, and either hang out in my room, or go for a drive somewhere. I didn't have much of a plan, but the crisp, cold air of the hill had done its job. I felt better. And so, I headed home.

As my coffee percolated, I decided to help out my mother. I'm not a complete jerk. I pre-heated the oven, and set the dishes out to begin warming. I texted Grace that I was home, and warming up the food. I told her I still wouldn't participate in the potluck, but I hoped that she could sneak away from the craziness to spend some time with me. I'd probably take a nap once the food was in the oven, since they'd be home within an hour.

****

I woke up from my nap, to the sound of Sabbath being closed. There were a few voices other than my mother's and Grace's. I heard the trademark hymn "Reste Avec Nous" ("Abide With Me") that every Haitian family closed Sabbath with. I didn't want to be awkward and just pop up in the middle, so I silently participated from my room, and then waited upstairs until the guests left.

D. Gloria Elysée

When I got downstairs, my mother was cleaning. I started helping her clear the table. "You were here this whole time?" "Yes mom. I was the one who warmed all the food. I was upstairs. I took a nap after I got back from my nature walk." She made a face as she scraped the remnants of her guests' food off the (real!) dishes. "Too bad. You missed the party. Everyone was asking for you." I loaded the dishes in the dishwasher. "It's okay. I'll see them next time. I'm good as long as you guys saved me that plate." She paused. "I didn't make any plates. You didn't make a plate before they came?" I looked at her like she was crazy. "You raised me better than that. I don't take scoops out of the food before it's served." She shrugged. "Oh. I thought you forgot how you were raised." I was over this conversation and the nuanced guilt trip she was aiming in my direction. "Where's Grace?" My mother pointed to the living room.

Grace was walking into the house, as I entered the living room. "Hey honey. How was the potluck? Why were you outside?" She gave me a death stare. "My parents just left with Peter. They were asking about you all afternoon." I was confused. "I told you I'd be upstairs, asleep, and that I wasn't coming to the potluck. Why are you so angry?" She shook her head. "It's nothing. I'm fine." Uh-oh. That's never a good sign. "Um, I know this is probably the worst time to ask but, where is the plate you made me?" She stopped fixing the couch cushions and turned, looking me directly in my eyes. "What plate? I didn't make you a plate." "Seriously hun? That's the *one* thing I asked you to do! Nobody could make me a plate, even though I came home early so I could warm up the food-" She rolled her eyes. "You came home early and decided to warm up the food once you got here. Don't even act like you intended to come home early. You probably got cold and decided to come back, and realized how it'd look if you didn't warm up the food. Don't try to act like you did this super selfless act."

Now I was angry. So what if she was right? How dare she assume the worst of me! I could've come home early with those intentions. She didn't know. And as my girl, wasn't she supposed to make my plate for me if I wasn't there to make it myself? Now all the food was gone, and I was hungry. Everything that *my* money had bought was now resting in the bellies of random people, and neither my mother or my girlfriend cared enough to save some for me. I was livid.

Of course, Grace and I began arguing. We argued about the potluck. She called me selfish and ungrateful. I told her my money paid for most of those groceries and if she was a good girlfriend, she'd have looked out for me. She told me she was too busy looking after the needs of her son, and that she only had one child. Of course, that pissed me off. She said she was hurt that I was so glad to not have to babysit Peter yesterday, and I told her I had a hard day and that it wasn't that I didn't care about him, but that I was relieved. She of all people should understand since she was always dumping him on other family members.

She said it was because she was working, not because she "didn't feel like being bothered." She

311

needed the money, which is why she didn't understand why I was trying to get her fired. I asked her where she got a crazy idea like that, which of course she glanced toward the kitchen where my mother was. I told her that I wasn't trying to get her fired, but that the insurance wasn't trying to cover a full-time person. Her agency wanted to give a part-time shift to another person, and I was stuck trying to negotiate. That's why we needed to penny pinch and not spend money on potlucks for people who didn't even care enough to call and check up on us.

She countered with my lack of communication skills, and "why didn't you just say so?" I told her I tried, but she never let me get a word in edgewise and always defended my mother without even hearing my side. If she and my mother weren't so busy being best friends, jumping to conclusions, maybe they'd know what was going on. She told me that someone had to be there for my mother, because she felt like she'd lost both sons, not one. I told her that I tried, but all she wanted to do was talk about my brother, so I tried to keep it at a minimum. Plus, I was busy with work. She said that was exactly the problem. That I became a workaholic and was spending too much time and energy on the pursuit of money. She said that I should've taken the job I was offered at the LLK, because I was so much happier then. She said that I was slacking on my responsibility to the boys, and never saw them since I started working at the call center.

Here we go again! I told her someone needed to pay for our outings, however few that we actually went on. Plus, the bills. She countered, "Then let me pay for dinner sometime! What's so wrong with that?" I reminded her that her money was to take care of Peter, and that I was the man in the relationship, so I needed to provide. Peter was where her money needed to go, and that was that. Clearly this irritated her and she snapped back, "What kind of 'grown man' avoids conversations with his loved ones? You can't even hold a conversation with your mother. But you wanna make all the financial decisions yourself?"

The argument had now spiraled into my avoidance of conversation about Junior- with an emphasis on how I needed to forgive. I told her that I was fine, and I needed support, not judgment. She said she did support me, but I reminded her of how little she actually did support me. She spent so much time judging me. She let me talk freely of my feelings for the first month, but since then, labeled me angry and bitter and negative, so no, I wasn't going to talk to her about my brother. And I didn't talk to my mother about him because he could do no wrong in her eyes, and I was the one who was always messing up, and I couldn't take being taken for granted anymore. I was ALWAYS there. ALWAYS. And she never appreciated it. She never congratulated me or applauded me. She only cared about one of her children, and I was tired of it, especially since he was the one who caused her heart attack and chose to live and die the way he did.

She told me I needed to forgive him, that I couldn't keep acting as though he never existed. And then I lost it. I shouted, "Like you do with your son's father? Like you pretend he never existed? You know Peter is asking me about him? When you start doing some communication and forgiveness of your own, then you can come at me." I knew it was a low blow when I said it and I instantly regretted it. It was so bad, it brought my mother out of the kitchen, and caused Grace to leave in tears. I can't even explain it. Something in me just snapped- trying to plead my case and be heard, but being judged and rejected and told once again that I needed to forgive him instead. It was my last straw. I'd been broken, and in return I lashed out. I was sorry, but the damage was done. She had left, in tears, without even saying goodbye to my mother. I stared at the door, hoping it wasn't over between us, but the sinking feeling in my gut told me otherwise...

Chapter 9
January 2015

The transition into the new year was uneventful. It had been almost a month since Grace had broken up with me after that stupid potluck. I had been avoiding people at my church by going to other churches. I'd mostly been avoiding her though. Being our home church, I'd surely run into her at Mt. Bethel, and I wasn't too fond of Mt. Calvaire (my mom's church), so I thought I should try an American church. First stop was Genesis SDA. I'd been there a few times, but not recently.

In all honesty, I was embarrassed. I'd lost control, and yelled at her, and said something really uncalled for. I felt stupid for my behavior, but I still felt like she didn't understand me.

=*Because she doesn't.*=

I wasn't asking for much, but she genuinely didn't have compassion for me. She didn't believe I was trying to forgive my brother. My pride was too much for me to apologize for anything other than my harsh words. I still

315

thought I was right. But she'd been avoiding me as well. The first week, she hadn't taken any of my (daily) calls or my text messages. I left messages, apologizing, asking if we could talk. But after a week, my pride wounded, I accepted defeat.

I knew that what we had was real, but I couldn't chase a woman who didn't want me. I even called every other day for the next two weeks, but by the time the holidays and the new year rolled around, it was a done deal. I still loved her though. Yeah, I said love. I really think we could've had something lasting. But part of me was glad, because *=I can't be with someone who doesn't support me. I deserve better than that. I mean, I should be with someone who lets me feel what I feel, no questions asked.=*

That broke my heart. Her unfair judgment of my situation. She'd never had to deal with Junior. She didn't know what it felt like to have your sibling screw up their life, but you get treated like the defective one. It hurt. And my mother, though she'd started being nicer since Grace and I broke up, still wasn't on my side.

Grace wasn't her visiting nurse anymore, and we had some older woman, Heather, who came twice a week. My mom was feeling down these days, because she didn't get the same level of care from the new lady. Sure, Heather did her job, but Grace had gone far above the call of duty when it came to my mother, and my mother loved her as her own child. Plus, Heather was Caucasian, so my mom didn't have the Haitian bond like she did with Grace. So my mother kept nagging me about seeing Grace and Peter. I sent Grace a text message, telling her my mother missed her, and my mother told me that Grace called her, the next day. I think that was the first time I'd ever been jealous of my mother.

All I know is that I'd never been affected by someone as much as I've been with her. This hurts. I think she really was falling in love with me, but I know what I said hurt her really bad. I didn't know if she'd ever forgive me. I think that's the most ironic part of this. The reason we broke up was because she didn't think I was willing to forgive my brother. And now she wouldn't forgive me. It was more than a little hypocritical, if you ask me. But I knew I just needed to move on with my life.

I arrived at Genesis SDA just in time for the service to start. I sat in the back, trying not to draw any attention to myself, but of course nosy old Mrs. Roberts (Gwen's mom) tried pushing me to the front. "He's not a visitor Sister Roberts." A familiar voice chimed in behind me. It was Heaven. She'd walked in just in time to rescue me from the crazy church lady. "Well, I haven't seen him at church in a while so he might as well be a visitor," she responded. "That's because my home church is Mt. Bethel. I'm just here for the day. Thanks for the program." I took it from her hand, and sat in the back row. Heaven nudged me. "You sure you don't want to sit up front with an old friend? Jonathan is on the pulpit today, so I'll be sitting by myself." I thought about it, but I declined. I needed to be inconspicuous.

I wish I could tell you what the sermon was about. I was really distracted. I should've known. I can't sit in the back pews, because I spend the entire service people-watching- especially when I visit a new church. Sitting in the back pews almost guarantees a limited church experience. I struggled with my attention during the sermon. My mind kept going back to Grace. I knew that I needed to do something about the situation. I just didn't know what it was. I could barely find motivation to make it through the days. I hated being at home because my mother was extra sad and moody all the time. I hated work because it was horrible, but we needed the income, so I spent more and more time there. And church wasn't the same since I'd been wandering. I felt so unsettled. I couldn't wait to get out of there.

I tried to hurry and leave after church, but Heaven caught up to me. "Hey King. You look a little down. Is everything okay?" "I'm sure you've already heard about me and Grace by now." Heaven smiled. "I think by now you know how I feel about hearsay. I don't mean to pry, though. In fact, I don't even need to know. Will you let me pray with you, though?"

I tried thinking of an excuse, but she grabbed my hand, and bowed her head before I could speak. "Dear Heavenly Father, we come before You so thankful for this day. Thank You for Your Sabbath rest, and for the life You've given us. We thank You for Your Will for our lives, the purpose You have placed in our lives, and the paths You've chosen for us. We ask for Your forgiveness, knowing that You will cleanse us from all our sins. Thank You for Your Son, and His sacrifice on the cross for us. Lord, I lift up my brother Solomon right now. You know the pain and struggle that he's had, and how hard it has been for him and his family lately. You know his inner struggles that no one else sees or understands. Please bring him comfort, joy, hope, and peace. Fill his heart with Your love, and Your Holy Spirit, and remove any thoughts that will crowd out Your love, Your Word, Your Spirit. Bless him and his mom, and continue to let Your will be known to him. In the precious name of Jesus we pray, Amen."

It was a perfect prayer. It said everything that needed to be said, but wasn't condescending. But Heaven was like that. A true woman of God. She'd gone through the fire a few years back, and it changed her for good. I gave her a big hug, but remembered to keep it "churchy" since her boyfriend was nearby, and plus, I respected the house of God. "Thanks Heaven. I needed that." She laughed. "I know. And I'm so sorry I never made it to the service. I was on call that day, and I couldn't find anyone to trade shifts with me. Did you get the card I sent?" I had. She was one of the few that had reached out. Mari came to the service, and so did a few others. "Yes, I did. Thank you so much. My mom and I appreciate the gesture."

The pleasantries went on for a few more minutes, until it was time for her to go. She invited me to Mari's house. It was potluck day. But I declined. Although running into her wasn't the nightmare I thought it could've been, I didn't want to be around others today. I couldn't handle a room full of pity and judgment, dependent on what they knew about my past few months. I told Heaven I had to go back to my house and make sure my mother was okay. To that, she and Jonathan exited.

I had almost made my escape before Sister Roberts came by with Gwen and Carine. That was all I needed today. "Hey there. I thought you'd like to see a familiar face. Well, a *better* one." Sister Roberts always took a dig at Heaven, even in her absence. "Hi King." "Hi Carine. Hi Gwen." "How are you? I heard your brother passed." "I'm fine. Actually, I'm headed home. So sorry. In a rush." I gave them each a quick, albeit awkward, one-armed hug before I rushed out the church. I needed no more exes today. I mean, Heaven and I weren't ever in a real relationship (which is probably why we were still in a pretty good place), but Carine and I didn't end so well, and Gwen was nosy like her mother, so I needed to leave before their prying yielded results.

I was halfway home when my phone began buzzing. Thankfully, I was stopped at a light. It was Carine. It'd been months since my brother's death, but *now* she was showing concern. I guess since I was no longer "out of sight," I wasn't "out of mind." In all actually, I'd forgotten that Genesis was her church. I knew I might run into Heaven, but I totally forgot about Gwen, and Carine. Had I remembered, I'd have gone to a different church. Her thirsty text message about "reconnecting" just made me uncomfortable and a little angry.

We'd broken up because I didn't see a future with her. Her personality was fake. Everything that had attracted me to her was phony. She was mean, gossiped and made fun of everyone, a hypocrite that was holier than everyone, and played pretend so well I wondered if anything she told me was actually the truth. After being with her, I took a long break from relationships. I had enough of crazy. I needed peace, truth, honesty, REAL things, not pretend. I'd found all that with Grace. I realized that even if Grace and I don't get back together, I don't want anything less than what she had to offer.

Grace was the gold standard. And it sucked that she was gone. But Carine and her phoniness could stay where she was. She sent me two more text messages by the time I got home. I was annoyed by her pursuit, so I ignored it and hoped she'd go away. She was annoying me, and there was no way I'd ever go back down that route.

I already had a lot on my mind. Grace had opened up to me about a very painful part of her past, and I threw it in her face. When she was younger, she fell in love with a guy who had been stringing her along for a year. He had convinced her to sleep with him, and when she did, he dumped her. Soon after, she'd found out that she was pregnant, and he wanted nothing to do with it. He told her that there was no way that the baby was his, and told her to get rid of it. When she was in the beginning of her third trimester, he was hit by a stray bullet and died. That caused her to go into labor early. She never got to attend his funeral, because she was in the NICU with Peter. She had Peter in June, so by the time the summer ended, she was back in school, finishing her nursing studies. She had never gotten over it, and had confessed to me that she struggled with forgiving him for a very long time.

She had such a hard time not blaming her dead ex for his actions, and for changing her life. She didn't know how to tell Peter about his father, so she avoided the conversation. So that's why my words hurt her so much. I really hit a nerve. And just like me, she was justified in her hurt and anger towards her ex. Too bad I couldn't tell her that. I just hoped that I could convince her not to hate me, and to give me a second chance.

****

My mother has been on the steady decline. I came home to her on the floor of her bedroom last week, but she told me she just slipped and not to worry. I thought something was off, but I trusted her. But today, I was feeling stifled at work and by noon, I'd decided to take the rest of the day off. Plus, for weeks I hadn't seen the replacement nurse, and I had a few questions for her. Every time I'd come home, there'd be no sign of her, and my mother would tell me that she had already gone for the day. Today I would hopefully catch her, and ask her about my mother's treatment- especially her fall. I was still uneasy about that, and I had a nagging feeling that I was missing something.

As I reached the house, I tried to push away a nagging feeling that seemed to be getting worse. The house was quiet, and the lights were off in the kitchen and living room. I turned them on, but nothing looked out of place in either room. "Mom!" I called out to see if she was home. "Mummy! Kote'w ye?" (Mom, where are you?). There was no answer. I went into her bedroom first, but all I saw was a disheveled pile of sheets on the bed. I went back into the hall, and went toward the bathroom. The faucet was running. It was a small trickle, not a lot, but that worried me even more. I looked in the bathtub, but it, too, was empty. I guess they'd gone out for a walk, but forgot to turn off that faucet.

I went to my room, and dropped my things off on my bed. I had just taken off my work clothes and plopped on the bed, when I thought I heard a wail. I cracked my door and called out, "Mom?" again. There was no answer but the wailing stopped. As soon as I closed my door again, the wailing started back up. I threw on some sweatpants, and ran out of my room with an aluminum bat. The wailing was getting louder. It was coming from Junior's room. I snuck quietly to the door, and then, in one quick motion, ran into the room while waving my bat crazily in the air.

She looked terrified. My mother had been laying on Junior's bed, curled in the fetal position, clutching his pictures, sobbing and wailing. But as I entered, she stood quickly, never taking her eyes off of me. But as we stared at each other for what seemed to be an eternity, she clutched her chest and passed out. I barely caught her before she hit the ground.

I could barely process what had just happened. I just knew we needed help. I called out for the nurse, but there was no answer. She was never here to begin with. I gently laid my mother on the bed and then called 911. As I waited for the ambulance to arrive, I tried to check my mother's pulse, and make sure she was still breathing. I had no idea what I was doing. I called Grace for help, but there was no answer.

I knew it was a long shot, since she still wasn't talking to me, but I knew I had to try, and that I'd try calling again. I was terrified. I tried not to hyperventilate as I watched my mother lying helpless. I did CPR until the paramedics arrived. The ambulance ride was a complete blur. I had considered driving, but I just wanted to be there with my mother, when she woke up. I needed her to wake up. I just needed her to wake up.

It was a long ten minutes until the ambulance had reached my house, and the fifteen-minute ride to the hospital felt like an eternity. My mind raced with thoughts like, " *=It's your fault=*" and " *=You did this to her=*", but I tried to push them away. I felt so guilty. I should've checked Junior's room from the beginning. And who did I think I was, bursting into the room like Rambo, swinging a bat and scaring the life out of my mother? And then I had to explain to the paramedics and to the ER docs what happened to her. I felt ashamed and guilty, and wanted to crawl under a rock. But my mother needed me, and I needed her to make it.

When we reached the emergency room, after I'd explained what happened, the doctor asked me to step out of the room as him and the nurses worked on my mother. Once I reached the waiting room, I checked my phone to see if Grace had called me back. I had no missed calls, so I tried her again, and left a message. I knew it was a long shot, since we weren't speaking, but I wanted to keep her updated. Halfway through my message, though, I decided that I didn't want to burden her with everything and she had no more responsibility to my mother or I, so I hung up.

I know it was awkward, but I was tired of hurting my loved ones. A nurse came to the waiting room and brought me back into the room where they were holding my mother. She was hooked up to machines to help her breathe, and hadn't woken up yet. They were going to continue to monitor her, and run some tests to confirm a diagnosis.

I don't know how long I sat there, whether it was for a few minutes or for a few hours, but I just prayed. I had grabbed my Bible before we had left the house and sat, staring at the pages. I couldn't focus on anything. All I could think about was that I couldn't lose my mother. Not after I'd lost so much this year. The words blurred on the page, swimming in a whirlpool until the doctor came in and startled me out of my stupor. It was a heart attack. I'd caused my mother to have another heart attack.

He saw my facial expression, and reassured me that everything would be okay, and that there was no way that I could've caused the heart attack. My mother's heart was so weak that it was imminent, and I had no influence on the situation. I heard what he said, but he wasn't there. He didn't see the look on my mother's face as I ran into the room with a bat. She looked so frightened, and then dropped. And it was all my fault. I wondered where the nurse was, but I couldn't blame her for this. This was all on me.

It was a few hours later that my mother woke up. I wasn't in the room. I was down the hall, as the nurse convinced me to get something to eat. We'd been there for almost five hours, and the cafeteria was going to close soon. I took some chicken tenders, fries, two bags of chips, some cookies, and a few drinks. I knew I'd be there for the long haul, and I didn't want to get hungry and have to leave my mother's side again.

I walked into the room and she smiled. She was sitting up, and the nurses were fussing over her. She waved them away, and as they left, I heard them talking about how her vital signs had suddenly improved and how they needed new scans because she didn't even look sick.

"Come here, Solo." She beckoned me to her side. "I'm so sorry mom! I didn't mean to-" She held up her hand to stop me. "You didn't do this, Solo. I was surprised, but you didn't make this happen. Don't even think like that." My head dropped to my chest and tears began streaming down my face. "I'm sorry for everything mom. I was so scared. I can't lose you mom. I just can't." She squeezed my hand. "That's not up to us to decide my love. That is God's decision. But I need to talk to you about something. It's very important." I slid my chair closer to the bed. "Okay mom. What is it?" I was hoping it wasn't about her funeral or anything morbid like that. She was the type to start talking about funeral arrangements and such, even though she'd just gotten better. But that's not where she began.

"Solo, I miss your brother more than anything." I began to pull away. "Seriously mom? Now?" She shushed me. "Listen to me Solo. Listen and then we can talk about it. I am still your mother." I nodded in silence, tears still streaming down my face. She began again...

D. Gloria Elysée

Chapter 10

"I miss Junior. And I miss your father so much more than I can express. I know they made plenty of bad decisions, but I've made my peace with the choices they made for themselves, and left what I could not understand in God's hands. I know that I am not to blame for all their choices, and I did the best that I could in the circumstances I was given. I can have peace in that. I still worry and struggle with guilt sometimes, but God gave me peace.

"What about you? I gave birth to you, so don't even think to lie to me. I know you haven't forgiven Junior. You won't even talk about him, or let anyone mention him without getting angry or leaving. You need to forgive your brother. Your life depends on it. You walk around so unhappy and so mean. So hurt and so broken. You are carrying a burden that no one meant for you to carry alone.

"You keep telling me, 'All these years I've [done everything you wanted] and never once refused to do a single

329

thing you told me to. And in all that time you never gave me even one [bit of credit or thrown a party for me]. Yet when this son of yours [came] back after [jail], you [celebrated] by [hosting a potluck in his honor!]'[60] I know you think that I give you no credit for all you've done, but can't you see that I know 'you have always stayed by me, and [you know] everything I have is yours. We had to celebrate [that] happy day[, because] your brother was [left for] dead and [had] come back to life! He was lost, but [then] he [was] found!'[61] You should be happy that he had an opportunity to turn his life around, even if he chose not to do right.

"You need to forgive him because, '[if] you forgive those who sin against you, your heavenly Father will forgive you. But if you refuse to forgive others, your Father will not forgive your sins[62]... [You must] love your enemies! Do good to those who hate you. Bless those who curse you. Pray for those who hurt you... You must be compassionate, just as your Father is compassionate... Do not judge [[Junior], and you will not be judged. Do not condemn [him], or it will all come back against you. Forgive [your brother], and you will be forgiven. Give, and you will receive... The amount you give will determine the amount you get back.'[63]

"Solo, '...[don't] neglect your mother's instruction...Come and listen to my counsel. I'll share my heart with you and make you wise.'[64] I know '[he wronged] you [what seemed like] seven times a day and each time [turned]

---

[60] Luke 15:29, 30
[61] Luke 12:31,32
[62] Matt 6:14, 15
[63] Luke 6:27,28,36-38
[64] Proverbs 1: 8, 23

again and [asked] forgiveness, [but] you [still] must forgive.'[65] 'If [you say], "I love God," but [can't stand your brother], [you make yourself] a liar; [because] if [you] don't love [your brother, who you] can see, how can [you] love God, whom [you] cannot see?'[66] You need to let it go for your own sake Solo. Let your anger go!

"**Do you think I didn't have the same struggle with forgiveness? Where do you think you got it from? Maybe I should tell you why I came to the United States, and tell you about your father so you can understand. I tried hiding it from you two to protect you, but it didn't work, so now you need to know.**

"**I was born in a small village just outside of Henche in Haiti. I lived with my parents and my two brothers. My grandparents died when I was a baby. I didn't know any other family except the ones I lived with. I was a good girl, very quiet, and I loved to learn. I did well in school, and was studying to become a doctor, but I met a boy when I was 21. He told me he loved me, and I believed him. Soon I became pregnant. When I found out, I was almost 3 months along. My mother called me a whore and beat me badly every day. My brothers would beat me too. My father was the only one who tried to make it stop. He saved me, and told me everything would be okay.**

---

[65] Luke 17:4
[66] 1 John 4:20

"Not too long after, I was in the yard and a group of men came to my house. They were Tonton Macoutes (the president/dictator Duvalier's private army). I could hear them telling my father that our house was theirs because he didn't give them enough bribe money in the past few months. I was scared, so I hid in the well until they left. They beat him pretty bad, and all I heard were screams from my mother, and gunshots. After about ten minutes of silence, I climbed out of the well to see what happened.

"They killed my mother and my brothers (presumably for fighting back), and shot my father. When I found them, my father was still alive. They let him watch as they killed the family so he would suffer more. I tried to help him, but he told me to go into a box under the bathroom. He said there was a paper with an address, his passport, and enough money to get me to my grandmother's house in Port-au-Prince. He said she never liked my mother, so she disowned him when he married her. He said go to her and I would be safe. There was enough money to continue my studies in the capital. I held him close, weeping until he died. I was so afraid and sad. Then I went and got the box. I took the money and hid in the well all night, terrified and heartbroken.

"The next morning, I walked the 7 miles to Hinche, and took a camion (bus) to Port-au-Prince to find my grandmother. It was worse there for me than it was at home. She hated me, and blamed my mother (and therefore me) for my father's death. She said my mother was trash, I was illegitimate, and had the nerve to be carrying a bastard child. I was an embarrassment. She accused me of terrible things, and refused to send me to school. She took the money I came with, and refused to give me any part of it. I couldn't go to school anymore. I had nowhere to go, and she dragged me and beat me when I would try to sleep in the bedrooms like a normal guest. So, I slept under the table in the kitchen with the other restavek (indentured servant) and cleaned the house and cooked meals so I could have shelter.

"I ate scraps of the food, after she was done. I wasn't allowed to speak to any of the guests in the house or I would get a beating. She almost beat me unconscious when she saw me reading, so I would have to sneak to read my medical book in the bathroom. She was wealthy enough to have a bathroom inside her house. She treated me much worse than the other restavek, even though I was her blood. She taught everyone else to treat me the same way. Everyone, including the restavek, the other servants, and any guests, treated me like trash. She'd call me names, worse than my mother had done. She said my mother trapped her son with a bastard baby, so who was I trying to trap with a bastard now?

"She was cruel, and I know this wasn't the protection my father expected I'd have. Part of me wished to go back to my village, but I knew that there was nothing left for me to return to. Plus, I had no money. I figured the streets of the capital were more dangerous than living in her mansion. My grandmother, Eve Clara Cassillion, told me I could never acknowledge

333

her in public. I'm sure I had relatives. People in the framed pictures on her walls visited her all the time. But after a short conversation with her, they treated me like the help. Any familial connection to any of them ended the moment my father died. That is part of the reason I never wanted to return to Haiti once I left. There was nothing to go back to, except painful memories, and living reminders of my nightmares.

"Soon, Madame Cassillion needed money, as she had to pay bribes to keep her land, so she sold me to the neighbors. I became their restavek instead of hers. My grandmother had sold me like a common cow. But I was worth less than a cow to her. I had only been there for a little over two months. But she sold me. Or maybe she was renting me. Either way, I was neither granddaughter, nor family to her. I was barely human. But the couple next door wasn't as cruel to me as she was. I'm sure she told them of my condition, and probably told them I had fleas, because I was not allowed to make physical contact with any of them. I saw the father eyeing me on several occasions, but thank God, he never touched me. I think she told them I had a disease.

"The couple only had one child, a young man a little older than I was. Their son took interest in me. He was an idealist who thought that no one should be a restavek. He always snuck around to spent time with me and talk to me. After his parents had gone to bed, he'd come downstairs to see me. We would speak about everything. He was surprised when he found out that I was going to study medicine, like him. His shock was overloaded when he discovered that I was the granddaughter of Mme Cassillion. It was then, I think, that he fell in love with me.

"That man was your father- David. He had applied for a student visa to the U.S. months earlier, so he asked his parents to send me along with him, and expedite a visa for me. They said no, of course, and then beat me because he asked about me. Because he noticed me. But David didn't give up. Since political exiles were granted amnesty in the U.S. he told me that he would find a way out for me. Three days before he was supposed to fly to Miami, he made me pack a bag, and handed me forged papers that he'd paid for with his tuition money. We left together, and never looked back. I was over 7 months pregnant by then, but I was really skinny because I was malnourished. I wore oversized clothes so they would let me on the plane without a problem.

"Soon after we got to Miami, I gave birth and called my baby David Junior. David had used up all his college money to buy my ticket, so he could only stay in school for one semester, while I tried to get citizenship for having Junior on American land. Once I got it, we tried to find a place to live. But there were too many people who knew David's family in Miami and New York, so we came to Boston. I changed my last name to Principle, because I didn't want anyone to associate me with Madame Cassillion.

"Things were good when we first got to Boston. He found work, and so did I. But he was used to being rich. Without his parents' money, he didn't know what to do. He had never been poor before, like I had been. So he fell in with the wrong crowd. They were some friends he'd made on the flight from Haiti, vagabonds of the worst kind. They convinced him to sell some drugs for them on his cab route. They also asked him to deliver questionable packages for them. I told him it was a terrible decision, but the money was too good for him to say no. He became addicted to the money he made, and started doing it full time.

"Nothing happened for the first few years. We settled down, and then I had you. We still weren't married. I would get better government checks that way, he said. I didn't mind. He still protected me. He reminded me of my father so much. I decided to use some of the money to go to school. I thought I could be a nurse, but could not afford to do that, so I became a nursing assistant instead.

"Soon, your father tried the drug he sold. They call it cracks. He tried it and then it got worse. He got addicted, and then got caught, and then was put in jail. They killed him because they lost money on the drugs he had when he was arrested. The same people who asked him to sell for them were responsible for him taking drugs, going to jail, and then his murder. Because we weren't married, he didn't have citizenship. So, they were going to deport him. Those men killed him before they got the chance to deport him. It was so scary. I thought they would kill all of us. So, when someone invited me to church, I said I'd go. I had two boys that I had to take care of. I was working so much that I couldn't watch you children like I needed to. I was trying to pay the bills and give you the life I never had. But it was hard, especially when your father got into the bad things.

"So, you see, I have had much hurt in my life. Many betrayals. It's almost like a movie, my life. But I need you to understand that if I let myself hate everyone who hurt me- my mother, my grandmother, the Principles, and even your father- I wouldn't have had any love left to give you and Junior. I wouldn't have any will to live. I would have been consumed. I would have been abusive, like my mother was to me. I chose to let it go, and though it was hard, I had to give it to God. That is why I tell you that you need to forgive Junior. It is not healthy for you to hold onto your anger.

"Do you not understand how much I love you? I wasn't playing favorites with you two. I just gave Junior a little more attention because he needed it. '...Healthy people don't need a doctor—sick people do.'[67] He needed a reminder that he could thrive, the way you did so well. Think about it, Solo. Your brother chose like your father did. '... [They disliked] knowledge and chose not to fear the LORD. They rejected my advice and paid no attention when I corrected them. [So] they [had to] eat the bitter fruit of living their own way, choking on their own schemes.'[68] '[They were

---

[67] Luke 5:31
[68] Proverbs 1: 29-31

337

held captive by [their] own sins; [the sins were] ropes that [caught] and [held them]. [They both died because of a] lack of self-control; [and were] lost because of [their] great foolishness.'[69] They chose their own path, but that's not what you chose. You chose God.

"I tried to force Junior into a relationship with God, but he didn't want that. I tried to warn Junior as best I could. I came to God after your father died, but I tried as soon as I got the message from God. That first day of church, He told me, '[when] you receive a message from Me, warn [your children] immediately. If you warn [them], saying, 'You are [in danger of] the penalty of death,' but you fail to deliver the warning, they will die in their sins. And I will hold you responsible for their deaths. If you warn them and they refuse to repent and keep on sinning, they will die in their sins. But you will have saved yourself because you obeyed Me.'[70] **I kept that message to heart, and I told God I would try my best to not leave you and Junior behind. But Junior didn't want to be like God. He was too much like his father. Trying to be a man, but not understanding what a man was.**

"Your father thought having money was what it meant to be a man, and then Junior and even you followed his lead. '[But you can't [focus on] [storing] up [wealth] here on earth, where moths eat[, and rust destroys] and where thieves break in and steal. [Build your [wealth] in heaven, where moths and rust cannot destroy, and thieves do not break in and steal. Wherever your treasure is, there [your

---

[69] Proverbs 5:22, 23
[70] Ezekiel 3:17-19

focus] will also be... [Understand that no] one can serve two masters. For you will hate one and love the other; you will be devoted to one and despise the other. You cannot serve both God and money... That is why I tell you not to worry about everyday life—whether you have enough food and drink, or enough clothes to wear. Isn't life more than food, and your body more than clothing?... So don't worry about these things, saying, 'What will we eat? What will we drink? What will we wear?' These things [dominated] the thoughts of [your father and brother,] but your heavenly Father already knows all your needs. Seek the Kingdom of God above all else, and live righteously, and He will give you everything you need.'[71]

"Money isn't everything! But your brother and father couldn't see that. They spent their lives chasing wealth. 'But [by doing that, Junior and your father] set an ambush for themselves; they [were] trying to get themselves killed. [That] is the fate of all who are greedy for money; it [robbed] them of [their lives].' [72] **I tried my best with them, but I couldn't save them. But don't be resentful of their bad choices. They have to answer to God now.**

"You don't think it breaks my heart to know that I may never see them in Heaven? 'Tears stream from my eyes because of the destruction of my [son]! My tears flow endlessly; they will not stop...My heart is breaking over the fate of [David and Junior].'[73] 'The thought of my suffering...is bitter

---

[71] Matt 6: 19-21, 24,25, 31-33
[72] Proverbs 1:18,19
[73] Lamentations 3:48,49,51

beyond words. I will never forget this awful time, as I grieve over my loss. Yet I still dare to hope when I remember this: The faithful love of the LORD never ends! His mercies never cease. Great is His faithfulness; His mercies begin afresh each morning. I say to myself, "The LORD is my inheritance; therefore, I will hope in Him!" The LORD is good to those who depend on Him, to those who search for Him. So it is good to wait quietly for salvation from the LORD.'[74] **That is my only hope.**

"I don't know how much time I have left on this earth, but I just want to make sure you're okay. Solomon, my dear son that I love so much, I am so proud of you. But you must be careful to make good decisions. I know you can do it. You are God's child. '[He] made all the delicate, inner parts of [your] body and knit [you] together in [my] womb. Thank [Him] for making [you] so wonderfully complex! [His] workmanship is marvelous—how well [we] know it. [He] watched [you] as [you were] being formed in utter seclusion, as [you were] woven together in the dark of the womb. [He] saw [you] before [you were] born. Every day of [your] life was recorded in [His] book. Every moment was laid out before a single day had passed.'[75]

"You are special to God, and He has a special calling on your life. You must seek Him in order to know His plans, and walk in His Will. 'Trust in the LORD with all your heart; do not depend on your own understanding. Seek His Will in all you do, and He will show you which path to take. Don't be impressed with your own wisdom. Instead, fear the LORD and

---

[74] Lamentations 3:19-26
[75] Psalm 139: 13-16

turn away from evil.'[76] Stop trying to take matters into your own hands. Listen to God. Choose what He chose for you and it will make life so much easier. The right career and the right woman you already saw. But you had an idea in your head of what they should look like, so you let them go. Do you think the money you make will compensate for your misery? Will that make you any less lonely? Will that make you any more righteous? No! It will only breed more unhappiness in your life. You will never be full, never have enough money. But if your goal is to have a life that is full of purpose, trust in God.

"You see Grace? She is a good woman. A woman of God. You should pray that you haven't messed that up for yourself. And if you get the chance, don't let her go again. She always tried to give you what you needed, and listened to God to give you advice. You think she was silly, talking about that job with the young boys? I heard you two argue. Don't you think God could use your testimony, and Junior's story to help keep these boys from ending up like he did?

The love of money made him into what he was. And his father told him that he was only worth the money he brought in. You don't think some little boy needs to hear that happiness from money is a lie, that '... the love of money is the root of all kinds of evil. And some people, craving money, have wandered from the true faith and pierced themselves with many sorrows[?]'[77] Maybe you'd be

---

[76] Proverbs 3:5-7
[77] 1 Timothy 6:10

able to teach them that if you believed it yourself. Son, 'I [am begging] you to lead a life worthy of your calling, for you have been called by God.'[78] Please Solo. You have hurt so much in this life already. Don't throw it all away for nothing. '[Tell me] what do you benefit if you gain the whole world but lose your own soul? Is anything worth more than your soul?'[79] Please son. Please. I just need to know that you will be saved. Promise me that you will keep going with God. Just don't waste your life."

I was speechless. What was I to say to that other than, "I promise, Mom. I promise"? She prayed with me then, a prayer of consecration. She asked God to rededicate me to Himself, and to reveal His will in my life. Then she leaned back in her bed, relaxed and told me she was tired and needed a nap. I sat quietly next to her, re-reading the story of the prodigal son[80]. I was definitely the older brother in that scenario- jealous of the concern his father showed his brother. Overly self-righteous and self-centered. I prayed and asked God to help me with my unforgiving attitude. It was time I let it go.

My mother, so strong, had suffered so much in her life, and yet still found it in her to forgive. There was no reason why I couldn't. I decided that my promise to my mom, before God, was real. I would choose God. I would choose forgiveness. I would choose change. The last thing I remember reading before I fell asleep that night was, "Don't copy the behavior and customs of this world, but let God transform you into a new person by

---

[78] Ephesians 4:1
[79] Mark 8: 36, 37
[80] Luke 15:11-32

changing the way you think. Then you will learn to know God's will for you, which is good and pleasing and perfect."[81]

---

[81] Romans 12:2

D. Gloria Elysée

Chapter 11
January 2015

My mother died that night. It wasn't anything dramatic- she simply slipped away in her sleep. I did manage to get another chance to talk to her before she passed. It was sad that this was the first time I'd had the chance to see her for who she really was. I had spent so much time in anger and frustration about my situation that I hadn't considered her feelings. I thought I was doing so well in the faith/Christianity department, but the truth was that I was lying to myself.

I spent most of my life judging myself against my brother's actions. I treated him like society did. And though I had a right to be frustrated by his selfish decisions, I compounded upon them when I refused to relay to him the same grace and mercy given me by God. And because I couldn't let my anger go, I resented the love and attention my mother gave him. So, I put up a barrier between us. I kept a parent-child relationship dynamic with my mother: constantly trying to prove my worthiness to her, instead of accepting the terms of our relationship. It made it difficult to see her as a human, not just "mom." This was the first time I'd seen my mother as an adult woman acting through the sum of her life experiences, and not just "my mother."

Part of my heartbreak was that I had waited so long to talk to my mother, to forgive her. I had been holding her love and forgiveness of Junior against her, and was angry for too long. I was so blessed and grateful that God gave me the chance to speak with her. It was what I needed, and just in time. I had been in "self-destruct" mode too long. I needed to know the truth, to see the truth. I'd been chasing money, approval, my own will. I had neglected the Scriptures about true Godliness, forgiveness, and had spent so much time in my feelings that I'd become a shell of a Christian.

It was time that I re-evaluated my purpose, and learned to choose God's Will. Well, once I knew for myself what it was. And this time, I would depend on God, and leave my pride out of it. I had to make better choices. As a man, I was called to be a leader. God had chosen a special path for me, and I couldn't lead like I was supposed to if I was headed in the wrong direction. I could not be strong enough to raise a family (eventually) if I couldn't follow God's Word on my own. If I couldn't do it single, what would happen when I was responsible for a wife, for children? I had to be confident in my chosen path now, before I added more people to my journey.

I was so grateful that my mother revealed so much to me, but it was a double-edged sword. I was angry about her past. I wanted to find the people who hurt her, and kill them myself. I'm sure she didn't mean for that to be my reaction, but she's my mother. No matter that these people were (most likely) all dead, but I was angry and didn't know what to do about it. Was I really supposed to forgive and forget it all, like she did? I suppose I had no real choice in the matter. These people all lived and probably died long before me. For that reason alone, I should let it go. And of course, because God said so. But as much as I had realized, and as much as I had learned, the application of forgiveness was *so* much harder than the theory. I understood what I needed to do, but it was harder to actually do it.

I decided to shift my focus off my negative emotions, to planning my mother's funeral. I needed to make good, smart decisions. Grace had not returned my phone call, but I shrugged it off. I decided to call the pastor of my mother's church to let him know the circumstances, and then the funeral home, to make the proper arrangements. I would do the full burial for my mom, and put Junior's urn in the casket with her. Honestly, I just didn't want to keep it at the house. I also had to decide if I was going to keep living in my mother's house. I considered asking some friends to stay there with me for a few days.

It was at a time like this that I really needed support. I had to pick the outfit my mother was to be buried in. I had no idea what to do. I didn't know anything about old lady fashion. So, I considered calling Mari or Heaven to help me pick one out. I had (thankfully) taken out an insurance policy on my mother, long before she'd gotten sick, so it was still valid. I had sat with her and chosen the casket and such then. But she'd wanted no part of it before. It was a good thing I convinced her to do it. Her last Medicaid and Social Security checks were not going to cover the bills, let alone a funeral.

I was exhausted. Physically, mentally, emotionally, I was spent. I still had a million things to do. I had to call my job and tell them what happened, and since I'd made a commitment to another volunteer session at the LLK, I had to call Mr. McFadden to cancel. I wasn't too happy about that, since I really didn't want to be seen as a flake, but Mr. McFadden told me I was being silly. "Of course you shouldn't feel guilty," he asserted! He assured me that he would explain the situation to the boys, and asked me to call him back once the arrangements were made. He'd like to attend the service, if that was okay with me. It was.

After my requisite phone calls were finished, and Mari and Heaven set off to find an appropriate outfit, I went back to my house. It was so empty. I decided to sleep with the lights on, not because I was afraid, but because I just needed it to feel like I wasn't the only person home. I struggled with sleep that night, and worried that my sleep would remain like this. So much loss in such a short time made me feel like I was spinning out of control.

****

The funeral service was, well- a funeral. It was nice. Simple. White flowers. Lots of crying. I asked for it to be on a Friday, since it would be small, and there weren't many people who would be coming. In fact, we only printed 25 programs. I was the only person on the "family" bench. I asked Ms. Joi if she would like to sit with me, because I was lonely. She did, and brought 2 other deaconesses with her. It was a good thing, though. I needed to be surrounded with someone.

I kept scanning the room for Grace. Every two minutes, I'd look until I found her. First, she was in the back. Then she was sitting in the bench across from mine. She half smiled when she saw me staring. A little wave. And then she put her head back down. Midway through the service was my time to speak. I had to do the eulogy and thank everyone for coming. I glanced at where she was sitting, once I started stumbling. She wasn't there. I felt so overwhelmed by everything. Here I was, laying to rest my last living relative that I knew of (with the exception of my niece). At 30, I had outlived my entire family tree. It was almost comical, thanking everyone on behalf of "our family." What family? I was alone. Completely.

As that thought began sinking in, resonating in every part of my mind, I began to sob uncontrollably. I felt a hand slip into mine, and heard a voice complete the reading that I'd begun. She wasn't in her seat because she was waiting in the wings, ready to rescue me when I needed her. Grace squeezed my hand, and let me weep on her shoulder. When she'd finished thanking everyone, she brought me into the side room of the church and sat me down. She rubbed my back, and pulled out a bottle of water. I could barely speak, but I tried to say thank you anyway. "Shh. It's okay, love," she consoled me. "I'm here. You don't have to say anything." I never appreciated anyone more in my life than I did Grace in that moment.

Eventually I regained my composure, and returned to the sanctuary. She sat with me until it was over, and it was time to close the casket. More tears, as I took the final look at my mother, and arranged the urn that contained my brother. The burial had its own tears, and I laid my mother in the ground, to rest peacefully until Jesus returned. All with Grace by my side. As the limo returned us to the church, I was silent. Though her hand had never left mine, I didn't know what to say. I wasn't sure if Grace was being compassionate, or if she wanted to be with me. I was afraid to ask. Every time I'd look at her, I'd look away, ashamed, afraid, confused, hurt.

She seemed to have as much trouble expressing herself as I did. So I decided to say the most neutral thing I could think of. "Um. I just wanted to say thank you. I can't even begin to say how grateful I am. So, thank you. You have no idea what it means to me." She smiled. "You're welcome." I wanted to say more, but I didn't want to ruin it. But I was determined to figure this out. Before I could speak again, we arrived at the church. The reception was inside, but I needed to wrap things up with the funeral home. Grace went in ahead of me, only after I insisted. A few minutes later, I was inside, sitting at a table with soup Joumou (traditional Haitian pumpkin stew), bread, ginger tea, and a Haitian patty in front of me. Then, the regular food was served. I picked at my food, barely hungry. Grace and Peter had sat next to me, her parents across from me, and Ms. Joi, Mari, and Heaven on the table next to mine.

I looked around the room. Once again, Trina had brought Kristal to the service, sat in the back, and didn't come to the reception. At least this time she went to the burial. I asked, begged Trina to let me come visit my only living relative, but something told me that I would barely get to. Still, I gave Kristal my information, and told her she was always welcome to call me or stop by. Trina was a good mother, but she clearly felt that my involvement in Kristal's life should be minimized. So much so that she gave Kristal a look when she took my information. I hoped that this wasn't the last time I would see my niece.

On my way to the restroom, I overheard Grace's parents ask her the question I'd been trying to ask all afternoon- were we back together? Unfortunately, I didn't hear a response, and by the time I returned to the table, the conversation was over. It wasn't until the end of the reception, when the older ladies were piling food into my car to take home, that I had a moment alone with Grace.

She quickly dismissed me before I finished my statement. "Not here. At your house. I'll help you bring the food. Just let me get Peter taken care of. I'll meet you there." So, I went home to wait for her. I declined the invitation for Mari and Heaven to come keep me company, and went by myself. It was hard to keep focused on the road, but eventually I made it home, and turned on all the lights, as was my new custom. Grace arrived twenty minutes later. She brought a cake. Apparently, she'd baked it for me, but left it at her house by accident. I put it in the fridge with the other food, after cutting each of us a slice, and returned into the living room.

We ate the cake and chatted pleasantly at first, but then silence. The cake was done. No one needed a beverage to be refreshed. Now was the issue at hand- our relationship or lack thereof. It was awkward, as neither of us wanted to bring it up. Me, because I was afraid of more bad news, and feeling foolish because of my stupidity. Her, probably because of past hurt, and because she might've felt it was a little unfair to bring it up at such a sensitive time. But I decided that I needed to speak on it. As a man, I needed to face my fear and if we ended up not together, at least I would apologize.

"I wanted to just say thank you for today. I know you didn't have to do, especially in light of the way we left things, and the way I treated you. I was hurt and angry and said really mean and horrible things to you, and treated you in a way you didn't deserve. I'm embarrassed at my foolishness. You were, hands down, the one person in my life who loved me enough to tell me the truth about myself. The one person who was concerned about addressing my needs, not my wants. I was incredibly stupid in my behavior and I lost the best woman I've ever had."

She began to speak but I interrupted her. "I really need to say this to you. You have done nothing but make me better. You have shown care and compassion, love, mercy, patience, and grace to me. I'm so sorry I let my immaturity and insecurity get in the way of my sense. I'm sorry I hurt you. The last thing you needed was for me to disrespect you like that. From the bottom of my heart, I apologize. I know my words are worthless, and you don't have to forgive me or take me back or anything. But I just wanted to make sure you know that I really do appreciate you. You are an amazing woman. Thank you for everything you did, and for just being so amazing. I'm sorry I had to ruin it to understand just how good I had it."

Again, we sat in silence for a few minutes- though it felt like hours. I braced myself for rejection, knowing that I'd messed things up and that though she was an amazing woman who would be there for me in my troubled times because she was a Godly woman, she had her limits, and I probably had surpassed them.

"I accept your apology. I am glad I could be here for you today. I would never leave you to deal with this alone, regardless of our status. I had to make sure you were okay. But you hurt me, Solo. You cut me deep." She was tearing up. "I love you, but how can I trust you? Your words cut me to the core. You threw my worst fear about myself in my face. You shut me out, after begging me to let you in. I let my guard down with you, and let you into my son's life, and you broke my heart. Why did you do it?"

What could I even say to that? I struggled to find the right words to say. "I was broken, and hurt, and lashed out. I can't explain it away. I shouldn't have done it, and there is no excuse for my behavior. I was angry, and scared. Angry at my brother. Angry at my mother. I thought she loved him more than me. I was worried about being poor. So I worked. And I buried myself in my work so I wouldn't have to deal with my feelings. I was scared of loving you too. Of what I would have to do to love you the way you deserved. I thought money would be enough, and when you were making more, I felt like less of a man. I realized my mistake, and tried to apologize, but I understand why you wanted nothing to do with me. I respected your space before. But honestly, now that my mother is gone and I've lost my entire family, I cannot deal with any more loss. I refuse to let you and Peter go. Even if I have to fight to convince you every day for a year, and even if I have to persuade you, and prove it, I will win you back. I cannot spend the rest of my life without you. There is no one other than you."

I think she wasn't expecting all that I had to say, but she smiled anyway. "You have a lot to prove. Don't think you'll have it easy. And don't even think of playing the sympathy card." She smiled again. I took that as hope. I wanted to grab her in my arms and kiss her, but I suspected that it would be too much. But she basically told me that there was hope. I could pursue and win her over. All was not lost. I still had a chance.

We stayed talking for another hour, but soon she had to go, and as she left, another wave of people came over. My friends came, under the suggestion of Mari, to hang out with me so I wouldn't be alone. They joked, laughed, and ate with me. They opened Sabbath and did a Bible study with me. They stayed pretty late that night, but by the time the last of them left, I felt encouraged, strengthened, and even a little happy. That night, I slept with the all lights turned off.

D. Gloria Elysée

Epilogue
June 2015

It took two months to get off of punishment, but I finally got my woman back. It was partly due to my relentless pursuit, and Mari's wedding. Witnessing someone else's declaration of love always does something to you. And of course, and most importantly, I got her back because of God's mercy. Either way, I'm happy, and I am determined to keep her happy.

I'm also glad to say that I am now fully employed (with benefits- Hallelujah!) by the League of Lost Kings. Mr. McFadden was looking for financial investors, and had gone to my former firm to ask for my assistance. When he found out I no longer worked there, he called me, and asked what happened. I gave him the full rundown, and to my surprise, he offered me a job as a financial consultant at the LLK. Of course, I'm making less than I made at Court, Locke, & Stone, but it's a good job, with a great purpose. I don't even need to mention how much better it is than working in that call center. I'm now able to keep my mother's house, pay my bills, and even have a little to put in my savings account. Since the LLK is a nonprofit associated with my former firm, they not only regularly donate to the organization, but also invite their clients to make donations as well. My former company is inadvertently paying for (part of) my salary.

In other news, I'm getting married! Okay not officially. In fact, I haven't asked anything yet. It is way too soon. But I have asked Mari to help me look for a ring. I probably won't be able to pay for it all at once, with my tight budget, but I will make small payments. By the time I'm ready to ask (or more accurately, by the time I think she'll be ready to respond yes) it will be paid for. And since we wouldn't be living together, there'd be no way she'd find it at my house. Plus, I swore Mari to secrecy, and made her cite this under attorney-client privilege (despite the fact that she isn't my lawyer). So, when I'm ready to make that jump, I'll be prepared.

In all honesty, I know there's a lot for me to work on before I can make a huge step like that. I know I need to be a spiritual leader. A good, Godly woman like Grace needed a strong, Godly man to lead. Not because she wasn't strong and smart on her own- but because she needed an equal, and not spiritual dead weight. Too often, in the church, men are content in being bystanders as the women are active in ministry. There already are too few of us in church, since most young men leave the church when they reach adulthood. In fact, most of my friends that I grew up with are no longer going to any church. Many don't even believe in God anymore. The ones that stay in church often do because their relationship, parent(s), or routines dictate they do. Many simply show up, with no real desire to work, to fix the current state of the church, but they are the first to complain.

It wouldn't be so much of a problem if the Word of God didn't call upon men to be the Priests and leaders of their homes. How can you lead your family if you're apathetic in church? How can you lead a church if you are consistently absent from church in body and/or mind?

A rising problem in today's churches is that men are refusing to rise to the Biblical standard of manhood. One that requires a clear head, that he be in control of his emotions. It is a standard that requires patience, vision, and direction. One that calls upon man to be sober and not use any substances that will cause him to have a diminished mental capacity. The standard requires that he be a hard worker, faithful with money (and in his relationships), sexually pure, and even-tempered. He should seek the wise counsel of others, and should not be too proud to ask for help. He should put God first in everything, and make it a habit to pray regularly for wisdom, discernment, and purpose. The Holy Spirit should be his constant guide, and he should be a good listener, obedient, and humble. A man after God's own heart should have only one fear- that he will break God's heart. His motivation should be the love, grace, and mercy of God. This is the standard to live up to.

Jesus said, "But you are to be perfect, even as your Father in heaven is perfect."[82] **This doesn't mean that you cannot make mistakes. It means that your intentions toward serving God must be pure. Your relationship with God should not be based on what blessings/miracles/favors you can get out of it. Otherwise your obedience to God, your tithing, the way you treat others, etc., will only be the bare minimum. You'll look to do only enough to "get by." That is not what it means to love God. That isn't even serving God. That is using God as if He is a genie, enslaved to our will, obligated to fulfill our desires no matter how sinful they are. But that will only hurt you in the long run. We should be seeking His desires for our lives, the purpose for which we were created. We need to remember that we are not in control, no matter if He's called us to lead.**

Though we are to be the head of our families, God is to be our head as well. Some guys like to demand respect, demand authority, and misquote the Bible often to elevate and falsely empower themselves. That does *not* a man make. A man does not need to demand for his wife to submit. In the same way that if he is holding a position at work or church, should not demand obedience from colleagues and/or subordinates. A man who respects himself and holds himself to a higher standard will *automatically* get the respect he deserves from his wife (so long as she is a real (mature) woman). She will follow the lead of a man she can trust to make good, rational, wise decisions. Perhaps if she isn't following you, it is not because she is being disrespectful, but that you are not showing that you

---

[82] Matthew 5:48

make decisions that are beneficial. Perhaps your decisions are selfish, immature, limited, and/or unwise. In the same way, a man who is a strong leader has an air of authority, proven by his work ethic, humility, integrity, and vision. A leader without a strong work ethic will not gain followers easily. Those with integrity will not follow a visionless, lazy, dishonest and/or arrogant person to their own demise. No one in their right mind would follow someone to their own peril. That's just insane.

That's why I needed to do better. As a man, I needed to make sure that I was honest, had integrity, and would be able to lead my future wife and children closer to God. As a man, I would be responsible for the spiritual atmosphere of my house. If I did not lead prayer, or make family prayer a priority, my children would devalue it, even if my wife was to pick up the slack and do a daily devotion. If I wasn't visibly praying, reading my Bible, and seeking God, my wife would not be assured that I was following God. A Godly woman will not easily submit to her husband if he is not submitted to God.

In fact, there are many times where a man who is not submitted to the Lord leads his family into spiritual darkness, because he refuses to seek the Light. They are usually quick to claim Bible verses such as, "For wives, this means submit to your husbands as to the Lord. For a husband is the head of his wife as Christ is the head of the church. He is the Savior of his body, the church. As the church submits to Christ, so you wives should submit to your husbands

361

in everything."[83] **True, the Bible says that, but before it jumps into the instructions for wives, it says,** "And further, submit to one another out of reverence for Christ."[84]

Furthermore, it continues, "For husbands, this means love your wives, just as Christ loved the church. He gave up his life for her... In the same way, husbands ought to love their wives as they love their own bodies. For a man who loves his wife actually shows love for himself. No one hates his own body but feeds and cares for it, just as Christ cares for the church...Fathers, do not provoke your children to anger by the way you treat them. Rather, bring them up with the discipline and instruction that comes from the Lord."[85] **God gave instructions for the whole family. If a man does not love his wife like Jesus loved the whole world (enough to die for us), the standard isn't held up either. My job is to love Grace enough to die for her. Surely if I'm willing to die for her, I should be willing to pray with her.**

I can't call myself a man and be lazy. I can't neglect my family because I'm tired from working all day. I can't ignore their needs because I don't feel like I'm at my best. I need to be willing to sacrifice for my family. I need to be fully invested, and do what I can to make life better for them. This doesn't just mean financially. I wouldn't be a good husband or father if I decided to work so much that my wife and children never saw me. Part of the temperance that the Bible speaks about is about finding balance in work too. I could use the example of many affluent men in today's

---

[83] Ephesians 5:22-24
[84] Ephesians 5:21
[85] Ephesians 5:25, 28, 29; Ephesians 6:4

society whose spouses feel neglected. People whose children act out because though they lack no material good, they value time with a parent who won't give them adequate attention.

In addition, an overwhelming amount of young males are being raised without a constant, dominant, (positive) male figure in their lives. How can a young boy be expected to turn into a man without the positive example of a good man? Not even adding the "Godly" requirement, many guys don't have any strongly positive male influences, and are left to learn about manhood from the streets. Trust me, I know. My brother was proof. My father went to jail, and set the example for him. His friends taught him about what manhood was- sex with lots of girls, selling weed, drinking and smoking. My mom's pleadings for him to focus on his education and his relationship with God fell on deaf ears. There was no voice but her own asserting the need to do right, so the older guys in the neighborhood outweighed her pleadings.

As a result, Junior dropped out of school, fathered a child, and went down a path that landed him in the grave. I believe I was spared only because of my interest in church, and my fear of becoming my father and brother. The truth is, even with a father present in a house, that doesn't mean the son is getting a good example. Some fathers (even in church) are saints in public- loving, caring, kind, and helpful. And at home they are abusive, unfaithful, selfish, and mean. They put

363

up a good front in public, but are private nightmares. Or, the man is lacking in work ethic, integrity, and a strong moral compass. Or they openly embrace a lifestyle or vices that do not lend to healthy relationships with their spouse, or otherwise. And throw in the fact that many children are being brought into unformed relationships and unhealthy marriages, and you see a reason why young guys are not finding many examples of true manhood.

As much as it pains women to admit this- a woman cannot properly raise a man by herself. This isn't to downplay the many women who step up and take charge of their responsibilities- working, and taking care of their progeny. Neither can a man properly raise a woman by himself. God's ideal was to have a team that balanced each other, and provided the foundation for their child. Half the team (man or woman) will not easily produce the full desired results. Women and men approach parenthood differently. Women are generally more cautious, nurturing, and tend to be more openly emotional. They are most active in the raising process, so of course a woman can raise a well-adjusted man, but it is much less likely than in a two-parent household with a dominant (positive) man. The truth is that men take more risks, and teach their children (especially sons) that risk-taking isn't necessarily a bad thing. You'll likely see men roughhousing with their children, throwing them up in the air with no abandon, and you see the woman telling him to stop, because he's going to hurt the child. Restraint is needed in risk taking, but a man who is emotionally unstable and unable to calculate and take risks is not really a man.

Unfortunately, the emotional openness of a woman can really work against raising a boy into a man. A real man is in control of his emotions, even in the presence of a nagging, weeping, or argumentative woman. A man is calm, seeking to diffuse the situation using clear and rational thinking- not one who throws gasoline on the fire by not keeping his tongue in check. But a young boy who sees their mother behave that way follows the example set for him. And even worse, many single mothers tell their young sons that they won't amount to anything, they are just like their (deadbeat or criminal) fathers/siblings/etc. They take their own bitterness towards men and project it to their sons. Or, they emotionally stunt their sons by telling them that boys don't cry, and cause their sons to lose the ability to emotionally connect, remaining repressed until a situation causes them to explode. I've met many guys who have no clue how to relate to women, who cannot maintain a healthy relationship with a woman because of the way they were raised. They are emotionally unstable, immature, and sometimes openly hostile to women because it reminds them of the nagging, angry, bitter woman they were raised by. Few actually go on to change their negative views on women, and have healthy relationships.

I'm grateful that I had a mother that never told me that I was good for nothing, and never told me that my father was useless. One of the reasons why I love Grace so much is because I saw the way she was raising Peter. I had never heard her mention anything negative about his father, and both her and my mother leaned on God for their support. They understood that they had to protect the fragility of their son's' manhood by nurturing them and still allowing them their freedom to explore, take risks, and be emotionally open. They also did not stand for tantrums, but chose to foster patience, and self-control.

And Grace does the same for me (in another way). She allows me to be myself, and though she is independent, intelligent, and strong, she doesn't mind following my lead. True, she holds no punches and tells me the truth, but I know it's in love, and that she only wants the best for me. With Grace, I know where I stand as the man in the relationship, and I know that we are equal partners. She does not mind deferring to me, and I don't always demand that she does. I can feel at ease trusting her instincts and deferring to her, as I trust her judgment and see her as my equal. We are balanced, but she knows how to make me feel like a man, and I don't mean sexually. It's so much more than that. She's my peace, which is rare these days.

Manliness is such a complex idea. No wonder God didn't just leave it up to man to define the terms! Good deeds are extremely important, but character is the key to manliness. The best examples are right there in the Bible. But it doesn't mean that men have to be perfect. Most of the men in the Bible that we hear about (like Moses, David, Paul and Peter) had *major* character flaws. Moses was a murderer, but God used him to do great things. David committed adultery with another man's wife, but was still referred to as "a man after God's own heart." Paul persecuted the church before he was converted. He relished in it. Peter denied knowing God, so much that he tried to prove it by cursing. But the main similarity in all these men is that they allowed God to change their habits. They were willing to change, to become better. They knew there was more to life than working, than ruling, than what they could see. And they trusted God, even when it was hard. I'm trying to be that kind of man.

I'm not trying to spend my life being mediocre, chasing *things*. I've already lost some of the most important people in my life. I've lost enough to realize that not only is life short, but that my comfort cannot be in things, it cannot be in people, and it cannot be in myself, because all of it is temporary. I can only find my comfort, hope and peace in God alone. That's the only thing that separates me from others.

Truth is, if you want to be different, if you want a life that isn't rooted in the temporary, you need Jesus in your life. Trust me. With so many males calling themselves "men," we need to be different. We need to think differently, speak differently, act differently, and live differently. We even have to love differently. But we don't have to rely on our own efforts. God is everything we'll need to be Kings among men.

D. Gloria Elysée

"...For you are a chosen people. You are royal priests, a holy nation, God's very own possession. As a result, you can show others the goodness of God, for he called you out of the darkness into his wonderful light."

- 1 Peter 2:9, NLT

D. Gloria Elysée

No Better Than You

D. Gloria Elysée

This book is for all of the people who've ever been hurt by people in the church. You've been manipulated, judged, and attacked by people who've falsely represented God- but know that His true followers act in love, and not in hate, fear, or hypocrisy. Remember, He said, "I am with you always, even until the end..."[86] Know that you can <u>always</u> depend on Him.

---

[86] Matt. 28:20

D. Gloria Elysée

Prologue

My mother never wanted me. She told me so herself. "I should've aborted you like the rest of them." That's why I'm an only child. When she married my father, he said he wanted children and threatened to leave her if she didn't have at least one. She got pregnant with me and when I turned one, he left anyway. She pretended he was in the military, stationed overseas, and lied to everybody. Her fabrications were so convincing, her church friends would tell me I needed to find "a good man like him!" If only they knew the truth.

He was dead by the time I was six, and my mother began spinning another fabrication about her life. She joined the Genesis SDA Church: a prominent Seventh-day Adventist church in Boston. She became so holy that you couldn't tell that she wasn't born that way- unless, of course, you were me. She still did her dirt. Under the guise of "men's ministry", she began tending to the specific needs of the men in her community. None of those needs had anything to do with God, unless you count the "Oh God!! Oh God!!! Yes!!!" coming from her room as she "tended" to them.

Why she made me stay home while she entertained, I don't know. But it was as if she derived pleasure in having someone else there to overhear. And equal pleasure in calling me a little slut, telling me, "I know you enjoyed it. You dirty slut. You speak a word of this and I'll kill you." It was the same script I'd later hear from one of her regulars after he raped me. I guess my mother took too long to get back home from the store. I didn't even know he was there when I got home. He waited until I was in my room, changing out of my school clothes to attack me. The worst part was when my mother got home. She took one look at my bruised 13-year-old body and tattered clothes, and turned away to take him into her room.

After he left, she beat me for being promiscuous with her man. I knew then that there was no hope for me in the world- except for Jesus. That became my life. My mom lived a life of lies, so I would live a life of Truth. My mother pretended to be holy, but I was going to do everything I could to be holy. Little did I realize that the sins of the mothers could be visited on the daughters...

Chapter 1
August 2016

I stared at her blazer jacket. It was so ugly. But then again, she wasn't that cute to begin with. But there she stood, in the front of the church, singing like she had any business being up there. I knew where she went last night. In fact, that's where she would be returning tonight. The strip club in Everett, MA, where she worked. Now I'm not calling her a stripper, but I can tell you that whatever she did there was *not* Christ-like. I was surprised that she made it to church on time, seeing how I caught her coming from the club so late last night. I was on my way home when I saw her. The weekly Bible study at my best friend Carine's house had run late. I saw her getting dropped off at her apartment complex nearby. She didn't see me, though. I recognized the logo on the car that dropped her off. And here she was, singing as though she was saved.

I know what you're thinking, but I had every right to judge. I saw it before. My mother used to do some

truly ungodly things, and then she'd come to church and pretend she was high and mighty.

But you have the same problem. Don't you browse those porn websites? Or do those not count because no one else knows about it?

I shook my head to silence those thoughts. I needed to focus. After all, I was at church, and I needed to hear a Word from the Lord. But not everyone at the Genesis Seventh Day Adventist Church got the memo. Some of these girls- I dare not call them ladies, were in extremely revealing, tight, short, low-cut clothing. Their full makeup, complex hair weaves, and stiletto shoes displayed full-on Jezebel mode.

I wouldn't be caught dead in those outfits. I mean, who comes to church in that stuff? This is not a club, even though the praise team tries to sing those super upbeat songs, causing some of these girls to end up dancing (suggestively). It's all too ungodly.

There are a few "outfits" you own that few have ever seen. Do they not exist because no one *here* knows about them?

I had to focus more on church. These girls were bringing up all types of negative and unnecessary thoughts in my head. I could only imagine the lustful imaginings the men of the church were having! Talk about being stumbling blocks: they were stumbling mountains! The worst offenders were a trifecta of un-holiness: the Jeze-Belles. I coined the name to describe Heaven Brown-James, Marianne Choux, and Grace Principle. At least they weren't on the worship team.

But bad as they were, none were as bad as her: Kennedy Robertson. We had similar last names, but I, Gwendolyn Ann Roberts was <u>nothing</u> like her. I had class, and more importantly, I was a *true* Christian. I brought my attention back to the service. I needed a special prayer over my life so that I could find a good, Godly husband. I wanted to have children that never had to suffer the burden of a hypocritical parent.

My mother was sitting in the front of the church in her usual spot. As the praise team sang she sat stone-faced. She (except in the case of the men she slept with) was an excellent judge of character. Since the incident when I was thirteen, she'd slowed down on the male visitors, and was slightly nicer to me. I guess her initial reaction had worn off. During a church revival when I was fifteen, she'd come into my room and sobbed about how sorry she was, and how she'd failed me, and promised that she'd never let anything like that happen to me again. She vowed to never bring another man home, and swore off men. I was a child, so I thought she meant it. Now that I'm older, I think it had more to do with the fact that that day, I'd chosen to be baptized, and was asked to give my testimony. I was next in line to speak when they said that they had to move on to the next part of the service, so I never got to speak. But I can't imagine what would've happened if I'd actually gotten to tell that story that day. She was much nicer to me after that, and stopped bringing men home, so I guess she meant some of it.

But I <u>never</u> forgot her betrayal. And I knew that indulging in sin meant that I would be like her. So, I prayed, fasted, and made sure to keep myself pure.

But what about those experiences you pretend don't exist? Do you really think you're pure because you don't acknowledge your own sexual experiences?

I don't fall into the traps that these girls do. I thought Heaven Brown was a real Christian, but my mom was right about her. And don't even get me started on Marianne. And Grace? All I know is that she recently got married, but has a child that's like fifteen years old. He's eight. **Her husband Solomon had the nerve to choose her over my best friend, Carine. I used to think he was a man of God, but** *clearly* **he has no discernment.**

I faithfully served God, yet these poor excuses for Christians were proudly displaying their lust and immorality. I couldn't believe that Heaven and Grace had gotten married before I did! Heaven was a Jezebel and Grace was a teenage mother. Marianne had almost gotten married, but that was a disaster. Kennedy wasn't married but she's a stripper so I'm sure that's why all these worldly men were chasing her. Yet I, a good woman of God, with standards, morals, and virtue- am hopelessly single. All the men in the church were not interested in my chastity. They were turned off by my modesty. And no wonder why! The worship team was a display of moral depravity, and self-adoration.

You really talk a lot of trash about other people. Don't you know you're a sinner, just like everyone else? Why are you so bothered by their existence? Could it be that you're jealous of their freedom?

These women claimed to be free. They gave testimonies about God saved them from their corrupt lifestyles- but I knew they were lying. I knew they couldn't let go of their issues.

Why? Because you're still struggling with your sins? Maybe if you admitted them-

I couldn't believe how I let myself get distracted by these women. I needed to pray and cleanse myself from these thoughts. Anyway, I've decided that the best way to help them is to continue to be a shining example of a servant of God, to pray for them, and to keep them on track spiritually. Their resentment towards me is just proof that I am in tune with God. They hated Jesus and mistreated Him when He tried to save others, so naturally, I can only expect the same level of disrespect from these women. Either way, their poor treatment of me lets me know that I'm spiritually sound. If they want to ignore me and go to Hell, that's on them. I'm just doing my part till I make it into the Kingdom...

****

After church ended, Carine and I stood by the door while everyone was exiting the sanctuary. I wanted to speak to Marianne, since she was the Jeze-Belle most likely to listen to reason. Heaven was a lost cause, and

Grace wouldn't even speak to Carine anymore. It's not her fault that Carine pointed out her teen mom status to the church. It's the church's business to know what the members are doing while they're out there representing the church. But Mari, having broken up with yet another man, was ripe for the taking.

"Mari," I called. "Can I speak with you? Alone?" I pulled her away from the pack. I noticed she rolled her eyes when I called her name, but I know that's the reception I'll receive while I'm doing the Lord's work. "Mari, I've heard that your relationship has, for lack of better words, "gone asunder." Would you like to join our singles prayer ministry? We meet weekly for Bible study. I know it must be hard now that all of your friends are married-" She became agitated. "Actually, not all my friends are married. And it's none of your business what happens in my relationships. Why are you even in my business? Don't you have any of your own?" As she stormed off, I called out, "So, I presume that's a "no" for joining the prayer ministry?" At that, the pack of wolves that are her friends surrounded her and left in a hurry.

"Did you really expect that girl to join a prayer ministry? Look at her so-called friends. How can you expect her to have any kind of spiritual success with those girls around her? She'll never be of any use in the Kingdom of God if she doesn't stop hanging around that pack of wolves." My mother had walked up behind us. "Those girls don't even bother wearing sheep's clothing. They're wolves in whore's clothing. Bunch of Jezebels. Especially that Kennedy. Just like her mothe- Oh, hello Pastor!" Her tone had changed. Her voice now dripped with syrupy sweetness. Pastor Rogers was retiring, but he knew who he was dealing with. Her fakeness gave me a bad taste in my mouth, but she was right about Mari. She was right about all of them. They'd need to be handled in order for our church to regain its decency.

My church had been around for over 75 years. It was the first Adventist church in Boston, and was replete with prominent African-Americans from the area. At least that's how it was in the beginning. These days, anyone can hold a church position. Now that the older generation has been dying off, younger, more liberal (read: less moral) people were running the church. Granted, I'm only 32, but I'm still very by-the-book when it comes to the Word of God. There seems to be an ongoing battle between the few of us who want to keep the church holy, modest and moral, and those who purpose to use their "freedom" in God to introduce false doctrine and immorality into the church. As a result, people are leaving in droves and our membership had never been this low before.

The first time I spoke to Heaven about the attire of the ladies on the Praise Team, she seemed receptive. But the more I mentioned the immorality, the less patience she had with me. She believes that her liberality and the reckless oversharing her testimony is helpful, rather than constantly distracting everyone. She claims she's trying to save the church, while unwittingly destroying it with her nonsense. Nobody wants to hear about her sins. We all have our own problems. It's

almost like she's glorifying her past indiscretions, instead of being ashamed of them, like a real Christian would. You don't see me going around broadcasting my sins and telling people that it's okay to struggle! She's so misguided...

****

She doesn't get it. She's so used to feeling guilty that she doesn't understand that I'm her redemption. She actually resents My children who've accepted my pardon, and no longer live trapped by their sins. Doesn't she realize that the key to freeing others is in her testimony?[87] Doesn't she know that she can't ever be "good enough" to earn a place in Heaven? Only I can do that for her![88] If only she knew how much I want her to feel at peace. If only she was as willing now to tell her story as she was when she was first baptized. If only she would let Me use her instead of trying to do it all by herself...

****

I have a love-hate relationship with my job. I love what I do. I just hate the environment that I have to do it in. I'm a CPA (Certified Public Accountant) for a very reputable firm in Boston: The Barton Group. I am super meticulous, and have a record of excellence in my field. The thing is, though, my job is full of people who don't believe in God. The ones who do say they do believe are often non-denominational, and don't even have a church home. They say they are "spiritual, not religious." What does that even mean? These self-proclaimed

---

[87] Rev. 12:11
[88] Rom. 6:23

"Christians" can be found at every holiday party getting super drunk, and carrying on like they've never seen a Bible before. I attend only the mandatory work events (i.e. the abominable Christmas Party, and the company anniversary), but still I cannot believe the things I see. On top of all the debauchery, the office politics are even worse! These people have no integrity! They're willing to lie, steal accounts, and they gossip about each other mercilessly! I'm glad it's such a big company that I can just keep my head down and do my work. My coworkers learned early that I was not to be trifled with. I had no problem with going to my superiors to report misconduct, so most people avoided me. Once again, my honesty and integrity made people stay away. Everywhere I go, the world shrinks back. I guess that's the mark of a true Christian.

There are some perks, however. Since my firm does the bookkeeping for many businesses around the city, I get to network with many people. I guess my scholarship to Boston College wasn't wasted. I've gone to gallery openings, start-up business launches, and conferences for free, thanks to my stellar record. But it is not easy being a Christian amid a bunch of heathens. I try to keep myself away from any and all negative influences. So, I spend most of my lunch breaks working or writing on a Bible forum group I started online. A group of atheists regularly cause trouble. I spend most of that time moderating the comments, and responding to them.

The mark of a true Christian is their love for Me. Instead of being a light to those who don't know Me, you insist on judging them. People stay away from you because you are unfriendly, not because of your alleged association with Me.

Anyway, I'm due to go to another conference in a month. I'm headed to Tulsa, Oklahoma. For two days, I will represent my firm, and learn about innovations in accounting. I have the opportunity to learn about relevant software that is being unveiled. My company trusts me because they know that I won't embarrass them or spend too much money when I travel. I often try to stay someplace other than the hosting hotel, so it usually costs less to attend. I usually stay at the long-term stay hotels with a kitchenette. My company covers the cost of my groceries and I prepare and eat my own food. I'm a strict vegetarian so usually room service and hotel food don't suffice. I don't use the company credit card, so naturally, I'm the best choice for the conferences and seminars.

I was walking into work on a Tuesday morning, and ran right into my boss, Graham Parker Dotson. He was a short Caucasian man in his mid-50s who, despite his height, was rather attractive. He had ice grey eyes, a winning smile, and had dark brown hair, peppered with silver-grey strands. He started this firm with seed money from his father-in-law, and named it The Barton Group after him. He had grown up in South Boston without much money, but at Boston University (on scholarship) he'd met his wife. She came from old money, but fell in love with him despite his poverty. After years of working as an accountant in her father's business, he'd decided to begin his own accounting firm. She'd convinced her father to invest in him, and using her father's connections he built a small empire. I admire him immensely, because he is a true philanthropist. He lives in a (relatively) modest home (in which he hosted one of the company anniversary galas a few years ago). He also donates to charity regularly. He carries himself with integrity (even though he, too, is not a Christian). He is one of the only reasons I am still at this job. When he hired me, he made sure I didn't have to work on the Sabbath. He even lets me work from home each Friday unless there's an important meeting. I love what I do. I still don't like the work environment. If my coworkers weren't so Godless, I'd love my job entirely.

When I bumped into Parker (he hated his first name), he asked me to stop by his office once I got settled in for the day. I wasn't sure what this was about, but I wasn't worried. Parker never had bad news for me. Within twenty minutes, I was seated across from him in his office. He told me what a great job I'd been doing, and let me know that if I was to keep it up, another promotion could be in the works soon. This was music to my ears! I'd be able to run my department, and in turn, supervise my co-workers. I would finally have the authority to stop the foolish distractions of my coworkers. I could see it now- productivity would increase, and soon I'd be a senior manager, or even partner!

As I drifted off into my fantasy, I gazed around the room. I'd definitely redecorate it if it became my office.

The old, heavy furniture, solid oak desk, and dark plaid wallpaper were not my particular taste. I'm not sure they were even Parker's taste. I preferred a simpler theme: black and white with bright color accents. Black desk, black chair, white walls, and red throw pillows for the pop of color. Parker leaned in and gave me an intense stare. "Is that alright with you, Gwen? I know you like to handle these kinds of things alone, but this one is rather important, and I'd like to have more than one person on the ground for it. Would you be opposed to this?" I had no clue what he was talking about. I didn't know what to answer, because although I'd probably agree with Parker on this, I wasn't paying attention. I had no idea what was going on, and didn't want to agree to the machinations of my own demise. But I had no time to ask him to repeat himself, so I replied, "I have no issue. I trust your judgment, and know you wouldn't put me in an uncomfortable situation."

He looked at me quizzically- disappointed even. "I expected you to be a little disappointed about not going to the conference alone. But, I thought you'd be a little more excited about going to Las Vegas for four days." I realized that he wanted me to attend the American Institute of Certified Public Accountants (AICPA) conference with him. He usually sent an upper-level manager to the conference. He had never attended it himself. I had to fix this. "Not at all sir!" I exclaimed. "I'm actually more excited about going to the conference than the location. Vegas intimidates me a little, but I appreciate the vote of confidence of letting me go to the conference." He smiled. "Now that's what I like to hear. I'll set it up for us to go to the conference. I know that you prefer the extended-stay hotels, but the resort has an amazing chef and plenty of vegetarian options. It'll be fun, I promise! I'm not as old and boring as I seem." I nodded in silence, stunned, but managed to eke out, "Let me know when you get things finalized. I'll prepare in the meantime."

This conference, though a way to win major points toward my promotion, would be putting me out of my element. I was used to small seminars that introduced software for small businesses. They usually lasted one day, and were never in a place KNOWN for sin. Here I was, a Christian, going to SIN city. I considered backing out, but I realized that my character and integrity had caused me to be selected for this trip, and Parker was putting his faith in me. Usually, the associate who would go to the AICPA Conference would come back with stories filled with drunkenness and partying. I believe I was selected because it would be different with me. I would be a shining example of how an employee should conduct themselves while representing the company they work for. I would also return with a complete grasp on the updated IRS regulations. I could make connections with the premier software companies and accounting firms across America. On this trip, I would be a model employee. I would make it easy for management to promote me to a Senior Managing Accountant, Accounting Director, and eventually a Partner. Perhaps then I could instill some integrity and sense into some of these people. Whoever did not abide by the code of conduct I would implement would be terminated. But I was getting far too ahead of myself. I needed to get back to work...

****

Carine and I had tried to start a weekly Bible study for Singles Ministry, but so far only our friends Jessica and Melanie attended. They hadn't arrived at her house yet, so I took the advantage to update her about the conference opportunity in Vegas. She was not pleased. "You know, I've been meaning to talk to you about your job. All these conferences are a lot. What do they have to do with your job description? And now you have to go to the hotbed of sin for four days? With your married boss? I don't like it." I was irritated. "No Rina. I don't have to do anything. I'm going because this is what will get me promoted. And you know full well that I know Parker is married. Who said we were going to be rooming together? Who said that I was loose like those other girls at church? I'm disappointed in you. You really think that little of me? Perhaps I should rethink your advice you always give, because clearly your spirit of discernment is lacking."

Her face tightened, and her body became rigid. "It's just that you talk about him- your boss, Parker, a lot. And I don't know about this. You said upper level managers go to this conference alone each year, and now, it's you and him alone in Las Vegas? It just doesn't seem right, and you know what the Bible says- 'Stay away from every kind of evil.[89]' I'm just worried about you." I sighed. "I understand, but you know me better than

---

[89] 1 Thess. 5:22

that. These conferences show my boss that I'm a team player. Plus, I spend the least amount of money, and never embarrass myself. If I go, not only can I get promoted, but think of how much of an example I'll be to the others by not partying and getting drunk. This is an opportunity to live my Christianity out loud in front of my boss. I'm going, and it'll be great. And anyway, Parker's not even like that. He loves his wife. And I respect the sanctity of marriage, as if you didn't already know." She narrowed her eyes. "But I just feel-" "So you think I'm just going to sleep with him, don't you? Have I ever slept with anyone before? Whom have you heard my name associated with?" I was getting agitated. "I didn't mean-" "Yes you did. You assumed the worst out of my job situation, out of my boss, and worst of all, out of me. You insinuated that I'm a whore. How dare you!" She stayed silent for a moment. "Well I wouldn't be a good friend if I just stayed silent. I would be a worse Christian if I didn't warn you of the possibility. Plus, you like him. You just don't want to admit that to yourself. You fawn over the man like he's the next thing to Christ. He's *married*, and not even a Christian!

"Sometimes I wonder if you're really about this Christian life, or if you're like the other girls at church. Last year you told Melanie how wrong she was for having feelings for a coworker was in a committed relationship. You almost kicked Jessica out of Bible study when you heard that she was having romantic dealings with an atheist. You told me that my job was compromising my faith in God when I had to stay until

391

6:30pm once a month. You have been hyper vigilant about what the rest of us do, but how about yourself? Since when were you okay with SIN city? You went from calling your boss Mr. Whatever-his-last-name-is to "Parker." No wonder I think your judgment is clouded!"

I exploded. "I have done nothing but set forth a good example of what a Christian is. I have been kind to those heathens, and have worked diligently at my job. I am close with my boss because he is the only person at my job that does not resent my honesty and integrity. He encouraged the seminars and presentations because I cost the company less money than the other attendees. They order room service, go out for drinks, stay at fancy hotels, and party. I stay in an affordable hotel, get groceries, and make my own food. I am now being rewarded for all my hard work, and you have the nerve to accuse me of this nonsense?

"Do you know how hard I've worked? Do you know how other managers promote people who are lazy, and hedonistic, and undisciplined? You want me to throw away my job because I have a good *working* relationship with my boss? Or because I was given an opportunity only senior managers have been given? Well, which is it?"

She looked like she was getting ready to respond, but then reconsidered. It didn't matter much anyway, seeing how the others came in. She glanced in my direction, and then faced the others. "Hi ladies! I'm glad you could make it!" Her tone had turned syrupy-sweet. It was no matter, I'm sure how I felt was written across my face. In fact, the other ladies kept looking at me until

I snapped at them. "Since you all are so intent on staring at me instead of paying attention, why don't you share why you were both so late today!" They glanced at each other, and then at Carine. Before they could respond, Carine said, "Ladies, let's just all stay calm and lift Gwendolyn in prayer. She's tired and has just been given a huge undertaking for work. Don't mind her tone. We just need to pray." She grabbed my hand and held it. I wasn't sure if she was saying this to draw the attention back to her sermonette, or if she was being sincere. She looked sincere, so I took a deep breath, and after they prayed for me, I apologized to everyone. I gave Carine a hug before I left her house, apologizing one more time.

The entire drive home I felt agitated. I couldn't understand why Carine's comment had gotten under my skin. Why I was so bothered by her statement that I "liked" Parker? I only spoke about him when she asked me about work. She always talked about her boss, so how could she insinuate an unhealthy relationship between my boss and myself? She had stolen the happiness I'd felt about my good news today, and I was upset. But I also knew how she was. She was steadfast and her position on this wouldn't change. Still, seeing that she didn't sell me out to the other ladies at the Bible study, I knew she was still protecting me like a best friend does. It's just this time, she has no clue what she's talking about.

Despite her methods, Carine is trying to protect you. There's something strange about this trip.

I guess I'm sensitive to her accusations because I strive to maintain a good character and integrity. I hate when someone questions that. It is completely off base, and I don't appreciate it- no matter who it is. But I've decided that I'm going to be excited about the conference. It isn't until January, so I have time to look up non-sinful activities in Vegas. Perhaps, I can find something that isn't related to gambling, prostitution, witchcraft, secularism, or pornography. I may just stay in the hotel, swim, and watch my nature documentaries while I'm there. Who knows, I might find something worth my time.

Chapter 2
September 2016

It's been happening since I was asked to go to Vegas. Not every night, but most nights. I dream about Parker: and not just any type of dream. That dream. The pre-pubescent boy's favorite kind of dream. I've never had them before. Yes: I'm familiar with those particular urges. I've have had nightmares of a sexual nature before, but never this type of dream. And now to have them at 32, and for them to be about my boss? I'm truly unsettles. In my dreams, we have done the unspeakable. Multiple times. In multiple locations. Sometimes even with another person. And I am ashamed. I can't even look at Parker in the eye anymore. He called me in for a meeting because I hadn't sent in my weekly report on time. Since my sleep has been terrible, my work has been suffering. So here I am, sitting in his office, trying to avoid eye contact while he asks me if I am okay.

He told me that he considered me more than "just an employee", and that he saw much potential in me. He said he was trying to mentor me (including going to the conference with me). This started the flashbacks of my first dream, when I asked him to "teach me." I quickly made up a story about how I was having an issue at home, and it was nothing he needed to worry about. I knew I'd get over this whatever-this-is soon. When he asked me if I wanted to cancel my trip to the conference, I quickly said no. I would need this time away to help distance myself from this plague, and get back into work-mode. I must've answered with vehemence because he looked taken aback, so I softened my tone.

I needed to fix this issue, and quickly. I was tired and falling asleep at inopportune times. I even fell asleep in church! And last week, I slept through Bible study. And of course, I can't talk to Carine about this. She'd never understand, and she'd tell me I should quit my job. But I know this is just a spiritual attack from the devil, trying to water seeds that Carine planted. I blame her for this! My life needed to get back on track. I thought my job was finally starting to improve, and even my coworkers were taking notice. Too bad, it turns out, they were mocking my friendship with Parker, and were gossiping behind my back. I was used to this behavior, though, so I remained indifferent.

Couldn't these dreams just be a manifestation of seeds that were already rooting, but Carine's inquisition pushed them to grow above the surface?

I definitely need to get away for those two days. I will be bringing some of the work I need to catch up on with me, but mostly, I'll just be using Oklahoma as a means of relaxation. I leave the day after tomorrow, so I still have a lot to prepare. My phone rang, but the phone number was blocked. "Gwennie!" A sing-song voice was on the other end. It was my mother. She only called me Gwennie when she wanted something. And since she hardly ever called me, I knew whatever it was, she wanted it desperately. "Hello mother. I wasn't expecting your call. I'm still at work." "Oh Gwennie, I'm sorry. I didn't mean to bother you." She really was laying it on thick this time. "Gwennie I just need a small favor. I need to come stay with you for a little while. Just a few days. I promise I won't get in your way." My mom never stayed with me. Since I moved out when I went to college, she hadn't spent more than two hours in my home. Plus, I was due to go to the conference and I wasn't about to leave her alone in my house to go through my things. So, I offered to put her up in a hotel while I was away. I told her she'd be more comfortable at an extended-stay hotel. I paid for one week's stay at a nearby hotel, and with that, my peace of mind returned. I might've had to dip into my savings a little, but as long as I didn't have to share my home with her I would be okay.

I never got a reason as to why she couldn't stay at home, but the truth was that I didn't really care. I didn't press the issue. I called her back to tell her that I'd set her up with the room. My only requirements were that she could only stay for one week, and would have to get her own groceries. She seemed offended when I told her that I placed the room charge on a prepaid credit card. I only own it for situations like this- anything that involves my mother. Last time she asked me for money, it was for a rental car. She kept the car for two extra days, and my account was overdrafted. Since then, I keep a prepaid account around in case I have to finance something for her. I call it my "Mother-proof" card.

Anyway, I was all packed and ready to go. I was planning to get a ride to the airport, but Parker told me that he'd arranged for a town-car to come get me from home. He said that the firm could afford to spend money on "one of our best." Especially since I was "meticulous about spending less than the budget called for." I happily obliged. The great thing about the conference is that we are splitting the seminars. Parker is letting me get first pick (excluding one executive-level seminar).

I'm going to use the seminars to carve out a future for myself. I have a plan to partner with a computer engineer someday, so that I can create some accounting software. The hope is to eliminate or drastically shorten IRS audits. I also want it to be able to recognize when fraud is occurring in real time. Plenty of software can provide checks and balances, but none can do so in real time. They still need someone to review the data in order to determine if fraud or misconduct occurs. I would've never known that if I hadn't been asked to cover someone's place at one of the smaller seminars two years ago.

Since then, I've been learning about software, and trying to test-drive as many as possible for the company. We have a department which functions to test-drive data encryption and accounting software. Based on recommendations, they get trial subscriptions of these services, and input test data to check the efficiency of the software. Then, they make their own reports which we relay to our clients. There is a lot of software out there, and we only want the best for our clients.

Six years ago, when I first started working here, I was only interested in accounting. Numbers are far more consistent than people. Numbers only change with human influence and human error. They do not have one meaning today, and another meaning tomorrow. There are constant, and unchanging. Truthfully, my attachment to numbers, counting, and formulas occurred after I was attacked. Numerical problems always had a solution, even when they did not. They were predictable and constant. I dedicated myself to my studies, and joined every after-school program I could, so that I didn't have to come home before my mother got off work. The math team, chess club, and choir were my choices. In one instance, I even joined the school paper (though writing is not my strong suit). I just didn't want to be home alone again. I could've majored in anything in college, but the numbers were my solace, so I stuck to what I knew. This branching out into computer software is huge for me.

I am hoping that maybe in ten years, I'll be presenting my own software innovations at an AICPA conference. Of course, I told no one of this dream I had. Most people won't understand why I want to leave the "safe" "boring" life of an accountant and risk a venture into technology. But I know that there will be great gain in creating a numerical safeguard for business- including my own. I would be in control of my own

399

D. Gloria Elysée

destiny, and wouldn't need to depend on anyone for a salary or anything else.

Now that I was free from my mother, I decided to switch up my luggage a little bit. There was a trunk under my bed that I wasn't taking with me. I had made a crawl-space under the floorboard, but not all the items could fit. So, I selected my favorite items, packed them into my luggage, and transferred everything else into the crawlspace. I filled the trunk with linens. Even though my mother wasn't coming to stay with me, I couldn't risk her (or anyone else) "dropping by" and finding the contents of the trunk. It's no one's business but my own...

****

Be careful. It's better to eliminate hidden situations that create secrets, or else you'll have far more than a trunk-full. They pile up in ways you can't anticipate. Remember, even when you try to keep them hidden, they always come to light.[90]

****

Oklahoma was nice. Warmer than I thought for this time of year. There were no tornado warnings or watches. In fact, I forgot I was in the land of 1,000,000 tornadoes. I enjoyed myself. So, by now, there's something you should know about me. About the trunk. It doesn't contain anything crazy. I'm not into kinky sex or anything. I'm actually still a virgin, but I do like to dress up in lingerie and sexy outfits, but mostly inside

[90] 1 Tim 5:24,25

the house. And rarely I'll go do an amateur night at a sexy dance club. It's actually quite cathartic to stand in a room and take command of it. Before you judge me as a hypocrite, first you have to understand something about me.

This began when in my first year of the MS in Accounting program at Boston College (BC). One February day, while at work as a cashier at a grocery store, I saw my attacker. He had aged badly, but I recognized him as soon as I saw him. He didn't see me at first, but when I saw him, my chest started to tighten, and I started gasping for air. As the customers began to call for help, he looked around. As he caught my gaze, he stared right in my eyes, raising an eyebrow, as if he was trying to remember who I was. That's the last thing I remembered before I passed out.

I woke up in an ambulance. After hours alone in the emergency room, and countless tests, they informed me that I'd suffered a severe panic attack. A psychiatrist came by to speak to me, but when she asked me why I thought I was having the symptoms, I began hyperventilating again. One hour and a Xanax later, I was finally able to tell her what I couldn't tell anyone else: the truth. In all honesty, I was prepared to share my testimony when I was 15, but I think my anger back then had given me the adrenaline to attempt talking about it. But in the seven years since, I had yet to tell anyone- not even Carine. I told the psychiatrist about the attack, my mother's response, and then told her how

I saw him that day. She recommended that I begin therapy immediately, and put me in contact with counselors at my school when I told her I couldn't afford it.

I went to therapy for almost a year (once weekly) before I quit. My panic attacks happened every time I spoke about the attack. I was formally diagnosed with a panic disorder, stemming from a latent post-traumatic stress disorder. My psychiatrist, Dr. Desaris, prescribed Xanax at first, and then Prozac for the long run. I actually enjoyed speaking to someone other than God about this issue in my life. After about 10 months, she referred me to a sex therapist. I was hesitant, but Dr. Desaris assured me that this was legitimate. She said I should try it, to address the issues I was having (fear of intimacy, lack of desire to date/have male contact). Within three sessions, the "therapist" told me that I needed to "embrace [my] sexuality" and begin "testing sexual boundaries to develop a healthy sex life." She also handed me a long list of prescribed activities to "reintegrate sexuality into the living being." It was then that I saw the limits of therapy materialize. There was no way I would allow her any more of my time. God said to abstain from sexual immorality, and here, she said in order to be healthy I had to directly contradict the Holy Word of God. There was no way. I never returned. When Dr. Desaris asked why I had cancelled my appointments with the other lady, I was very frank. She insisted that I take it seriously and not be afraid. That was when I decided to stop going to therapy altogether. I just kept taking my Prozac until my refills finished.

Both of them made it seem like I was an alien for never having had sex or even kissed anyone, and for burying my sexual desires. What use were they if I wasn't married? What was the point of living for God if my so-called counselor was advising me to fornicate? Her first exercise I had already tried out: I had bought lingerie and worn it. I had to admit it gave me a sense of strength and confidence, but now she was pushing the limits further than what I was comfortable with. At that time, at 23 years old, living alone in an apartment I rented in Brighton, buying lingerie was not an issue. That's how I began my collection. She'd also included recommendations to watch or read pornographic material. She recommended specific books and videos. In addition, she emphatically recommended taking an erotic dance/striptease class. I chose the lingerie, as it was the most reasonable option, and no one would see it. Plus, it was the least sexual (to me). When I purchased my first set, I bout a large trunk to keep it in. I threw the paper in the trunk along with the lingerie and costumes, and eventually filled the trunk.

I had been discreet, ordering the lingerie online. That did help a little bit. When I'd wear it underneath my clothing I kind of felt like I had armor on. I felt like I was a woman- no Superwoman. I felt confident and in control of my life. No one would see this, but it was my secret protection. So, when a guy from school asked me to dinner, I said yes. Unfortunately for me, I wasn't prepared for what would come next. I thought I'd experiment, live a little, and try to branch out. I even

D. Gloria Elysée

tried tasting his wine! I ended up drinking two glasses-his, and my own. I don't believe it mixed well with the Prozac I was still taking, because things became fuzzy after that.

We ended up back at my apartment, and started making out. (My first kiss!) I probably wouldn't have stopped him on my own, but God had intervened and caused me to vomit the partially digested contents of my stomach onto his lap as he was trying to take my shirt off. That ended the night. He rushed out, and I went to sleep. I woke up the next day blissfully unaware of the memory of the embarrassment I'd caused. A few days later he texted me about going on another date, joking about the mishap. It was then that I remembered that night's events. I went out of my way to avoid him until he stopped trying to contact me altogether. I felt so ashamed and dirty for what almost happened. I vowed to not drink alcohol ever again- especially with the Prozac.

Unfortunately for me, the floodgates of sexual feelings I had long suppressed had been opened. One evening, while trying to find more lingerie online, I stumbled upon a porn site. I must've watched porn for the next 4 hours. As much as I wanted to look away, I was captivated by it. There was so much of it available. I cycled between binge watching it and masturbating, and then feeling guilty and cutting it out for months at a time. Soon, it went from being an occasional binge to a daily habit. It was almost like a drug- I had to have it, and felt high off it. Once it became incorporated in my life, I began seeking more stimuli. It began with chatting with strangers online. I created an alter-ego. With my anonymous online persona, I flagrantly expressed the sexuality that I was too afraid and ashamed to express out loud. At the suggestion of one of my new online friends, (and the recommendation of that sex therapist) I decided to try a strip-tease class.

I decided to try one in New Hampshire just to ensure that no one saw me. I took to it immediately. It actually helped curb my appetite for porn. I felt more of a high by dancing, and I didn't even feel guilty about it afterwards. I'd even stopped chatting with strangers online. Every subsequent Tuesday, I faithfully attended this pole dancing class. After about 12 classes, my instructor Kelly asked if I'd like to take a field trip. We ended up at a small, seedy strip club in the middle of nowhere called Sweetie's. I had never seen anything like it. She bought me a lap dance, and then asked if I'd like to sign up for amateur night the following week. Kelly told me that I had a special talent that she hadn't seen in any of the other ladies. She told me that I'd never feel more powerful than when I commanded the attention of everyone in the room.

I wasn't ready for this challenge, though, so I declined. I continued attending the class, but as my semester progressed, coursework became more intense. As a result, I attended the pole dancing class less and less until I stopped. A few months later, attempting to attend class, I found out the little dance studio had closed permanently. The flyer stating where the class had been relocated to had gotten destroyed by the most recent thunderstorms. So, I went to the only place I thought I could find Kelly: that seedy little strip club.

As it turns out, she was there, hosting amateur night. As the next performer came onto the stage, I noted that I had better dance technique than she did. When Kelly came by, she told me that she couldn't afford to rent out another studio for her class, and would be discontinuing the class altogether. She suggested someone else's class, but I wasn't interested. My time spent with her had given me the confidence to begin dating, and though it was unfruitful, I was actively participating in adult life again. So, when she asked if I'd like to try one dance, I said yes. As a final farewell to my secret hobby, I would dance on that stage. But first, I made sure there was not one recognizable soul in that place. Satisfied, I added my name to the list of performers.

I was super anxious, and wished (out loud) that I still had my Prozac. The girl next to me told me she could help with that, because she took Xanax for her anxiety, and handed me three pills in a small plastic baggie. I took one, and wrapped the other in a napkin and placed it my purse. I didn't feel any change yet, but rather than taking another, I ate a small order of fries while I waited for them to call me. They were terrible, but I had to eat something! I saw the other girl, Janet, and asked for a recommendation for a fruity drink, and let her know that I didn't drink alcohol. She told me to ask for a "Simply Sweet." It tasted like candy, and was so good I had two more. By then I was feeling super relaxed. I figured it was because the Xanax finally kicked in and I'd eaten something. I didn't know that the fruity drink was rum punch.

I had worn my favorite lingerie, so I didn't need to borrow an outfit for the dance. I did, however, have to decide on a stage name. I couldn't think of anything, so I asked Kelly to pick one for me. She wasn't much help, but in my inebriated state I came up with "Chastity Belle." By the time they called me, my drunkenness was in full effect. My performance was awesome. Something about being able to generate the lustful stares, and control every man in the room made me feel twice as high. Chastity Belle was born to dance, and boy did I dance! I'd even considered taking my top off, but though I teased like I would, I didn't. Kelly didn't call me her prize student for no reason. In fact, I made quite a bit of money that night. I even got a marriage proposal, but I laughed that away, still giddy from my performance.

Kelly noticed I was acting differently, and pulled me aside. I told her that some girl had given me a Xanax and that she told me to order a "Simply Sweet," of which I had three. She asked if I was okay and if I wanted to leave. I told her that dancing was so exhilarating that I didn't want my night to end yet. She asked if I wanted to get back on the stage, but I walked onto the floor, and saw girls giving guys lap dances. I pointed in their direction and told her that I wanted the full club experience. As I was scanning the room, a Caucasian man beckoned for me to join him. As I walked toward

D. Gloria Elysée

him, Kelly called out "Hey Short Stuff!" and mentioned that he was a "high roller." She told me that he was a regular, who would want to be taken into the back room. When we reached him she grabbed his hand, but he was staring at me. He asked if he could just take me into the back. She mentioned that it was my first night and that he would much prefer someone more experienced. But he was firm in his stance, so Kelly (her eyes narrowed) said sure and brought us into a private room in the back. As she was leaving, she called out, "Church girl, huh?" To him, she said, "Call me when you get bored with the first-timer!" To that, she left the room, and closed the door.

The man was attractive, though I cannot remember what he looked like. I was angry about what Kelly had said. But my focus quickly shifted to the subject at hand: my first lap dance (well, the first one I'd ever given). One dance turned into so much more, and soon, I noticed Kelly had returned. He whispered something to her, handed her a stack of bills, and left the room. She came over and said, "I guess it's *both* of our lucky days." She took me back into the changing room and told me to get my stuff. She said I was too out of it to drive, and so I'd be staying the night with her. She drove my car to her house. As I sat on her couch, she began fixing up the room: mood lighting, music, and setting up what looked like an ice cream bar. By now I was still a little drunk and was starting to get a headache. When I told her this, she said, "You're not about to ruin this night for me," and promptly handed me a pill. It didn't look like the Tylenol I take, but plus I figured this was the generic brand. Unbeknownst to me, she had given me ecstasy. I didn't know what was going on, but drank some water and started to feel better. I decided to take a quick shower, and threw my clothing in her washing machine.

When I came out of the bathroom, Kelly was exiting her bedroom tying a satin robe. I could see she was wearing a bra that had no cups, and panties that didn't have a bottom. I asked if she had something I could wear to sleep. She threw me something that looked like a bunch of strings tied together. I declined. She said, "It's his favorite." I didn't understand what she meant but was still too out of it to argue, so I nodded and put it on anyway. I had started to feel more alert in the shower, but due to my empty stomach, the pill she gave me was kicking in strong. She also gave me a robe, which I gladly accepted to cover up the stringy outfit. A few moments later, the doorbell rang. It was the guy from the club. She looked like she was expecting him. I certainly was not. As I started to panic, she told me to calm down, and handed me a drink. She told me to drink it quickly and it would help my anxiety.

The last thing I remember about that night was watching her undress, while he was untying my robe. The next day, around 1pm, I awoke with a massive headache and more questions than I could think of. The night before felt like a dream, yet here I was: alone, naked, and sticky on Kelly's couch, covered in a thin white sheet. The living room (other than where I was sleeping) was spotless. No one else was home. I quickly grabbed my clothes out of the washing machine and put them in the dryer. I felt gross, especially considering I had no idea why I was so sticky. I threw the sheets I'd slept on in the washer and took a quick shower. My whole body hurt. Everything was aching. I tried to use the bathroom and it felt like I was about to rip apart. It was even painful to wipe. When I looked down, there was blood on the tissue. I rummaged in Kelly's cabinets until I found a maxi pad.

I was less sure about last night than ever before. I couldn't remember anything that happened, but I knew it couldn't have been good. My phone was dead, so I put it on the charger. I looked around for a house phone, and thankfully there was one in Kelly's bedroom. I had to call work and tell them I was sick, since I was supposed to have been there at 10am. Thankfully, I had graduated a month before, so I didn't have to worry about school. After I got dressed and put the linens in the dryer, I remembered I had driven here. I searched the living room frantically for my keys. They were nowhere to be found! I looked outside and my car was gone! I had no idea where I was, and how I was going to get home. I decided to search the house for any clues. I'd just walked into the kitchen when I heard someone enter the house.

Kelly had returned. "Hey Gwen!" She smiled cheerfully. "Sorry I took your car. I had an errand to run, but look- breakfast!" She placed her groceries down, and handed me a paper bag and my car keys. Before I could even speak she continued, "I filled your tank. I hope you slept well last night. I know I did! Can you do me a favor and put these groceries away? Thanks. So, I have to be at the club in an hour. Can you drop me off? I left my car there last night. Oh, I have something for you!" With that she disappeared into her bedroom. When she returned, she tossed me a thick white envelope, and went into the bathroom. I put the envelope in the bag with the breakfast sandwich and went into the kitchen. The sandwich had bacon on it, so I placed it back in the bag and grabbed a banana instead. Something in me felt uneasy, so I put the banana back, and just proceeded to put the rest of the groceries away. I decided against eating anything while I was here. I'd pick up some fast food on the way back to Boston.

Moments later, Kelly stuck her head out of the bathroom door and called out "Can you turn on the TV and check the weather for me please?" I did. This June day was going to be sunny and warm. I still had another month before I had to sit for my CPA exam, so today was going to be a rest day. Studying could be put off until I recovered from last night. I continued watching the news until it was time to go. I grabbed the food, and the envelope and stuffed them inside my purse once I got to the car. I let Kelly drive herself to the club. During the 10-minute drive, she asked me how I enjoyed the "full club experience."

I said I could barely remember what happened, and asked her what she meant. She then described (in great detail) the undertakings of the previous night. The "high roller" who had taken me into the back room had asked her if he could extend the night. She detailed how

411

she had made arrangements for him to come to her house. She said that was why we left the club so early. When I asked her about why I couldn't remember any of this, she casually said, "Oh. It was probably the X that did that." I stared blankly at her. "X? What is that?" She laughed. "You know, Ecstasy? The feel-good drug? I knew you'd need a little encouragement for the threesome, so I gave it to you before he came over." My head was spinning. "Threesome? I can't have a threesome! I'm a virgin! Wait, you drugged me?" My head was spinning. "Well, yeah. You asked for the full club experience. That meant the pole, the lap dance, the threesome after the party, and the X. But don't worry. I told him you were a virgin, so we only did anal last night. Well, you did anal. I did everything else. No worries though, he used a condom. Oh, and you're still "intact," though I wouldn't say you're a virgin since you slept with both of us. But technically, I guess you are. By the way, your cut from last night is in the envelope. You did good, kid. You should come back next time."

I opened the car door and threw up (though there wasn't much to throw up). We had arrived at the club, and she had already pulled in front while we were talking. I began sobbing uncontrollably while I was still dry heaving. I felt another panic attack coming. I grabbed a water bottle from the backseat, and took the last two Xanax at once. I had to get out of there. Kelly stood outside, looking concerned, but then told me she had to get inside. When she asked if I'd be okay to go home, I had no words to answer her with. My breathing had calmed down, and I nodded, just before I peeled off.

I raced home, stopping only to buy some food and coffee at Dunkin Donuts. Thankfully, there were no police on the road, and I got home in record time. As I sat on my bed, I started going through my purse. I had forgotten about the bacon sandwich until I saw the bag. I remembered the envelope inside, so I put it on my bed and went to throw the sandwich away in the kitchen. I had charged my phone in the car so I returned to my bed and began to check for any missed calls or messages. While I listened to voicemail, I opened the envelope. There was at least $1,000 in there! I knew I hadn't made that much at the club. There was about $100 made up of ones, fives and a few twenties. And then a separate bundle of $2,500 with a note paper-clipped to it.

The note said,

"Worth every penny!

- Shorty!"

I was mortified! I cried until I fell asleep. I prayed and fasted for two weeks. I heard a sermon about how God doesn't blame you for the things that you couldn't help, and that He'll forgive you for the things you do. I decided then that I was forgiven, and that He understood that I was just trying to heal from my childhood.

The next day, I called Dr. Desaris and re-started therapy. I told her that I wouldn't be seeing a sex therapist, but that I did want to continue. I told her that I had tried experimenting with lingerie, and the dancing class, but that my panic attacks were not being well managed without my medication. She put me back on Prozac. But as time went on, she began to press me about my sexuality (as she'd done in the past.) I didn't want her invading that part of me again, so I pretended to have a "healthy" sex life just so that she'd leave me alone. I only had to go to routine appointments to renew my prescription.

Within a year I had stopped going altogether, but kept 3 full bottles of Prozac on hand in case I ever needed it again. Those also lived in the trunk. I never returned to that little club, and I deleted Kelly's contact information from my phone. In case you're wondering, I kept the money. I put it in a savings account, only removing my tithes and offering. (Yes, I still tithe, like I do on all my earnings). I add to it whenever I dance. Yes, I still dance once-in-a-while, but only on my out-of-state trips. I safeguard myself and make sure to never drink anything that I didn't bring myself. The high of dancing is enough, and I never want to have another "full club experience" ever again. I make sure I keep two pills with me, that I take before going inside, and only bring in my coat and ID. I only go to clubs that either keep the lingerie on, or only take off their tops. Yes, I have standards still. I may be "Chastity Belle," but I'm still Gwen Roberts.

I had started dancing again a few months after that experience because I wanted to see if I was cured. I realized that dancing sober (I was still taking Prozac) still gave me that original high. As crazy as it sounds, dancing (I can't call it stripping) helps me stay a virgin. I release all my sexual tension without needing another person to do it for me. It's all on my own terms, and if I feel uncomfortable, I just leave. It's really empowering, and I only need to do it once every few months. So, I save my tips and put them in that bank account. The account info goes into the trunk as well. I know God understands my situation, and that I'm only doing it to stay pure. But since I started having those dreams about Parker, I began watching porn again. This time, though, it's been harder to kick the habit.

****

Oklahoma was a nice break, and I even got to go to a club, though I didn't dance. I never dance when I'm in major cities- only in small towns. Since I didn't feel up to looking for a small-town club, I went to one in the suburbs of Tulsa and watched for about an hour. On my last night in Tulsa, I considered entertaining a guest, just to distract me from my dreams. His name was Mike, a patron at the hotel. I didn't care to get any information other than making sure he wasn't here for the same conference as I was. I simply needed a release. I stopped by his room, gave him a private dance (fully clothed). After making out with him for a little bit, I made up an excuse to leave and went my way. But it didn't do the trick. I wanted more. The high I used to get wasn't high enough anymore. I craved more, but I knew that I wouldn't cross that limit. I could dance for them, even take off my clothes, but I would not have sex with anyone until I got married. At this point, not even porn could calm down my hormones. In fact, it made me more frustrated than satisfied. Aggravated, I decided to go to sleep.

****

The dream was more vivid than before. This time, I saw myself, Kelly, and Parker doing the unspeakable. We were recording it on a camera and simultaneously watching the playback on a TV. It felt so real! By the time I woke up, I was a mix of hot-and-bothered, angry, confused, and guilty. I said a quick prayer of forgiveness and headed out to the airport. It was of no consequence though- I was headed back home, and would have to see Parker on Monday.

Chapter 3
January 2017

I stood in the airport waiting for him to finish checking us in. We had arrived separately, but I'd waited until he arrived to check into the flight. Parker smiled and handed me my ticket. "You ready? Security is over there!" He pointed towards the right, and began walking to the line. The past few months had been brutal, and last night I couldn't even sleep in anticipation of the trip. Finally, it had arrived- four days with Parker, at the AICPA Conference in Las Vegas.

At the counter, the attendant informed us that plane would be delayed due to a mechanical issue. He had managed to upgrade my ticket to first class so that I could sit next to him on the flight. As we waited, we decided to grab a bite at one of the airport bars. Service was slow, and I was anxious, but it was unnecessary- the delay was almost two hours. As we finished our meal, we heard the announcement for our flight to begin pre-boarding. It was finally time to go. The meal exhausted me, so as soon as we boarded the plane, I fell asleep.

Six hours later, we arrived in the desert. It was sunny and really hot out, so when we deplaned, I went to the restroom and took off the hooded sweater I was wearing. I had a T-shirt underneath, but the sweat had made it clingy. I contemplated changing my clothes, but decided to wait until I could shower in my hotel room. Because our flight was delayed, it took time to get off the plane (as our original gate was occupied). Then, it took forever to find the carousel with our luggage, due to our tardy arrival. Parker made a few calls while we waited at baggage claim. Thankfully, after we'd finally retrieved our luggage, a car was waiting to take us to the MGM Grand Las Vegas Hotel. It was beautiful! I was a bit overwhelmed, seeing how I'd never stayed in a hotel like this before.

Almost by instinct, I stood aside as Parker checked us in. I was busy scanning the ornate lobby when I heard Parker say, "What do you mean 'overbooked'? Both rooms were supposed to have been paid in full!" I turned around quickly. Parker stood, fuming. The hotel attendant said that though his two-bedroom suite was ready, my room hadn't been booked. Now there were no more rooms available. Apparently, the reservations were made separately, and his was paid in full at the time of booking. Mine was to be paid upon checking in. Since we were three hours late, they gave the room away to someone else. There were no available rooms because of the conference.

The man apologized profusely, but I heard nothing. I came all the way here, and now I was unsure if I could find accommodations. Of course, most of the hotels were full, or out of my price range. I would have to go to something farther away. Any other time I would've been fine with a less ritzy hotel in the outskirts of town, but this time I was disappointed. Nonetheless, I told Parker I'd be fine at an area inn. I volunteered to pay for hotel and travel to/from the conference if I was reimbursed when we got back to Boston. He told me he had a better solution. He offered me the second bedroom in his suite. "I have the extra room. There's no need to for you to have to go through the hassle of paying for a sub-par hotel, transportation, and a daily resort entry fee. Plus, it would be weeks before you were reimbursed by the company. You are more than welcome to stay in the second bedroom of my suite. Unless you are uncomfortable with this idea. It's entirely up to you."

I thought about it. It would be awkward sharing a "living space" with my boss, considering the dreams I'd been having about him. I also wouldn't be able to get around like I usually do on these trips. On the other hand, I hadn't planned on spending so much money, even though I would be reimbursed. Plus, I wanted to stay in the big fancy hotel for once. I felt like I deserved it, because of my diligence in being fiscally responsible on every other trip. My anxiety was beginning to mount, and the heat was sweltering. I just wanted to shower and change, and Parker's room was already available, so I decided to take Parker up on his offer.

Are you sure you want to do that? This is your boss. He is married. This is a violation of your professional boundaries. This could be dangerous, considering your current position. The inconvenience of staying at another hotel is a better solution than rooming with him. Trust me, it's not worth the potential consequences for either of you.

The concierge gave us each a glass of champagne while the bellmen were arranging our luggage. I refused, but Parker told me to "live a little" and accept the drink. I took an obligatory sip and placed the drink back on the counter. It took a while to get to the room since the elevators were so busy. During the wait, I had finished my glass of champagne. I had finished my bottle of water during the wait to check in, and I hadn't eaten since we'd left Boston, so I was starving. When we finally reached our skyline suite, I was tired, cranky, hungry, and a little tipsy.

I stood in the entrance waiting for Parker to choose his room. He was super friendly (and generous) to the staff, so it took him a little while to pick a room. I quickly went into the other room, dropped my things, and began to unpack. I just needed to lay out some clothes before I hopped into the shower. As I was in the middle of my task, I heard a knock at the door. "Hey. It's me. I'm just checking to see if everything is okay with you. You seemed a little distressed throughout this whole check-in process. May I come in?" I opened the door. "Wow, unpacking already? You waste no time I see!" I chuckled. "Actually, I was about to get in the shower, but figured I should find some clothes first." He paused. "Oh! I didn't mean to disturb you. Would you like me to leave?" "No, it's no bother. I'll just finish unpacking everything while we talk. And *then* I'll shower and most importantly- eat. I'm starving!"

We spoke for almost 30 minutes. I had finished unpacking in like 5 minutes, but we sat in my room and laughed at the craziness that had happened. When the subject switched to our extracurricular plans for the trip, I told him that I wanted to see a gospel show. He wanted to catch a Cirque de Soleil show. I told him I was most excited about the restaurants here. So many notable chefs had restaurants in the hotel. I wanted to try as many as I could afford since I probably would never return to the den of sin again. When I mentioned food, he exclaimed, "Oh no! You were supposed to shower so you could go eat. I'm sorry! I'll let you get ready now." As he walked away, I called out, "You should join me! We can figure out a plan for this week." He turned around and flashed me his signature (brilliant) smile before walking away. I never realized how white his teeth were before. Like gleaming pearls.

You are too invested in him. You should be treating him as your superior, but you are acting like friends. And flirting. Keep it professional and courteous. Nothing good can come from crossing this professional boundary.

In the duration of the conversation, I had forgotten how hungry I was. I showered quickly (and thoroughly) and switched my outfit twice before I settled on a cute dress. I did, however, put one of my favorite lingerie sets on. Sure, no one was going to see it, but I needed to feel in control while I was in Vegas. I was totally out of my element. I had no desire to gamble. No desire to see any of the millions of sex shows available. I just wanted to eat good food, and sit in the room and relax.

We ate lunch at one of the non-famous-chef's restaurant, although I wanted to go to Tom Colicchio's at first. I intended on going to each restaurant with a famous chef I'd seen or heard of on TV. I decided to make the reservations for all the restaurants I wanted to go to. I had saved up enough money to splurge on this. The food was great! Parker and I talked the entire way through lunch. There wasn't one awkward silence the entire time. After lunch, we headed back to the room to make a game-plan for the rest of our time there. As we sat in our little living room, I let him convince me to let him take me to dinner and the Cirque de Soleil on our last night. I also realized that I'd missed the gospel show since we'd taken longer than we were supposed to because of the check-in fiasco. I had budgeted my time to arrive/check-in, shower and change, and grab a quick bite before the show. In all the craziness, I'd completely forgotten about it, and now it was too late. I made the concession to go to Zumanity since I couldn't catch the show I wanted to go to, and plus Parker been so great to me.

****

The days had flown by and now it was our last full day. Parker had been a perfect gentleman all week. In fact, he went right back into "boss" mode. We were busy with the conferences so I didn't see him most of the day, though we did check in with each other from time to time. He wanted to weigh-in on the information I was gathering at the seminars. I wanted to go to the fancy restaurants, but the seminar schedule wouldn't allow me the time to go. He'd insisted on ordering room service so we wouldn't be distracted during our "business dinners." I don't know why I was so worried about sharing the suite with him. He was the consummate professional.

Today was only a half-day of seminars, so I went back to the suite to get ready for dinner and the show. I wasn't sure if Parker had remembered that he'd invited me (seeing that he'd made no mention of it since Sunday). When I walked into my room, he'd left a little note on my bed:

"Gwen,
Be ready by 7pm for dinner. Attire is formal. The show is at 9:00. There will be limited time to change after dinner, but you're welcome to change if you'd like.
-Parker "S""

I had a few hours to make myself "formal." I usually never spent much money on my clothing. I felt that excessive spending was contrary to the will of God, so (apart from the lingerie) I saved my money instead. I did have a few gala-worthy gowns at home, due to the events I am invited to attend from time to time. But I hadn't brought anything with me on this trip, so now I'd have to go shopping. And do something with my hair. I thought the last night would be dressy, but nothing on this level. Good thing I still had a few hours until dinnertime.

At the recommendation (and direction) of the concierge, I went to a nearby mall. I saw a beautiful black gown, but the neckline was too low, and it had a side split. Plus, it was a little too form-fitting for my taste. It was far too sexy for someone of my upbringing. I needed to find something that was less "come hither" for this dinner. Unfortunately, I became distracted in a store that had the most beautiful lingerie sets I'd ever seen. I purchased two lingerie sets: bra, panties, garter belt and stockings to match. I had very little time to purchase a gown before I had to return to do my hair and makeup. I could not be late for this dinner. So, I returned to the store with the black dress and bought it. I could stand to be a little sexier tonight. I'd still be far classier than many of the other women milling around Vegas anyway.

****

The dinner was amazing. We'd been seated at a table with two CEOs and their wives. It appeared that the men all knew each other, and were quite nice, but the women weren't very friendly, so I didn't interact much with them. The conversation about investment ventures seemed to bore the other ladies, but I happily chimed in. Parker had taken the liberty of ordering drinks for the table. He'd ordered wine for me (I didn't want to embarrass him by saying no, so I politely sipped), and a bourbon for himself. The night took a turn, however, when the men began challenging each other. The wives dismissed themselves, but having nowhere else to go, I stayed and included myself in the boy's club. During the conversation, I ordered dessert, finished my wine, and had another glass. I was tipsy. I still had my sensibilities about me though. Parker and I then left to go to the show.

When Parker had first suggested the show, I went online and researched Cirque de Soleil. It seemed like a circus-themed acrobatic performance, so I wasn't too worried. I probably should've looked up this particular show. Zumanity was basically a beautifully choreographed orgy. I had difficulty keeping up with the going-ons of the show due to my inebriated state. As much as I hated the show, my body loved it- I was super turned on. And I wasn't the only one. I found myself inching closer to Parker, and he toward me throughout the night. His hand had accidentally grazed mine, sending a chill up my spine. It didn't help that I was freezing, because the air conditioner was on. Somehow his hand ended up on my thigh, and was working itself up.

When the show was over, embarrassed, I jumped and ran to the awaiting car. I was more embarrassed at how much I liked his hand placement, and that I did nothing to stop him. Mostly it was that had the show not ended, I wasn't sure I would've stopped him. I didn't want to- I liked it so much. I guess he had a headache too, because he took two pills once he got in the car. The drinks had worn off and my head was throbbing so I asked for two as well. He looked at me quizzically, with an eyebrow raised, but he said nothing. I stuck my hand out, so he handed them to me and watched me swallow them down (with no water).

The car ride back was silent until we reached the hotel. Once inside the suite, however, that changed. He began apologizing profusely, to which I quickly told him it was okay. Truth is, I wanted him badly, and felt guilty knowing he was married, knowing he was my boss, knowing that I was failing God. Maybe it was the way he was staring at me, or the wine that I'd consumed, but my resolve was diminishing by the millisecond. I ran into my room, determined to change quickly and put on the least sexy thing I owned. Unfortunately, he followed me and caught me, dress lowered, in the new lingerie I'd just bought. From the look in his eyes I knew- I would no longer hold claim to the title of "virgin" after tonight.

****

The flight home was uneventful. At least on the surface. Once again, Parker had me bumped up to first class, and I was seated next to him. But this time he was the one fast asleep. Meanwhile, my mind had never been so active. I kept playing the previous night's events in my head. I was no longer a virgin- officially. Since no one else knew about what happened with Kelly, (and she assured me that nothing vaginal had occurred) I could still claim my virginity. But last night made sure that I could never claim that status again. Parker and I had had sex multiple times last night. And I hated myself because not only did I thoroughly enjoy it, but I wanted more. I couldn't shake the thought that I was an adulterous whore. It made me want to burn my lingerie, swear off alcohol (like I was supposed to have already done), and lock myself into a literal chastity belt.

The passionate throes of last night had stirred up memories of a distant past. The night with Kelly was at the forefront of my mind, along with a persistent nagging feeling that I couldn't place. Dismissing it, I tried to force myself to fall asleep. My head was throbbing from the prior night's events, and I knew I needed to make it home in one piece.

I awoke to a hand on my breast. Apparently, Parker had decided that he wanted to rekindle last night's flame. I, however, was neither that drunk, nor that stupid (again). When I pulled away, he looked surprised, and then with a knowing look, said, "True to form, you never change. Chastity Belle, you are still the same minx you were all those years ago." My stomach did a backflip and dropped to my toes. "H-How do you-? Why do you-? Why did you call me that?" I stammered, shocked. "Oh, come on!" He whispered, "I met you years ago! Don't act like you forgot! It's me, Shorty!

427

Don't you remember? From Sweetie's! We had so much fun that night. You were my best yet! After that, I tried to get Kelly to find you, but you'd disappeared. I thought I'd never see you again, but then you popped up for that job interview."

He continued, "You looked so familiar, but I couldn't place you. It was only until a few months later, while watching the tape, that I realized who you were. I played along this whole time, thinking you just didn't want to mix business with pleasure. And I respected your decision to act like it never happened. But you devilish little minx! You knew exactly what I wanted. You kept dropping hints! You were so enthusiastic when you agreed to come to Vegas with me. Showing me your sexy lingerie while you were unpacking, and that dress last night! I knew you wanted me too! That's why you didn't pull away from me at the show. That's why you asked me for the Ecstasy. That's why we couldn't stop ourselves last night. We're magnetic, you and me. We couldn't stay away from each other if we tried. You know, I still have the video of us from that night! I wish we made a new one last night."

At this, I began hyperventilating. Parker, my married boss, was Shorty, the man I couldn't remember from that encounter all those years back! This was my nagging feeling. This was what I was being warned about. As my panic attack grew, and a flight attendant was called over, I grabbed my purse and took my Prozac. I suspected I'd need one today, but didn't know that I'd need a double dose! "Are you okay?" the flight attendant asked. I couldn't even look past him at her, let alone look him in the eyes but I nodded, grabbing the paper bag to breathe through.

He waited until the flight attendant walked away before he began speaking again. "Was I wrong? Do you not want this? I thought we were on the same page. You mean to tell me that you really didn't know it was me this whole time? That you forgot that night? I thought you were just trying to be coy." I shook my head, "no." "I didn't know. I couldn't remember anything from that night. All I knew was it was some guy name Shorty, and that Kelly slipped me some kind of drug. I have almost no memory of that night. I did have some confused feelings at the show last night, but this can't continue. I'm already a whore in God's eyes. You're married! And you're my boss! This would be a disaster if it continued. It simply isn't worth the consequences. And what do you mean I asked you for Ecstasy? Those weren't pain pills? I had a headache! Those were drugs??" "I thought you knew! Why do you think I looked at you like that when you asked?" I was stunned. "I just had a headache. And then you came into my room while I was changing. I just wanted to put on my sweats and go to sleep. I should've closed the door. I- wow. I don't even know what to say."

He sat back, deep in thought. He seemed very disappointed. "So that whole thing with the lingerie last night was an accident? This whole time you weren't just playing innocent? No. You wanted me too. I know that much. It was definitely mutual. You practically tore my clothes off my body. You should've seen the look in your eyes. And you were so receptive, and loud! It was amazing. We can't just stop now. Plus, the damage is done, so there's no harm in keeping this going. The sex was amazing. It'd be a crying shame to deprive ourselves of great sex just because it was an accident the first time. Do you really want to say no to the greatest sex of your life?" "You're the *only* sex of my life, and you're married. I wanted it- yes, but not at this cost. So, yeah. No. This isn't happening. Ever again. It should've never happened in the first place- even back then. In fact, I'm going to need a week off. I need to pray. Oh, God! What have I done?" He seemed put off by my reaction, but I had no care or concern for his ego. I had real problems to deal with...

****

I fasted for every day that week until 6pm. I ate no food, drank no water, watched no TV, stayed away from the internet. In fact, I stayed away from everyone- including Carine, my mother, and the church as a whole. This was the first time in years that I'd missed church. Carine called, asking why I'd missed Bible study and church. I told her I was under the weather- but highly contagious, so she wouldn't try to come by.

I knew that missing church seemed counterintuitive, but I couldn't go without getting my life right with God first. I had to fix this mess. And most importantly, no one could know about this. I couldn't believe I was back in this situation again. The alcohol had gotten the best of me again. I felt so disgusting. And dirty. And worse, I still wanted Parker. I craved sex with him again. In fact, it was a battle to not email him during my time at home. I was confused, aroused, and completely enveloped in shame.

You still don't get it. You can't get right and *then* come to me. I'm the <u>only</u> way you can get right in the first place. Don't try to blame this on the alcohol. It was just a vessel you used to do what you really wanted to do in the first place. You made small, seemingly insignificant decisions that led this to happen. This started long before you'd taken any drinks, or swallowed any pills. You have to own up to your desires or else you have no chance of ever controlling them. You have to trust Me. Stop fighting on your own, and trust Me.

I'd considered calling out for another week, but knew it was time to face the music. Running away hadn't help thus far, and would only make things more difficult in the long run. I had a job to get back to, and hopefully Parker wouldn't make it awkward.

****

I returned to work feeling extremely apprehensive. I took a Prozac before I left home, and planned on taking another before the day was half done. Thankfully, Parker was professional, and left me to do my work. In fact, he had emailed me the projects I needed to work on, and left me to it. All I had to do was either email him the necessary items or drop off the information to his assistant. He made it so that we didn't have to see or speak to each other the entire time.

For the next few weeks, I'd be working independently. My anxiety finally subsided when an office announcement stated that Parker would be on vacation for the next month. With him gone, I would be able to breathe easy, and get back to normal on my own terms, at my own pace. My prayers had been answered. I would soon be free.

Chapter 4
March 2017

"You've got to be kidding! Please say you're joking right now!" I stared in disbelief at her. Dr. Plarta looked surprised. "I wouldn't joke about this. You had unprotected sex. How could you- an educated, cultured woman, not consider this a possibility? Did you wear a condom? Did you take the morning-after pill? You need to get tested for everything." I began to hyperventilate. "Gwen, I need you to calm down. Breathe deeply. It's okay. You'll get through this." But I wouldn't. After telling her everything that had happened, she'd given me the news I'd feared most. I was six weeks pregnant- an unfortunate by-product of my tryst with Parker.

I hadn't even considered the fact that he might not have been wearing a condom. It never crossed my mind. In fact, I'd tried so hard to pretend that it never happened, that I never went in for a check-up. I had spent all my time trying to forget. When I started feeling ill, I assumed it was a virus. I only came in because my symptoms got worse. I wanted to make sure that it wasn't a result of the cold medications counteracting with the Prozac I was taking. And now I was facing this.

I had no idea what I wanted to do. You would think my reaction would be, "I guess I'm having this baby," but it actually was a horrified, "I can't have a baby. What will everyone say? I can't have this baby!" The fact that I was considering an "A-word" made me vomit. It could've also been the combination of the morning sickness and the terrible news. Or realizing my extreme lapse in judgment I'd been exhibiting for a while now. Either way, I was pregnant, and had a few decisions to make.

I couldn't believe I was in this position. After everything I had done to make sure that I stayed chaste, I'd failed God miserably. And now I had this to add to my burdens. I wanted children, but just not right now, as I was unmarried and nowhere close to being in a relationship. My head was reeling with questions. What would people say? My mother would sure have a ton to say about this. I wouldn't be able to show my face in church again! I'd be a disgrace, and surely, my mother would make me pay for ruining her good name in the church. How would I take care of a baby? Sure, I made enough money but that was beside the point. I couldn't be a mother. I had goals.

Each question brought up a new question. And then the realization sunk in: the father of this child was Parker, my boss. My _MARRIED_ boss. I began sobbing. Dr. Plarta had left the room to get me some information (and crackers). She returned to find me crouched on the ground, in the fetal position, sobbing and dry heaving. After about 15 minutes of her less-than-helpful platitudes, I pulled myself together and left. As I was on my way home, my mother called. I let it go to voicemail, however she called back. I thought about not answering, but if I didn't respond, she might have the idea to drop by the house. That was the last thing I needed, so I answered. "Were you screening your mother's calls?" This was already a bad start. "No mom, I was getting into my car, which is why I missed your call. What's going on?" I was tired of her already. "How are you? Is everything okay with you? I heard you were sick." She almost sounded like she cared. "No mom, I'm fine. Just a little virus, but I'm okay now." "You shouldn't be by yourself when you're sick. I'm coming to stay with you for a month, so you can recuperate properly." A month? She must have lost her mind. "That won't be necessary mom. Like I said, I'm fine. But I would like to know why you can't stay at your house for a month."

That angered her. "Who said I can't stay home for a month? Here I am, showing concern for the well-being of my only child, and you're accusing me of ulterior motives. You are such an ungrateful child. You are so selfish and self-centered! Why do I even bother trying to be such a good mother to you? I-" "That's *enough*, Mother." I cut her short. "I don't have time for this. You're going to have to figure out your living situation out, and solve your own problems. I don't have the patience for your shenanigans anymore." She became irate. "You are so disrespectful! What did I ever do to deserve a child like you? I've been a good mother to you! You know you can't get into Heaven if you keep disrespecting me, right?" That was the last thing I'd heard as I hung up the phone.

435

D. Gloria Elysée

I was grappling with the possibility of parenthood, and my mother only solidified my confusion. If I ever thought I would become a mother like her, I'd tie my tubes immediately. I could never have this child if it meant that the child would be subjected to my mother's antics. And she had the nerve to ask what she deserved to have a daughter like myself. What, indeed? But the better question was how an evil hypocrite like her could end up with a daughter like me. I'd bailed her out financially, backed her up, and prayed for her when everyone else would've just turned their backs already. She's lucky- no <u>blessed</u> to have me.

I could never think of bringing life into this world if she would be anywhere even breathing near it. I hadn't forgotten who she was for a moment. Even though she was my mother, her betrayal was something I'd never forget. She had let her boyfriend rape me and then defended him. She treated me like a whore, while lying to everyone else about her own whoredom. She constantly expected me to cosign her antics, and was completely corrupt. That made me sure that no child of mine would EVER be left alone with her. She had some nerve trying to rewrite history! She acted as though she'd been a saint, an innocent mother victimized by her malicious daughter. And to tell me of all people that I wouldn't get into Heaven! She should be the last person trying to condemn anyone else. As I drove the rest of the way home, I fumed and vented my anger towards the other drivers on the road. But when I finally reached my apartment, I was exhausted. Unfortunately for me I was having difficulty sleeping (at night- that is).

My mother's insinuation that I was a bad daughter left me livid. Her insistence that I'd be barred from entering the Kingdom of God was preposterous. But there was a nagging feeling in my gut that she was right about one thing- I was selfish. My entire condition was because of an unspeakable indiscretion with my boss. He knew nothing of my current state, but however undecided I was, I figured it's be best to try and speak to him about it. I'd have to wait until he'd returned from his trip, but I needed to tell him face-to-face. I wanted to keep this child, and do the right thing by God and raise it. But it was a daunting possibility to consider undertaking. I was unwed, and the child was the result of a tawdry (yet brief) affair with my married boss. Things couldn't have been worse for me right now! Or, at least, that's what I thought...

****

You spend so much of your time organizing and attending prayer groups and church, yet at the time you need Me the most, you don't even consider Me as an option. I'm trying to be here for you, but you need to acknowledge Me so I can help you. I know you're scared and don't know what to do. But "[come] now, let's settle this....Though your sins are like scarlet, I will make them as white as snow. Though they are red like crimson, I will make them as white as wool."[91] You don't need to be afraid- I got this. You are mine, and there's no

---

[91] Isa. 1:18

437

changing that. Just come talk to me. I promise, I'll make things better for you. Trust me. Or at least just talk to me.

****

His mouth was agape. His eyes, glossed over like he'd just been in a terrible accident, narrowed. "There's no way it's mine. Absolutely not. My wife and I tried for years, and she never got pregnant. It can't- No! There's no way! You're lying! What do you want? Money? Is that what this is about? You're really trying to blackmail me?" I knew Parker wouldn't be happy about it, but I didn't expect this! "You realize that about two months ago, I was a virgin, right? Before we went to Vegas and did the unspeakable," I replied. "I've never had sex with anyone else. You think this is about money? I'm scared out of my mind, and you think I'm trying to extort you? Parker, I would never do that to you. Plus, I'm a Christian. We don't do those things." He snorted. "Christians definitely don't do what we did that night, and especially not virgins. You forget, we've met before *Chastity*. You can keep your virginal Christian scam to yourself. I know that baby isn't mine. You can go pawn that bastard child onto someone else. Now get out of my office before I make you wish you never worked here!"

It was a quiet, whispered snarl, but vicious indeed. I'd never seen Parker like this before. He was shaking. Sweat glistened off his brow, and his face was contorted in a grimace that made him resemble a monster. He *was* a monster. This was not the same man I'd shared that passionate night with. And definitely not the sweet, caring, friendly boss I thought I'd become close with. Whoever this was, I did not recognize. I stood my ground and stared into his eyes. "All I wanted to do was tell you what was going on with me, and let you know I plan on keeping the baby. I didn't want anything from you. I still don't. But let me be clear. You were the one who initiated sexual contact. You were the one who invited me to share your hotel room with you. You did. Not me. So, don't even think of putting me in a position where I have to fight you. I *will* win. The paternity test itself with exonerate me. Now, if you'll excuse me, I'll be leaving now."

He jumped out of his chair, and ran to stand in front of the door, blocking the exit. "This is one fight you will lose. I have the receipts from the hotel. You know, from the room you chose not to sleep in?" My face must've looked confused, because he smirked. "Oh, the mix-up at the hotel? Never happened according to this document." He went to his desk and grabbed a paper from it. He was right. The record said I checked into my room, and checked out according to the duration of the Vegas trip. Confused, I stammered, "H-h-how?" He chuckled. "Simple! I had your hotel booked at the same time mine was, and I even checked you in when we got to the hotel. I have the concierge a little "incentive" to "lose" your reservation, and told him to play along. I wanted to see if you would agree to stay with me in my suite. I figured that since you were always flirting with me, you might want to rekindle what we had that night at Sweetie's. I thought you could use a little "encouragement," so I made up the room issue to test and see what you really wanted to do. When you agreed to share the room with me, I knew it was because you wanted me as much as I wanted you.

"Your room was always there. If you had insisted on booking your room elsewhere, the concierge would've "magically" offered you your original room. But I *know* you wanted me then and now, and you know it too. Now you're coming up with this story to blackmail me but it won't work. It will be your word against mine. Oh, and you try to bring up this child, or sexual harassment, or anything of the sort, I will sue you for libel. Everyone here sees how you've thrown yourself at me. How you flirt with me and call me "Parker" instead of Mr. Dotson, like everyone else. No one likes you here. They'll be quick to dismiss you like some disgruntled stalker. Furthermore, if you sue me for paternity, I will sue you for full custody of the bastard and win. And I'll make sure you never see it again. You'd be better off just getting the abortion."

I was shocked. This was surreal. I told Parker, "You are evil. Pure evil. I suggest you begin looking for my replacement and consider this my notice. I assume I'll be getting a decent severance package for my trouble." "The only severance you can expect is being blacklisted from all the other firms in Boston. That is unless, of course, you are willing to sign an attestation absolving me of paternity of the child. It also requires for you to bring documentation of an abortion. Plus, a nondisclosure agreement that states that you won't pursue this matter in the future. Then you'll not only get severance, but my glowing recommendation. Don't worry. I'll have the papers drawn up by tomorrow," he responded.

He'd switched again from a monster to a charmer, but I knew the snake that lay beneath the attractive exterior. I'd be able to walk away from this situation if I signed away my life on the dotted line. But I didn't want anything to do with him at all. I walked away with my head high, until I reached my car in the parking lot.

I collapsed in a barrage of tears, unable to regain composure until an hour had passed. How did I get myself into this mess? I try to be a good Christian, a good employee. I faithfully tithe. I do my best to stay away from gossips and the ungodly. How did I find myself in this situation? Who could I go to with this problem and honestly get help? Maybe Carine. She'd probably judge me a little harshly, but she's a real friend.

I knew I needed to call someone, but I really couldn't think of anyone. Everyone would either ask too many questions, and I was too fragile to let Carine know right now. I needed someone neutral- like my former psychiatrist. Somewhere I wouldn't get any judgment. But I had burned ties with my psychiatrist. I had one too many no-shows, inconsistent attendance, and a general disregard of her counsel. I no longer felt welcome, though legally she couldn't say it. I'd have to seek out new counsel if I wanted someone.

****

You could always just come to me. You don't have to do this all on your own. I told you that you are not alone in anything you do.[92] I'm always here for you. Why do you continue to ignore me and suffer by yourself? Don't you know that I can heal you? That I can free you? That I can save you? Only I can give you the strength to have this child, and face the storm ahead of you! Don't try to do this all on your own. Please don't do it like this...

****

But my issue lay deeper than conversation could handle. I needed someone to tell me what to do. I needed someone to tell me that my feelings were valid, and that I wasn't an evil person for considering the "A-word". But I wouldn't find that today. I'd have to pray instead, and hope that God didn't smite me for not quite considering this fetus a blessing. I'd always been pro-life, staunch and enthusiastic in my support of fetal life. I believed that life began at conception, and that every child was a blessing from God. It was a responsibility that was given to few. There were so many women in the world who were barren, and spent all their time, money, effort, and emotion trying to conceive. Women who'd cried bitter tears because of their infertility. And here I was, a champion of fetal rights, disappointed, no-repulsed by my own pregnancy.

I couldn't bear to think of the fetus as my baby, my child, my own. Emotional detachment hat pervaded

---

[92] Deuteronomy 31:6; Hebrews 13:5

my perception of this pregnancy. Guilt overshadowed the situation. Disgust at myself and Parker clouded my judgment. Lastly, there was a selfish nagging thought of the inconvenience this life would bring. I couldn't stop thinking of the damage it would inflict on my lifestyle and reputation. I could not think of this child as a reality. I could not think of this child as a child. It was a fetus, a surprise guest at a party to which I'd invited no one. A parasite of sorts: unreal, unimaginable, unwanted.

Before, I thought that when I became pregnant, I'd immediately start thinking up baby names. I thought that I'd search tirelessly for clothing and items necessary to welcome my new child. Then again, I'd always thought I'd be married to the father of my child. That we'd be welcoming in new life as a symbol of the love we already shared. The last thing I'd wanted (or expected) was to be an unwed mistress of my employer. If I'd thought this was even a remote possibility, I'd never have even gone on the Vegas trip. Carine was right about that- it was an evil I should've avoided at all costs.

I'd allowed myself to be wrapped up in Parker's smile. In his charm, I'd forgotten who I was, and who I needed to be in God. I'd gotten caught up and now I was paying for it. But the worst part is that I knew I had a difficult road ahead of me. No matter my choice, my life would never be the same...

****

"Yes." My voice creaked out. It sounded so foreign, but then again, this all was so foreign to me. The clinic was quiet. I had to get through two security doors just to sit with the doctor. That, in itself, was daunting, but now she was asking questions. I nodded, unable to look her in the eyes. She asked repeatedly, "Are you sure?" But I wasn't sure. In fact, I was most *definitely* unsure. Everything inside of me was screaming "No!" and I had every urge to turn around and go back home. But here I was, surrendered to the choice that I had made, even though there was still time to reverse it.

"Okay," she said. "There will be some cramping and bleeding for the next few days, like you would have on your period..." As she continued, my mind wandered. I had been advised to bring someone with me, since I'd be very groggy afterwards. But I had no one. No one I trusted with this information. Carine, my best friend, would never have accompanied me. She was the type of person who would stand outside of these types of clinics with signs that said "Repent" and "Abortion is Murder." I couldn't tell her. And my mother was definitely out of the question. I didn't have many friends. Okay, any friends. And I couldn't ask Parker to come. I'd returned the day after our argument (if you can call it that) and had agreed to sign the paper. I could make no mention of the pregnancy, and I'd receive a generous severance package.

I mostly wanted to do it because I couldn't bear to face him anymore and wanted a fresh start. Seeing his face or his name everywhere was mentally damaging. My panic attacks had returned with a vengeance. With the baby, I couldn't take the high dose of my meds that I was accustomed to, and was honestly too afraid to take them at all. Plus, I was running dangerously low. So hopefully after this ordeal I'd be able to reclaim some bit of my sanity.

I had no one to bring me home, so the clinic gave me a waiver saying that I allowed myself to be put in a cab/Uber back home. I chose the Uber since I knew it would come out of my account. I unlocked my phone so that the nurse would be able to access what she needed. I gave her express instructions to not call my mother in the case of an emergency. This was one person I needed never to know about my situation, even though I know she could relate. Too bad I realized that she'd be more inclined to come than Carine. I reconsidered and gave my mother's information. I selfishly prayed to God that He'd bring me safely through this procedure so no one else would find out.

I followed the nurse into the other room, and they began the procedure. I dreaded having to go back to the office with the written proof of this procedure so I could show Parker. I'd considered faxing it, but who knows what could happen if I did. The wrong person could end up with that information in their hands. Plus, I wanted to be done with it. I'd decided that I'd meet with him and his lawyers on Friday. It would give me two days to recover before I had to see him again.

After the procedure, I barely understood the written instructions given to me. They made me sit in a room until I could walk/ talk appropriately. As I left the waiting room, I thought I saw a familiar face, but she quickly turned away. When I looked back, she was gone, so I thought I imagined it. The entire way home, I tried to place her face. But I was still so drowsy that I struggled to remember where I'd placed my house keys. Thankfully the ride was only a few minutes long, and my keys were in my coat pocket. As I finally climbed into my bed, I had a fleeting sober moment. I did see someone at the clinic, but who was it? A wave of dread came over me as I thought, "Who could it be?" That was my last thought before I passed out.

Chapter 5
March 2017

Kennedy Robertson! I woke up in a cold sweat. The face: it was Kennedy. She was at the clinic when I was leaving. What was she doing there? Did she see me? Did she know it was me? I could barely remember going to the clinic in the first place. Did I speak to her? Acknowledge her existence? Was my secret out? The way I'd treated her thus far told me that if she had recognized me, my secret would be proclaimed on every high mountain and in every low valley. I had ostracized her for her impropriety, and here I was hoping she hadn't discovered my own.

After all the time I had spent calling Kennedy a Jezebel, I was now at her mercy. If she did see me (which my gut told me she did), my entire reputation was at stake. It would be up to her discretion to choose to bring me to the church board, and cause me to be disfellowshipped. I could lose everything: my reputation, my position in the church, my bible study group. Everything. I'd already quit my job, so this was the final straw.

I had no one to blame other than myself. I'd pretended that I was a victim of my circumstances. But the truth was that those weren't mistakes I had made. They were choices. Deliberate, intentional, and determined. I wish I could lie and say that I was forced to have an "A-word" but the choices I'd made prior to that day had set me on this path. I wasn't sexually assaulted. I wasn't a victim of incestuous rape. I had chosen to engage in a passionate encounter with Parker. Even more, I wanted to continue with the affair- that is, until he showed his true colors. I had become the very thing I'd hated: a phony Christian who engaged in premarital sex. Unwed and pregnant by a married man, and committing murder through abortion. I would only be worse if I engaged in homosexual activity during all of this!

****

How can you continue to speak so lowly about others, while in the situation you are in? Do you not realize that I saw you as no different from them before any of this happened? Do you not see that all sin is the same? No matter what sin is committed, you are guilty, just like they are guilty. [93] You really need to stop putting yourself on a pedestal. Your sins are catching up to you, and they will continue to if you don't repent and have compassion on your fellow man. "**All** have sinned..."[94]

****

---

[93] James 2:10
[94] Romans 3:23

I had a choice to make. I had to see Kennedy, just to know if she had seen me at the clinic. I'd play it cool, though. I'd just pull her aside after church and ask her about singing for the upcoming church banquet. That way, she'd be more willing to hear me out. I could get a good read on her that way. I had to make sure to isolate her from the other Jeze-Belles in case she tried to divulge too much information. This would definitely pique their interest, and they'd try to join the conversation. Our church banquet was set to be in June, but being on the planning committee, I had already started planning. No one would be surprised if I pulled Kennedy aside about the banquet. They already knew how meticulous I was.

So, I came to church only a few days after my "A-word." (I know it's childish, but I still couldn't bring myself to even think the word). I wish I could tell you that I was listening to the sermon. I mean, I was, but other than a general "You shouldn't judge others" theme, it was all lost on me. Plus, I was tired of both Christians and the Worldly whining about judgement. I'm in this predicament, but you don't see me carrying on about how unfair it would be if people knew what I did. I know what I did and I judge me! Why would I expect anything else from any other person, especially God?

Anyway, I was tired and was still cramping, so I hurried to catch up to Kennedy before she left. "Hey Kennedy. Can I speak to you for a moment, please?"

"Sure," she sighed. She stopped and faced the other Belles and handed them her purse. I also assume (from the reactions of the other girls) that she rolled her eyes. "Okay Gwen. What exactly do you need?" We were alone. "I just wanted to speak to you really quickly about something. It's important." She interrupted me, "Let me stop you right there. It's none of my business what you were doing there-" "Whoa, whoa, whoa!" I exclaimed. "I didn't call you over to ask you about that! I just wanted to know if you could sing a song for the banquet!"

Before I could finish my sentence, Carine walked up to us. "Hey Gwen. What's going on?" She stood beside me, across from Kennedy, but didn't speak to her or acknowledge her presence. Kennedy scoffed, and rolled her eyes. She started to walk away, but I grabbed her arm. "Kennedy, wait! I'm not done yet. Sorry Carine, I can't talk to you right now. We're having a private conversation. I'll call you later, though." Carine stared at me, confused, but then turned and walked away. "You're that pressed to talk to me that you can't even let your best friend in on the conversation? So much for the 'I'm here to talk about the banquet' story. I know you'd let her stay for that conversation, especially since she's on the planning committee too. She must not know about your situation, does she?" I looked down at the floor, unable to maintain eye contact with her. "I don't know what you're talking about," I mumbled.

She spoke with an air of disgust. "So, you're just gonna stand here and pretend like you don't know what I'm talking about? Like nothing is out of the ordinary? Like you're still little miss perfect? That I didn't see you leaving an *abortion* clin-" "Keep your voice down," I hissed. "I was there for research. And like I said, I'm just trying to confirm performers for the banquet, not discuss what you were doing at that *place*. I know how you get down. Always trying to create and spread salacious rumors with no regard to your own hypocrisy and sinfulness. I don't know why I'm even asking you to sing for the banquet. With your track record, you shouldn't even be allowed to be a member here." She leaned closer and sneered at me. "*You're* judging me? I can't believe you'd sit here in the middle of the church sanctuary and lie to me, like I wasn't there myself. Like I didn't see you with my own two eyes, being led out the clinic by a nurse. Are you serious? You're trying to be self-righteous right now? You know, you're just like your mom-"

I'd had enough. Whisper-yelling I said, "First of all, don't you even go there. I'm nothing like her. Never, ever say that again. Second of all: like you said, you were at that clinic too. If anyone even gets a hint of this I will take you down with me and expose you too. Especially in light of that "job" at that club you think no one knows about. This ends now. You will never mention this to anyone or I will see to it that your days at this church are ended. And don't think it won't follow you wherever you choose to go after you're done here. I'm sure you'd like to keep certain things about your life private- so don't tempt me."

She laughed in disbelief. "Oh. Is that right? I didn't know you had it in you." She laughed a little more.

451

"I guess it's no joke when you're the one hiding skeletons in the closet. But you don't have to worry about me putting your business out there. That's not even my style. I know I'm a work in progress, so I don't judge. You, however, missed the whole point of today's sermon. Honestly, if I were you, I'd be more careful about how I treat other people. You might find yourself in another situation like this. Needing someone to keep your secrets for you. They might not be as willing to be "Christ-like" like I am right now. I can almost guarantee that they'd want to knock your hypocritical self off your high horse. But, no worries! Like I said, it's not my place. God will handle you for me."

As she walked away, still chuckling, I struggled to contain the rage I felt from showing on my face. When she reached the doors of the sanctuary, she turned and called out to me, "By the way, my answer is yes!" My confusion must've registered on my face because she laughed again. "Yes, I will sing for the banquet." And with that, she exited the sanctuary. I stood inside, still fuming. She was mocking me. How dare she call my bluff! And then for her to say that I was just like my mother! I was livid. But as I looked around the sanctuary, I realized that there were still a few people standing around. So, I masked my emotions and put on a smile.

As I was walking out, I saw the Jeze-Belles gathered around Kennedy. She quickly glanced around her and then leaned in to speak to her friends. As I stared at her, someone stood directly in front of me, blocking my view. "So, we need to talk. Why have you been avoiding me?" Carine looked exasperated. "You've been acting weird for months now," she continued. "You haven't been to the Bible study group in ages. And suddenly you have to "visit" other churches every Sabbath. I come by your house, no one answers even though your car is in the driveway. You don't respond to my calls, texts, or emails. When you finally do show up at church, you sit in the back. And since when were you so friendly with Kennedy? And why did you send me away earlier? What is going on? What did I do to you?"

I guess the day of reckoning was upon me. I hadn't even had a chance to process what Carine said when my mother approached us. "Well, well, well. It looks like Gwen has finally decided to make an appearance at Genesis. So glad you finally have time to return to your home church!" I bristled at her sarcasm. "Well *Mom,* some of us are actually welcome at other churches in the area. Anyway, I can't stay and talk to either of you right now. I have to attend an important afternoon program at Corazón Spanish SDA church so I'm going to have to go now. I'll call you later Carine. Happy Sabbath Mom." My mother had an odd smile on her face. "No worries my dear. We'll speak soon." My mother walked away, and left Carine standing alone. Hurried, I told her, "Meet me at my house in two hours. We'll talk then. I promise I'll tell you everything." The last thing I saw as I exited the church was a dejected, furious Carine staring at me as I left. I could no longer put off the inevitable. But judging by the way she was looking at me, this would not be good!

****

Carine should be here in no time. I played the part of a good hostess and laid out a vegetable platter, and some apple juice for her. I added a small box of her favorite raw vegan coconut macaroons. There was still twenty minutes left for her to arrive, but I knew she couldn't be more than five minutes away. She'd been my best friend (and often, only friend) for years. We met as children when I first began attending Genesis SDA Church. She was vegetarian (well, now a vegan), modest, and a true Seventh-day Adventist. As teens, we never went to the movie theatres. We stood firm on our decisions to not celebrate X-mas, and bonded over the lack of teenage sexual experiences we were "supposed to have had." She was the only person I'd ever discussed my trauma with, and the only one who came close to knowing my mother for who she really was. Though I'd left out the details of my mother's involvement in my trauma, she still could see the hypocrisy that oozed through my mother's pores.

BUZZ BUZZ BUZZZZZZ My trip down memory lane was interrupted by the door buzzer. With fifteen minutes left until the time I'd asked her to come, Carine had arrived. When I let her in, she sat across from me, in an armchair. I motioned to the food and said, "Help yourself." No response. I was seated on the couch, and patted the space next to me so she could come sit closer to me. Stone-faced, she didn't budge. "Okay. I guess I'd better tell you what's been going on. You know, this is supremely difficult for me. Acting like this isn't helping the situation. I know you're upset. You don't need to glare at me like that. It's not going to make me any more forthcoming."

"You're supposed to be my best friend, Gwen. Why have you been avoiding me for months? What did I do to you?" Her voice broke, like she was holding back tears. I guess I had never realized how affected she was by my behavior. "Rina, it's not you. I've been dealing with so much lately. You were right about Parker." I started crying. Over the next hour, I told her everything. I told her about how I learned to use lingerie to cope with my feelings of anxiety and powerlessness. I told her how I used dancing to feel a sense of control. I told her about that night at Sweetie's and how I met Parker/Shorty. I told her about Vegas and that I'd gotten pregnant and had an abortion, and how scared I was. I poured out the contents of my soul to my best friend, sobbing. I left out seeing Kennedy at the clinic, and my mother's reaction to my rape. I figured that everything else was enough information. I spoke for an hour, only stopping once to take a Prozac, and blow my nose.

When I was finished, she stayed silent. "So all these years, you've been lying to me?" She finally broke the silence. I began to protest but she held up her hand. "No. I let you speak. Now it's my turn. All these years, you've told me nothing about your supposed addiction. I think you're trying to find any excuse you can to explain your affair with a married man. I told you he was dangerous, but did you listen? I told you he was no good. That you were too attached. I told you not to go to

455

Vegas. But you always have to be right, so you never listen. And then you compound your sin even more by committing murder? Your crocodile tears mean nothing to me."

I felt my chest tightening, as a huge panic attack began mounting. But she continued. "You're the worst kind of hypocrite. I bet that's why you were talking to Kennedy. Getting advice? Or perhaps a job, since you're a stripper. You know, you're the worst kind of Christian! You pretend to be so holy, but you're doing the same thing as all these other girls. I never thought I'd say this, but perhaps you need to take a lesson from Heaven Brown. At least she embraced who she was, and has done better for herself. But you? You even had me fooled! I bet you that's why your relationship with your mother is strained. You never told me what happened but I can guess it's because she knows who you really are. And you had me thinking she was a problem this entire time! What, am I supposed to believe anything you've said to me over the past decade?" My chest pain was worse now. My breathing was labored, and the room started spinning. The last thing I heard was her say, "You really think I'm stupid, don't you?"

****

I woke up, strapped to a stretcher in the middle of my living room. Carine was seated next to me, her face grim. I grabbed her hand, and she whispered to me, "I can't believe I lied for you." Confused, I tried to sit up, but my head was throbbing. "You sure gave your sister here a scare!" One of the paramedic spoke up. "Good thing she's quick on her feet. It could've been bad for you if she had waited any longer to call us." I had an oxygen mask on my face, but I pulled it down. "I'm okay. Just a panic attack, I promise. See, that's my Prozac prescription!" I pointed so Carine could show them my pill bottle. "Please, I'm okay. I don't need to go to the hospital. I'm fine." The paramedic looked skeptical. "Ma'am, we're legally obligated to bring you to the hospital if we're called for an emergency."

I protested. "Isn't there some form or waiver I can sign, like at the hospital, that says I'm going against medical advice and accept all consequences of my decision?" "Sure," he grunted. "Wait here. You have to sign the waiver." 20 minutes and a few forms later, Carine and I were alone in my apartment again. I looked at her, but quickly looked away. "You are my sister. As angry as I am at you, and as disappointed as I am in your behavior, you're my sister. I don't know what I'd do without you." Her voice broke. "Don't ever lie to me again. Or keep secrets from me. I need you to promise me that you won't."

Tears streamed down her face, and as I reached out to grab her hand, I felt the tears springing from my eyes. "You know I didn't mean it. I'm so scared and confused. I hate everything I've done. I messed up so bad, and I don't even know who I am anymore. I just don't know what to do!" She nodded. "We need to pray. And after that, we need to throw away all of the things that could be a temptation. No more lingerie for you. Maybe put a block on your internet so those sites aren't accessible. And I think you need to pray harder and stop taking the Prozac. You should depend fully on God to fix this. I'm glad you're not working there anymore because you need to be away from any and all negative influences. And I know that you don't like this, but we should take this to the Pastor and elders so they can pray with you. It's-"

Her voice trailed off. I assume it was because of the look that was registered on my face. "You can't tell anyone about this!" I spoke a little too loudly, almost shouting. Embarrassed, I calmly continued. "No one can know about this. Promise me that you won't tell a soul, Rina. Promise me!" "But there's power in their prayers, Gwennie. Don't you want to beat this? They are the leadership of the church. They should know!" I stared at her like she had three heads. "Rina, they will disfellowship me if they know. They'll gossip about me. They'll tear me to shreds. And you know that those Jeze-Belles would love nothing more than to see that happen. No. You can't tell anyone about this." She persisted. "But what about the prayer circle? At least they can be a support for you." "No, Rina. No one. Absolutely not!" "Okay Gwennie, what about your mom? I know-" "NO!" Now I was shouting. "No one Rina! NO ONE!"

She wasn't taken aback by my behavior. She just sat quietly with a thoughtful expression on her face. "Okay. I understand. I'm sorry for pushing." I sighed, relieved. "Good. Can we talk about something else now? I'm so tired of being in my own head." She laughed and grabbed a macaroon. We spent the rest of the evening talking and laughing.

For the first time in months I felt at ease. Maybe I could do this after all- beating my addictions, redeeming myself from the mess that I've made. I feel like things will actually get back to normal. I know I probably seem like a hypocrite because I don't want my business out there, but that's because I'm a church leader and it would cause all manner of confusion if people knew that I fell from grace. People would stop trying to strive for Christian excellence, and would not try to keep a standard of righteousness and holiness. Or even worse, people would look at my example as a way of life, something to emulate and not flee from. I couldn't be responsible for causing someone else to sin. The Bible talks about not being a "stumbling block"[95] to each other. I wouldn't be able to live with myself if I caused someone else to do what I did.

****

The saddest part about all of this is that you still think you can do this on your own. Your job is not to redeem yourself- that's MY job. You're still trying to work your way into Heaven. You think that your idea of "righteousness" does any good to Me?[96] Even more than that, you pretend like your need to keep your sin a secret is from a noble desire to not cause anyone else to sin. You and I both know that you just don't want to be treated the way you've treated others. The same ridicule, humiliation, and degradation you subject My other children to is what you fear

---

[95] 1 Cor. 8:9
[96] Isaiah 64:6

the most for yourself. But you cannot hide the truth for too long. Like a beautiful sepulcher[97], you have hidden away your corruption for too long.   You do everything you can to complicate the Gospel[98], and remove grace even though that is the only way anyone can be saved. You make others feel as though they'll never be good enough to be My child, and yet, you elevate yourself still, after all the sinning you've been doing. You harshly judge others, leaving no room for My love to comfort and encourage them into right living. You'd rather block them entirely, telling them they've fallen too far to return, they're too broken to be fixed, too dirty to be cleaned. You block out My voice saying, "Come now, let's settle this... Though your sins are like scarlet, I will make them as white as snow. Though they are red like crimson, I will make them as white as wool."[99] The same voice that says, "My grace is all you need. My power works best in weakness."[100] I wish you would finally figure out that I Am not the God you think I Am. The God you make Me out to be is a direct reflection of your own character. You project your own ideas about godliness and righteousness onto others. Even worse, you propagate a false image: a vindictive, unloving, menacing Being who you have to slave for, in order to reach Heaven. You verbally abuse My other children, telling them that they aren't good enough for Me, when you aren't able to meet any of My standards yourself. You do not know Me at **all**!

But- I still want you to know who I am. There's still time. If only you'd stop being so stubborn...

---

[97] Matt. 23:27,28
[98] Matt 23:4
[99] Isaiah 1:18
[100] 2 Cor. 12:9

Chapter 6
April 2017

I stood in the center of the church, looking at the mayhem ensuing. "Pastor, she should be disfellowshipped!" One elder shouted out, jumping from his seat. "She shouldn't be allowed back!" A woman chimed in, yelling from the choir loft. They were staring at me, talking about me. "Get her out of here!" They began chanting over and over again, until it became a thunderous roar. "Guess the apple doesn't fall far, huh?" My mother appeared beside me, sneering, letting out a bellowing, sinister laugh. In the sea of faces, I saw Kennedy and the other Jeze-Belles laughing menacingly and pointing. My chest began to tighten, and I could feel the panic attack coming on. I turned, ready to run out of the church, but Carine was standing directly behind me. She opened her arms to me, and I sobbed with relief. As I fell into her arms, clenching her tightly, the yelling behind me started fading away. As she wrapped her arms around me and tightened her embrace, she leaned into my ear and whispered, "Whore." I immediately awoke in a cold sweat.

It was Friday night, almost a week after I'd told Carine everything. Even though she'd agreed not to tell anyone, I still felt this overbearing guilt that was now manifesting itself in my dreams. My worst nightmare was to be in that situation- exposed and humiliated in front of those who had always respected me. I couldn't think about what could happen at church tomorrow. My emotions were on high, and I felt like I was, but as I let my mind wander, I slipped back into a heavy drowsy sleep.

I saw her. A beautiful, cinnamon-skinned little girl stood before me. She was about seven years old, wearing the prettiest black and white plaid dress. Her curly brown hair was affixed in loose pigtails, and shiny black barrettes. She had grey eyes that matched her winter coat. She looked like she was headed to church. As I stared at her, my heart began to ache. I felt a strange emptiness in my belly. That's when I knew. She had been staring at me, sizing me up as I looked at her, wearing an eerie, yet familiar smile. She was my daughter- the one I'd just aborted. She began walking towards me, but I felt frozen in place. When she stood next to me, I felt like I couldn't breathe. She reached out her hand to grab mine, tilted her head up to me, smiled (creepily) and said, "Hi mommy. My name is-"

I woke up screaming. There was no way I was going back to sleep after that. It had to have been the most disconcerting, unnerving, and terrifying dream I'd ever had. I felt sick to my stomach, throwing up on my floor as I ran towards the bathroom, and soon, my vomiting turned to sobbing. As I lay on the bathroom floor, curled in the fetal position, I felt the weight of the universe bearing down on my uterus. As much as I knew that realistically she couldn't be my child, I still felt connected to her. She was so beautiful and creepy at the same time. I ached knowing that she (or another child) could have- should have been in this world, but I chose not to have her. Now I know many women have made this same decision, and I'm sure there are many who feel okay with their decision. But that's not how I feel. Not even close. The guilt was choking me. Literally choking my spirit, my energy. I felt the walls closing in, and the darkness around me growing deeper. I decided to turn on the lights, and play some music to calm my nerves.

I stayed up all night. I was too wound up to fall back asleep, so I listened to song after song until my alarm went off at 8am. I wasn't looking forward to church today, but I knew I'd be due for a visit from my mother (and Carine) if I didn't show up. I stared in the bathroom mirror unable to come to grips with my reflection. I looked haggard. I knew I was tired, but I didn't know I looked as exhausted as I felt. I'm dark-skinned, so the puffy dark circles under my eyes surprised me. My eyes were rimmed with red, a telltale sign of my difficult night. I wasn't accustomed to wearing makeup, but I needed to hide my flaws. It was nothing a little concealer, foundation and some eye drops couldn't fix- at least on the outside.

My tossing and turning had caused my hair scarf to come off of my head during the night. Now my hair was a mess, and I had limited time to re-straighten my edges and curl my hair again. I decided to press the front edges of my hair with the flat and put the rest of my hair in a half-updo. After showering and changing my clothes, I was finally ready to go. My eyes weren't as puffy, but I still needed a little concealer for the dark circles. I put a thin layer of foundation over it, and then grabbed my keys to leave.

Something told me to look down, and when I did my clothes were peppered with marks. The foundation powder had fallen onto my stark white blouse, and my grey skirt. When I grabbed my shirt to brush it off, the remaining concealer/foundation combination added brown streaks to the symphony of stains. I groaned, knowing how late I was going to be for church. I knew I had to change, but I didn't have a backup-outfit. Tomorrow was laundry day, and everything was either dirty or wrinkled. I knew I'd need to iron something or wear what I had on. I opted to grab a cardigan from the "worn" pile, and put it over my shirt. The wrinkles and slight odor made it look worse than before. I decided I had to iron anyway, even though I felt like that was breaking the Sabbath.

I'd already incurred enough guilt with everything else that was going on. I needed to hurry up and get to church. I grabbed a grey plaid wool dress from the back of my closet. I hadn't worn that dress in over a year, and it was a little too snug for my liking. It must have shrunk in the wash because it was shorter than I remembered, but at this point, I had no other choice. I was finally out the door. At 65 degrees, the March weather was unseasonably warm, making my outfit even more uncomfortable. By the time I'd arrived at church, I was sweating. Parking was all but gone when I arrived, since I was so late, so I parked a few blocks away, and walked to the church.

The service was already halfway over by the time I walked into the sanctuary. I had no choice but to sit in the back. There was only one row that had space, but someone was blocking the end. Unfortunately, I'd chosen the row where Kennedy was seated. She rolled her eyes when she realized who had asked to sit next to her. I tried to be pleasant, cheerily whispering, "Hi! Happy Sabbath Kennedy!" She smirked, "Late *and* wearing that short, tight dress? Your life must be in shambles, huh Gwen?" With a chuckle, she slid aside so that I could sit. The sermon had just begun, but I couldn't hear a thing. Part of me was embarrassed for coming to church so late. Part of me was annoyed at Kennedy's snide remark. And one part of me couldn't stop sneaking glances at her.

When Kennedy first began attending Genesis two years ago, she'd tried to be my friend. She had extended an invitation for lunch, which I'd accepted. My mother had told me to stay away from Kennedy (she "had a bad feeling" about her), but I didn't share the same sentiment, so I ignored my mother and went anyway. The lunch went really well at first. It went so well that a stranger, hearing our laughter, asked if we were sisters. I laughed and said no. Just then, the waiter returned, and Kennedy ordered an alcoholic beverage. As an

465

ambassador of Christ, I spoke up. I told her no good Christian should be drinking anything alcoholic, and that she should stop. I knew she was new to Christianity, but I told her I had to put my foot down. She laughed, until she realized I was serious. Then she became defensive. She told me that I was free to leave since she was still going to enjoy her beverage, and she didn't want to "violate [my] conscience by being so ungodly!" I tried to reason with her, but she was adamant, so I paid for my portion of the meal, and left.

After that, things were very hostile between us. We were the same age, only about 4 months apart (her being older) but somehow, she seemed far less wise than I. It was of no consequence. Since she did not want to be spiritually mentored by me, I left her to her own devices. That's how she fell victim to the Jeze-Belles. She'd been friendly with them when she first began attending. They bonded over their mutual enemy (me), and became a tight-knit group of friends.

I remember when I discovered she worked at that club. I was at a really low point. I'd decided (against my better judgment) to go to a local strip club, and see if I could relieve some tension. As I walked inside, I saw her across the room. Immediately, I asked the bouncer if he knew her. "Who, Ken? Yeah she works here." That was all I needed to hear. I quickly exited the club, and made my way home. Thankfully, she never saw me.

As I now sat next to Kennedy, I couldn't help but remember how our relationship had begun. I wish things had turned out better, but I couldn't re-write the past. I stared at her face, and realized how similar our features were, with the exception of our skin tones (she was much lighter than I was.) She was exceptionally pretty (in a more obviously sexual way, whereas I was pretty in a more muted, demure way). I wondered if she was possibly mixed with something. I swear she had small flecks of gold and green in her eyes, and her short honey blonde afro was a softer, curlier pattern, versus my coily kinks.

"What? Why are you looking at me?" Suddenly, I zoned out to find her frowning at me. I didn't mean to, but apparently, I had been staring for a few minutes, lost in my thoughts. "Sorry," I mumbled. I tried to focus during the remainder of the service, but it was to no avail. After the final prayer, I stood to scan the room for Carine. She was making her way over to me, and had a frown on her face. "So first, you come to church late and then you sit with *her*?" The contempt in her voice was palpable. Kennedy rolled her eyes and turned away. "Looks like someone's in trouble with her mommy!" As she walked away, I turned back to Carine. "Rina, I've had a terrible morning, and I didn't know I was sitting with her until it was too late. Stop being dramatic." She stiffened.

"I'm not being dramatic. I care about your relationship with God. Now I know telling your mother about you was the right thing to do." My face blanched. I couldn't see it, but I knew if I looked how I felt, I'd be passing out in a millisecond. I half-shouted "You what?!" Thankfully no one seemed to notice, since there

D. Gloria Elysée

were so many people around. Unfortunately, my mother was quickly approaching us. "Carine, let me talk to my daughter. I'll call you later." She grabbed my elbow and squeezed hard, pulling me away. She wasn't satisfied until we were standing outside of the church, away from everyone else.

I stood, rubbing my sore elbow as she began her tirade. My mother had a certain way of being masterfully mean and manipulative in the most Christian way. "So, I see you've been doing your fair share of whoring around. And apparently, I didn't teach you anything because you got pregnant and had to have an abortion? And to make matters worse, you told your oblivious little friend about it? She's more stupid than you are! I had to spend an hour convincing her that I'd talk to the Pastor about you just so she wouldn't go do it herself! How stupid can you be? Did I teach you nothing all those years ago? Does anyone here know my business? No. Because I know how to keep my mouth closed. Now I have to figure out a way to keep your stupid friend from putting this all out in the open."

"Why are you so stupid? This is why I didn't want kids: so I wouldn't have to clean up all their messes for the rest of my life. How old are you now, that you don't know how to use a condom or get on birth control? How stupid must you be to sleep with your boss? Don't you know better than to sleep with someone that close in proximity? You do your dirt elsewhere. You never track it back into your home. And you never, ever, tell people what's going on! You have got to be the most moronic person I've ever met. Stupid! Just stupid!"

I stood quietly as she berated me in front of the church, because I knew I deserved it. I had messed up, and even though at first I was okay with sharing with my best friend, I regretted saying anything to her. I wish I'd just lied and pretended that it never happened. I wish I'd done a better job of not telling anyone anything, and that I could control my hormones and feelings better. I wish I was better at being me. Maybe then I wouldn't find myself emotionally overextended, overwhelmed by my life. At that moment, I wished I could be someone else. Anybody other than myself. I wish I wasn't a failure, having destroyed my life, and still waiting for consequences to rain down upon my head. I felt like I was teetering on the edge of a cliff, and Carine had the ability to push me over. My mother was watching it happen in anticipation.

No doubt I had disappointed God, my best friend, and myself. I wondered how I ever got to this place. I used to spend so long listing all the things I'd never do. "Oh, I could *never*..." "Oh no! I'd *never* even consider..." "Never in a million years would I..." And the judgment I reserved for those who did any of those things: premarital sex, abortions, extramarital affairs, homosexuality, et cetera. They, and the people who engaged in them were counted (to me) as the bottom of the barrel. Not worthy of forgiveness. Not worthy of acceptance. They should be made a spectacle of so "good" Christians wouldn't get the wrong idea and copy the behavior, and then they should be exiled into the category of spiritual lepers: King Saul, Balaam, Ahab,

469

and Judas. The unworthy, unforgivable sinners who would never again be included in the ranks of God. They were disloyal to the Kingdom of God and deserved every bad thing in life they received.

So, your loved one died during an abortion? Oh, she probably deserved it for killing her child. Your neighbor's kid killed himself? Well, he was gay. I'd probably kill myself too if I knew I was contrary to the will of God. You have HIV? Maybe you shouldn't have been sleeping around with people. You overdosed? You're a criminal drug addict and people like you make the world as terrible as it is. I counted sin as sin- and did not excuse people who were "just human." I was human too, and I wasn't gay, a drug addict, or indulging in any of the other amoral lifestyles I'd mentioned.

But I was no better. In fact, I was worse. I, who was supposedly held to a higher standard because of my relationship with God, had done the things that I hated in others. And I realized that just as I had no mercy for them, there would be no mercy for me. And what made things worse was that I didn't even need to be publicly humiliated. Did I deserve it, sure! But the fact that as my mother told me I should've kept my business quiet, I stood agreeing with her, I knew I was wrong. I had become like my mother, indulging in all types of indiscriminate secret sin. That was all the reproof I needed. My spiritual life was officially dead.

****

You still don't get it, do you? I created everyone on this planet, and I don't play favorites.[101] You claim to know Me, but you miss out on the most important fact- the love I have for all My children is EQUAL. You speak of those who are hurt and broken by life, rejected by others, and trapped by their own sins (and often the sins of others) as though I were not the One who created them, who loves them with an everlasting love.[102] I am their provider and comfort, and their protection from people like you- people who claim to know Me, but have no idea who I actually am. How I would love to shield my little ones from those who claim to be my representatives! You seem to think I differentiate between their sin and yours? Is that what you read in My Word? Because I said nothing of the sort. The fact that you are still so intent on judging others despite your current situation tells Me that you will not change unless more drastic measures are taken. Your arrogance is appalling, but there is still hope for you. I just hope you end up choosing Me...

****

"Gwen, I'm sorry. But this is the way it has to be. You know that." I sat across from Pastor Rogers and the Head Elder, Brother Collins. Carine had spoken with them last week, after my mother had pulled me aside. They had called my mother on Sunday (which she took full advantage of to call me all types of "stupid"), and now, this Thursday evening, they were in my living room. I felt anxious, fearful, betrayed. Carine didn't have the decency to call me and let me know that she told the

---

[101] Romans 2:11
[102] Jeremiah 31:3

Pastor about me. I thought she might do it, but I figured she'd at least tell me that she was going to do it.

Nonetheless, the Pastor came in and told me that I'd have to step down from all the positions I held in the church. He said that I wouldn't be able to hold another elected office in the church until the next nominating cycle had gone by. We'd just finished one in December, for a 2-year term, so that meant that I was barred from public ministry for at least two years. He said that he hated the practice of disfellowshipping members unless absolutely necessary. I'd counted it as weakness of character before, but was grateful for at this moment. He said that if I conducted myself accordingly, there would be no scandal. I could still choose to do ministry outside of Genesis church, so long as I didn't try to use the church name or logo to do so.

Knowing Carine, however, she wouldn't even consider letting me stay on as a leader for the Bible Study. I was officially stripped of my duties, even as Banquet organizer. I was to attend a rehabilitative Bible Study for at least 40 sessions: either the regular Wednesday evening service, Carine's weekly study, or (God forbid!) the Sunday evening Bible study at Heaven Brown's house. If I went to all three, I'd be able to hit 40 sessions in no time. But I'd have to get a signature in order to prove I did it. The ladies at Carine's study would ask too many questions, and Heaven's house would be far too humiliating and debasing. So, I chose the weekly Wednesday night service at Genesis. At least this way, I could sneak up to the Pastor or Elder and have them sign it directly.

I knew I should be grateful: my soiled reputation wouldn't be aired out for the entire world to see. But I didn't feel grateful, or happy, or relieved. I was angry. Since when did I have to check-in to prove my relationship with God? I was a lifelong member of this church! I'd joined Genesis as a child, and had been there longer than either of these two men had. What right did they have to tell me I had to sit down? Pastor Rogers had a chronically weak hand when it came to controlling the church. Plus, I'm sure everyone was aware of the rumors of Elder Collins beating his wife. Surely, they were in no position to declare me unfit for ministry!

I assume my hostility showed on my face, because Pastor Rogers added, "We just want to be sure that you're doing okay spiritually. We want the opportunity to address your spiritual needs before we throw you back into the forefront of church ministry. Too often our leaders complain that they didn't get adequate support from the church when it came to their spiritual life. They say they were burdened with trying to help others grow spiritually while they were becoming stagnant or backsliding. This is not a condemnation. Consider this a spiritual refresher course."

I know I rolled my eyes, but I nodded. At least this wasn't the public flogging I'd experienced in my nightmares. I guess I could deal with this. I just wish I knew what to say to people, who would ask me why I was suddenly not participating in everything. I felt like that could lead to a scandal if we weren't careful. As the Pastor and Elder prayed with me before they left, I didn't hear a word of it. After they left, I called my mother back. She had called me four times since the Pastor had arrived, knowing this meeting was tonight. I was beyond annoyed, but thankfully, my phone was on vibrate the entire time.

"Why are you stalking me? Didn't I tell you I'd call you as soon as they left? You're sitting here making me look super disrespectful, which didn't help my case any. You're so aggravating!" She scoffed. "Well, you don't have to be so rude, Gwennie. I just wanted to make sure you were okay." I knew she was lying, and of course, she needed something. "Gwennie, huh? What is it now mom? *Clearly* you weren't calling because of my meeting." "You really don't know me at all, child. After all I've done for you, you treat me like this? You are so ungrateful-" I was already irritated, but this took me over the edge. "Mom, WHAT DO YOU WANT?" I roared into the phone. It was almost as if I could see her shocked expression. "I just called to check up on my daughter. But since you asked, if you could lend me $500, I'd really appreciate it!"

I scoffed. After everything that had happened so far, I was done. "No. You will no longer get anything from me. I should've told you no the last time, but kept letting myself get sucked into your guilt trap. But I'm done. I hold no obligations to you anymore. You spend all your time calling me stupid and ungrateful, and then expect me to go out of my way and fund your foolishness? How much of my money have you borrowed so far, Mom? Just this year? I'm not even working, but you sure don't care about that! No, mom. No more. I'm officially done supporting your habit. You're a middle-aged woman. It's about time you start learning how to manage your money, and stop depending on me to fix your messes" "Of all the things you could do to your mother! Don't you know I carried you? I wrecked my body to have you, so much that your daddy didn't want me anymore. I threw my life and my plans away so I could take care of you, and this is how you repay me? I AM YOUR MOTHER! YOU OWE ME!!! You hear me? You little ungrateful whore. I did everything for you and this is the thanks I get?" "Aren't we being a little dramatic, mom? You still lived your life how you wanted to, regardless of my presence. Have you forgotten how you let your boyfriend rape me and then slept with him right after? And now you have the nerve to say I should be grateful-" *CLICK* She'd hung up.

I knew I'd awoken a sleeping dragon, but I no longer cared. She felt like she had permission to say and do to me whatever she pleased. I was tired of it. I was tired of everything! But even that small release didn't help. Instead of making a bad situation better, I made it much worse. Having my mother as an enemy meant that any weakness I had that couldn't cause her embarrassment was free game. My abortion fell under that category. I just knew she'd make a martyr of herself, and spend her time lamenting, "I did my best to raise her right in the Lord. I can't imagine why she'd turn out like this!" With this information at her fingertips, she

475

could (and probably would) ruin my reputation and not even give it a second thought.

Carine was not much better. I knew I couldn't call her after this, because she'd only make the situation worse. She had no clue how reality worked sometimes. She was far too idealistic to be of any help. As much as I wanted to scream at her for reporting on me to the Pastor and Elder, I knew it would be of no use. She wouldn't accept responsibility for her betrayal and instead would blame me for it, and then run back to them to complain about my behavior. Telling her the truth now about my mother would cause her to call me a liar, and then she'd try to confront my mother. When that didn't work, she'd also run back to the Pastor and Elder, and by that time, more people would have to get involved. Plus, if my mother knew her lies were exposed, the situation would get out of control. She'd lash out and reveal any and everything she knew about anybody to deflect from her situation. She was the type to attempt to bring down as many people as she possibly could.

I didn't know who to turn to. There was nobody I could talk to about my life. I felt super lonely. I'm self-sufficient, and very determined. My independence is one of my most marked attributes. But my "Jesus first, everyone last" attitude had isolated me from a lot of people. Carine was the only person I communicated with on a regular basis. My mother was my only family. And now I felt I had neither. I wasn't regretting finally standing up to my mother. But I also wasn't relishing in the fact that I'd alienated my only living relative either. I wished I had someone (other than Jesus) to talk to, to spend my time with. Not that I didn't love my Creator, but I craved human companionship. I had to come to terms with the fact that I had no friends, and a difficulty connecting with others because of my uncompromising attitude. That's what made that blossoming friendship with Kennedy so rare. I had felt at ease with her, even as a new Christian. Had I not been so rigid, we'd probably be good friends by now. Well, maybe not. My mother hated her and insisted I stay as far from her as possible, and Carine was a jealous friend. Plus, I'm not comfortable knowing she works at that strip club. It probably wouldn't have lasted anyway. What I needed most right now was a friend, but all I had was myself.

****

You are far too self-centered for your own good. You say Carine won't accept her betrayal, but you won't accept that these consequences are resulting directly from your own actions. Carine, though misguided, is just trying to help you. And up until recently, you saw the world almost exactly the way she did. You, too, thought it was your duty to report on the goings-ons of others, and "save" others from themselves and their sin. You mock how idealistic she is, but you shared the same ideology- at least until you did something you felt needed to be covered up. It's not until then that reporting on other people's sins became the wrong thing to do. Your own uncompromising attitudes isolate you from others, and it has nothing to do with Me. It is your own choice to mistreat others, judge others, and to punish them for sinning against Me (not you). They did nothing to you. Your offense on my behalf is unfounded. I can fight my own battles, and it is I who convinces and convicts people of their sin.[103] THAT IS NOT YOUR JOB. Because you've been so busy trying to be Me, I cannot be Me in your life. That's how you got here. But you have very limited time. You need to see the errors in your ways or else you will never change. Your trial is not like Joseph in the prison, a result of choosing integrity.[104] Your life is like Saul, accusing the saints of God, placing yourself on a higher plane than they because of your perceived spiritual and social standing.[105] If you do not become converted like he did, and continue on this path, you'll become more and more blind to your own sins: unrepentant and, therefore, unforgiven. My dear, dear daughter: PLEASE do not keep going like this. I love you FAR too much to let you destroy yourself. Perhaps if you felt the weight of your decisions it would cause you to change. But nothing, so far...

---

[103] John 16:8
[104] Genesis 39
[105] Acts 8:1-3; Acts 9

Chapter 7
May 2017

I needed a job, and soon. Since I had quit my job, I'd been having trouble finding a new one. It had only been a few weeks, but I found each interview troubling. No one wanted to match my previous salary. One lady expressed surprise that my salary was so high since I didn't have a managerial position. She said she'd hired someone from my firm before who had the same position as I did. They had better credentials, and their salary was still significantly lower than mine. $10,000 lower, to be quite honest.

I was surprised, but after thinking about it more, I realized I knew why. Parker had been paying me more to keep me around, hoping to bed me one day. I didn't even know how much I was supposed to be getting paid, and was nervous. I budget pretty well, and I take care of my bills, but I'd have to take a pay cut in order to work again. As the woman continued, offering me the job at a much lower pay rate, I had to ask to return her call later. I needed to pray on it, and see if it was worth it. Distraught, I fell asleep during my prayer. My phone rang loudly, jarring me awake from my impromptu

Tuesday afternoon nap. I assumed it was another company, either calling to schedule an interview. Or, most likely, following up to say they were unable to offer me a position at the pay rate I'd requested.

Kennedy was on the phone. I didn't know she still had my phone number, but here she was, on the line. "I really need to talk to you. In person. Can I come over?" This request unsettled me. What did she need to see me for that couldn't wait until Sabbath? I didn't want to be bothered but she sounded very upset, like she'd been crying. I agreed, and gave her my address. Thirty minutes later she was at my house, and I was wishing I had never answered the phone.

She prefaced her statements by asking me to wait until she was finished to comment. Hesitantly, I agreed. She also asked for my utmost confidence in the matter, and reminded me of the secret she held for me. I felt like her request was a hair short of blackmail, but I agreed to it anyway. After she was comfortable (enough) with my response, she began. She told me that today was the anniversary of her father's death two years ago, and that her mother had died a decade ago. It was after her father's death that she became a member of Genesis SDA. I knew that already, but she restated it anyway. She continued, rehashing her and my history. She spoke of how we were almost friends once, how my mother hated her, and how she and I stopped speaking to one another. I had to resist the urge to interrupt her in my exasperation, but I didn't have to because she stopped talking on her own.

She then took a long deep breath and exhaled. After pausing for another moment, she blurted out, "Gwen, I didn't come to Genesis by accident. Or by random chance. Or "by God's providence" as you'd put it. I came to Genesis to find you. You're my sister. We have the same father: Gary Robertson." I chuckled, dryly. "My father's last name was Roberts, not Robertson. We're not related." She paused and said, "I know what this must sound like, but I promise you, I can prove it. Gary Roberts and Gary Robertson are the same person."

I was extremely skeptical as to how she'd arrived at this ridiculous conclusion, but I stayed silent, as promised. She continued, "My parents were high-school sweethearts. They got married right out of high school. They'd been married only a few years when my dad met your mom. Then he started having an affair. My mom found out and then kicked him out, but he promised to stop seeing your mom, and they went to counseling. Things were still rocky between them when she became pregnant with me. She found out in her last trimester that he had still been seeing your mom, and that she was pregnant too. It caused her to go into labor early- almost two months early. She was so angry and hurt that she kicked him out for good, and filed for divorce.

"Daddy came back and begged for her forgiveness, stating it was an accident, that it happened when he went to end things. He told her your mom was crazy, and promised to make his life miserable by

481

calling and harassing my mom if he'd left her. She didn't believe him at first, but your mom started stalking them, calling at all hours of the night, and destroying their property. That's when she realized he must be telling the truth. She decided to try and work it out in counseling. She ended up taking him back and letting him move back in when I was one. A few years later, we moved to Atlanta. After that, your mom left them alone, and they were happy together until she died ten years ago.

"When my mom died, we were devastated. She was killed in a tragic car accident. Some drunk teenager slammed into her car. He didn't make it either. All of my mother's family was back in Cuba, so we didn't have many options for a funeral. Daddy decided to have a service here, and then cremate her and send her ashes back to her family so they could grieve too. Only her sister lived in the States (in Florida). The rest of the family wasn't able to fly Stateside. He and my Tía Maria planned to take a trip to Haiti and meet the extended family on the week following the funeral. We had planned on making it a private event, but the accident was a bit high-profile and was on the news. They interviewed us and the funeral home posted the obituary online. I'm guessing that's how your mother found out about it.

"Your mother showed up to the funeral home towards the end of my mom's wake." "EXCUSE ME! What are you even talking about? This is absurd!" I interrupted her. She took in a deep breath. "I know this is hard to hear Gwen, but please, let me finish! I didn't know who your mother was back then, but it was hard to miss the chaos that happened after her arrival. I was in the restroom for most of the drama, but we did cross paths while she was walking in, and I was headed to the restroom. First, she came wearing a tight, white midi dress and high heels. Everyone was making their rounds, consoling the family, so it was rather crowded. She walked to the front where Daddy and I were sitting, skipping the lines who were waiting to pay their respects. She paused at the casket for a moment, and then came to stand next to where he was seated.

"Your mother tried to console him I guess, but it backfired. Daddy flew into a rage, calling her all types of names, and even attempted to hit her or something. Everyone there was shocked, since he never reacted to anyone that way. Plus, no one knew who she was. As they restrained him, he called out for security, amidst the flurry of curse words he spewed out at her. By the time I came back from the restroom, security was escorting her out. I called out to my dad, and she turned around to look. When she left, we finally got him calm, but he refused to tell any of us who she was. She never popped up again, which was a good thing.

"A little over three years ago, Daddy was diagnosed with an aggressive form of pancreatic cancer. Unfortunately, it was discovered when it was too late to do anything about it. I had just moved to Boston to work as a graphic designer. I flew back to Atlanta as much as possible, and when that became too much, decided to move him in with me. I heard the medical care here was stellar, and there were many acclaimed

Cancer treatment centers here. We were desperately trying to save him. After he was rejected from a last-resort clinical trial, he realized he wasn't going to survive the cancer. That's when he told me about you and your mom.

"Daddy told me that he had tried looking for you, but your mother had done everything she could to keep you from him. She said that his biggest regret was taking the job in Atlanta, because once he moved away he never saw you again. I think that's because your mom changed your name to "Roberts," rather than "Robertson." Such a small change, but it was difficult to find you. He said that he tried to contact any family or friends, went back to the old apartment you used to live in, and then eventually just gave up.

"Daddy said that I should still try and find you, because even though he has a few cousins, he had no close family, and didn't want me to be alone after he died. I still had family on my mother's side, but I'd only met my Tía Maria, Tío Marco and my cousins Esperanza and Jorge a few times. Before he passed, he made me promise that I'd still look for you. He gave me your mother's name, your name, and your date of birth. It was all that he had. He didn't have any pictures of you. Apparently, your mother had destroyed all the photos you had taken together during one of their arguments.

"I tried to look you and your mother up online, but I found nothing, so I decided to pay an investigator to do it for me. Daddy hadn't considered that route, but I found success. Unfortunately, he passed away a week before I got the results. I was so devastated that it took me three months to open the letter with the results. It hurt me, not just because I'd lost both parents, but also because he never had the chance to find you. It took about six months before I got the nerve to show up at Genesis to find you. I didn't know what to expect, or how to broach the subject with you, but I figured I should attend for a little while so I could figure it out.

"I showed up one Sabbath morning, and stayed for the whole service. Your mom recognized me, I think, from the moment I arrived. I had no clue who she was, but had a nagging feeling that she was familiar. She approached me when the service had ended, made some small talk about welcoming me to church, and then asked for my name. When I told her, she looked angry and disgusted for a few seconds. But as quickly as her veneer fell, she regained composure and her face changed back to normal. Before I could react, we were interrupted by another group of women, who came and asked if I wanted Bible studies. I said yes, and let them shuffle me away.

"I had never really been involved in church before. Just the occasional Easter or Christmas, and weddings and funerals, so I was interested in getting to know what you knew. They were all so nice that I almost forgot why I came. I pulled an older woman aside, and asked for your mother's name. When she told me, I froze. Before I could begin to ask about you, your mother came back and pulled me aside to talk. She and told me she knew who I was, and to stay away from you.

She said that she'd ruin my life if I breathed a word of this to anyone, much less you. So, I just did my best to avoid your mother at all costs."

She began to cry. "Your mother is so hateful! I almost didn't come back to Genesis because of her! But the older women impressed me by how nice they were, and realized that the God I'd found there was worth going back to. I chose to get baptized, and tried to ignore your mom as best as I could. I was super excited when you volunteered to be my church "big sister" because we could finally be close. I thought I could finally tell you who I really was! I thought we were getting along great, until the day you decided I was "beneath you" and you didn't want to associate yourself with me.

"Thank God for Heaven, Mari and Grace! They encouraged me, and helped me keep going. They told me about their struggles with God, and I started feeling like I was understood, and that I wasn't alone. I came to Genesis for one sister, but I found three in them. They even helped me find the strength to break up with my ex-boyfriend Travis. He owns a strip club in Everett. We met when he hired me as his promoter and graphic designer. I didn't originally work for him. In the three months leading to Daddy's death, I had lost my job because I had to take too much time off to take him to his appointments. I was grateful for the job Travis gave me. The downside was that people always assumed I was one of the strippers, and treated me like an object, unless he came to my defense.

"Eventually, I began hating my job, and when I'd stopped drinking, it lost any appeal it had ever had before. I really loved Travis, so I didn't want to let that part of my life go. I think it was because he stood by me after Daddy died. Unfortunately, he didn't like that I was changing and getting closer to God. He didn't trust religion, so he tried everything in his power to get me to stop going.

"The past two years have been so difficult! All I had wanted was to get to know you, and bond with you, but none of that has happened. Somewhere along the line, you decided I wasn't good enough to acknowledge or speak to. You completely wrote me off, and that hurts, being that you're the only family I have around here. You know, after that last lunch we had, I swore I'd forget you and I had any blood relation, and that I'd stop trying to speak to you-"

"I HAVE HAD ENOUGH!!! I've stayed silent long enough. I've sat here and listened to your lies, and I've seen your crocodile tears. I'm not buying it. My parents were married. My dad had no kids, which is why he begged my mother to have me. And then he died when I was six. I don't care what you say. You're just another Jezebel stripper-whore who's looking to illicit sympathy from me. How dare you make up lies about my family! You think I'm stupid, don't you? Get the hell out of my house!"

I was so angry, I didn't even think twice about the fact that I'd just swore. Tears were streaming down her face, but she stood up straight. "You might not like the truth, but this is it. If you don't believe me, fine. Ask your mother. In fact, do it in person so you can see her reaction. As for me and you, I'm done. You won't ever have to worry about speaking to me again. As far as I'm concerned, you're as dead to me as *our* daddy." With that, she got up and left.

I didn't know what to think or feel as I watched her leave. I didn't call after her- she'd just ruined my day! She was either boldly lying to my face or... Or nothing! It *couldn't* be true! But the backflips my stomach was doing were quite telling. My mother's story about my father had never sat right with me. I always felt like there were huge gaps of missing information. She had claimed he left us (for good) when I was two, but if Kennedy was telling the truth, he'd never lived with us to begin with. None of our neighbors in the Boston suburb where we had lived knew my father. I couldn't remember attending the funeral at all. When I kept asking where my daddy was, an urn appeared in the living room, and my mother told me (and my neighbors) he was in it.

But if Kennedy was right, *that's* why mom couldn't find my dad's birth certificate, death certificate, or marriage certificate when I'd asked her for them. *That's* why she had no wedding photos. I had only three pictures with my dad, and she was only in one of them. I wanted to know what happened to all the memories of the "love of her life" since there was barely a trace of him. She had claimed that the box containing the important documents and photos was destroyed in a fire. That's why we had to move to a different house all of a sudden. The rest of his personal effects were lost by the moving company during the move itself. In fact, every time I tried to ask about my father she would become extremely agitated and tell me to stop asking questions.

Then, at sixteen, I got a copy of my birth certificate as I was getting ready to apply for a driver's license and passport. My certificate had no name listed under "father." There were also two addenda noting name changes: she had legally changed both of our last names from her maiden name "Cooper" to "Roberts." But (other than the last name) there was no sign of him on my birth certificate. When I asked why his name was missing, she said she had her reasons. She said that when they had me, she suspected he was cheating on her, so since she hadn't yet changed her name, she left it that way. But I was confused as to why she waited until around the time he died to change our names. She claimed to have done it when she was overwhelmed by his death and no one would refer to her by his last name because she still used her maiden name. I thought that was a strange reason, but when I inquired further about her decision, she lost it. She forbad me to speak about him again, and ignored me when I asked about him until the day I stopped asking. In fact, she only brought him up if she was trying to guilt trip me about something.

D. Gloria Elysée

It pained me how little I knew about my father. Per my mother, I knew his name was Gary Roberts, that he was born on September 16th (year unknown), and that he was from a small town in Texas. I knew what he looked like, and that I looked more like him than my mom. I knew very little else. I had very little contact with my former neighbors, other than the two I ran into occasionally. They didn't know much about him either, other than what my mother told them. The only information anyone had about him was his name. Any search was fruitless.

Mom said he didn't have any relatives, that he was an only child and his parents had died when he was younger. She said that she was all the family I had- and all that I'd ever need. I thought that was quite ironic, seeing how she kept telling me how she never wanted kids, and how he forced her to have me. Now that this new "information" has come to light, maybe she means that he "forced" her to have me as a last-ditch effort to keep him around, since he went back to his wife.

What was worse was that (if this was true- which I still doubted) my mother somehow kept my father away from me. That my father and I were robbed of the opportunity to know each other, and that he died, not when I was six, as I'd previously thought, but two years ago. TWO YEARS AGO. We could've had a relationship. I could've had some support! I could've asked all the questions about my past, my heritage that I've always wondered about! I could've had a whole different life! That is- if Gary Robertson and Gary Roberts were the same person.

Unfortunately, the more I thought about it, the more plausible Kennedy's story seemed. I really wanted to call my mother and confirm the truth. I'd stopped searching for answers as a child, and the trauma I'd experienced was enough for me to distance myself from my past in general. I barely spoke during the sessions that Dr. Desaris wanted to concentrate on my childhood. I didn't remember too much. All I had was a father who'd left when I was two, three pictures with him, and a few years later he was dead. There was nothing to talk about. He had no family, and my mother was stonewalling me. She had squelched any possibility of me finding him.

Dr. Desaris thought I was avoiding the subject, but she didn't understand that my mother would never budge on this topic. It had been long since I'd given up my futile search. I simply rested on the fact that I had God, my Heavenly Father, and was fulfilled by His presence in my life. What good would it do to fight my mother, on a quest to discover a dead man? But with the onslaught of this new and unsettling information, I began to reconsider my decision to stay in the dark about his life.

My entire life I'd built up a barrier against any and everything related to my "father." I was hurt that he left my mother after begging for her to have me. I was angry that he hadn't come back to visit much. But what bothered me most was that he had left me alone with her, and hadn't taken me with him. With no one else to act as a buffer to distract her, I received all her attention-good and bad. When she went on a rampage because her latest boyfriend had left, or when she joined the church and decided that I would have to share in her "penance," there was nothing to divert her attention from me. I was either completely vilified and blamed for her situations, or I was ridiculed for trying to stick to my guns when it came to God. Whatever the situation, though, she was never satisfied. In life or death, I resented my father because he didn't protect me from her wrath, and left me to fend for myself.

Now to see the story from a different light, was to change my perception of both my parents. My mom, ever the resentful mother, was now a liar, homewrecker, and her deceit was unmatched. My father, no longer a deadbeat- but a father who tried to do the right thing by me, even though I wasn't part of the plan. A man who wanted nothing to do with my mother, but still made an effort until she'd kept me hidden from him. Her deceit and pettiness, though not a surprise, disgusted me entirely.

I think the day I was going to tell the church about my attack was the first time my mother had ever been "sweet" to me. Even if it was only to get what she wanted. I guess having that "power" over her (to expose her lies) caused her to tread carefully. Even if the sweet demeanor was fake, I wanted to experience as much of it as possible. I didn't mean to blackmail her, though. I just wanted to keep her verbal attacks to a minimum. Every time she'd start a tirade, I'd remind her that I could tell the church her story and ruin everything. She hated that

I could do so, but she would soon acquiesce and I'd have some semblance of peace.

This whole time I'd thought that her fear of discovery was about the rape. Never had I considered that this was just one of the loose threads that could unravel the tapestry of lies she'd woven about her life and mine. If I told people about the rape, they'd probably figure out the truth about her (many) boyfriends. Then, they might become curious and dig deeper and find out the truth. I was illegitimate: the unwanted bastard child of a married man and his desperate mistress.

I was a last-ditch effort for her to control and manipulate someone who didn't care about my existence more than a few hundred dollar bills tossed in her general direction along with the words "take care of it." That was how I had imagined his reaction to her pregnancy. Him, clinging on to a flailing marriage, and her: deceptively planning to trap him with a mistake no one wanted. I don't think she decided to get pregnant on purpose. I just assumed she chose to keep me just so she could keep him. When her plan backfired, and he left, she tried to extort him. When that no longer gave her the feeling of power she craved, she chose to hurt him in the way she hurt, taking me away from him, permanently. She changed her name and mine to something very similar. It was probably her way of being petty: "You'll never find me. I'm taking on your name and hiding in plain sight." And it now hurt me more that both him and I were pawns in her sadistic game.

493

I'd never really dug deeper into my feelings about my parents because it hurt that I had no father and an abusive mother. As a child, I used to imagine that he was a caring man that just couldn't bear to live with my mother. It was easy to imagine him as being benevolent because he was nice the few times I'd seen him. Plus, I could barely stand living with my mother, and I figured him and I had that it common: he loved me, but hated her. But as I got older, I became embittered with the thought of my abandonment. For reasons of self-preservation, slowly tucked him away into the recesses of my mind.

Now the bandage had been ripped off again. It'd hurt that I had no father around growing up, but nothing like this. At least before I had my delusions: though I resented that he didn't take me with him, there was comfort in the thought that he at least wanted me. That he begged her to have me, to keep me. That I was special. But the truth was that I was a trap set for him, a pawn to force him to choose my mother over his wife. She didn't want me- this I knew. But he didn't either. I was the failed plan that they were stuck with, that devastated a family, and ruined lives.

The worst part about the news was that I was clearly following in my mother's footsteps. With everything that happened between myself and Parker, I was barely any better. I guess I was destined to be a mistress of some sorts. This was harder to deal with than the web of lies my mother had woven. All I wished for now was the truth. Was I a product of a flailing marriage between my parents? Or was I a sinister plot to destroy a marriage, dividing the spoils of war?

Uncovering the lies would likely leave me devastated, but I needed to know the answers as badly as I needed air to breathe.

This was too much for me to handle. All I had known or thought about my life was turning into a lie. My knee-jerk reaction to Kennedy's revelation was proof of that. Did Kennedy deserve my wrath? Of course not! But I was my mother's child. I projected all the pain, rage, and hurt I had thought was locked away in her direction, so I wouldn't have to bear the brunt of it alone. Even if her facts weren't 100% correct, *any* truth to it was a devastating blow. What I needed to do I dreaded most of all: call my mother. She didn't answer the first time I called, so I left a message. I knew she was still upset with me, and I didn't want to speak to her, but with this new turn of events, I had to at least make the effort.

When she finally answered, I didn't give her the chance to speak. "Mom I need to talk to you. It's important. Can I come over?" I immediately regretted the decision to call her. "Oh? So, you have a mother now? Are you sure? Last time I checked, your mother was an evil witch who never loved you and who abused you every chance she got. Now, all of a sudden, you *need* to talk to me?" Her smug attitude oozed from her voice. "Look, I'm sorry I hurt your feelings, but this is important. I just heard something about my father that doesn't make sense. I-" "Your father? Are we back to this again? I thought you were over asking questions about him years ago. What brought this on?" I knew she

495

was deflecting, but I answered her anyway. "Well, actually Kennedy just came over, and we were talking, and-" "THAT GIRL IS A LIAR! DON'T YOU BELIEVE ANYTHING SHE SAYS! SHE'S A LIAR AND SHE'S JUST TRYING TO DESTROY US! I TOLD YOU NOT TO TALK TO HER! WHAT WERE YOU DOING IN THE FIRST PLACE?" She went on yelling for 5 minutes before I could even speak. "MOM! MOM! CALM DOWN! Why do you think I even called you in the first place?" Her meltdown, however amusing, wasn't what I needed right now. I needed answers that only she could provide. "Mom, I just need you to tell me the truth. Could she really be my sister?" "That lying slut is just a scammer trying to ruin our lives! Gwennie I need you to believe me: there is ABSOLUTELY no way that she is of any relation to you. Just forget about everything she said. She's a liar who is trying to get back at me through you. Her mom always hated me because I got your father and she didn't."

It *sounded* plausible enough, but Kennedy was quite convincing. I knew I'd have to talk to my mother in person. Though she did a good job of fooling most people, I could always tell when she was lying. As I listened to my mother continue her campaign against Kennedy, I let my mind drift towards the memories of my past conversations concerning my father. My mother was always on the defensive when I brought him up. There was never one moment that she didn't end up yelling about how I was ungrateful, and that she was no liar. She always ended up saying how unfortunate she was to have been left by him and end up with such a terrible daughter. This time, however, she'd laser-focused on Kennedy and made her the common enemy.

Soon enough, though, she'd switch her focus from the "horrific lies" Kennedy told me, to the "I can't believe you actually gave thought to her lies" guilt trip to keep me from asking anything else.

Ten minutes later, the moment arrived. "I cannot even imagine why you, my child, would take anything she said seriously. You know her reputation. You know how she decided to drop you for those Jezebels at church. How could you even think to give credence to her lies? Were you that angry at me? Did your thirst for revenge become so great that you would conspire with a person you don't even *like* to fashion these lies against me? Do you know how hurt I am to know this is what you think of me? That I'm a homewrecking liar who-" "MOM!" I sharply inhaled. "Immediately after I mentioned her name, you started ranting. So how do you know that Kennedy accused you of being a homewrecker if I never told you what she said?"

She was silent for a few seconds. "Well, she called me one before, so I-" "When, mom? When did she call you a homewrecker?" "I don't remember. It was a long time ago. She came up to me at church and- Wait! Why are you interrogating *me*? She lies about me and insults me and you do nothing but accuse and interrogate me as if I'm at fault here! Don't tell me you believe her? I can't believe you believe her? I'M YOUR MOTHER GWEN. I GAVE BIRTH TO YOU. I TOOK CARE OF YOU BY MYSELF ALL THOSE YEARS SINCE THE DAY YOUR NO-GOOD FATHER LEFT! HOW DARE YOU-"

I knew the conversation had reached the end. I had no desire to be a party to her victim charade. "You know what, mom? I can't even do this right now. I have to go." I hung up the phone before she could respond.

After all that denial, her true colors showed. Kennedy, as far as I knew, wasn't the type to accost someone at church and call them out their name. And even if I didn't want to believe my mother, her trademark "bait and switch" routine had proved one thing: her defensiveness was definitely a cover. And based on her explosive reaction, this was something *huge*. I knew there was just one thing left to do.

Chapter 8
May 2017

Kennedy wouldn't look at me, much less speak when I saw her at church. She wouldn't answer my calls. It had been three weeks and Kennedy's active avoidance was maddening. At this rate, I might have to go to the den of Undesirables (Heaven's house) to meet her after their Bible study. I haven't been there since she'd first moved to Boston, and never had a desire to return since our falling-out years ago. But I needed to speak to Kennedy, and at this point, I was willing to do whatever it took to make her respond.

My mother, still raw from our last conversation, wouldn't answer my calls either, so I knew she had no answers she was willing to give. I had barely spoken to Carine since she turned me in to the Pastor, so she had no idea about Kennedy's revelation. I needed to talk about it. I needed to figure out what was truth and what was a lie. Kennedy's story, though eerily realistic, was still just a story. My mother's denial and refusal to talk about my father (both now and in the past) left me little information to actively refute Kennedy's accusations. Now I was left with two conflicting ideas of who my

499

father was, and no real way to separate it into a complete portrait of his character.

If I took Kennedy's idea to heart, my father was a philanderer and adulterer who violated his marital vows for my mother. A willing participant in the destruction of his household. That made me not a product of love, but a lustful consequence, a pawn of a scorned lover, to destroy any remainder of love and happiness in said marriage. But, he also was a caring man who thought about me and tried to stay in my life until my mother pushed him out. That meant that he has a redeemable character, and that he did, in fact, love me.

If I took my mother's story, their love was volatile, brought on by the fact that she never wanted kids. He forced her into having me, and then left because the resentment that had built before my conception had caused too great a rift between them. I was an idea that was better in theory than in reality. Then, he only came by occasionally so he could see her and sleep with her, and take the few pictures with me. Then he died, leaving me with little memory of him, and a dead end about who he was.

In either scenario, my conception was the factor declaring the end of a marriage: my parents or Kennedy's. Neither scenario left room for the other's claims, and both focused me as a clear-cut point of contention. My very existence had broken up a marriage any way you slice it. That was something I couldn't stomach, so I was determined to figure out which of these were the most accurate. Thus, I decided to ask Kennedy for tangible proof. If she consented (which she

wouldn't if she was lying), I'd know the truth. Either way, it had to come out somehow.

****

The more time you spend unearthing the truth, the more you expose your true character. I know you are looking for answers, but be careful of the manner in which you seek out the answers. It will all come out in due time,[106] but accusing multiple people of lies and deceit will only hurt you and everyone involved. What you find may cause you a great deal of pain. Be careful to not alienate others in your quest for truth. You may need them more than you think. And remember, if you are looking for Truth to complete that void you're feeling, to make your life make sense again: turn to Me.[107] I will take care of you.

****

She stared at me in disbelief. "You want me to do what?" I kept my composure calm. "I just want to know the truth, once and for all. I'll pay for it, but I would like you to take a DNA test. If you're really my half-sister, you should have no problem doing it. It would only validate your story." I was on a roll. Earlier that day I'd accepted the job offer (and pay cut) at a small accounting firm in Needham, MA. Now I was standing in front of Heaven's apartment asking Kennedy to take a DNA test. Photos and mementos could be forged or

---

[106] Luke 8:10
[107] John 14:6

doctored. There was no way to falsify DNA. If she was telling the truth about my father, we'd be a partial match. If not, I would confirm the fallacy of her story. Her hesitancy was making me calmer by the second. She knew she couldn't do it because her lies would be exposed. I had no doubt that in any moment, she'd be recanting her ridiculous story.

"Okay." I stood, confused. "Okay, what?" "Okay, I'll take the DNA test." I was taken aback, but there was little time to deal with the shock. "I'll have to choose the DNA test. Who knows what type of tampering you're capable of when it comes to the results. I don't need to-" "Seriously? You're still questioning my integrity even after I've agreed to take the test? If I was lying, why would I set myself up for that? And how would I even be able to tamper with results? That doesn't even make sense!" I had every urge to scream at her until she felt as unsettled and insecure as I felt in that moment. She may have had a point, but I wasn't about to let her know that I agreed with her. "People who are desperate to destroy others' lives always seem to find the creativity to discover new lows. Lord knows my mother told me that your mom was jealous of her marriage to my father, and you seem to have inherited her spiteful nature."

I know that was an unnecessarily low blow, but there was no way I'd let her stand there and make a fool of me. And there was no way she was my sister. I don't even know why I suggested the test. I thought she'd back down and confess as soon as I suggested it, and this would be all over. Unfortunately, I was far too impulsive and headstrong, and now I was stuck. I didn't really care about the test. I just wanted to prove

Kennedy was lying. I accepted that my mother, however imperfect she is, was telling the truth. So, I gathered myself, and prepared to leave, saying, "I don't need to take this test. I don't even know why I bothered with you. I'm not giving you the chance to fake results and really ruin my life."

"How about you just go to a doctor and use a blood sample for whatever DNA test you need? If anything, I could do it for you. This week, even. It would only take a few minutes to do. Maybe then you'd-" Heaven was standing a few feet away on her stoop. My rage mounted. "Who even asked you? See, Kennedy! I knew you couldn't even be trusted to keep this to yourself. Always running back to your friends like the weak little-" "Actually Gwen, had your discussion not been so loud, I wouldn't have known a thing." Heaven responded, as Kennedy looked on, angrily." "I came outside to see what the commotion was, and I heard about you not trusting a DNA test. I figured, being a doctor and all, if you're worried about results, I volunteer to take blood samples of *whomever.* So, you can go home now, and stop embarrassing me in front of my neighbors. It's late. My husband and I would like to go to bed. Go home. Figure out your mess on your own time, on your own property."

She turned and looked at Kennedy. "You okay sis?" Through gritted teeth, eyes welling up with tears, she responded, "I'm fine." As she turned to leave, a worried look came across Heaven's face. "Gwen, can I speak to you for a second?" I was still livid, but I nodded in agreement and walked up the stairs to meet her at the door. "Look, I don't know what's going on with you two, but you'd better fix it. And fast. Kennedy isn't like me. I've been through enough to know that people like you don't accurately represent God, but she hasn't been a Christian for that long. If you do anything, and I mean *anything* to push her away from God, you will have to deal with me. I promise: that's not something you want for yourself." With that she turned and went back inside, closing the door behind her.

My great mood, caused by accepting a new job, was now officially ruined. Somehow this exchange had left me exhausted, and now my anxiety was beginning to mount. I decided to just go home, feeling defeated. As I drove home, my phone began dinging. A few moments later, at a red light, I pulled over to read my text messages.

"Whatever you two were arguing about seems important if you are carrying on outside my house about a DNA test. I think it's worth exploring the possibility of the blood test. I assume you both have health insurance. Tomorrow, call to schedule an appointment with me at Klinton Hospital on Thursday at 3:30pm. Pay whatever co-pay and I'll override the appointment so you can be seen. The turnover for results shouldn't be more than a day. Bring whoever needs the blood test. Let's end this nonsense now."

It was Heaven. She'd made a group chat with Kennedy and myself, and made an appointment for us to come get our blood drawn. I wrote back, "This is highly unusual. And most likely illegal. Plus, Kennedy is your friend. I know you'll cover for her and skew the results in her favor. Anyway, I am not going to lie and create a medical necessity for this test. That is fraud. I'm not as comfortable with dishonesty as the both of you are, so I'll have to say no."

"Are you kidding Gwen? I'm willing to open my schedule to accommodate this issue you're so absorbed with, and you're accusing me of possibly tampering with the results? Do you really think I'd willingly jeopardize my career by faking a blood test? For you, no less? Wow. And here I was, expecting you to say, "thank you." Gratitude really isn't your thing at all, is it? That's cool though. Go ahead and see if anyone else will care enough to try and help you. Go ahead and spend a few hundred dollars and wait weeks for your results. That'll help your situation."

I didn't want to admit it, but I'd prefer her way if only it was someone else. But thankfully, I'd remembered that doctor-patient privilege would mean she wouldn't be able to talk about this to anyone. Ever.

"Okay. Fine. I have a physical at Klinton on Thursday, anyway, so I might as well stop in before. Can we make it for 3pm instead? My other appointment is for 3:30."

"Whatever Gwen. Fine. That works for me. When you've booked the appointment, I'll put a note in your chart that I ordered the generic labs as well as a DNA profile, so you won't have to draw blood twice that day. Just make sure that you don't eat within 12 hours of the appointment so we can get everything."

Throughout this exchange Kennedy had stayed silent. Considering the fact that Heaven was doing this for her, I was appalled at the lack of gratitude she'd displayed. But perhaps she was texting Heaven on a separate message thread, and wouldn't be responding to me because she was still upset about the previous conversation. Either way, it would've been nice to receive confirmation that Kennedy was coming.

Heaven must've felt the same way because she sent another text message directed towards Kennedy. "Ken? You're not even going to respond? Are you coming?" All we received was a "I'll be there." I don't know why, but the thought of Kennedy being miserable because of Heaven's suggestion made me feel so much more at ease with the situation. Don't get me wrong: there was nothing comfortable about this situation. This was extremely risky, involving Heaven. True, she was bound by the law, but if I wasn't so sure that Kennedy was lying about this paternity situation, this would give me *extreme* cause to worry. Thank God I'm sure about this...

****

Thursday should have been a simple day. I should've woken up at my leisure, and gotten ready for a few quick medical appointments. The pandemonium that ensued, however, was quite the opposite of simplicity.

Let's begin with the fact that I awoke to my mother calling me, cursing at me because I hadn't paid her bill. I was far too groggy to be able to decipher which exact bill she was upset about, but it was of no consequence anyway. She would call back once she had realized I hadn't paid any of her bills. Every time she had asked me for money, she had ignored the vehement warnings that I was no longer working and could no longer afford to carry her financial burden. She assumed I was willing to finance her financial irresponsibility. Over the past few years, her spending became reckless, and her lies bold. My mother thought I hadn't noticed when she asked me for $200 three times in one month for the same bill. So, this morning I let her yell, and then I reminded her that she could just as easily get a job if her disability checks weren't cutting it anymore.

Before you lambaste me for being cruel, may I remind you that my mother is far from disabled- in any way. She'd gotten herself on welfare years ago, and when they'd ended it (after I'd turned eighteen), she was forced to get a job. Unfortunately for them, after almost 10 years of working in a medical office, she'd "slipped" and fallen while carrying a box of medical supplies. Her dramatic fall caused her to roll down some precarious looking stairs (about 5), hit her head, and bruise a disc in her spine. Truth is, she was fine. She was back to picking up boxes around the house within a week, possibly trying to re-injure herself. She only moaned in pain around other people. Around me, she'd command me to pick up heavy boxes, and help her move furniture. When I couldn't do the task alone, she'd mock me mercilessly and show me "how it's done" by doing it herself- with ease. She was faking her injury because she didn't think she should have to work, after her life didn't turn out like she had hoped.

Of course, she successfully sued the company. She'd received a hefty settlement, but of course that wasn't enough for her. She applied for disability and played the part of the helpless invalid until she was awarded enough to help pay her bills long-term. Her rent was ridiculously cheap. She'd gotten an apartment in an independent living apartment building, and had very little bills. Disability all but covered rent. With the money from her structured settlement, she was comfortable. At least, she should have been. Yet her money always seemed to run out. I recognize that she is my mother, and the Bible says I have to honor her. But I was tired of being scammed out of my hard-earned money by someone who only called when she needed money or needed to gossip.

Thus, beginning my day with an irate mother was not conducive to my day of simplicity. As the day progressed, it did not improve much. The encounter with my mother left me with a pounding headache. Since I had the physical later, I couldn't eat anything, and therefore couldn't take any pain medication. Also, I had to go do a training at my job, which ran over time, so I ended up rushing to the hospital, and paying for parking just so I wouldn't be late.

I arrived after Kennedy, and as I entered the doctor's office, I found her seated, silently sulking on a rolling stool next to Heaven. I was surprised that they weren't chattering away like they usually do at church. Nonetheless, I watched as Heaven asked the nurse to draw Kennedy's blood. I craned my neck to try and see if the sticker label read the correct name. Of course, the other two rolled their eyes at me while I did so, but I was on a mission. When the nurse returned to draw my blood, Kennedy stood and silently left, tapping Heaven on the shoulder, and giving her a slight wave. She barely glanced in my direction, but I didn't mind. As I sat there, daydreaming, Heaven typed away on her computer until I cleared my throat. "Gwen, you're free to leave at any time. I'll call you when the results are in." I gave her a pointed look. "I still have my physical today with Dr. Jones. She's in this department, so I thought I could wait it out here, but *clearly,* I should go elsewhere. Your bedside manner needs work. Anyway, apologies for inconveniencing you so greatly!"

She turned around and stared at me for a few seconds. "Dr. Melissa Jones?" I nodded. She sighed. "Dr. Jones is out today. I'm covering her patients. No one called you and let you know? You'll be seeing me instead of her today. That is, unless you want to reschedule, if you're uncomfortable seeing me." "Unlike you, I am mature enough to separate whatever issues we have for this potential doctor-patient relationship. I mean, I know you've had your trouble in the past, but I hope you're competent enough to perform a simple

509

physical. I assume so, since they still let you be a doctor." She was vexed, but held her composure. I was almost impressed, but it would take far more than her silence to impress me. She looked extremely uncomfortable, but she began the physical.

Unfortunately, I had forgotten the many invasive questions I'd have to answer in a typical appointment. It had been two years since I had been to a non-psychiatric doctor. That's when the tables had turned. Since my new doctor was in the office she worked in, she had access to all my medical records. She began asking if I was still taking the medications prescribed to me by my therapist, and I became extremely nervous.

When she began reading through my gynecological notes, as they were the most recent medical encounters I'd had, I could hear her tone change. She must've seen the information about the pregnancy (and the termination.) I know she did, because her query began with the question: "When was your last pap smear?" When I paused, she'd said, "Never mind. Your records are here so I'll just check your his-to-ry." Her words slowed as she clicked through the links on the computer. It was only for a moment, because she quickly regained composure, but the damage was done. A panic attack, sudden and violent, set in, making my day infinitely worse. I was embarrassed to have Heaven not only read my medical history, but to witness my panic attack and treat it as well. How utterly humiliating!

Once the nurse (called in with medication to ease my panic attack symptoms) left the room, Heaven turned and looked at me. I tried to speak, to explain, but my breathing was still really rapid and I couldn't make out any words. I didn't have the words to say, anyway, but I tried to give some form of explanation for the information in my medical chart. She held up her hand to stop me from speaking. "Gwen, you don't have to say anything. It's okay. Trust me, I am in no position to judge you. And this information is covered by law, so as far as this is concerned, this conversation never happened. From a personal standpoint, are you okay? This couldn't have been an easy decision for you. I know you love God <u>so</u> much, and how important it is that you are obedient to His will. Do you have anyone you can talk to about it? Because if you need someone, I'm here. I know we haven't been on the best of terms for the past few years, but I'm here for whatever you need."

Still unable to speak, I began sobbing. I couldn't believe what I was hearing. Part of me was still burning with shame that she had found out about my secret. Another part of me was angry at myself for crying: feeling raw and exposed. But the overwhelming feeling I felt (at first) was relief. That gave way to a deep (albeit irrational) anger at Heaven's reaction to the information she'd just received. Who was she to offer me compassion? Who was she to go beyond the limit of professional indifference to try to reach out to me on a personal level? Who was she to be nice to me, even though I've been nothing but condescending and insulting. For years I've belittled her, told her that her Christianity was weak, flawed. Who was she to repay

511

**that with kindness? It made me feel weak, eclipsing me
with thoughts like**

This is what I've been asking of you. Compassion for those who
have made mistakes. That way they know there is no
condemnation for them,[108] but forgiveness and hope. This is
the call. This is what it means to follow Me. This is what living
in Christ looks like. You've hurt her. You've talked about her.
You've openly denounced her. And yet, she is choosing to care
about your well-being in this moment. You chose to hurt her.
She is choosing to love you. This is what I meant by "love your
neighbor."[109]

**My tears showed no sign of subsiding. Heaven
stood beside me, and wrapped me into a hug. She then
began praying for me. For ten or so minutes she prayed
about my life. She asked God to give me comfort and
peace. To bless me and my family. To bless my job and
my social life. She asked God to give me the desires of
my heart. She asked God to bless me with health and
prosperity. And then she got deep. She asked God to
heal the brokenness in me. She asked God to help me
forgive those who had caused a world's worth of hurt in
my life. She asked God to help knock down the barriers
I'd placed to protect myself after being hurt and violated.
Shea asked Him to heal the places I wouldn't even allow
my own mind to access. She prayed for me to restore
the relationships I'd broken and severed due to fear,
shame, and distrust. She asked God to melt my heart
with His love, and change my character to reflect His
own, more and more each day. She told God that He had**

---

[108] Romans 8:1
[109] Mark 12:29-31

made promises that He would deliver, unshackle, and restore His children, and that we were holding Him accountable for them.

As she continued, a small nagging thought kept trying to distract me from the prayer. *=Of all people, she's praying for me? Her?=* But I pushed it away. Prayer was sacred, no matter who it was that was doing it. But I was surprised that at my own reaction to the prayer. I can't explain it, especially since I didn't really like her, or believe that she was *that* great of a Christian, but I felt lighter. It was as if a weight lifted- one I didn't know was there. What I found most appalling is that I'd never felt that way after a prayer before. Not after prayers in church, prayer in Bible study, or even when I prayed for others. I'd never felt this unburdened and powerful. It was almost as though my prayers, up until this point, weren't really prayers. While Heaven prayed, I felt like I was literally sitting next to God. It can't really be put into words, but it was a feeling that left me deep in thought, long after Heaven had said "Amen." If this prayer made me feel so close to God, feel so unburdened, and so fulfilled, why had I never felt this before? Was the distance between myself and God so vast, and my ignorance of this so great, that I'd fooled myself into thinking I was closer to God than I was?

As I wondered about my standing with God, Heaven pulled back and looked at me with a worried expression. "Gwen?" I snapped my attention back to the present, remembering that I was still in a doctor's office.

I chuckled to myself, finding humor in the fact that my most religious/spiritual experience to date occurred in a medical office, with a woman, whom I couldn't stand, praying for me because I had a panic attack about her finding out I had an abortion. I thought this was hilarious! Here I was, piously decimating her character for *years*, and yet, her prayers were far more powerful than mine had ever been! I wasn't jealous, per se, but it made me want to know why her, and not me? Was I really that bad of a Pharisee? Was I the one from the parable[110]: self-absorbed, self-loving, self-condemning while I paraded my outward status of a Christian? Did I use others' mistakes as validation that they didn't deserve God's mercy, and therefore none of my own?

Heaven looked even more worried when I began laughing. She was about to reach for her phone, to call the nurse back in, when I stopped. "I'm okay! I'm not having a mental breakdown. This is just too funny! Wait! Let me start again." I took a deep breath. "Thank you. Thank you so much, Heaven. That prayer was-. Thank you. You didn't have to do that. Especially after how I've treated you all these years. I can't believe you did that! This is so funny! I don't think I've ever had an encounter with God before. I mean, I felt the urge to get baptized when I was younger, sure. But here I am, sitting in a doctor's office with nary a Bible in sight, and I've had an encounter with God that rivals every single church service I've ever been to. Even funnier, this is a result of the prayer of someone who hates me!"

---

[110] Luke 18:9-14

As I broke into another fit of laughter, Heaven started to smile. "It's not that I hate you Gwen. You just know how to get on my last nerves. Extremely well. We were acquaintances once. But you judge people very quickly. And very harshly. That's why I decided it would be best for myself (and you) to cut off all contact with you. But I've always prayed for you. And I certainly don't hate you. My heart is breaking for you. You must have been so scared dealing with all of that on your own." My laughter slowed to a stop. "Terrified. Especially with the thought of it getting out, and becoming the subject of church gossip." "I hear you," she responded. "Listen, I have a full schedule most days, but how about you come by for dinner sometime? There are some things I'd like to discuss with you. I should have the results of the blood test by then. Are you free, let's say Saturday evening at 8:00ish? Before you object, the sun sets at 7:15."

I was caught off guard. "Just me and you?" I asked. "Yes. My husband is away visiting his family this weekend, so it'll just be the both of us- unless you wanted to include someone else? Kennedy, perhaps?" "No thanks." I replied quickly. "No, you don't want to invite Kennedy, or no you don't want to come over for dinner?" Her question was slowly drawn out, like if she'd said it any after, I'd get skittish and run. "No to Kennedy. Hmm. Okay to dinner, I guess." I couldn't believe myself. It involuntarily flew out of my mouth. I had no desire to eat with someone who'd been my "enemy" for so long. But the prayer had clearly

515

disarmed me (and clouded my judgement.) As soon as she received an affirmative response, she shuttled me outside of her office, making apologies about her busy schedule. "See you at 8:00 Gwen." And with that, she shut the door.

I was still on my prayer high when my mother called me back. With my mood still elevated, I answered. Unfortunately, the curse words she screamed out at me were more than enough to jolt me back into reality. I held the phone away from my ear as I walked back to my car. I placed the phone on the passenger's seat, and waited until she exhausted of her tirade.

I was halfway home by the time she hung up the phone. I had half a mind to text her "I decided to get a DNA test with Kennedy," just so I could give her a heart attack. But that wouldn't make me any better than she: vindictive, petty, always hitting below the belt. I feel like as hard as I try to escape any of her qualities, I dig my feet in them and become more like her. I tried to abstain from all sexual contact, which isn't a bad thing, but I took it to the extreme. Perhaps that was just a result of the PTSD from the rape. Maybe it was a result from my mother's reaction to the rape. She punished me, and coddled my rapist. She was an indiscriminate, loose woman, so I decided to become the closest thing to the female Jesus. I wouldn't allow myself to be tempted. I wouldn't talk to men. I'd avoid them at all costs, unless they were in church.

Unfortunately, most of men in the church did not appreciate or respect my boundaries. They told me that I was taking it "too far" with my demand for absolutely no sexualized physical contact. I wanted nothing more than a simple "church hug" (one armed, from the side), and the occasional hand-holding. Absolutely no kissing. No pressing my body up against theirs. Nothing of such kind. I didn't bother acknowledging any of those men after the fact. In fact, if they flirted too much, used profane language, drank alcohol, or said dirty jokes, I'd effectually cut them off. I had zero-tolerance. Eventually the word spread and no one would pursue me. I told myself it was for the best. Their lackluster standards wouldn't be able to match my Godly standard, so they obviously weren't marriage material

But here I was, a reformed stripper, prostitute, and murderer in the same. The things I tried to bar from my life had taken over. I'd become my mother. Maybe even worse than she is. The first taste I had, making out with a man, was at the end of graduate school. But it clearly wasn't enough. Had I not been drunk that night, who knows how far it would've gone! I should've learned my lesson then, putting away all the lingerie, the dating, and just promised myself to the Lord. But I was weak. Apparently, I still am. I still crave male companionship. I still want a husband. I still want to have sex. And it confuses and angers me.

After the damage I've done, the damage that has been done to me, I still have sexual urges. Do you know how much I begged God to take them away from me? Do you know how many nights I've yelled at God for giving them to me in the first place? How I love and hate sex?

517

It's ruined my life on so many occasions, but I still don't want to stay away. How it's like a drug, more than any other drug, but the withdrawal, the guilt, and the shame make it completely not worth it. Not even a moment. I just wish I could remember that before I do it. While I'm in the heat of it, in the middle of the craving or while I'm hot and bothered. I just wish I could remember how the aftermath feels before it gets too far.

Carine wouldn't understand that. She was still a virgin. She hadn't disgraced herself like I'd done, sleeping with a married man (twice apparently), getting pregnant and having an abortion. I was sure that if no man wanted me before, when I was chaste, they sure wouldn't want me now. If I'd ever disclosed my past to a man, I was sure he'd run for the hills. Especially the ones in the church. Even worse, if one did stick around, he'd be sure to pressure me into the very behavior I was ashamed in, using the excuse that I'd done it with others. Surely, he'd tell me that I was damaged goods and had to prove my love for him. I had to be grateful for whatever love he'd give me because no one else would want me, and he was taking a chance on me by accepting my past.

I'd heard it before. Not from my own suitors, but from the girls in the Bible study. Foolishly, as a teen, I'd counsel other women to accept this type of "love," not understanding the abuse it truly was. I'd tell other girls they would have to settle for whomever would want them. I thought that once their virtue was gone, their worth would decrease exponentially, and at a certain point, cease to exist. And here I was, past that imaginary line I'd drawn for others. A line of no forgiveness, no redemption, no hope of a decent man ever considering me marriage material. Now I understood the angry and sad reactions of the girls I spoke to. Now I clearly saw that I was extinguishing hope, and leaving no room for mercy when I told them that their value had permanently decreased. I was being cruel, heaping onto them shame and guilt, hurt, and brokenness with judgment.

My prayer high was demolished by the time I had arrived at home. I replayed the last few days in my head. I had accosted Kennedy and convinced her into getting a DNA test. But I also (inadvertently) included Heaven into it, so I couldn't even pretend I didn't get the results. It was all out of my hands and I was terrified. On top of everything I was feeling, I was living my worst nightmare. I had basically become my mother, and the girls who I'd ostracized knew my deepest and most shameful secrets. I wish I could take it back. Every word I said. Every action of cruelty. Maybe then there'd be some mercy for me. Carine in her naivete shared my secret with the Pastor of the church. But Kennedy had no obligations to me. No threats I could make would change the fact that she knew, and so did Heaven.

Why did I make her into an enemy? Why did I constantly try to break her down? Why did I do that to basically everyone? I'd never questioned why I treated people this way before. I had combined it with my righteousness and gave myself permission to talk to anyone any kind of way. I'd been so focused on anger at Kennedy, and accusing her of being a liar, that I'd forgotten that she knew about the abortion. What was I thinking? Constantly goading her, provoking her into breaking down and admitting she was a liar, when I was the liar. I had the most to lose in this situation. In fact, I had everything to lose...

****

"I always thought I had to maintain these super high standards of righteousness, to be a living example of what a Christian should be. I hated the example of Christianity you represented. It seemed like you were giving everyone a free pass to do whatever they wanted if they went to church and claimed to be in a relationship with God. I felt it caused confusion for new believers, and gave them permission to continue in their life of sin and call it a struggle. I guess I didn't respect your point of view because it looked too much like my mother's."

Heaven sat across from me at her dinner table. She'd made a vegetable lasagna for me, and some sort of meat dish on the side for herself. After small talk and obligatory pleasantries, she'd asked me why I was always so "unapproachable" (her word, not mine.) I told her, I was trying to live up to a Godly standard. That led to why her and I weren't friends. I slipped and said too much, however, because she began asking what I meant by the comment about my mother.

I figured now was a good time to change the subject. "So, you said you had the results of the blood test. Were you planning on sharing them with me?" Not that I wanted to talk about this either, but it was better than getting into the topic of my mother. "I was hoping we'd get to that a little later, but if you'd like to know now I can tell you. "Yes, I'd like to know. Wait- have you told Kennedy the results yet?" "Yes. I called her this afternoon, and she asked me. I was hoping she'd come tonight, but she thought it would be best if she didn't." I smiled on the inside. That meant I was right. She was lying about the whole thing. I was so content with myself that I didn't hear Heaven continue speaking.

"I can't believe you guys are sisters. How is this even possible? Did you know her before she came to Genesis?" "Wait, WHAT?! Sisters? Who are sisters?" She paused. "You and Kennedy had a positive match on your blood test. You share an identical DNA strand. I printed the results for your records. "That's impossible. The lab made a mistake. Or you're covering for your friend, and doctoring the results for her. But I know you're lying." She sighed. "Neither this test or myself are lying. Your blood sample was fresh. If both vials were your blood, the match would be 100% identical, rather than a 50% match. If your blood was mixed in with hers, there would be two separate DNA profiles, and the lab would denote it. And for the record, you watched as the nurse came, drew her blood, sent it to the lab, and then came to draw yours. I had nothing to do with this. All I did was print the results for you and Kennedy. In fact, the results are also on the online patient website, so you can cross reference with that. I don't know how, but Kennedy is your sister."

I felt sick to my stomach. Worse than when I found out I was pregnant. Okay, nothing could be *that* bad. But she continued anyway, "I just don't understand it. But you both have the same last name, so I assume you have the same father. Thing is, I remember you telling me about your parents being married until your father died, and Kennedy said the same thing about her parents. And you guys were only born a few months apart. How can you both be telling the truth? Unless… Your dad was a bigamist?! Or somebody's adopted!" I'd had enough. "YOU DON'T KNOW WHAT YOU'RE TALKING ABOUT!" My shouting brought her to silence. Or the tears that had begun to stream down my cheeks. "I'm sorry, Gwen. I meant no harm. I know this must be rough for you. I know it was for Kennedy. But you and her will have to get through this. You're going to have to have to sit and talk, and work out whatever issues you have. You are sisters. You have to figure it out."

"She's not my sister." I barely spoke above a whisper. We sat in silence for a few minutes, before Heaven said, "Do you want to pray about it?" When I didn't respond, she grabbed my hand and began praying. "Dear Heavenly Father, I'm so grateful for this day you've given me. I'm grateful for the love and the blessings you've given in abundance. Thank You God for everything You have done for me. For the life You've given me, providing for all my needs, and still giving me the things I desire, according to Your will. I thank you most for the sacrifice You made on the cross for my life, even though I don't deserve it. Today, I am coming to

You on behalf of my sister-in-Christ, Gwen. You know all the troubles she's had lately. You know the burdens she's had to bear. You know, more than anyone, the pain and suffering that she deals with, and the fear of alienation from you she's had. God, please remind her that You are more than enough for her. Please remind her of the community she has access to, if only she'll ask. Please show her the love that she desperately needs, and teach her how to love others with the love You've shown. This is a rough time for her, and she has more questions now than answers, so please protect her mind and her heart while she seeks out the answers. Since You are the Truth[111], give her the truth she seeks. Give her the strength to withstand whatever is coming her way. Whatever this information may uncover, help her do Your will despite any opposition. Comfort her and give her peace that passes understanding[112], and a hopeful future.[113] You promised you would, and that you would never abandon us,[114] so right now I'm holding You accountable for Your words. You said that You never lie,[115] so I believe You will come through for her. Bless her home, her family, her friends, her job, and every aspect of her life. Forgive her sins, cleansing her from anything that isn't like Your character, and restore her through the righteousness of Christ. And more than

---

[111] John 14:6
[112] Phil. 4:7
[113] Jer. 29:11
[114] Deut 31:6,8; Heb 13:5
[115] Num 23:19; Mal 3:6; Heb 13:8

anything, Father, please let Your will be done in Gwen's life. We pray this, not because we are worthy in any way, but because You are the Master of Everything. Thank You. Amen."

"I think my mother lied to me. I think she and my father were never married, and I think she used me to try and trap him into leaving his wife." Those were the first words on my mind (and out of my mouth) when Heaven said "Amen." She sat in a stunned silence, allowing me to continue. "I know that's the truth. Kennedy's story makes too much sense. There were too many plot holes and inconsistencies in the stories my mother would tell me about my father. She said he wanted kids, but he left her when she had me. She said she should've aborted me 'like the rest of them' whenever she'd get angry. I have his last name, and so does she, but he's not on my birth certificate. There's no copy of her marriage license, but I bet you there's a record of her name change. He never came around, except for the two times from my only pictures of him. My former neighbors still think that he was working out of state, and that's why he was never around, because that's what she told them. She told me he left because of me. I'm pretty sure my mother was the homewrecker in this situation."

Heaven didn't say a word. Though she didn't react outwardly to my monologue, I was pretty sure there were wheels turning in her head. It's not that I noticed. Words were pouring out of my mouth faster than I could dissuade myself from revealing my business. Especially to someone who wasn't even a friend.

"Did you know I was raped? Of course you didn't know! I never told anyone outside of my therapist. The only people who know are my rapist and my mom. I was thirteen, he was her boyfriend, and she spanked me after it happened. Called me promiscuous. Told me if I didn't keep it in my pants, she'd put me out of her house. Don't look so shocked. She did eventually break up with him, and apologize to me. But that's why I've always been so... so prudish- is what I'm told. I guess that's what makes this so ironic. On one hand you have my mother, the whore of whores, who beat me after her boyfriend raped me, telling me I was being fast. And then you have me, prude of prudes, aborted the baby that my married boss impregnated me with!

"I hated my mother! Part of me still does. I judged her for her boyfriends, her abortions, her lies, her hypocrisy. And now it's confirmed she used me in her attempt to break up a marriage? And then lied about him being dead? I have no words. I guess I'm not surprised, though. She beat me because I was raped so I guess that's as low as anyone could possibly go. But I can't judge. I have done just as bad. I repressed my sexuality because I hated it. Went to therapy and they tried to unleash it. I would control my sexual urges by wearing lingerie, which worked until it didn't. Then I tried a pole dancing class, until the studio closed. And then I tried Amateur Night. I was great, too. I only did it when I was out of town. Never anywhere noticeable- in the middle of nowhere. That used to be enough to keep those urges satisfied. But then my boss requested that I join him in a conference in Vegas.

"Carine told me I shouldn't go. I should've listened. I went anyway. It was good for my career. At least it should've been. But then I got tricked into sharing a suite with my boss. And then I drank too much. And then I slept with him. And then I did it again.

"I used to pride myself on my virginity. I literally used to feel like I was a better person than others because I hadn't even kissed a man before. In college, when I finally did, I almost went too far. I thought that was the worst of it, but clearly it wasn't. Did you know I met my boss before I started working for him? When the dance studio closed, my dance instructor invited me to amateur night. One of the girls there drugged me and apparently, I had a threesome with my instructor and my former boss. And it's on film. But they supposedly left my virginity intact. Even worse, he paid me for it. But that Vegas trip took the cake. He remembered me from back then. He thought I remembered him too, and that this whole time I was being coy and flirtatious. That's why he chose me to go to the conference. And then when I found out I was pregnant, he extorted me by saying he'd ruin me if I told anyone. He threatened to take away the baby if I had it, and offered a hefty severance package in return for an abortion. I guess you see what option I chose.

"I was stupid and told Carine about the abortion, thinking that I could trust my best friend. She went straight to the Pastor. He sat me down and told me that I had to step down from all my ministry positions. On top of that, I was obligated to attend at least 40 Bible studies before I could be re-instated in any of them. I've been attending prayer meetings just so someone else can sign off on it, as if I'm on parole! And Carine was even more dumb and went to my mother. My mother! So now she knows about the abortion too. I am a walking billboard for hypocrisy and disaster!

"Funny thing, I've never put all the pieces together before. Not like this, at least. My therapist was insufferable in trying to get me to explore my sexuality, so I stopped going. Stopped being vocal. Carine would publish it to the entire church board (like she did before with the Pastor). My mother, well she can't be trusted with anything. So, I've been bottling it up. Until now. And now I've revealed it to you. Isn't it ironic, given our relationship, that you now have me in my most vulnerable position?"

I began to laugh, but not a happy, healthy laugh. It was a manic, tortured, laugh. A laugh-to-keep-from-crying laugh. But I cried anyway. Loud, chest-wracking sobs that made me feel lightheaded, like I was drowning in my own tears.

"You were a terrible person." Heaven spoke, grabbing my hand. I pulled it away, but she grabbed it and held it tighter. She began speaking, as she used her free hand to wipe my tears off of my face. "I used to think you were absolutely horrible. You were mean, judgmental, and just terrible! I thought you were a do-gooder who had never been through anything, so that was why you had not even a shred of compassion for anyone else. Remember when I was going through the worst depression in my life, and you came to my house to pray for me? You called me a sexual deviant in your prayer, and made me so angry that I kicked you out. I almost gave up on God because of you. You were horrible! But that's not all your fault. Your behavior is just a product of your environment, a result of all the trauma you've experienced. Don't get me wrong- you've been purposely antagonistic to everyone except your little Holy Roller crew, and your behavior isn't at all excusable. But wow. I never thought..."

Her voice trailed off, and she stopped wiping my face. I looked up at her. She had stopped wiping my tears because she was wiping her own face. "Gwen, I am so sorry for everything you've gone through. My heart breaks for you, not only because of everything that's happened, but even more because you haven't had a support system to help you through this. You remember everything I went through, attempting suicide and all. I know what it feels like to have nobody to talk to. To feel betrayed by your best friend. To feel like everyone is staring at you, judging you when you walk through the church. I know what it's like to feel broken, and hurt, and want to lash out at others because of it. To try and preserve your dignity and your image, because that's all the worth you have left. I know how it feels."

Her voice broke, under the weight of her own tears. I remembered the time she spoke of, though it felt like forever ago. She had just moved to Boston, and we were acquaintances. I'd invited her to an event where she had run into a former boyfriend. Not long after, they'd rekindled their romantic relationship. I was partly responsible, as he was a co-worker and told me she was his first love. Plus, I saw Carine's ex-boyfriend milling around her, so I knew I needed to act fast. I gave him her phone number so he could try to win her back. He turned out to be a snake, though, and was caught sleeping with her best friend Mari. She had almost stopped coming to church after she was fired from her medical residency. Her final straw, however, was when she was publicly humiliated at church by her former (and now current again) best friend. I came to pray for her, but all I could think of were the sexual experiences Mari had described during their shouting match. So, I prayed for God to forgive her sexual perversion. That's when she kicked me out of her house. Not long after she attempted suicide. But somehow, she'd found God in all that mess. When she came back to Genesis, she came back in full force. By then, of course, she'd have nothing to do with me.

So, the fact that she was standing next to me wiping my tears and her own said a lot about the growth she'd made. She wasn't the same person she was eight years ago when I'd met her. She had grown exponentially. As much as I hated to admit it, she was spiritually anchored, hosting weekly Bible studies in her home. She was now married, working as a doctor (again), and active in the church. She was in the choir, and helped plan youth and young adult events for the church. She even hosted "girl talks" for the young girls in her home. I was never invited. Apparently, I make everyone "uncomfortable," so I always found out after the fact.

Eight years ago, Heaven's life fell apart, and yet she was thriving now, as if none of it had ever happened. Meanwhile, I was still in the same place as I was back then. Correction: I was worse off than I'd been. I was stripped of all my ministerial duties at church, lost my lucrative job, and went back on the promise of sexual purity I had made to myself. I couldn't even recognize myself through the choices I was making. It seems like everything I said I never wanted to be, I've suddenly become. A liar. An adulterer. A murderer. I don't even recognize myself. I don't know who I am. Clearly, I'm not the same. And now, I have to grapple with the facts that I was a "Venus flytrap" baby, my mother was a homewrecking liar, and I had a sister.

I think Kennedy hates me. I've ostracized her, called her names, speculated (and planted rumors) that she's a stripper, called her a liar, promiscuous, and much more. No wonder she wanted nothing to do with me. I could see why she opted out of being her while Heaven told me the news that we were blood sisters. She doesn't want me for a sister. I've been terrible to her. My only other living blood relative, and I'd alienated her. What family did I have that wasn't a manipulative user, or Kennedy? I wanted to talk to her, see her. Hopefully she'd let me talk to her. However, if the shoe was on the other foot, I certainly wouldn't think to extend that grace to her.

Heaven was right. I am a terrible person. I know she thinks I'm getting better, but the truth is nothing has changed. I feel like my life has been set back eight years and now I have to figure out my life again. Everyone else around me is living- thriving, even. People are making headway in their careers. They're forging ahead with relationships, marriages, pregnancies. They're forging ahead with relationships, marriages, pregnancies. They're buying homes. Going on vacations. Trying new ventures. Starting businesses. They're generally being great at life. Meanwhile, I've done none of those things, suffered a ton of setbacks, and I feel like I have nothing to show for the past eight years.

I felt more like a failure than ever before. How was it that I, a "Child of the Living God," was worse off than I'd started? After all these years of serving God, of being faithful, and of trying my hardest to live righteously, I was left behind in this race. All the people I'd thought were less than honorable, less than worthy, were now all leaders in the church and in the community. I was unemployed (soon to be underemployed), and miserable. I was where Heaven was, just a few years ago. But where she had a support system, I did not. I had done such a good job of alienating myself from the "world," that I'd deemed almost everybody too worldly to interact with. The only motivation I had to even speak with anyone was because I was lonely. And now with all the time that had passed, was I really expected to go and try to cozy up to people and forge a relationship? There was no basis for a relationship with any of them!

By this time, I'd gathered myself together, stopped crying, and stood up. I was more than ready to leave. Heaven, on the other hand, wasn't finished with me. "Gwen, I know this is a lot to ask, but I think you'd really benefit from the Bible study at my house. I know you'd rather go *anywhere* else, but I honestly believe you should come to mine. At least once before you write it off completely." I had absolutely no desire to spend time with any of them, especially now that Heaven and Kennedy knew my secrets. "No thank you," I replied torpidly. Heaven recoiled from my tone, but recovered quickly. "Suit yourself. Well, it was an interesting evening. The offer stands, but something tells me you won't be making any appearances. I guess I'll see you around church. Have a good night!"

I collected my things, and rushed out the door. I knew I had been rude, but I no longer cared. The magnitude of emotions I felt about walking into the lion's den was insurmountable. So what if I was okay with Heaven? What did that have to do with the rest of them? Perhaps Heaven was suffering from a memory lapse. She had never really liked me, but the rest, I was sure, unequivocally hated me. Kennedy was automatically at the top of the list. Then came Mariannne and Grace, both of whom I'd never associated with because of their ties to Heaven and Solomon.

The rest of the ladies in Heaven's Bible group were the ones who didn't last in mine and Carine's group. I knew for sure that they'd have it out for me. I was angry that Heaven could be so naive to even suggest such a thing. What comfort, what hope would I find in the presence of women who I'd alienated? I was better off going to Carine's study and offering up myself as tribute. At least the suffering I'd endure there would be from a friend.

As I drove home in silence. No hymns playing on my car radio. No phone conversations. Nothing. I'd been so exhausted for such a long time. The thought of discussing my secrets with other people- people I didn't trust, and who didn't trust me, was completely absurd. It was never going to happen. I needed to talk to someone who could understand the absurdity of this situation, so I called my mother.

She didn't answer, so I left a message on her voicemail, asking her to call me back. I'd totally forgotten about the argument we had gotten into earlier. I guess that was a lost cause, anyhow, so I hung up the phone and continued to my house in silence. Perhaps if I had learned how to abide in silence as a child, I wouldn't have spilled all my business out to a bunch of women who want front row seats to my destruction.

Either way. it had been a super long night, and I was exhausted. I had far more dragons to slay, and I didn't have time to waste on thoughts of my enemies. I just wish I could figure out what this next Sabbath would bring. I'd try to get some sleep tonight however being that it was certainly an emotionally taxing, but wildly informative day.

****

I really wish you'd stop building walls that I've worked so hard in breaking down. I chose you to be a part of a community, not like a country club: exclusive, with arbitrary and exclusionary rules. I chose you to be different, not isolate yourself and ostracize anyone who isn't like you. I called you to be holy, not self-righteous and impertinent. You have pushed yourself out of the reach of others, no matter how many times I attempt to draw you back over the line. No matter how much Heaven reached out to you in your brokenness, you chose to slap her hand away. She's one of the last people willing to try with you, willing to fight for you. Clearly you haven't been getting the picture. If you continue at this pace, there won't be much left I can do to help draw you back into my fold.

Chapter 9
June 2017

It was happening: scandal had broken out at Genesis SDA Church! I walked into the sanctuary on Wednesday evening. It was my habit since the Pastor and Elder had mandated rehabilitative Bible study. Unfortunately, due to oversleeping, I'd arrived almost twenty minutes late. But rather than the fifteen or so regulars who came week, the church was packed. Pastor Rogers and Elder Collins were seated next to a table in the front of the sanctuary, looking pensive and fatigued. Elder Johnson stood, motioning for silence, trying to hush the crowd, but it was to no avail. I saw Sister Karen Phillips, my mother's "best friend" standing at the small podium in the front of the church. She was far older than my mother, retired for at least a decade. But she, too was a busybody, along with the other member of their wolfpack: Sister Angelica Courts. Their mutual friendship consisted of minding other people's business, gossiping, and being holy hypocrites. I knew that seeing her, my mother wasn't too far away. After scanning the room for about two seconds, I saw her. My mother was seated in the front of the church, in her usual spot.

I tried to make sense of the scene before me. I noticed Jessica Cannon (from Bible Study) seated a few feet away from where I was standing at the sanctuary entrance. I sat by her, still confused by the happenings of the evening. "Jessica! What is going on? Did someone get possessed? Is this an exorcism?" She laughed. "Nope. Just your regular 'ol church-lynching." "What? Excuse me!?" She could tell I wasn't amused by her comparison, so before I could begin my tirade she quickly spoke. "Calm down. Apparently, Sister Phillips and your mother have found out where Kennedy's been working. Since then, they've magically obtained proof of the allegations, and made the announcement to everyone few minutes ago. Now they're calling for Kennedy to be disfellowshipped and kicked out the church. And, for once, your mom is sitting down and letting one of her friends take the lead."

I wanted to ask more, but the Pastor had stood up to speak. "I am not willing to condemn anyone without first taking their account. I will reach out to the appropriate parties and draw my own conclusions. Until then, we will not allow the judgment and condemnation of a party before its time. Furthermore, this prayer service will continue as planned." Sister Phillips went and sat next to my mother, with a dejected expression. My mother leaned in and whispered in her ear, and a few moments later, rose to exit the church. As she passed me, she scowled, and hurried out the door before I could speak to her. Sister Phillips followed suit about five minutes later.

I pondered the possibility of another interaction with my mother. I decided against it, as I'd come to church to worship God, and I certainly didn't want to get mixed up in whatever this was. It would be best for all parties if I stayed out of it and kept my mouth shut. No good could come from my involvement with a Kennedy scandal- especially if my mother was the one spearheading it. I'd thought my mother would find a way to retaliate against Kennedy because she told me the truth about my father, and my parents' relationship. I'm sure her fear of being exposed caused her to bare her teeth and sabotage Kennedy. I did feel bad- Kennedy was only trying to tell me the truth about hers and my life. A truth that I had persistently denied until that blood test forced me to confront it as reality. I had yet to embrace the truth, and attempt to forge a relationship with my "sister." But despite the tension between us, and the ill feelings we carried for one another, this brewing storm was unmerited.

A minute part of me felt like I had to warn Kennedy. I wanted to call her and let her know what was going on, what she'd be up against. I doubted that she would believe me, given our history. In fact, I was sure she would find a way to make this my fault. My mother was spearheading this. Of course it was my fault! But this impending disaster would have to wait for the time being.

I had been suffering in the throes of anxiety and depression since I had received the blood test results. I was the equivalent of the relational "anchor baby," desired only to achieve status and permanency rather than being conceived out of love. My mother never wanted me, and neither did my father (even if he changed his mind later). I was thrust upon his life as a scourge to his existing family. I wasn't wanted by anybody. Well, anybody other than God. Although my mother was still alive, part of me felt orphaned. Often enough, she'd repeated her lack of a desire for children. She blamed my father for his desire for children. She'd left out his desire to have a child with his wife, not the crazy ex-mistress he had been trying to end all contact with. And most importantly, the fact that up until two years ago he was still alive.

I had no idea how to process my feelings, while dealing with the new sibling I'd acquired. She was everything I wasn't. Kennedy grew up in the South, unchurched, but happy. I grew up in the North, a child of God, but terribly unhappy. She had grown up with a set of married parents who loved each other (and her). I grew up with a mother that I was convinced hated me. I knew at the minimum, my mother strongly resented me for my existence. As far as I knew, Kennedy had never been assaulted, molested or abused. I had been, in many ways. She had plenty of friends who supported her. I had just one. She had the life I had wished I had.

Kennedy grew up with the father I had been told was dead. I had an urn with dirt (or something else) in it to call "father." She was a daddy's girl who was super close to him, spoiled by his love and affection. I grew up having only the love of God to keep me warm. I learned to depend on God because, truthfully, no one liked me.

Growing up, I didn't have friends. A few (nice) people would talk to me in school. I had Carine at church. That was it. Everyone else I encountered, I managed to rub the wrong way. Everyone. My therapist didn't even like me! I know she'd never admit it, but I saw when she had to catch herself rolling her eyes during my session. She'd always pretend there was something in her eye and blink furiously to cover her slip-up. But I knew she didn't like me. Just like I sensed it when others would stop speaking whenever I came around. When they'd make up excuses as to why I wasn't invited to things, or would generally avoid me (or openly mock me). School, Work, Church. It always happened. That's why I learned to depend on myself and God.

I was stuck with my mother. Though I knew she resented me and didn't like me, she still fed, housed and clothed me, so that was what I focused on. She loved me enough to do those things. What need did I have to be liked as long as my fundamental needs were met? There were people out there who had no food, clothing, or shelter. There were people out there whose parents had kicked them out and left them destitute. There are people whose parents were physically and/or sexually abusive. My life was *not* unbearable, and my mom really wasn't *that* bad.

That's what I had thought until now. Or, more accurately, until the moment Kennedy's story was confirmed. Before, I had convinced myself that my mother was misguided in her love for me. I thought she

539

didn't always express it appropriately, but that she did love me. That she was telling me the harsh truth about my life in order to protect me. But now, I no longer knew what to think about my life.

Kennedy could have easily taken the truth to her grave. I had accepted that I wasn't going to know anything about my father, and had decidedly ended all inquiry into matters concerning him. But she felt the need to tell me the truth about my heritage. Though part of me was grateful for the answers to my longstanding questions, I felt burdened by the truth. That was part of the reason I couldn't tell her about the impending dramatic confrontation at church.

I didn't want her to feel like there was an axe swinging over her head, perched for her destruction. I felt that way once I had received the call from Pastor Rogers after Carine had told him about my issues. Even if I didn't like Kennedy all that much, I still didn't want her to be unfairly attacked like this. I didn't think she'd believe me, but maybe Heaven would. So, I decided to call her once prayer meeting was over (and I'd gotten my required proof of attendance signature).

Heaven and I spoke for ten minutes. Long enough for her to question how I knew about the drama at church. I understood that she was being protective of Kennedy, and that I was a prime suspect in the turmoil that had ensued. Her tone, however, was harsher than I'd thought. I knew that the ladies would blame me for the chaos, not only because I was the messenger, but because my mother was the ringleader. It didn't help that I had threatened to expose Kennedy's place of employment a few months ago. But that was just a desperate attempt to ensure her silence regarding my own skeletons. The Belles did not trust me, and I was certain that now, more than ever, I'd officially become Public Enemy #1.

****

Sabbath afternoon was absolutely gorgeous! The warm summer weather had finally arrived, with plenty of sunshine, and a slight cool breeze appeared every so often. It was a perfect day. Unfortunately, the climate inside of Genesis SDA wasn't so perfect. During the morning service, I'd sat by myself. Carine was on the pulpit, slated to do the morning's welcome. The Jeze-Belles sat together on the opposite side of the church. Pastor Rogers had a sermon prepared about love, and how it covered a multitude of sins.[116] I figured he was playing his usual game of preaching subliminal messages that he believed his congregation needed.

That was an annoying trait of Pastor Rogers'. He was always trying to discretely single people out during his message, rather than just being a messenger from God. He always had to try to make a point. It happened more frequently than before, most likely due to the fact that his term of service at Genesis SDA was due to end. In a few months, we'd be getting a new Pastor, and he'd be assigned to another church. It would be his last

---

[116] 1 Peter 4:8

before he retired. I think Genesis might have encouraged him to retire sooner rather than later.

Honestly, I heard only fragments of the sermon. I was distracted by the restlessness of the congregation. My mother kept turning around to look at the Jeze-Belles. Every once in a while, I noticed Heaven reach over and squeeze Kennedy's hand. Just before the final benediction, I looked over and caught Kennedy's eye. I smiled nervously at her, trying to show some support, but she glared at me until I became uncomfortable and looked away. I hope she didn't think I was mocking her. Maybe a few months ago I'd be scowling self-righteously like my mother was, but today? Today I just wanted to let Kennedy know that everything would be okay. I knew that she wasn't the kind of person that my mother and Sister Phillips were claiming she was. I knew that her place of employment seemed overwhelmingly condemnatory. But where I had been promiscuous, she had made every effort to cut ties with her employer/boyfriend. Any feelings of superiority I had felt had been squelched by her revelation about our relationship.

The turmoil in the church reached peak highs once everyone gathered after the potluck for the business meeting. As I looked around the room, I saw groups of people impassioned by their perspective. Kennedy, was surrounded by Heaven, Marianne, Grace, Jessica, and a few others. She looked steadily ahead, while her support system milled around her with words of comfort and cheer. Sister Phillips, my mother, and Sister Angelica Courts stood at the front of the church. They were attempting to hide their self-satisfied grins with mock outrage. It looked like a cat deliciously licking its lips at a bird, nearby and unaware. Carine walked up behind me and began expressing her outrage to the other women in our Bible study, and others nearby.

The pastor looked contrived, burdened by this scene. His eye caught mine, and his shoulders sagged. I don't think he could tell whose side I was on. Would I stand, self-righteous and self-important, with my mother? The side of everyone who had laser-focused on this ill-proven rumor to call for judgment before the accused could even speak? Or would I stand with those who counted me an enemy, my long-estranged sister and her friends whom I had gleefully persecuted not too long ago? This middle ground was unsettling, but I could not make a choice. My own sins could be exposed if I stood by Kennedy. It would expose the sordid past of our parents.' But if I stood by and did nothing, I might as well have morphed into my mother's clone. I would be deflecting my own sins to highlight someone else's. Either way, this seemed like a lose-lose situation.

Pastor Rogers reluctantly began the proceedings. My mother and her pack of wolves raised their hands to speak first, bringing the accusations to the light. The pastor would only allow one of them to speak, so Sister Phillips took the microphone and began her discourse.

"I do not like to speak out of turn," she began. "And you all know how much I despise gossips and the ever-turning rumor mill-" The audacity to lie so boldly! "-

but I must be honest about what I have seen, and confirmed with my own eyes and ears. As you know, I live in the Everett area. If I am unable to make it to the Tuesday morning service, I will go and do the Lord's service by passing out Bible tracts to the people I meet on the street. This past Tuesday, I went near that disgusting cesspool of prostitution, alcohol, and drugs called "The Kandi Shop." I had hoped that I could possibly rescue someone from that life of abject wickedness. When I approached the building, I saw that Kennedy Robertson fraternizing with the security personnel outside the club, and entering the establishment. I approached the club, as the security guard noticed me staring. I overheard one of the riffraff claim that I was 'trying to get me a piece of that young thang.' Of course, I had to set him straight. As I came forward with the Bible in hand, I told him that I did not, in fact, 'have a thing for that young piece', but that I recognized her. I asked them if that was, in fact, Kennedy Robertson, and they agreed that yes, her name was Kennedy, but they did not know her last name.

"I then attempted to go inside, but the riffraff would not allow me to enter their establishment. They said I was bad for business. Fortunately, as I stood, ready to call down the powers of Heaven onto them, a polite, handsome young man approached and told them to leave me alone. It was the owner of the establishment, Travis Springer. I told him why I had approached, to see if our dear Kennedy was inside the den of sin, partaking in the riotous lifestyle we choose to abstain from. He confirmed that it was her, and that she had been employed there for over two years. He also informed me that she was his girlfriend, and that they had been cohabitating for at least six months. As you know, she has been attending Genesis SDA for far longer than that, and knows that we do not accept those kinds of lifestyles here. He was kind enough to let me borrow a photograph of them, in which she was dressed quite provocatively! He even volunteered to attend today's meeting! I told him that it wasn't necessary, but he is here anyway. Travis, please stand honey."

The congregation erupted in a sea of murmuring and chatter. Kennedy looked as if she was going to pass out. The rage on her face amplified the depths of her feelings tenfold. Travis made his way to where Sister Phillips was standing, and began describing (in cringeworthy detail) the nature of his relationship with Kennedy. What he failed to mention, however, was that their relationship had long ended, and they no longer were living together. He insinuated that she was a dancer at the club, rather than a graphic designer who helped create his advertising campaign. Like the serpent he was, he aided and abetted Sister Phillips in her quest to tarnish Kennedy's name. I was disgusted by his display of half-truths and obvious lies. He had no respect for the house of God. I couldn't believe my mother was so desperate to ruin Kennedy that she would enlist the aid of a snake willing to tell lies in the house of God. Was there nothing sacred at all to her?

In any case, he was brief, and sat down. Pastor Rogers dejectedly called Kennedy and asked if she'd like to speak. She was barely able to, as she choked back tears. I recognized them to be the mounting rage at the lies that were told about her, but others, like Carine, assumed they were proof of her guilt. Kennedy refused to let her friends stand with her at the front. She chose to face the lions alone. As she stood, Elder Johnson asked, "Do you know this man?" She nodded. "Do you work at his establishment, the Kandi Shop?" She nodded, tears drenching her face. Once again, the church was in an uproar. "Is there anything you'd like to say?" She hesitated. I could see that part of her felt that any defense of hers would be futile at this point. But as she reached for the microphone in Pastor Rogers' hand, my mother ran up and grabbed it. "She doesn't need to speak! She's already admitted it! She's guilty! Don't let her stand here with these crocodile tears and fake penitence. She's guilty and should be disfellowshipped!"

Kennedy stared at my mother intently, her rage on the brink of boiling over, and then turned and began walking towards the exit. As my mother shouted more damage in her direction, something came over me. The next thing I knew, I was in the front, holding the microphone. "I can't believe this is happening right now. My eyes and ears *must* be deceiving me! Is this really who we have become? Kennedy, wait! Please don't leave!" I took a deep breath. Things were about to get really hairy.

"Over my lifetime, I've sat through many of these types of meetings. I've usually gone along with them: seeking for a member to be disfellowshipped because of some public sin they've committed, or a secret sin that has come to light. I have been openly disgusted at the mere thought of their public sin, vocalizing my outrage, feeling as though it was a personal betrayal of my trust and esteem. And over those years I have not thought twice about the motives behind it. But today, I cannot sit idly by and let this happen.

"I know that the responsibility of the church is to watch out for one another, correcting faults in love. We are to and ensure that our brethren do not fall to the wayside, giving up on their Walk and putting their salvation in danger. But now I believe that we've strayed drastically from that responsibility. I believe we fear being seen as spiritually lenient so much that we go full force into merciless cruelty and shameful display.

"I understand the need for censorship. It makes an example, and publicly states that some things are not okay to do. But the difference between disfellowshipping someone and censoring someone is based on intense contemplation, prayer, and an assessment of intention/heart condition. Because by their actions, you will know who they are.[117] So when they agree to re-dedicate their lives to God, continue to show up to church, struggling with their own issues, inviting others to church, and showing their remorse by agreeing to step down from their visible positions in the church until an appropriate time, I don't understand how that is not enough, and they must be kicked out anyway.

---

[117] Matt. 7:16-20

"Disfellowshipping has its place and its own necessity. But the way it's misused is either directly intentional or a result of misunderstanding its purpose. Especially because the church manual states that disfellowshipping is a last resort.[118] Too bad it is most commonly the first suggestion. It should be reserved for a person who shows no sign of remorse, no intent to change paths, and no care for the traditions of the church or the ways of God. Contrary to popular belief, this tradition of radical disciplinary action is a result of an egregious misunderstanding of the Bible.

"The situation in the Bible with the man proudly cohabitating with his step-mother is an extreme example[119]. Note that no show of remorse or repentance was mentioned, and it was a sin that was ongoing. See, remorse and repentance are different, but necessary. I can have remorse that I did something wrong, but not repent. I can be remorseful because I didn't like the consequences, and wish I never did it. Or I could repent. I could have the same remorseful attitude, but recognize that I hurt God, and thus the source of my remorse is a deep-seated unrest due to the disobedience of my God. Your attitude to your sin is reflected by your intentions. Not to mention, the fact that we sin against God and not against each other most of the time. The Biblical model for addressing sin was meant to highlight our broken relationship with God. To show His grace, mercy, and restoration available to us and through love for one another, hold each other accountable to God for our sins.[120]

---

[118] SDA Church Manual pg. 193-197
[119] 1 Cor. 5: 1-13

"Secondly, I have come to see that it is CRUEL beyond measure to have such a large group of people publicly vote on the fate of its members. In the time of Ellen G. White, a large church was considered 50 members. Nowadays, that barely makes a storefront church. The smaller the church was, the more intimately acquainted the church members would be with one another. It would help foster an environment of familial bonds and accountability. If a member went astray, discipline was to come from those who were very familiar with them, able to accurately call them into account.

"These days, churches like ours have over 500 members. Most people are not that familiar with each other, and that breeds mistrust. So, the business meetings in which we are to determine someone's guilt and punishment have become akin to the Roman tradition of feeding people to lions in front of a roaring audience. Even worse, it mirrors the last day of Jesus' life, crowds pressed around yelling, "Crucify Him!"[121] I'm sure that the overwhelming majority were expressing mock outrage. Many wanted to distance themselves from someone who was so publicly denounced. It wasn't because they believed his guilt. They didn't want to stand up for his innocence in fear their own guilt would be brought to light.

---

[120] Matt 18:15-19
[121] Matt. 27:15-25

549

"Even to mention the life of Christ, we cannot ignore the telling story of His compassion and grace for the adulterous woman.[122][123][124][125][126] She was an involuntary pawn of the Pharisees to try and trap Jesus. He offered her mercy instead of condemnation, and after forgiving her, he told her to "go and sin no more." That wasn't a free pass. It was grace and mercy, a lesson to us all to recognize what it means to treat others with love. We have now become Pharisees. We make the substantial claim of be the remnant church. But just like Israel, that didn't keep the door of God's mercy from closing on those who operated out of tradition rather than love. Jesus said, "Let he that is without sin cast the first stone."[127] Jesus had spoken many times to prove that he didn't want us to become like the Pharisees in their hypocrisy, and their judgment. Well, I have sinned egregiously enough, and God has been gracious to me in spite of it, so I refuse to be a hypocrite that casts stones.

"You are taking the place of God by condemning a person who shows the signs of remorse/repentance. Especially if they accept punishment for what they have done (good fruit)[128], and humble themselves. By not allowing a person to live out a repentant heart, and condemning anyway, you assume to read their hearts and intentions, which only God is able to do. When you

---

[122] John 8: 1-11
[123] Matt 7:1-6, 16
[124] Matt 6:12, 2, 5, 16
[125] Luke 11:52
[126] Romans 2:1
[127] John 8:7
[128] Matt. 12:33-37

excise their membership, and make them a pariah, you eliminate important avenues of communication with them. It can even alter their perception of church, and endanger their relationship with God. But we don't think of these things. We only seem to think of the "image" the church has to uphold. The ONLY image the church needs to reflect is of Christ, and when we don't so that, we lose our very purpose.

"Our methods are not of God. In the Bible, only one person is described to be an accuser: the devil.[129][130][131] We shouldn't be slandering others, using gossip and rumors against each other. The Bible says that unforgiveness is a sign of a lack of the Holy Spirit working in us,[132] and states that we should not do such things.[133] When we are on a mission to expose others' sins, we shine a light on the unconverted hearts we have, and the sins we desperately are clamoring to cover. Jesus said all things would be brought to the light. He wasn't lying. Take me, for instance. In the past few months-"

My mother interjected. "You need to sit down right now! How dare you insult God by making a mockery of this! The Bible and the Church Manual are

[129] Rev. 12:10
[130] Job 1:6
[131] Zech 3:1
[132] 2 Tim. 3:1-5
[133] Titus 2:3

clear-" "Sister Roberts! SIT DOWN" The Pastor's voice boomed. Startled, she stood as he took the microphone from her hand. He looked directly in my eyes and nodded, so I continued.

"In the past few months I have learned why Christ said not to judge one another. I have always sat on my high horse, proud of the fact that I was a virtuous woman. I scorned those who asked about support and prayer regarding their sins, especially sexual sin. I have ostracized women who came to Bible study, with repentant hearts, or questions about God. I have ridiculed women who have sought restoration from God after giving in to their temptations. And a few months ago, I committed the very acts I found so deplorable. In my pride, I expected that my attachment to God was enough to keep temptation from overpowering me. My virginity was proof (to me) that I was successfully dominating my sinful desires, and that I should teach others to do the same. Never did I consider that my virginity was not indicative of my spiritual purity, nor was it a safety from my own temptation. So, when I was faced with temptation, I was not successful and chose to succumb to sexual immorality. Even worse, I was unable to face the consequences of my wickedness, and chose to dishonor God and my body even more. I made a decision so deeply selfish that it still haunts me to this day.

"When reproached about my actions by those who loved me, I became prideful and resistant. I equated their grace and mercy as weakness. I spurned their rebuke because I thought they were incorrectly handling my trespasses. I assumed that because the tradition to publicly humiliate others was common, it was right. But humiliation doesn't serve as a warning to others. It doesn't keep anyone from falling into sin. All it does is create an atmosphere where we cannot come to one another for prayer and spiritual assistance when we need it the most. It makes us dishonest about the true state of our spiritual journey, and hide the sins with which we struggle or revel in. It causes us to become hypocrites: the finest actors of spiritual abundance, while we fester and rot in our wickedness.[134] We have no accountability, and therefore no change.

"After being found out, I expected to be publicly humiliated, because that was what I would have done if the roles were reversed. But that experience, and a few more humbling encounters with God, showed me what He *really* meant by "My grace is sufficient."[135] and that His mercy was "new every morning."[136] I realized that as much as I tried to work for my righteousness, I couldn't. And as long as I judged others by my own righteousness I could never have a real relationship with Christ.

"I'm now learning how to make amends for the most egregious of sins I've committed: hurting my fellow brothers and sisters in Christ. I've done damage to so many in the church because of my judgmental

[134] Matt. 23:27-28
[135] 2 Cor. 12:9
[136] Lament. 3:22-23

mindset, including and especially Kennedy. If anyone deserves a little mercy right now, it is her. Especially since that man, her <u>ex</u>-boyfriend, has done everything in his power to keep her from coming to church. He has always hated that she chose to love God more than him. She's a graphic designer, hired by him in a time of financial need, not a stripper. The picture my mother and her friends have painted for you is a lie. That being said, let us remember what Christ said: whatever we do to those who are the most spiritually fragile among us, we do to Him.[137]

"Now that I've said this, I just hope that you truly think on these things. And please, I implore you, postpone voting on this until we've fasted and prayed over this. Two or more must agree in the Spirit in order for something to be held as true.[138] So I am imploring the help of many to confirm or deny the allegations and to either ratify or refute this. All I can ask is your intentional, focused thoughts, prayed about, and inspired by the Holy Spirit, and possibly a change of perspective when you are faced with a decision like this. I know I'm the last person you'd expect to say this, and definitely the last person to be so open about my own life, but God really impressed it on my heart to say something. This cannot continue in the House of God, as though God has approved any of this. But I'll let you pray about it, and come to a conclusion."

Most people in the congregation were silent. Kennedy was in the back, silently weeping. Grace and

---

[137] Matt 25:31-46
[138] Matt 18:15-20; Deut. 17:6

Marianne had their arms around her, comforting her. Meanwhile, Heaven was smiling at me. Like, at me, not just in my general direction. Carine looked confused. My mother, however, looked as if she was going to have a heart attack. She sat, mouth agape, eyes burning with fury. Sister Phillips, not one to be outdone, stood and yelled, "Maybe we need to disfellowship you too! You clearly just confessed to sexual indiscretions, and you have the nerve to not only defend her, but to accuse us as being unrighteous?" But Pastor Rogers held up his hand and she stopped speaking.

"I have been at this church for a very long time," he began. "I was blessed enough to serve two consecutive terms here, and my time at Genesis SDA is coming to an end. One of the things I have worked tirelessly for was to bring God's will to the forefront, and use the Word of God to transform lives. I've been accused of being too lenient on public sin, though I have never condoned sin and always made efforts to accurately depict how God sees it. Today has shown me that my efforts have not been wasted.

"First, Kennedy chose God, despite all the pain she's been through in the past few years. Having spent a great deal of time with her, I see that she has grown tremendously in the Spirit and power of God. And now Gwen, who at times felt like a thorn in my side, so judgmental and proud, has shown what a repentant heart really looks like. I met with her, and knew that public defamation wouldn't do anything to address the roots of her sin problem. She needed to see God's grace and mercy in action. So, I mandated my rehabilitative Bible study for her. And now to see the change in action, I know that this church is headed in the right direction.

"In any case, *no one* is being disfellowshipped today. In fact, I am now proposing the implementation of my 40 Day Spiritual Rehabilitation Program©. Each spiritual offender will have the option of enrolling into the rehab program. They can also choose to disengage with the church entirely and, in essence, disfellowship themselves. Censure will still be prescribed as deemed necessary, but we will not permanently remove a member unless they are rebellious and unwilling to repent. This way God can restore His willing children into a healthy spiritual walk with Him. I move that this be accepted and implemented immediately. All in agreement, say aye."

I didn't stay to hear the results of the vote. I rushed out of the church, ran into my car, and headed home. The adrenaline of the moment was fast fading, and what was left was a gnawing sensation in the pit of my stomach. I couldn't believe that I had stood and said all of those things. Even if I hadn't gone into detail, the fact that I revealed so much about having fallen into sin mortified me. True, there were no pitchforks, torches, and stones, but that didn't mean the threat wasn't still looming. Even if Pastor Rogers had enough votes to pass and implement his "rehab" program, he'd be gone in less than a year. Most likely, the new pastor would be convinced to overturn his program and return us to the same misguided tradition of harsh spiritual discipline.

Realistically, Kennedy and I could be disfellowshipped anyway.

I hadn't said anything to anyone when I left. As soon as my vote was counted, I slipped out as quickly as humanly possible. I knew my phone would soon be inundated with phone calls and text messages, but I wanted to be home before I had to deal with it. My level of embarrassment and shame was rising by the minute. How could I have said all those things? I wasn't even trying to be noticed during the meeting, which is why I sat close to the back. What could've possibly gotten into me to make me do that? All I knew was that I needed to get away, and hopefully (someday) I could return to the church.

****

I know it doesn't feel like it right now, but you did the right thing. You stood up for your sister. You spoke out against traditions that have evolved into a sinister method of breaking apart the church I am trying to build up. You feel every urge to run and hide, because though you stood up for what was right, you inadvertently made yourself a target. But, my child, you stand among the ranks of Elijah[139], Shadrach, Meshach, Abednego[140], and Paul[141]. Each stood for what was right, and became targeted because of their faith in Me. Do not let this

---

[139] 1 Kings 18, 19
[140] Daniel 3
[141] Acts 9

discourage you from doing right. You have no idea how many people have been impacted by your decision tonight. You don't know how many people were blessed by your words, and by your testimony. There will always be people who choose to use your testimony against you, but remember, I said that ALL things work for the good of those of you who love Me.[142] Your growth in Me has only just begun...

---

[142] Romans 8:28

Epilogue
December 2017

The world is still in chaos. There are mass shootings, bombings, natural disasters, and threats of war. There are the usual, run-of-the-mill crimes: domestic violence, rapes, assaults, thefts, etc. Depression, anxiety, helplessness and hopelessness are rampant. But amidst all the pain and struggle around me, in my life, and in the lives of those I love: I am at peace. After that disastrous meeting at church, I went home and spent about 3 hours in prayer. Honestly, I was terrified of the outcome. I thought that everyone would hate me, I would still get disfellowshipped, and that I would never recover from the hurt and shame I felt because of it. I assumed that neither my mother or Kennedy were interested in maintaining a relationship with me. I could do away with the notion of family almost entirely.

This wasn't a pity party I was having for myself (in my prayer). I was trying to cope with the magnitude of what happened. I hadn't planned on getting up to speak in front of the church. I found myself there, shocking myself as I spoke. It was almost an out-of-body experience. And hours later, I was alone in my room, prostrate on the floor, sobbing my prayer to God.

I prayed for the hurt I'd inflicted on those around me. I had finally seen what it looked like when I judged and dismissed others who were just trying to get to know Christ. In that moment, standing in the church, I saw the pain in Kennedy's eyes. After having fought many personal battles to get to know God, she was constantly being told her devotion to God would never be enough. Even though the Bible told her that her belief in God was acceptable to Him[143], I told her that she required more.

Since I'd met her (and many others as well) I had reinforced the notion that you needed to be perfect[144] in order to access God. The truth was that it was only the presence of God that could purify and heal and save you. You had to acknowledge your flawed and fallen state in order for God to be able to work in you to produce the obedience, love, and holiness He required. I'd always believed that God would reward my efforts to impress and serve Him. I thought if I was eager, strict, and rigid, I would reap the rewards of holiness. I thought that I was supposed to fight on God's behalf, and uphold the standard of purity in others, so that I could become that which I preached. I thought that I was helping people by calling into question their devotion to God. I assumed that if they wavered because of my discourse, they were never really children of God to begin with.

---

[143] Acts 16:31
[144] Matt 5:48

I waged war, and rather than directing my weapons on the enemy, I had focused all my self-righteous rage on my fellow brothers and sisters. I had utterly disgraced myself and my God, in His own name. Even worse, I had done the most important work of the enemy by not only grossly misrepresenting the character of God, but using that as a means of alienating people from accessing the forgiveness and love that God had made freely available to them. If even one person had felt separated from God due to my actions that was enough to condemn me. And I *knew* that there were much more than one in the church that I'd done this to. I felt the weight of this burden that day, as I walked away from the church.

I had no excuse. The apostle Paul was zealous and persecuted the people of God, but he wasn't a hypocrite like me. I blamed and judged my mother for so long, for never practicing what she preached, and I realized just how much like her I was. I, too, did not walk in the same manner that I required everyone else to walk in. I didn't abide by the standards of purity, chastity, or even love that God had set forth, and yet I demanded others to do so. During this prayer, I saw my truest self as if I was in front of a mirror. On the outside, the look of a Christian: modest in apparel, carrying a Bible everywhere I went. I didn't drink or smoke. I didn't do drugs. I was as straight-laced and prudish as a Christian stereotype could get. Or so everyone thought. In reality, I was a shameless hypocrite who slandered others, gossiped "in the name of Jesus," had zero control over my sexual desires, and lied constantly. I was a self-important, self-righteous, malicious bully.

But I couldn't bear to pray for myself until I'd prayed for the damage I'd inflicted on the church as a whole. I had many people under my sphere of influence. Rather than using my service and ministry to aid the people of God, I weaponized it into a way of damaging those who just wanted to know God a little better. Those who were struggling under the weight of their sin I made sure to inform them that they had already been judged. Those who differed in method or opinion from me, I openly criticized as being doctrinally unsound and a danger to the Body of Christ. And as my influence and position in the church grew, so did my following.

While I plead for God to heal those whom I'd hurt, I had to add in the fruit of my spiritual warfare. I asked God to forgive those under my influence whom I had made disciples of my spiritual terrorism. Although I was not the first perpetrator of these heinous offenses, it didn't matter. I had followed the example of many who were unloving and unkind. I chose the path of attacking my spiritual brothers and sisters. I shot down their faith in God's love and forgiveness. I invalidated their relationships with God because it didn't mimic my own. I crushed their spirits until they gave up their last spiritual breath: leaving God altogether.

I had weaponized the Bible into a tool of division and destruction. I told people that because they were LGBT that God had nothing to offer them. That they were already condemned and there was nothing they could do about it. I told people that they had to get "right" and change their habits before they joined a church: as though God didn't declare the opposite.[145] I told people that God only valued their worship if it was in silence, with heads bowed and hands folded. Not too noisy or it was fake. Not too excited or you were being a distraction. I had rules and standards for every situation and gladly taught it to anyone with an ear to hear. I spied and reported on others, thinking my duty was to weed out those "wolves in sheep's clothing," never realizing that I was the leader of the wolfpack.

I had to pray to God to forgive those in whom I had planted, fertilized, and watered the seeds of spiritual destruction. Before I could think of praying for myself, I had to pray for everyone I'd hurt, whether I could remember it or not. I felt so far away from God in that moment. I knew the punishment I deserved. I knew that I had hurt so many people, but no one more than I had hurt God. I couldn't fathom asking Him to forgive me. Not after everything I'd done. Especially since I had spent so long misrepresenting Him, and then fighting to ignore Him when He tried to correct me. I knew that whatever bad things life had in store for me, I deserved. But even in that stance I knew I was wrong. I had spent so long painting God as unforgiving, vindictive, and spiteful that I didn't want to ask Him for anything when I needed Him the most. But as the burden weighed heavily on me, He began to speak.

---

[145] Isaiah 1:18

"...Come to me, [my daughter] who [is] weary and [carrying] heavy burdens, and I will give you rest. Take my yoke upon you. Let me teach you, because I am humble and gentle at heart, and you will find rest for your [soul.][146] I AM still your Father...If [only you, my child] who are called by my name, will humble [yourself] and pray and seek my face and turn from [your] wicked ways, I will hear from heaven and will forgive [your] sins and restore [you.][147] I am still the God of love, faithfulness, and hope. I will never fail you. I will never abandon you[148]... [Though you feel] hunted down, [you are] never abandoned by [Me.] [You got] knocked down, but [you] are not destroyed.[149]

"All this time I have been striving to get your attention. [You], like [a] sheep, have strayed away. [You] have left [My] paths to follow [your] own.[150] You ignored my advice and rejected the correction I offered.[151] But there is still hope for you. I AM not finished with you yet. But, the choice is yours: your foolish pride, or My fruitful love. You can't keep trying to save yourself. You will fail. You need Me. Admit it. Your pride is only going to cause you more pain. Refusing My help to ease this burden will crush you. You won't be able to withstand the pressure and will die trying to get yourself together.

"Don't you know that I love you? Don't you know how much I AM willing to do to save you? To restore love, peace, and hope in your life? Don't you know Me at all? Why do you

---

[146] Matt. 11:28-29
[147] 2 Chron. 7:14
[148] Heb. 13:4-6; Deut. 31:6,8
[149] 2 Cor. 4:8
[150] Isa 53:5
[151] Prov. 1:25

keep thinking I AM like you? My precious child, [...you don't have what you want because you don't ask [Me] for it. And even when you ask, you don't get it because your motives are all wrong—you want only what will give you pleasure.[152] Forgiveness is waiting. Peace is waiting. Love is waiting. But you have to want it. And you have to accept it on my terms, not your own.

"If only you'd ask Me to do for you what you desperately want, I would change your life so drastically that everyone would notice. But even that doesn't matter. Remember, [fearing] people is a dangerous trap, but trusting [Me] means safety."[153] If you trust Me, I can help your life shine so bright it begins to reverse the damage you inflicted on others. It won't all go away, and some people may never trust you again, but if you focus on me, and continue to follow me, ...I will draw everyone to myself.[154] I promise, my love, I can make things right again.

"[My dearest daughter,] listen! Today I am giving you a choice between life and death, between prosperity and disaster. For I command you this day to love the [Me] and to keep [My] commands, decrees, and regulations by walking in [My] ways. If you do this, you will live and multiply, and [I,] the Lord your God[,] will bless you...But if your heart turns away and you refuse to listen... then I warn you now that you will certainly be destroyed... Today I have given you the choice between life and

---

[152] James 4:2-3
[153] Prov. 29:25
[154] John 12:32

death, between blessings and curses... Oh, that you would choose life, so that you... might live! You can make this choice by loving [Me], obeying [Me], and committing yourself firmly to [Me]. This is the key to your life...[155] So will you trust Me to take care of you, to forgive you, to love you?"

I finally saw an accurate glimpse of God. Not in full, of course, but like Moses[156], just a taste. I realized that by not asking God for forgiveness, I was not only rejecting His appeal, but also His salvation, and His love. The very act of not asking for forgiveness was one of disobedience and rebellion. I prayed for forgiveness then. If God still saw enough in me to salvage a relationship with me, who was I to say I wasn't good enough for His grace and mercy? Who was I to judge and condemn myself when God wouldn't? It was my same issue that I had with others, but in a different form. I was still judging with finality, still trying to do God's job for Him. So, I prayed. And I kept praying past the aching knees and tired limbs. And when I finally got up, body throbbing, tears crusted on my face, I finally felt relief.

He did it for me when I deserved it the least. After everything I'd done to Him and to His children, He still chose me. That love, I was never going to let myself forget. I'd have to find a way to remind myself of what it felt like to be truly seen, truly loved. And I knew that I had my work cut out for me. If He showed me this love, it was so that I could extend that same love for other people. People who thought differently than I did.

---

[155] Deut. 30:15-19
[156] Exod. 33:12-23

People who lived differently than I did. People who openly rejected me. People who openly mocked my God. People who I didn't like. I had to learn to love them all. Because at the end of the day, it wasn't about me. This love, this life, and my existence were not about me. They were a gift from God, so that through my experience I could show someone else that true love exists. That forgiveness is possible. That redemption, hope, and peace are not theoretical, but actually attainable. I was finally beginning to understand what real love was.

****

I won't pretend that my life has drastically changed in the past six months. I did not walk into the church the next Sabbath met with rousing applause. All the people I'd hurt didn't automatically forgive me and now I am friends with everyone. My mother didn't suddenly see the light, change her ways, and start living right. No major changes took place. Carine and I are still best friends. She was surprised at everything that happened at the church, but she reached out to me and told me that she would support me through prayer. She said I was bold for choosing to tell the truth, but I had to stop her. I told her that I hadn't been fully honest with her about my situation, and told her the truth about my relationship with my mother and Kennedy. I didn't tell her I saw Kennedy at the abortion clinic, but I filled in all the gaps. She cried when she heard what I had been through. Like a true friend, she prayed with me and let me know she was always available for me: whether my needs were spiritual, emotional/mental, or physical. She has been my accountability partner since. She's helped keep me honest about my spiritual journey, and isn't afraid to call me out on my mess, but as a true sister, makes sure that I know it's done in love. The best part is that she's shared with me some of her own struggles, ones she had never felt safe enough to divulge. So, we support each other in honesty and love. I couldn't have asked for a better friendship with her.

One thing that has also improved is my relationship with Heaven. Her kindness to me in the past few months has made it really easy for me to talk to her. In fact, she is the person that Pastor Rogers assigned to be my peer counselor. After the day of the infamous business meeting, I restarted my spiritual rehab plan. I decided on the forty-week plan instead of the more intensive daily plan. Pastor Rogers teamed up with a few members and elders, including Heaven and Grace, and created a guide booklet for the plan. That's when he assigned Heaven as my peer counselor.

Since then, her and I have spoken at least once weekly. She checks in with me, but not in a correctional officer type of way. I can tell that she sincerely cares about me. That is probably the most surprising thing about all of this. She is very open and honest about her own spiritual journey, and is transparent about her mistakes and struggles both past and present. I never thought we would be friends, especially after the way I treated her. She said that when I came to her job a few months ago, and "finally let down that facade," she saw a real person with real struggles. She'd been praying for me ever since.

It's not easy having to consider her a spiritual authority (of some sort) over me. Even though I know she serves God, I still disagree with some of her methods and theories about God and Godliness. Plus, as a matter of pride, I used to instruct *her* on spiritual matters (or at least *try* to). So sometimes it is especially difficult to hear what she has to say about God. We might argue about some things, and she may get exasperated with my discourse, but eventually we agree to disagree (or concede). She challenges a lot of my opinions about God. Sometimes I think she's too radical. Sometimes I don't think she's radical enough. But despite the times when my pride gets in the way, I appreciate her help.

Although Heaven is still being nice to me, but the majority of the rest of her friends still want nothing to do with me. I understand that I've hurt people deeply and they won't trust me to not revert to the same vicious tactics I was using before. It does sting to know that I've caused people so much pain that they're unwilling to give me a chance, but this is a consequence to my actions, so I have to take it. Maybe in the future, if I am sincere, they'll see the changes in me and we might become acquaintances. Until then, I'll continue to strive for what's right: not because I care that much about what they think, but because I care about what God thinks of me.

Kennedy is still coming to Genesis SDA Church, although not as often as she was before all the drama. I get it. I wouldn't want to come to a place where people have tried to slander and humiliate me either. Notwithstanding, the strength and bravery it took for her to return must have been immense. It took me a month to come back to church after that meeting. Heaven told me it took Kennedy half the time to return. She no longer participates in the Praise Team ministry (by her choice) and she leaves soon after, but she shows up. Her love for God is that strong. I know she's probably looking for a new church home, but her commitment to God in the face of ridicule and personal loss is laudable. There was nothing negative anyone could say about her as far as I was concerned. I wasn't so sure if she could say the same about me.

After the meeting, I tried calling her. I tried again after I prayed and once more a week later, but to no avail. She wasn't responding to my phone calls. Who could blame her, after everything I'd done to her? I decided to text her one last time.

"Kennedy,

I know that I've been horrible to you. I know that you've suffered great losses, and I've only added to it in spite of the fact that we are sisters. Words cannot express how truly sorry I am for everything I've done to you. I am so sorry for doubting you and accusing you of being a liar. I'm especially sorry for attacking your character and integrity. I am the least of all people who has the right to say anything to you about your life. I was absolutely terrible to you, and my mother was a nightmare. I had nothing to do with that meeting at church, but I'll still apologize because she's my mother, and I didn't do enough to protect you from her. I am not seeking your forgiveness, I just wanted to make sure you were okay. If you ever decide to speak to me again (and I don't blame you one bit if that never happens) I am here. I would like to begin getting to know you as a sister (if you wish.) I will continue to pray for you, though I know I'm probably the last person you'd want praying for you. I hope that someday, eventually, we can reconnect and move forward. May God bless you.

-Gwen "

I wasn't expecting her to ever respond, but about a month later she texted back.

"Gwen,

I don't know what to say to you. I don't know why I'm even reaching out. Maybe it's because Grace says that I need to forgive so that I can heal. All I know is that I'd like to resolve this permanently. At the current moment, I do not wish to have any type of relationship with you, especially due to your proximity to that toxic woman. She's made mine and my parents' life miserable for so long, and I can't be around anyone who can give her access to my life. I am willing to let bygones be bygones with you, and I will be cordial should we run into one another, but that is as far as I can go. Please understand when I say do not contact me again. If I decide to contact you in the future, it will be on my terms. In any case, I hope life treats you with more kindness than you have shown to others, and I wish you well. Goodbye.

-Kennedy"

Of course, that hurt me, but what could I say? I couldn't explain how much my mother had poisoned my life, and that her and I had virtually no relationship since that showdown at the church. I couldn't make her see me any differently, and had to accept that my actions had put me in the same category of my mother. The very woman whose identity I despised, I had assumed. But I couldn't dwell on that. I had to take what I could get with Kennedy. If she didn't want to have anything to do with me, it was her choice, and my consequence.

I feel like God had tried to warn me about the consequences of my actions, but I had no desire to listen. There were so many people who I was now closed off from as a result of my own behavior. My own decisions. I couldn't ask God to spare me the dislike, the repudiation of others just because I was sorry *now*. He had to allow me to be humbled so that I could learn from this experience. So that I wouldn't take others for granted, or prematurely judge others. I had to deal with the mess I had made of my life and my relationships. If I hadn't gone through this, I would not value others the way that I'm learning to now. I would not love others the way He wants me to. I would never be motivated to make this change.

But thank God for His grace, because it could be much worse than it is. About two weeks ago, Kennedy reached out to me. She let me know that she was ready to sit and talk. I didn't want to waste time or give her too much time to change her mind, so I agreed to meet with her last Thursday.

Our meeting was brief. Well, at least according to my perspective. She came by the house. We sat and I offered her some refreshments. She declined. She asked me to (once again) stay silent as she spoke her piece. Not in a place to negotiate, I complied.

She told me that her absence from Genesis Church for the past month had been intentional. She had joined another church in the Boston area. It was smaller than Genesis, but she said that it met her spiritual needs, including that of fellowship and spiritual support. She said that she had a lot of time to think over the past few months. Though she wasn't fully comfortable with the idea of reaching out and trying to forge ahead with a relationship, she had felt compelled to do so anyway. It was especially due to the holiday season. (It's hardest on those who have lost loved ones. Losing both of her parents must've made this season nearly impossible, especially with everything that had happened lately.)

She told me that she'd switched jobs and found a new apartment. She was still a freelance graphic designer, but had taken an office receptionist job while she was looking for something in her field. She had gone through the same spiritual rehab program as I did. Grace was doing double duty as her peer counselor and accountability partner. She was still looking for one in the meantime. She looked like she wanted to say more about that, but decided against it. She concluded by telling me that she was hurt by my actions. Thankfully, she felt the relationship was salvageable based on how I stood up for her at the church business meeting. She said that we still had a long way to go, but she was willing to take small steps. So, she extended an open invitation for lunch when we could get our schedules together.

Before she left, I asked to speak. I let her know how sorry I was, and told her that my mother and I hadn't spoken since the day of the meeting. I told her that over time, she'd understand why my mother and I were never on the best of terms, and that I was sincere in trying to make amends. I told her that I, too, was following the program, and that Heaven was my peer counselor. "Yeah. I've heard." She let out a short chuckle. I smiled, shrugged, and replied, "Karma." She laughed harder and responded, "You mean consequences." We broke out in peals of laughter.

575

Before long, we were parting ways with smiles on our faces.

It turned out far better than I had thought it ever could. I wanted to invite her to spend Christmas or New Year's Eve/Day with me, but I wasn't sure she'd accept. I still have time to ask, but I want to respect her boundaries, now more than ever. Her invitation to lunch was more than enough, but I wanted her to know that I was here for her. I decided to ask Heaven what she would do if she were in a similar situation. She responded that she didn't want to be placed in the middle of our situation, and that she didn't want to discuss the other person with either of us. I had no choice but to respect her stance, since she was trying to be fair to both of us, so I decided to pray about it instead.

Perhaps prayer should've been my first step, but I was still learning how to lean on God's guidance, and not on what I *thought* He wanted to say to me. Each and every time I thought I took a step in the right direction, I'd do something else and mess up. I restarted therapy, but then I started gossiping. I read my Bible every day, but said quick, rushed, "microwave" prayers. I was nicer to people, but then began valuing myself based on how people saw me. I was, in short, a mess. But one thing stood out: every I acknowledged that I was a mess and that I needed help, I got the help I needed. Some way, somehow, God provided help for me just when I needed it the most. I still struggle with how other people see me, but I'm learning that reputations mean nothing. At least, not in the grand scheme of life.

When you worry about what others say about you, you begin to tailor your life according to their opinions. You begin to compare yourself to other people, celebrating when you are doing "better" than others, and hurting deeply when you are doing "worse" than others. Your conversations, self-perception, and your existence become wrapped up in other people: who they are, what they're doing, what they think of you. When you make mistakes and bad decisions, you are terrified that people will speak lowly of you: as lowly as you speak about other people. So, you try to hide it. You can sometimes be successful in hiding your faults from other people, preserving your reputation. The thing is, you cannot hide who you really are from God.

I forgot that God values character: who I really am. He saw who I was pretending to be, but He saw even clearer who I was when no one else was around. He tried to show me that I could not live my life for others. I celebrated my outward righteousness, demeaned others (including my mother) and compared myself to them to "find my place." The truth was that humans have never been (and will never be) the benchmark by which we are measured. Our standing in God is marked by where we stand compared to the perfect life and supreme sacrifice of Jesus Christ. None of us can compare to the standard He set, and therefore we cannot and should not compare ourselves and our merits to each other.

The Bible is clear: no one meets the standards that God set.[157] If meeting God's requirements were an exam in school, no one would receive a passing score, let alone a perfect one. That's why His grace and mercy are so important. When God sees us, His Son Jesus Christ takes His perfect exam score, and says, "This is [Insert Name Here]'s exam. This is [Insert Name Here]'s righteousness. These are [Insert Name Here]'s works. This stand in the place of [Insert Name Here]'s life." He offered up His own life for us. Jesus substitutes our sin, our mistakes, our stubborn, unrelenting pride, with His own perfection, so that is all that God sees when He looks at us.

We have no better mediator and savior than Jesus Christ. But that's why we cannot afford to get caught up in any form of "respectability politics." The Bible is clear that God doesn't care who you are: we are all factory defects, suitable to be recalled and destroyed. But Jesus loved us so much that He gave us the most important gift: the gift of a fresh, sinless start. The best part is that He renews the gift. We, who constantly mess up, can constantly ask for forgiveness and be granted a clean slate. Every time. All we have to do is ask. But some of us, like me, are so proud, so stuck in our ways, that we don't ask. Even worse, we won't let anyone else ask either. We choose to let people feel condemned, because it gives us the illusion of superiority.

I learned this lesson the hard way, though I am most grateful that I have finally begun to understand. I am just like everyone else. I am privileged to know God, but that's it. He does not favor me over everyone else if I obey every commandment or tradition with His name

---

[157] Rom. 3:23; Isa. 53:6; Isa. 64:6

attached to it. Nor does He hate everyone who is disobedient to His will. He is a God who loves us no matter where in life we are. Christian, Buddhist, Atheist. We are all His children. He will love, bless, and protect us all. Does He have special affection in His heart for me because I chose Him- sure. But that doesn't mean He'll bless me more than others. Especially when I take His love for me and try to elevate myself higher than everyone else. When I begin to consider myself the Godly standard on Earth, rather than Him. When I begin to treat any of His children as though they were beneath me because they don't live how I live, or do what I do, or speak how I speak, or look how I look, or love whom I love.

He'd rather remove His favor from be and bless and prosper the atheist who is out serving the homeless and taking care of the sick. The gay man who went and bought his elderly neighbor some groceries because he noticed that they cut her social security allowance. The Buddhist monk who teaches others to love and nurture each other. While I profess His name, carry on my shoulders His identity, using it as a platform to hurt, maim, and destroy His other children (whom He loves deeply.) I'm supposed to be telling people that He exists and that He loves them. That there is hope, peace, love, and joy available in abundance when you take the time to get to know Him. I'm not supposed to use His name to tell the crushed, oppressed, and heartbroken that the most powerful Being in the universe is disgusted by their existence and hates them. That He's waiting,

579

thirsting after their destruction. That He doesn't care what happens to anyone but me and people like me. Those things couldn't be further from the truth.

I've done so much to prove that I'm better than people. I've made huge errors in judgment just to hide the fact that I make mistakes and bad decisions. I've gone through enormous lengths to cover up my flaws and avoid consequences. But God saw me anyway. The same way He sees you. The real you. And He'll do everything in His power to save you, just like He did for me. Don't get caught up in the comparison game. You'll either be depressed because you don't measure up against where you think you should be. Or, you'll have a false sense of superiority and security based on what other people have and what other people are doing. Social media is one of the biggest proponents of this. There is a lost art (and huge blessing) in minding your own business[158] and focusing on God and the purpose He has for you. When you do that, you won't have time to gossip. You won't waste your time with activities, things, projects, or people that do not benefit your end-goal, further your purpose, or grow your relationship with God. Do yourself the favor of being the best you can possibly be. Find your purpose, and then focus on making it a reality.

Most of all, remember that God took special care in creating you.[159] He values you immensely, and needs you- just as you are, to make His world right. No one else can fill the role that He has planned for you. They

---

[158] 1 Thess. 4:11
[159] Psalms 139:13-18

can try, but everything that makes you who you are is what He needs to be successful. He is dependent on your voice, your hands, your mind, you as a whole to make a difference in the world around you. He knows how far you can go, how great you can be, and just how much this world desperately needs you. You are valued. You are favored. You are necessary. Never forget how much God loves and values you. Never forget the sacrifice He made to save you so that you get to spend an eternity with Him, in peace and joy that cannot be compared. Never forget that you are special in His eyes. There is no one else that has ever existed on this planet (or will exist in the future) that is exactly like you. God made us with a unique plan and purpose in mind for each of us. He made us all different yet equal. So, don't let depression make you feel like you're worse than anyone. And more importantly, don't let your pride fool you into believing you are superior to any of His children. I learned this the hard way, but I can never forget: you're no better than I am, and I (for sure) am no better than you.

D. Gloria Elysée

Because of the privilege and authority God has given me, I give each of you this warning: Don't think you are better than you really are. Be honest in your evaluation of yourselves, measuring yourselves by the faith God has given us. Just as our bodies have many parts and each part has a special function, so it is with Christ's body. We are many parts of one body, and we all belong to each other. Don't let evil conquer you, but conquer evil by doing good.

-Romans 12:3-5, 21 NLT

D. Gloria Elysée

D. Gloria Elysée

www.ingramcontent.com/pod-product-compliance
Lightning Source LLC
Chambersburg PA
CBHW020622020726
47494CB00001B/9